For Tsune,
my real live soul-mate,
and to my daily inspiration,
my daughters, Elaine and Emily.

DARKNESS FALLS

Magikos Alliance

Ann Marie Kazutomi
Illustration by Khenaton Rainey

K.U. INTERNATIONAL, INC.

Darkness Falls
Magikos Alliance
All Rights Reserved.
Copyright © 2013 Ann Marie Kazutomi
v2.0

Cover Photo © 2013 Khenaton Rainey All rights reserved - used with permission.

ISBN: 978-0-578-11420-0

Library of Congress Control Number: 2012919162

PRINTED IN THE UNITED STATES OF AMERICA

CONTENTS

ACKNOWLEDGMENTS

I want to thank my family and friends for their undying support, and encouragement; for them putting up with my late night writing escapades; and for listening attentively about my passion for history, even though I know it bores them to death. Without them this book would have never been completed.

Thank you,

To my husband, Tsune a.k.a. Tom, who not only made sure I stayed on track, but endured a paranormal romance to become my first reader and editor.

To my daughters, Elaine and Emily, who not only inspired some of my characters language, but gave me ideas when I was stuck in a scene.

To Catherine for finding a way to make me look photogenic.

To the many people, who are too numerous to name that took their time to read "Darkness Falls" and give me their honest opinions.

To the many successful authors who took their time to answer my questions, and inspire me to continue with my dream.

And last but not least, I thank God for giving me the gift of imagination, and my grandmother, for teaching me how to use it.

I hope you enjoy the world of the Magikos Alliance, and my favorite species, the Cruetians who inspired it all. I would love to hear from all of my fans, and you can contact me at:
annmariekazutomi@gmail.com

Ann Marie

PROLOGUE

A legendary warrior! The crown prince of the Cruetians! The sole
leader of the Magikos Alliance! Alexander Valerius Maximus is
a revered man in every aspect of the word. He's a man of great strength
and power; a man respected and honored by his soldiers; desired and
cherished by all women; loved and admired by his people; and feared
by his enemies. As a general, he commands with intelligence and
compassion; as a prince, he devotes his life to his people; and as a
leader, he is sworn to protect all moral beings. If not for the curse,
his wife had inflicted upon his race centuries ago; he would truly be
a man of content. Now Alexander walks the earth with guilt, looking
for a way to lift this horrible affliction, and finally fulfill the destiny
he was born for.

Over 2300 years ago, Alexander was born into two of human's
greatest civilizations ever to inhabit the earth; and one of the strongest
civilizations to ever walk the earth. His father, Avitus Valerius
Maximus, was a very powerful man, not only a Roman senator in the
human world, but King of all Cruetians. A strong but compassionate
leader for both Dark-Souls and humans alike, Alexander's father held
the respect of all beings. Avitus was strong enough to protect his
people from harm, but compassionate enough to protect all innocents,
including Alexander's mother from certain death. Upon the death
of her father, a great Macedonian King, Alexander's mother and
grandmother were marked for death.

Determined to protect herself from her husband's greedy generals,
the Macedonian King's first wife, decided to execute his other two
wives. Parysatis, Alexander's grandmother, was barely able to escape.

She located a Cruetian named Demitrius in Babylon, and demanded protection for her unborn child. As royalty, he could not refuse her request, but Demitrius knew, as long as she was on Greek soil, he would never have the power to ensure her safety. For he understood, that the dead King's first wife would never stop hunting Parysatis, not until her unborn child had been eliminated, guaranteeing the first wife's child the throne. Demitrius realized, the only place Parysatis would be safe, was in a territory equally as strong as the Greeks. Somewhere the Greek generals and the Queen would be unable to order or command the people's loyalty.

Rome!

They traveled to the only person Demitrius believed could and would be strong enough to protect Parysatis. The Cruetian King! His King, Avitus Valerius Maximus. At their meeting, Parysatis confessed that she had deliberately sought out Demitrius. Explaining that she believed him to be a Cruetian, or as the humans liked to call them…a Dark-Soul. A legend of the Great Titans. A race of people thought to have been created by the three Titan protectors.

The protectors were believed to have gone into hiding among humans, after Cronus was overthrown by Zeus. It was said, that the Titans living in a peaceful time did not believe they needed great armies, so they created three immortal beings to protect them. These protectors survived off the blood of human sacrifices given to the great Titans. Human blood was away for the Titans to insure that their protectors remained loyal to them, since the only other blood available in the heavens was Titan blood. Naturally this blood was poisonous to the protectors, which made them dependent on the gods for their survival. This was just the way the Titans liked it, it assured complete obedience.

When Zeus ousted Cronus and the other Titans, it is said that the goddess Hecate helped the three protectors disappear. It's assumed these three protectors created the Cruetian race. A race of immortals that survives off human blood.

Parysatis begged them to protect her unborn child, offering her own life as a sacrifice.

"I do not need your blood" Avitus snarled. "There are plenty of men dying in current battles to supply my people's needs." He took a deep breath calming himself before he continued, "However, I will exchange your services in my household, for my services of protection. Since you come from a royal home, I will not make you my slave. You will be registered as a free slave; allowing your unborn child Roman citizenship. I will not allow your King's child to become a slave. He was an honorable man, his accomplishments legendary. His child deserves more than the treachery it is being shown. You will live in my home, work for your room, board, and a small wage. If this is satisfactory, then I will protect you and your unborn child."

Parysatis knew her choices were limited. As a woman she had no rights, and it would only be a matter of time before she was hunted down and killed. Her only option was to accept Avitus's offer.

With her blood oath, the deal was forged. A deal that ultimately brought Alexander's mother and father together...16 years later.

◊∭◊

At 16, Alexander's mother was an extremely beautiful woman. With her golden curls and teal eyes, she was definitely her father's child, and as such, afraid of being discovered. Even though Hypatia was a Roman citizen, she led a solitary life, living in the small room given to them by her mother's employer, the master of this villa. Hypatia had never actually met the man, but appreciated everything he had done for her and her mother. She knew he had to be a kind man, for not only had he protected them from being assassinated, he made sure Hypatia was tutored in Latin and her duties as a patrician. It was his kindness that created the loyalty she felt for this stranger, and the reason Hypatia was so willing to take over her mother's duties tonight, while her mother lay ill in bed.

Their master was hosting a large dinner party. Knowing the stress it would cause being short a server, Hypatia assured her mother she would take her place and pour the guest's wine.

Hypatia was amazed how many people attended these functions, and how beautiful the architecture on this side of the villa was. She never came to this part of the villa, always staying hidden in the servants' areas, unsure if it was safe. Even after 16 years of hiding, Hypatia rarely left their small room.

What if her father's generals were still hunting her and her mother? They had heard that her father's first wife and son had finally been killed by his generals. These were the same generals that had divided up her father's territories. What if they hadn't forgotten about her and her mother?

That was a chance Hypatia was unwilling to take, so she never strolled far from their room. She did make a mental note to explore the beautiful gardens on this side of the villa the next morning, however. For this area of the villa, Hypatia would make an exception to her rule. It was quite beautiful here, and she enjoyed the gardens wonderful floral smells and the many fountains adorning it. This part of the villa was decorated to its finest, with white marble floors, that had gold inlaid throughout, beautiful red silks hung about, and it had the most exotic statues she had ever seen. Hypatia was completely in awe over its exquisite beauty.

Since Hypatia never left the villa, she had never seen *patricians* before, for that matter she hadn't associated with *plebeian*s either, but these men and women all seemed just like the servants she was used to associating with. They just wore nicer clothes, seemed to have better manners, and spoke more confidently. The women were breathtakingly beautiful, and the men were absolutely gorgeous. Hypatia was approaching one now that looked to her like a god in the flesh. He was tall…very tall. Hypatia could tell he would hover over her if he was standing. His hair was black like raven's wings, and his eyes were as blue as the sky on a clear day. His beauty took her breath away.

As Hypatia approached him to fill his glass, she couldn't help noticing the closer she was to him, the more handsome this man became compared to the rest of the guests. As she stood in front of him, she would have liked to have been able to touch his hair. She wanted to know if it was as silky as it looked, and his beautiful blue eyes were even a deeper shade than she had originally thought. She had never seen a man so delicious. Of course, she had never been outside of the villa…but still…compared to the other guests. No contest! He was glorious. He was obviously a general, for the air around him commanded respect. His body was all laced with ropes of hard, sinewy muscle. Hypatia didn't see any visible scars; still, she could tell he had killed men. Many men! Yes, she thought, definitely one of the Roman Generals. An important guest in her master's villa.

As Hypatia finished pouring his wine, he reached out and grabbed her arm. As beautiful as this woman was, and she was extremely beautiful, with her long golden blonde curls that kissed her waist, and her teal eyes that reminded him of the sea, he did not know her, and Avitus knew every one of his servants. This woman did not belong in his home.

"Who are you?" he demanded. "I do *not* know you."

Hypatia tried to step away from him, but Avitus tightened his grip around her arm. She quickly looked around trying to find someone to help her, but realized no one was paying attention to the altercation.

Avitus noticed her looking around for an escape, and pulled her into a corner away from his guests. He had no intention of allowing her to escape her clear invasion of his home.

Avitus could smell the fear rushing off her and saw the nervousness in her eyes, as she finally answered him. "I am a servant of this household."

Avitus hated liars and knew instantly she was lying. He knew every one of his slaves, and he did not remember her. Furthermore, he would never buy a slave this beautiful; it just created havoc amongst the male slaves. "You are not a slave in this house." He scowled, refusing to let go of her arm as she struggled against him.

"I *am* a servant in this house, and I do not believe my villa's master would approve of you bruising my skin, but you may ask him when he arrives." Hypatia countered, hoping her bravado would make this man release her. She knew from her mother, that their villa's master was feared by most men. Hypatia hoped the man gripping her arm feared him enough that he would release her. As handsome as he was, and by the gods he was handsome, she was still not going to allow someone to hurt her in anyway.

That statement alone proved to Avitus that she did not belong in his home; otherwise she would know who he was. He did not want to cause a scene with his guests present, but he wanted answers from this woman and by the gods, he would have those answers.

"Who are you? I demand your name." Avitus growled in her ear "Either tell me your name, or........."

Knowing this was getting out of hand; Hypatia decided she had better answer him, so then maybe she could get away quickly. "Hypatia" she said confidently. "My name is Hypatia."

Avitus couldn't have been more shocked if she had slapped him. Could she really be...Why hadn't he noticed her in his home before? She had to be about...what? 16 years old...and why was she here serving his guests?

"You are Parysatis's daughter?" he asked amazed. Cupping her chin, Avitus lifted it to search her eyes.

Instantly Hypatia's heart stopped. How did he know her mother? This was bad...very bad. Was he an assassin? Had her father's generals finally found them after all these years?

"How do you know Parysatis?" She jerked back from him, trying to find an escape away from this huge mountain of a man. Avitus could see the fear in her eyes and smelled her sheer terror. It was then he realized she truly did not know who he was. How odd. She had lived in his home for 16 years, but had no idea who she was speaking to. It would make sense, of course, for he had never seen her either.

"I am..." he gave her an amused smirk, "Avitus Valerius Maximus, akribos."

Oh, No! How could I be so stupid? My mother's going to kill me. I just embarrassed our master in front of all his guests.

Hypatia immediately dropped to her knees. "I apologize, please forgive me. I have never seen you before I...I...I did not know. Please." Avitus was unsure why she was crying on her knees in front of him. Had he frightened her so badly? "I did not know. Even though I am not a slave, you may punish me for my ignorance. Please do not make us leave. My mother is ill today, so I told her I would do her duties. Please forgive me."

Avitus had not meant to scare her; he was just surprised, for he had never seen her before, and had always taken the security of his villa very seriously. He knew Parysatis had a daughter, he even knew her name was Hypatia, for he had put her *bulla* around her neck at her purification ceremony, but he had never seen her.

Avitus remembered the day Parysatis had brought Hypatia to him. She had presented the baby to him like one of his slaves would have presented their children. He remembered his words to her. "Parysatis, I told you when you came here she would not be a slave, and I meant it. She is the daughter of a great King and Queen, and she will never be made a servant or slave. Lay her at my feet, woman." As Parysatis obeyed, he picked the child up into his arms, accepting her into his home. "I will pay for tutors to teach her Latin, and anything you are unable to teach her to prepare her for her role in society. I will continue to protect her as long as she stays in the villa with you. Go now and raise your daughter."

Neither when Hypatia was presented to him, nor at her purification ceremony, did he open the cloth to look upon her. Seeing her now, he had always assumed correctly, as the daughter to the once great king of Macedon, she looked like a Greek goddess. Her beauty was beyond anyone's he had ever encountered, and being one of the Titan protectors, Avitus remembered the goddesses well. Even they couldn't compare to her. She was exquisite.

Avitus reached down, lifting her chin, as he helped Hypatia stand up. He didn't want her bowing to him, and he definitely didn't want her groveling on her knees. As he rubbed his thumb over her cheek, he noticed her skin was as soft as silk. Looking deep into her beautiful teal eyes, he instantly realized he was looking into the soul of the woman in his prophecy. Hypatia was to be his Queen. The woman he had waited for. The woman the gods had destined to become his in a prophecy thousands of years earlier.

You will find your one true mate,
unlike yourself in every way.
A great female born to nobility,
She will be a strong survivor,
With beauty beyond imagination.
A woman created for you,
who will bare you many children.
And your first born son
will hold a great responsibility.
For he will be the protector of all moral beings.
The greatest fighter and uniter to ever walk the earth!

From the moment Avitus and Hypatia looked into each other's eyes, they've never been a part.

Their love for each other…legendary.

Then in 301 BC, their first son was born, Alexander Valerius Maximus.

Named after his maternal grandfather… another great uniter.

1

Alexander was exhausted. He had been up all night trying to find the common denominator in his warriors' reports. Over the last 6 months, Dark-Soul renegades, or Vampires, as Cruetians called their criminals, had killed 127 human females all over Europe. Alexander had his best men, his Vici Warriors, out hunting these Vampires, but so far the Vampires had eluded them. Quite a feat when they were up against his best hunting force.

Since the victims were from so many different jurisdictions, the human police hadn't discovered that it was Vampire's committing the murders, and Alexander wanted to keep it that way. It was imperative that they figured out what these women had in common, so they could put a stop to this murderess rampage.

Maybe with a little rest, Alexander could see what he was missing. As a Dark-Soul, he could shift from one location to another. All they had to do was picture where they wanted to go and with one simple step, they were there. He could shift himself into his bed without a second thought, but Kalab, his bodyguard would panic if he returned and Alexander was missing, so instead he opted for the couch in his office.

As tired as he was, Alexander easily fell into a deep sleep and right back into his recurring nightmare. The last few weeks he had dreamed about his people's curse over and over, as if the memories were trying to tell him something. Every time he closed his eyes, it was like watching a movie of his life. He moved from one nightmare right into another, until every dark memory of the last 800 years was replayed with devastating detail.

Today, Alexander was watching himself walk the streets of Rome in 1205 AD.

Alexander was raised in the constant reminder of his duties. As the Crown Prince of the Cruetian people, he had been schooled in both Greece and Rome. He had studied many subjects, including politics and negotiation skills, and had naturally trained in the disciplines and skills of a warrior. Over the centuries, he dedicated himself to studying all worldly fighting techniques. He had even studied in Asia and Egypt with both of his uncles.

Alexander was an accomplished warrior through and through. He had fought numerous enemies and always won. Sometimes with heavier losses than others, but he always prevailed. Most of his people considered winning these battles his greatest accomplishments, but Alexander knew his greatest achievements were in the alliances he had forged, which is the exact reason he was back in Rome today.

On Alexander's 16th birthday, he had been summoned by his father's advisor, Tamarinda, a talented soothsayer, where he received his prophecy.

Millenniums ago your Destiny was forged by the gods
Chosen to be the protector of all moral beings
You will live a life of turmoil
Fighting battle after battle, war after war, to solidify unity
Forging great alliances
You will bring peace to your own kind
Leading many of the gods children into a promising new age
You are a warrior at heart
A leader of mind
and a protector in your soul
Unite them together as one to fulfill your destiny
As all three men
You will achieve great success and ultimately peace

Over the centuries, Alexander had contemplated the meaning of his prophecy. As he fought each battle and lost numerous comrades, he believed more and more that his destiny was truly in establishing a peaceful existence with the otherworldly races. Alexander hadn't always understood this. For the longest time, he believed wielding his sword was the incontrovertible way to peace. It took centuries of fighting and loosing good warriors, before he realized that conquering your enemies' only lead to enmity. If you actually wanted peace, you needed to form alliances instead.

How young and naïve Alexander had been in his youth. Unable to fathom any of the horrors of his prophecy, all he heard and imagined was the glory. He could still remember the excitement that rushed through his body as Tamarinda had finished speaking. He kissed her cheek, thanked her, and ran all the way back to his father's villa. Extremely passionate for life, Alexander intended on fulfilling his destiny as soon as possible.

At the conclusion of Alexander's coming of age ceremony, he immediately joined the Roman army. By the age of 20, he was already a revered General, possibly the youngest of his time.

Alexander commanded Roman legions in the Pyrrhic War, while at the same time, leading the Cruetian military. Sometimes they fought for the Greeks, sometimes for the Romans, sometimes against otherworldly beings, but they always fought to protect themselves or humanity. In fact, Alexander has led the Cruetian military in every war that has touched the earth since he became a warrior.

Finally as he came to terms with his true destiny, he negotiated a great alliance with the Magusians. A race made up of many unique beings that the humans like to call fairies. Once, one of the Cruetian's greatest enemies, it took years to get the Magusians to agree to an alliance, but once they had, Alexander had been able to slowly negotiate similar alliances with some of the different Auraian, Lycanthrope, Agerikian, and Daemon clans.

Now in Rome, all the monarchies of these alliances awaited his proposal. A proposal Alexander hoped would lead to his greatest achievement yet.

The Magikos Alliance!

A council of otherworldly races similar to what the great Roman

Senate had once been. A place where otherworldly representatives could unite under peaceful circumstances, to learn about each other's cultures and traditions; discuss issues, alliances, and the needs of their civilizations, while allowing objectivity and fairness to prevail. This had become Alexander's dream, a dream that was now on the verge of reality.

"Alexander, everyone has assembled." Hypatia was stating as she walked over to him. He looked up at his mother, just as she reached out and cupped his cheek. "gios, do not worry. The gods are with you, for this is your destiny. They gave you the wisdom to create an amazing idea, and the skills to convince even the most difficult monarchy. You have nothing to worry about. Did you read your grandfather's oath at Opis?"

Alexander kissed his mother's cheek. "Yes, matris, I did. It never ceases to amaze me what a great man grandfather was. He was a true visionary, a fierce warrior, and a great King that believed in peace and equality for all men. I am truly sorry you never had a chance to know him."

Hypatia sighed with a weak smile, "Yes, I would have enjoyed knowing my father as a person, instead of from manuscripts, but your grandmother passed down stories that only the people close to him knew. I believe this helped us all know him better. He held wisdom far beyond his age. Just as his grandson does." She lovingly squeezed his hand. "Remember whose blood runs through your veins. That strength will help you succeed. Besides, your father and uncles are already in the chamber, and they believe in your alliance. That already gives us three votes, so go out there and get the rest." She reached up and kissed his cheek, before she turned and left him standing at the entrance of the chamber.

Hypatia left so quickly, he hadn't even had a chance to tell her thank you for believing in him. Alexander had always gained strength from his mother's faith in his abilities, and with her saying ' us', he knew she was putting her stamp of approval on the council as well. She never failed to amaze him. Even after all these centuries and 33 children, she was still able to make each of them feel special. There was no denying Hypatia's love for her family, and she showed it every day. She was an exceptional mother, and a wonderful Queen to their people.

After 3 days of harsh negotiations, there seemed to be one issue that continued to stop the proceedings...The Stregians! Like the Magusians, the Stregians were comprised of many different species, what most would equate to cousins. Like the Magusians, where there are many different types of fairies, the Stregians have equally as many different types of witches. The Magusians noticed that even though there were many different types of breeds within the Fae-world, they understood they had more similarities than differences, which led them to believe they were cousin species. With that realization, they began forming their own alliances, discovering that fighting together made them stronger against their enemies. The same exact realization the witches had when they bond their covens together and formed the Stregians. Unfortunately, most of the otherworldly races had been at odds with one or more of the witch species. When they united, it meant they were now at war with the Stregians, all the witches, instead of a particular species, and unlike the Cruetians, not all of Alexander's allies had armies filled with talented warriors, as his did. Over the centuries, Alexander had tried to place his armies near his weaker allies, but the world is an awfully big place, even the Cruetians didn't have enough Dark-Souls to protect all of it.

Alexander and his parents sat in their library discussing today's proceedings. Both his father and mother strived in educating themselves and their children, so over the centuries, they had accumulated a significant amount of scrolls and manuscripts. The library had been designed specifically for studying. It was settled in the depths of his family's castle, in the side of a mountain, protecting the documents from extreme temperatures. The room was circular with high vaulted ceilings. The documents were aligned around the room by subject, reaching as high as the stone ceiling. In the middle of the room was a long hand carved wood table, with numerous chairs surrounding it. At the moment, Alexander and his parents all occupied one of those chairs.

"You two cannot possibly think that Alexander should go and try to negotiate an alliance with the Stregians?" Alexander crooked an amused eyebrow at his father as his mother continued her ranting. "We all know they are not rational people. They do not even fight hand to hand. They use those...spells, or curses, or whatever they call them. Avitus, you cannot seriously expect Alexander to negotiate with such unreasonable people."

Avitus understood his wife's concern for their son. He didn't like the idea of Alexander going to the Stregians either. They were a very unpredictable race, and their Queen had proven more than ruthless on numerous occasions. "akribos, I understand your concern, however, neither of us sees another way. The other monarchies are unwilling to create the council without the alliance with the Stregians."

Hypatia threw her hair over her shoulder and slapped her palm on the table. "The other monarchies are using this to their advantage. They're all tired of fighting the war, and they know none of them stand a chance at negotiating an alliance themselves. Their only chance is Alexander, so they are using his council against him."

Alexander hated seeing his mother upset. She was always such a pleasant and kind woman, and normally had an extreme amount of patience. It was one of the reasons she was such a great mother. He wished he could ease her fears, but he already knew he would go to the Stregian Queen. He honestly didn't see another choice.

Avitus took Hypatia's hand hoping it would reassure her, as he spoke in the loving tone he only reserved for her. "akribos, Neither one of us are incompetent. We understand the monarchies motivation. This is Alexander's choice. You of all people know, I would never force our son to take on such an unpredictable challenge. However, Alexander and I both agree, if he concedes on this issue, the monarchies may capitulate on their other desire."

"patris!" Alexander castigated, at the same time Hypatia asked "What other desire?" Giving them her 'I-am-not-taking-anything-less-than-a-full-explanation' look.

Exasperated, Alexander rubbed his fingers back and forth over his forehead. "patris, I thought we agreed not to discuss this here."

Avitus understood this was not a topic Alexander wanted to discuss with his mother. They both knew her opinions on arranged marriages, and had no interest in listening to a lecture about other races antiquated ways, but he also had a hard time keeping secrets from his wife, and she had to understand the full ramifications of the other monarchies proposal.

"filius, I am sorry. I know what we discussed, but I believe your mother needs to know everything."

Alexander nodded, clearly unhappy, before looking at his mother. "matris, the monarchies have decided that they want me to lead the Magikos Alliance once it is formed."

"An intelligent decision........."

Alexander raised his hand, interrupting his mother's speech. However, they have two demands before they will agree to the council. One, an alliance with the Stregians. Two, they want me to wed. They want their leader to produce an heir. They are..." He paused dreading his next words, "requesting I marry the Magusian Princess."

"You will not!" Hypatia jumped out of her chair and stalked over to her husband. "Avitus you will tell those self-centered monarchs that the Cruetian people do not believe in forced marriages. We never have and we never will. The thought of our son, the Crown Prince, being forced into marriage is absurd."

"He will never be forced, akribos. I will not allow it. Even marriage must be his decision."

Hypatia swung around to face Alexander. "Is this what you want? Do you want to marry this...this...fairy princess? Do they even understand that she would have to become a Dark-Soul? Is she willing to live our life? What about you and Catherine? Are you willing to give up your happiness?"

Alexander had never seen his mother so angry. This was the exact reason he had not wanted to tell her about the second stipulation. They all knew and respected their mother's feelings on arranged marriages. No one wanted a loveless marriage. Since his father and mother had a fairytale relationship, well...most the time. Every one of his siblings, including himself had dreamed of that forever love. No,

he didn't want to marry the fairy princess, but he did feel the Magikos Alliance was worth the sacrifice. "No, matris. I do not want to marry Tanya, and she has assured me, she has no interest in marrying me either. Which is why, we believe if I am able to negotiate an alliance with the Stregians, the monarchies will concede the marriage. As for Catherine, we occasionally see each other. Nothing more. At this time, I am not serious about marrying anyone. When the Magikos Alliance is formed, I will have enough to deal with between my current responsibilities, and the councils. I will not have time for a wife. I promise someday I will give our people their heir, just as I will give the Magikos Alliance theirs, but for now, I am not interested in any one woman."

Well! That took the wind right out of her sails. "gios, I am so proud of you. Someday you are going to make some lucky woman a fine husband." She patted his cheek. "I see how important this council is to you, and I understand why you have to try for this horrible alliance. Just promise me you will be careful." Alexander nodded. "Then I will allow you and your father to make plans. Hurry back home!" She reached up and kissed his cheek, "I Love you, Alexander." And she shifted out of the library.

Both Alexander and Avitus let out a long sigh of relief. That had actually ended better than either could have imagined.

For the next 2 hours, they examined every aspect of Alexander's strategy. They decided that he should leave immediately, to begin tracking down the Stregian Queen. In the meantime, Avitus would ask that tomorrow's meeting be postponed until Alexander returned.

Alexander's nightmare drifted in and out of memories, until he found himself walking through a dense forest towards the traitor's castle. He tried to stop, but his body continued forward. If only he could halt, the curse would never happen. Why couldn't he stop?

It had taken a week to finally arrange a meeting with the Stregian Queen, and since then they had been in negotiations for 5 days. Alexander had shifted every night back to his family's castle to speak with his father and give him an update on the negotiations. It seemed his father's assumptions had been accurate. The other monarchies had agreed that they could live without Alexander's marriage if he was able to forge an alliance with the Stregians. It seems that the monarchies conceding that one stipulation might be the only way he was going to be able to reach an agreement with Queen Miander. It was obvious, the Magusians and Stregians think more alike than he had anticipated. Queen Miander was insisting on the exact same stipulation the monarchies had demanded, an arranged marriage between him and her daughter, Princess Fiona. Since Cruetian law only allows one union, he could not have agreed to both marriages. Not that Alexander approved of arranged marriages, and he definitely had never wanted one for himself, but he could appreciate the thought process behind it. Naturally, if the witch princess married the Dark-Soul crown prince, no Cruetian or Stregian would ever attack one another again. It did make sense; he just hated people playing with his life. Furthermore, he knew how his mother was going to react. She had just had a fit over the idea of an arranged marriage with one of their allies; he could only imagine her reaction to an arranged marriage with one of their enemies.

Alexander sat in the Stregians thrown room, trying to persuade the Stregian monarchy against the marriage. Queen Miander was the middle sister of triplets. When the Stregians formed, this family had become their monarchy, and since Miander seemed to have the strongest powers, she had been named Queen. They were definitely not what Alexander had expected. As triplets, he had assumed they would all look alike, they were actually quite different. Queen Miander was tall with straight jet black hair that graced her shoulders, and golden eyes that resembled honey. Her older sister, Satyria, was short, no taller than 5 feet, and had crystal blue eyes that reminded him of lapis, with long silver hair that sparkled like moonlight. Their younger sister, Lailee, stood somewhere in between the two. She had flaming red hair, and light green eyes that sparkled like peridots. Of the three, their Queen was the most difficult to get along with, and Alexander was afraid they had reached an impasse.

"Prince Alexander, this is not an option. If you want the wars to cease and the Stregians to join the Magikos Alliance, you will marry

my daughter. I can assure you, she is a worthy woman to hold the title of the Cruetian Crown Princess."

Alexander knew they were at a stalemate. Either he married her daughter, or he would have to wait to establish the council. "Your majesty, I am not insinuating your daughter is unworthy as a wife. I am simply inquiring, if she herself is willing to follow through with this union. As I have explained, your princess will have to become a Dark-Soul herself to conceive my children."

Miander laughed and clapped her hands twice. "My dear sweet prince, of course Fiona understands her responsibilities. She will be honored to marry such a fine commander, and into such a distinguished monarchy. If you doubt me, you may ask her yourself."

As Miander pointed towards the entry way, Alexander saw a woman walk through who could have passed as the Queen's twin. The only difference between the two was Fiona's long black hair. Braided it hit below her calves, loose it must drag behind her. Pity! As attractive as Fiona was, she stirred nothing inside him.

Fiona walked over to the man her mother had chosen as her husband. He was extremely handsome; he wore his golden blond hair a little longer than the traditional pageboy style, his eyes were a bright teal, as she walked around him they seemed to change from blue to green. Even under his armor, she could see his taut muscles. He was a fine male specimen. Any woman would be proud to call this man her husband.

Fiona stood in front of Alexander and curtsied. "My Lord, I am well aware of my duties, and what a marriage to you entails." Alexander shivered as her long nails traced his jaw line. "With such an attractive and virile man," she traced his lower lip, "how could I refuse?"

Alexander was also well aware of his responsibilities. He knew not only did his own people depend on him, but so did his allies. He just hoped his mother would understand when he brought home his new wife.

Alexander tried to push the next memories away. His nightmare had just become pure horror, as he relived the last thing Fiona bestowed upon him before her execution.

Her memories!

Alexander stood in their bed chamber watching Fiona give herself to Seth. Alexander knew it was 1208 AD, just days before Fiona's execution. If her desire had been to torture him, these memories had accomplished that.

It had been 2 1/2 years since Fiona gave up her life for her people, marrying Prince Alexander and enduring the painful transformation to become a Dark-Soul and his wife. Somehow in the last 2 years, she had even been able to earn Alexander's love. Not that she loved him, she never had. This union was her mother's plan to take down their worst enemy from the inside.

Alexander had been the only obstacle in her mother's way to conquer the rest of the otherworldly races. His alliances had united them, making them difficult to defeat. Just as the Stregians were stronger by uniting all the witch covens, Alexander's allies were virtually indestructible. What they hadn't anticipated was her. Fiona was raised knowing her duties and the sacrifices those responsibilities might require, so when her mother explained her plan to rid the otherworldly races of Alexander's leadership, she immediately agreed. What neither of them had anticipated was being able to ruin the Cruetian race completely.

Not long after her marriage, Fiona met Alexander's cousin Seth. Seth was older than Alexander and the first born son to Alexander's Egyptian uncle, Amun. It seems when the goddess Hecate helped the three Titan protectors escape Zeus's wrath, she split them up between Asia, Egypt, and Greece. Since Alexander's father was the first Titan protector created, it was agreed that he would become the Cruetian King. Fortunately for Fiona, Seth disagreed with Amun, his father, on this issue, and believed since he was the first born son of any of the Titan protectors; he should be the heir to the Cruetian throne. Utilizing Seth's desires for her and the throne, she was able not only to assure Alexander's demise, but also the entire Cruetian monarchy.

Fiona stood behind Seth, running her hands through his long slick black hair. She knew every sensual spot on his warrior body, and knew how to make him beg for his release. It was how she had earned his loyalty in the first place. Sex and Seth's desire for the Cruetian throne. Fiona slowly circled him, gliding her long nails over his sensitive flesh, delighting in each of Seth's tremors.

"Are your people in place for the raids?"

Seth grabbed Fiona, spinning her around before plastering the temptress' back to his chest. "Just as you have set the stage for the family gathering, my part of the plan is secure." He slowly rubbed his hands up and down her hips, "Tomorrow many will have died, and the babies you need for your sacrifices will be secured." He nuzzled her ear as he plunged deep inside her. With each pounding stroke, he staked his claim. "Three. Days. You. Will. Officially. Be. Mine."

Fiona's body burst just moments before Seth growled with completion. Truly, sex was the one thing she was going to miss; both Alexander and Seth were exceptional in bed. What a shame all Dark-Soul's must die.

Seth could sense Fiona concealing something from him. What, he was unsure. Everything seemed to be playing out precisely as planned. His part was the raids, on the unsuspecting Cruetian families with babies. Babies she needed as powerful sacrifices for her rituals. In exchange for his part of the plan, she had called a gathering of the royal family. Cruetians always announced a royal heir at a gathering of the entire sovereignty. It was a long standing tradition. Not that Fiona was pregnant, but that would be the assumption, since she called the gathering. With the entire Cruetian monarchy present, Fiona would poison the wine, debilitating them, allowing his warriors the opportunity to sever their heads. In one move, she would wipe out every royal Dark-Soul leaving the throne to Seth. There couldn't have been a more perfect plan.

Fiona reached for her clothes as Seth seized her arm. "Kyria!" She knew something was wrong when he used her official title. The Cruetians distinguished their royalty by titles. Kyria meant Crown Princess, where Kyrios was Alexander's title, Crown Prince. All of Alexander's siblings and cousins held the titles Basilo or Basila. "Do not try to deceive me. I have waited a very long time for my throne."

"Basilo, Never raise your voice to me!" Fiona blared. Calming

herself she took a deep breath. "You know I would never deceive you, Amayo." Using the Cruetian endearment 'My Love', she teased his lips with her tongue "Remember in 3 days, this will all be ours."

Seth couldn't think as Fiona kissed him. "I am sorry, Amaya. You are right, we are so close. I am just nervous." He smiled as he grabbed his clothes. "I should be going. Tonight we begin."

Kalab shifted into Alexander's office. At first glance, he didn't spot his Commander, but he could hear his distress. He silently unsheathed his sword. Staying in the shadows, he slowly moved around the room. He found Alexander tossing and turning on the couch, moaning in pain. Kalab could see there was no danger. Alexander was just caught in another nightmare. Should he try to wake him? He reached out to touch Alexander's arm, and was grabbed in a bone crushing grip. He looked down at his Commander who was still asleep, still caught in his nightmare. He pried his way out of Alexander's grip, and decided to leave him alone.

Alexander hated leaving his warriors during battle, he knew his generals could handle the Lycanthropes, but it wasn't his nature to walk away from a fight. As much as he loathed the idea of leaving, he was also extremely excited. His wife had called a family gathering, which could mean only one thing. At last, he was going to be a father.

Alexander had waited until the last minute to leave his warriors. He shifted directly from the battlefield into his bed chamber, determined to clean up before meeting his guests, and hoping Fiona would be waiting for him. Instead, it was Kalab, one of the royal guards, waiting inside his chamber with Fiona held as a prisoner.

"What is the meaning of this? Untie her."

Kalab heard the death threat in his Commander's words. "I am sorry, Kyrios. I cannot. I caught....your wife poisoning tonight's wine. I was unsure how to handle the situation, so I restrained her here until your arrival."

Alexander was confused. Kalab must be mistaken, because Fiona would never harm his family.

Kalab could see the disbelief in Alexander's eyes. "Kyrios, I can prove it." He pointed to the floor where a trap lay with a rat inside.

He poured a small amount of wine into the rat's mouth, and within minutes it was dead. "I am sorry, Kyrios."

Alexander was shocked. The disbelief wayed heavy on his mind, but he had seen it with his own eyes. "Fiona?"

"Do not look so stunned, Alexander. Did you honestly believe I could love my enemy? I could never love you." She laughed.

"Kalab" Alexander choked back the lump in his throat "Take her away. There is only one punishment for...Treason. Execution!"

Kalab could see the hurt in Alexander's face. He could barely speak the words, as he condemned his wife to death.

"Yes, Commander! Kyrios, there is one more thing you should know. Prior to your arrival, she confessed more of her treason. Your cousin Seth was her lover and accomplice. Together they plotted to kill the monarchy. It seems they are also responsible for the raids on our people." He bowed his head. "Since we found no survivors, we assumed everyone dead. Kyrios, they kidnapped the babies...for sacrifices."

Alexander closed his eyes, not wanting to believe what he was hearing. "Are they alive?"

"Seth has them hidden."

"Find them!"

Kalab hated being the one to tell Alexander about his wife's treachery, but was dreading his next revelation even more. "Kyrios, Seth escaped. We have guards tracking him as we speak."

Kalab knew the betrayal was wearing heavy on Alexander's soul, as he watched his prince struggle to gain control over his emotions. Alexander had lost a lot tonight, but Kalab knew his Commander wouldn't rest until the children were found, and the traitors were dead. No matter how difficult it was on him personally.

The loss was overwhelming, as Alexander understood the full ramifications of his wife's betrayal. Innocents had died, and the only one to blame was himself. He had to pull together. His feelings would have to wait, for others needed him. "The traitor was my wife. I will execute her myself...in the morning. If you need me, I will be in the court explaining the situation."

Alexander wasn't even sure if he was dreaming anymore, everything seemed so real. The anger, the pain, the guilt, the realization that Fiona had never loved him, all came crashing down on him. He felt the weight and could barely breathe. This felt too real to be a nightmare. Alexander felt like he was reliving it all over again.

A bright light flashed, as Alexander's blade sliced through Fiona's neck. On the platform beside him stood Fiona's mother and a tall beautiful red head, he recognized her immediately as Cerridwen, the Celtic Goddess of Magic; before Alexander could speak, Cerridwen through her arms towards him.

"I grant your revenge, Miander, and empower your curse. I abolish the Cruetian way of life. No longer will they turn others into their kind, their children will be a thing of the past. In time all Dark-Soul's will cease to exist." With the slap of Cerridwen's hands, another beautiful woman appeared behind Alexander.

"Cerridwen, what have you done to my people?" She walked forward, her long black hair swirled around her body.

"Hecate, they have been punished for killing the witches princess unjustly. As the Greek Goddess of Witchcraft, are witches not your people. Should you not protect them?"

Hecate laughed as she pointed to Miander. "Cerridwen, you are a fool. She and her daughter tried to kill my Cruetians. They also are my people. Titan blood runs through their veins. I will not allow you to destroy them."

"You are too late, it is already done." Cerridwen jerked Miander's arm "but I assure you, she will pay for her deception, and her punishment will be harsh. Oh, and Hecate...DO NOT EVER CALL ME A FOOL!" With a flash they were gone.

Hecate turned, flashing Fiona's body away. She looked down at Avitus and Alexander, who were on their knees before her. "Sweet Alexander, do not blame yourself. Fiona was like her mother, a vile, evil woman. Avitus, my loyal protector, I cannot vanquish another goddesses curse. However, I can alter it."

Hecate laid her hands upon their heads. "Cerridwen wishes to punish, so only your lawless will meet her true fate. Stay true to your beginnings, protect the innocent and never intentionally take their lives, this will change Cruetian fate. As the other Dark races must find their one true mate to procreate, so must you. Follow your heart and with a kiss, a matching sign will appear on your chosen one's left hand. To protect our people, I allow you to turn dying warriors into Dark-Souls, but only upon their last breath. Nothing else has changed. The sun will still weaken you, and the moon will be your strength." Helping them stand, she flashed a sword in each of their hands. "Alexander, follow this sword to find the one that is reborn in fire, for he will help you find your mate. As you need her, so does our people. Avitus, my old friend, you have done us proud, continue to protect us, and with this sword, we will continue to protect you."

Alexander felt himself falling as he landed in a meadow surrounded by large stones. He looked around realizing he was in the Stregian homeland in 1572.

Naturally after the curse, a war broke out between the Stregians and the Cruetians. A war that lasted three centuries, until humans started hunting and killing witches. Humans captured Miander and burned her at the stake, freeing the Stregians from her control. The new governing Queen decided they could not fight the humans alone, and asked for this meeting with Alexander.

"We need your help, my lord" Naitaya, the new Queen was pleading. She was tall for a Stregian, over 6' with black hair and black eyes, and very young compared to the others.

"Release the curse on my people, and we will protect you." Alexander replied, clearly happy that the witches were in need of his services. Maybe now, he could remedy his mistake from all those centuries before. He should never have married, or trusted Fiona, not even for an alliance. A mistake he would never make again.

"We cannot!" Satyria, Miander's older sister tried to explain. "Not that we are refusing to, but without Miander we cannot remove the curse. The curse was instated by a cone of power. Cerridwen requires the original three to abolish it."

"My apologies, ladies!" Alexander continued "My warriors will not fight for a people that holds a curse over our heads."

"What if we can change the curse?" Lailee, Miander's younger sister asked "what if we can ease the curse?"

Alexander hadn't really paid any attention to her until now, he remembered their first meeting, and how quiet she had been.

"How?" He asked unconvinced.

Lailee looked between the other two, both nodding their heads in agreement, as if they were able to hear what she was thinking.

"We could give your Amara the power to find other chosen ones. We would be willing to bestow Stregian powers upon her. If the other Magikos Alliances are willing to do the same, she would be powerful enough to find your people's Amaras. We have foreseen this prophecy. Since you are the leader of the Magikos Alliance, I do not think they would refuse your request, do you?"

"That will not help me." Alexander argued. "I still have to find my Amara, and as you know, that is the most difficult task. I might never find her."

"Wrong!" They all three said simultaneously.

"Naitaya is half Lunarian" Lailee revealed "we reached an alliance with their Council last year."

"Then why do you need the Cruetians." Alexander asked.

"My mother's people will not harm humans. Not even in self-defense." Naitaya explained. "Satyria and Lailee have been trying to lift your curse. I even tried to help them acting as Miander, but without her, Cerridwen has not appeared. With my Lunarian power, we can ease it as Lailee stated, but no more. We are truly sorry."

Naitaya could see Alexander contemplating her offer. "We could create a cone of power. Using your blood, we would raise your Amara's mark. We also know where you can find...the Phoenix. We are aware of Hecate's mandate. The goddess has given us the location of the Phoenix."

"If you can do this, why not do it for all my people?" Alexander prodded.

"A cone of power uses a lot of energy; it's not something we can do very often." Naitaya added, "but as Lailee suggested, we can change the curse, by giving your Amara a gift of Magikos powers."

Alexander studied Naitaya for a few moments. She could be part Lunarian, it would explain her features. Not much is known about this warrior race, except they are vicious fighters and have amazing powers. It's said they were created by the goddess Morrigan to cull her shape-shifters, the Morfians, and that she gave them powers of the Blue Moon. If they could substantiate their alliance with the Lunarians, then a truce with the Stregians would prove very beneficial. For their allies would become his.

Alexander had agreed to alliances with both the witches and warriors. Even after 400 years that alliance has remained strong. They have always kept their side of the truce, even helping him locate the Phoenix, Kelmar. This time his dream drifted and Kelmar stood before him, just as he had done the day Kelmar foreseen Alexander's Amara.

As was spoken long ago, you live in turmoil.
A life with many achievements and successes,
a life utterly alone.
You will ultimately find peace in your... Kara.
She awaits you in another time.
Small and beautiful,
her strength, love, and compassion will equal your own.
As will her spirit, power, and intelligence.
Balance will be bestowed upon you, as the Darkness Falls.
Your Kara will be different from you in many ways,
her gifts will make you whole.
Your children will be like no others
that have ever walked this great earth.
As you are now the protector, they will be the uniters.
Find your chosen one in a human.
Born in the year 1986,
in a land called the United States of America.
Find her in a place called Fort Collins, Colorado.
She will become a woman in the year 2004.
Find her and show her the man you truly are.

Kalab relaxed, as he saw Alexander's breathing return to normal. He had been worried, as it seemed his Commander had been gasping for air a few minutes earlier. Maybe now that Alexander wasn't attacking everything, he would try to wake him.

Alexander kneeled in front of the goddess Hecate. This was a memory he didn't remember.

"Kara" Hecate said "Find Kara! You must hurry, Alexander. Open your hand." As Alexander obeyed her request, he felt something hard and cold placed inside his palm. "As your mate, she must wear this rare stone, this extremely rare diamond will protect her. Hurry! Until you and Kara blood bond, many will die."

Alexander could hear someone calling his name as Hecate began to fade. Just before she vanished, he saw a face. A blond haired angel and he heard "Kara!"

Could this be his *Amara?* Had he finally seen her?

He felt someone shaking his shoulder. Alexander slowly opened his eyes, finding himself looking into his bodyguard's dark glare.

2

"You all right?"

Alexander sat up, noticing the layer of sweat dampening his body. No wonder Kalab's glare looked concerned. "Nightmare!" He croaked. "It was just a…" Alexander looked down, he was holding something, opening his hand…he discovered the pink diamond. "Damn! She was real."

"Who?"

"Hecate! She visited my nightmare. She's trying to tell me……" Alexander jumped up, ran to his desk, and began shuffling through reports in lightning speed. "Sonofabitch!" The reports went flying off his desk. "Seth knows. He's after her. Every woman murdered was born in 1986, the same year as my *Amara*." Alexander looked up in horror. "Kalab, this is not a coincidence. *Seth knows!*"

Kalab gripped the hilt of his sword. Like hell was some low-life going to get their hands on Alexander's *Amara*. Alexander has already lived through enough pain. It was time his Commander had a little happiness in his life. "What does he know? Do you think his assassins know why we're here?"

Alexander became a human doctor, to not only care for his human *Amara*, but so he also had a viable excuse to move to Fort Collins, Colorado. As a doctor, he convinced the human authorities that there was a need to research the differences and similarities among their species, and that research should be done at the university here in town. It gave them the perfect ruse for moving there 10 years earlier.

Alexander built a fortress outside of town, with his youngest brother and sister, Nathaniel and Adelina. Hoping when the time came it would be enough to protect his *Amara*.

"I'm not sure. By the females they've murdered, they obviously know she's human and born in 1986. Since they've been killing in Europe, I would assume they're not aware she's here, but it won't take them long to figure it out. It's more important than ever that we find her. Inform my father...*Regis* of the situation, he'll lead them away from us. I'll send for reinforcements."

Alexander strolled over to the window overlooking main street below. It was spring in the Rockies, and everything was beginning to bud. He enjoyed all the green, and the smell of the pine trees as the wind came across the foothills. He watched the humans stroll by, having no real idea of the dangers that encompassed their world. If only he could be so naïve. Damn his enemies! Again, innocents were dying because of him. He had to find his *Amara* and bond with her, it was the only way to stop the killings and save his race, but would this woman be a blessing or another curse? If his *Amara* was as selfish as his first wife, she would never help his people. On the other hand, if she wasn't, this would be their salvation. Salvation, in yet another woman destined to be his. Could he trust this woman, or would he be making *another* huge mistake? A mistake he swore he would never make again. In yet, here he stood, possibly getting ready to do the exact same thing. Could this new woman truly love him? This woman the fates chose as his. Would she be kind, compassionate, and caring, or would she be deceitful, calculating, and manipulating like his last wife? A greedy, heartless witch, a *putalla* who had all but destroyed his people.

Alexander let out a frustrated sigh, as he plopped down into his black leather executive chair. Everyday, Fiona haunted him and his people. It's too bad the bitch's memory couldn't stay dead. Even after 800 years, Fiona still pissed him off. No! She didn't just piss him off; he wanted to kill her all over again. Except this time, he wouldn't just execute her. He'd torture her ruthlessly. He'd make sure she felt the pain she had put his race through. The pain Fiona continually put him through, the destiny she had robbed him of. Alexander was well aware that nothing good came from remembering his wife. In yet, for the

last five years, those memories had been eating away at him every...
single...day. No matter how hard he tried to banish them, they were
always sitting right at the back of his mind, waiting for a chance to
besiege him, and today, it seemed the flood gates had opened.

Alexander scrubbed his hand over his face, and closed his eyes.
Had anyone else noticed the similarities of his current situation, to the
circumstances that had caused their curse in 1208? Or was he the only
one concerned with the fact, that again, he would be trusting another
foreign woman, with the future of his people. Granted in 1205, it had
been his decision to marry the Stregian princess, Fiona. Alexander
had basically sold the Cruetians for an alliance. An alliance that most
of the otherworld deems his greatest achievement, simply because the
council has been such a success, but all he sees is the centuries of pain
it has caused his own race, along with...how many innocent deaths?
How stupid he had been.

In the 800 years since the curse, only a few Dark-Souls have
actually stumbled across their chosen ones, causing Alexander to hate
himself and Fiona more and more each day. He hated seeing his people
suffer. They could fall in love with someone, but if they're beloved's
not immortal, they have to watch them die, unable to turn them, and
if they weren't their chosen one, no matter how much they love them,
they are *never* able to have children. For a race that thrives on families,
this has been the worst part of the curse. Again...All...His...Fault.
Again...the reason Alexander's here. To make amends.

It took his people centuries to understand that the mark could be
on any race not just Cruetians. Alexander figured the fates enjoyed
toying with their minds. The marks are always hidden on the left hand,
and only revealed during a kiss, making it virtually impossible to find
your *Amara*. To make matters worse, the Cruetian and their chosen
one have to become blood bonded, it's the only way to make their
Amara immortal, tying them eternally to their Dark-Soul. It wouldn't
be so bad, except some races view drinking blood disgusting. Causing
other issues altogether.

"Damn!" Alexander slammed his fist onto his desk.

Frustrated, he got up and walked to his window. Where *is* his

Amara? 10 years they've lived here, and he was no closer to finding her. No closer than the day he had arrived in this small college town.

Alexander chuckled to himself. The residents here would chastise him, if they thought he considered their town small. They're very proud of how much their town has grown. Still not as big as Denver, but they claim, it's no longer a town…it's a city. Of course, he would always think of it as a town. Rome, Paris, New York, these are cities; Denver is even small in comparison.

Considering how tiny Fort Collins is, it shouldn't be this difficult to track down one woman. If Kelmar was correct, and there was no reason to doubt him, than his *Amara* will turn 23 years old this year. If only Kelmar could see more than his *Amara's* location. Her name would have definitely been helpful.

"You know prophecies don't work that way."

Alexander chuckled at that. Kalab, his personal guard had returned. Kalab was standing in his favorite corner watching Alexander like he always did. After Fiona's treachery, Alexander's father insisted on a personal guard, one that was not part of the royal family. Kalab had been the royal guard who exposed Fiona for who she truly was, so even though he had been a very young guard at the time, Alexander had entrusted his life to him. It was the best decision he had ever made. Kalab is an honorable warrior and a strong fighter. He towers at 6'5" and is built like the ancient Gladiators. Of course, Alexander was a feared warrior in his own right, but it never hurt to have Kalab watching out for him, especially when he was working and somewhat distracted.

"I know you're not a telepath, but sometimes…I sure in the hell wonder." Alexander replied.

"You are constantly standing up and sitting down, just to repeat the action a few minutes later. *Kyrios*, after 800 years, I believe I can read your body language without having to read your mind." Kalab sighed and plopped down into a chair, knowing this was going to be a long day. Anytime his Commander began blaming himself for their people's situation, the guilt would eat at him for hours. "*Kyrios*, we will find her, and she will be everything Kelmar promised. You will truly be, a very lucky man, and our people will be fortunate to have her."

Maybe Kalab was right. The fates are Greek goddesses after all. It's not like we're dealing with another pantheon. Could the fates be so cruel? Alexander snorted. Of course they could. They've done it before. Look what happened with Fiona? Hopefully Kalab was correct about his *Amara*. Since his allies have agreed to bestow powers upon her, she is destined to become very powerful. It was one of the reasons he decided to bring an envoy to Colorado in 1999. They began searching for his *Amara*, hoping his enemies would not realize why they were actually here. Unfortunately, as they found out today, someone has acquired her information, or at least part of it. They know she's human; a fact that still shocks Alexander after 400 years. No one wants his enemies to locate her first. Yes, If Kelmar said his *Amara* lives in this town, than she definitely walks these streets. He just needs to hurry and find her. No matter what his personal fears are, the curse demands he claim her.

Alexander felt his brother enter the room, but he didn't turn around. Nathaniel was his youngest brother, only 850 years old. He still fully enjoyed life. How Alexander wished he could be so care free. Nathaniel appreciates, what he calls, the current trends. Right now, that equates to black leather and Harley's. It actually matches his personality pretty well.

"Seeing that you're at that window again, and Kalab's frowning. You must have discovered something in the reports."

"Seth knows about my *Amara*." Alexander admitted, sounding somewhat defeated. "All the females that his warriors are killing are humans born in 1986."

"Shit!" Nathaniel sunk down into a big white leather chair. Alexander's taste has always been impeccable. His office has a large mahogany, hand carved, antique desk with a white marble top. Hanging behind it, are built-in matching cabinets. In the corner, where Nathaniel was relaxing, are two big white leather chairs facing a hand carved mahogany coffee table, and a white leather sofa.

Alexander turned around looking at his brother, who was now

lounging, on the other side of his office next to Kalab, looking over the reports himself. Nathaniel must have grabbed them off the desk before he sat down. Unlike Alexander, who took his blonde hair and teal eyes from their mother, Nathaniel looked like their father, with black hair and deep blue eyes. Most people never even realize they're brothers, until they see the tattoo, three arrows crossing each other and tied with laurel leaves, on the inside of their right wrist. The Cruetian insignia!

Frustrated, Alexander combed his fingers through his hair. "Nathaniel, I have to find my *Amara*. You know this will only get worse until we find her. They will keep killing human females until she is my wife, or until they kill her."

"The good thing is, they're obviously unaware she's in the U.S. Apparently your plan is still in effect. Coming here 10 years ago, under the ruse of research, was a brilliant cover. Only the immediate family, your trusted generals, and Kelmar knew she would be born with the sign, so no one will be looking for it. I have to admit, whoever is murdering innocents, I'd love to put my blade across their treacherous necks. I can't believe Seth has so many followers. If only we could find *him*."

Sighing discouragingly, Alexander turned back around to the window, watching the people below. "*fratellino,* you won't have to kill him. I will. Thank the gods no one's decided to look here, but how long until they figure it out. It's bad enough women are dying in Europe, simply because they were born the same year she was, but what would happen if they find out we know she's here. This is not a very big town. Nathaniel, they could wipe out the entire female population in less than a week."

Nathaniel heard the stress and worries in his brother's voice, and knew Alexander was right. What worried him more, is that Alexander's chosen one is an American female. That in itself could pose a whole different set of problems. She's already 23 years old. Americans tend to commit themselves fairly quickly. What if she is already taken? What is she refuses Alexander? American women tend to be more independent and stubborn than European women, but he didn't want to add to his brother's worries. Not yet, they hadn't even found her…yet.

"Don't worry *adelfos*. We'll find her." Nathaniel vowed. Kelmar had made it clear, Alexander and his *Amara's* children were destined to be uniters. Without them, wars will continue and millions will die. A fate the world did not need. They *had* to find her.

Alexander chuckled. Not a happy chuckle, one of resignation. He stepped back from the window and walked to the sitting area, putting his hand on Nathaniel's shoulder. "I know your right, *fratellino*, it just doesn't change the fact that people are dying." He walked over to his coat and started putting it on. "I have a few errands to run. Any sign of her at the club yet?"

Their sister, Adelina, had suggested opening a night club 2 years ago, assuming at her age, Alexander's *Amara* would end up through their doors. All college students' party, or so they had thought, but after 2 years…nothing. It made them all wonder if she still lived here. Maybe she had moved. Americans tend to move around a lot, but Kelmar insists the information is accurate, and that she's still living here.

"No, not………"

The door slammed open as all three of them ducked into their attacking crouches, ready to spring at any impending danger.

"Whoa…guys." Adelina through her hands up in the air. "It's just me. Aren't *you* guys a little jumpy today. What's going on?"

"Damn you, Adelina." Alexander spat, coming out of his crouch. "Could you stop with the dramatics, we could've hurt you."

"Well, aren't you just *Mr. Appreciative* today. I didn't mean to scare you guys; I was just a little excited. Guess what?" She looked between all three of them smiling and biting her lip while waiting for them to guess. When they didn't say anything, she again yelled "Guess what? Come on you guys, you look so discouraged. Guess what I found?"

Nathaniel laughed, rolling his eyes at Alexander "You might as well hang up your jacket and sit back down, *adelfos*. Adelina's so excited, you're not going anywhere without guessing her secret. She's probably found some new light fixture for the Denver club or something useless like that."

"Shut up, Nat! Or I won't tell you guys my *life* saving news."

Kalab chuckled. "Life saving? I thought that's my job."

Alexander was laughing when he hung up his coat and plopped down on the sofa, stretching out with his hands behind his head. "I think your right *fratellino*; she must have found a new dress. What color is it, *sorella*?"

"You guys are completely stupid. I said this was *life* changing and you three........."

"Did you tell him?"

They all turned to see a beautiful woman standing in the door. At 5'9" she looked every bit the goddess she was born from. With her pale skin, black hair, and dark eyes, she had the distinct features of all Lunarians. The same features as the goddess Morrigan.

"Namorita?"

"Hey, Nam." Lately Adelina had started cutting everybody's names short. She said in today's world their names were too long. "I should have known you'd show up. No, I haven't told them because their idiots. They think I'm excited over a new dress or something, but don't even think about stealing my thunder, Nam. I found it, not you."

"Adelina, I'd never steal your thunder." Namorita winked at her "but wasn't it a red sweater you found?"

"Nam, what the hell are you talking about? Oh, OHHHHH! Yes, you're right it was a red sweater." It had taken Adelina a minute to understand what Namorita was talking about. There was a red sweater involved in her discovery. Cute...Nam. Really...cute. If her dumb ass brothers wanted to treat her like she's ignorant, she could play along. At least for a little while.

"You're right! I found this great red sweater. Although I don't think it was cashmere. No, definitely not cashmere."

"What the hell are you talking about, Adelina?" She recognized Alexander's tone, he was running out of patience, but *he* was the ass that wanted to act like she was an idiot.

"Commander, maybe you should give your sister a little credit. You might want to listen to what she has to say." Namorita advised, while walking to the other chair. "I'm curious as hell what she found, aren't you?"

Ok! This was becoming very strange. First, Namorita shows up out of nowhere. Then Adelina and Namorita begin talking in some woman's code that he clearly doesn't understand. It was all really starting to piss him off. Unless…Why was Namorita here? Had something happened? She was one of his Lunarian Generals. He had reassigned her just this morning to patrol Colorado, watching for Seth's warriors. Were his enemies here? Surely not, if that was the case she wouldn't be sitting here so calm. Would she?

"Namorita, why are you here?" Alexander asked, watching her eyes for any sign of her true intentions. Namorita was one of the Lunarians who was able to see current visions. Not things happening far in the future, but visions of things that are currently taking place or will take place in the next few minutes. Namorita gave him a sly smile. "I was wondering when you were going to ask me that. I've come to see your reaction to Adelina's news."

Alexander's heart stopped. Adelina's news? He thought she had found some…Shit! He jumped up and flew to Adelina. "What did you find?"

Adelina gave Namorita a wicked smile. "Now he wants to know." Rolling her eyes, "Give me a minute. I need to get back into my excited mood." She turned around and around in a circle, jumping up and down she yelled "I found her, I found her, I fooooouuuuunnnnd her." Both Adelina and Namorita broke out into hysterical laughter.

Alexander was too stunned to move. All he could do was stand there and watch his sister jump up and down. Her auburn hair flapping on her shoulders with each movement, her bright green eyes sparkling with excitement, and her high pitched screeches, as she continued to yell. This wasn't something Adelina would joke about. This was too important, and the fact that Namorita had showed up…Adelina must have found her. He was finally going to have a life, a wife, a family. Alexander finally pulled himself together to ask.

"Are you positive?"

"Yep! She's wearing your mark. The exact same mark that is on your hand, and your sooooooo lucky, she's cute. More than cute, she's pretty. I was actually getting worried, because we have the hottest club in town, and since she'd never been in, I was afraid she might be really ugly, but nope, she's beautiful. Kelmar was right, she's so small and delicate, she's adorable."

Kelmar had walked in during all the excitement. So it was his turn to roll his eyes. "I'm always right." In all honesty he *had* begun to worry. Kelmar had always seen this place when he had his visions of Alexander's *Amara*, but after 10 years of searching, even he was beginning to doubt himself. It was a huge ego boost to finally find her.

"Adelina!" Alexander scolded. "Why didn't you immediately tell me?" As Adelina started to protest, he shook his head "and don't tell me it was because we were teasing you. This is too important." He pointed a finger at her. "Oh, and I never worried about what she would look like, she is my mate, my chosen one, my *Amara*. I accept her the way she is. Now where is she?" He asked impatiently.

Adelina was still beaming, as she noticed the astonished look on Nathaniel's face. She couldn't believe they'd found her. No. *She* had found her. All these years of searching, and finally they had her. She couldn't believe their luck. She had agreed to meet one of the local Dark-Souls to discuss Alexander's research. He had asked her to meet him at his favorite morning spot. A local tea shop that he had breakfast at every morning. He is friends with the owner, and did not want to disappoint her by not showing up. He had explained that they have been having breakfast together for over twenty years, so it was imperative that they meet there, or wait until lunch instead.

"She owns a tea shop right here on North College, and you're going to love this. Her name is Kara…Kara Spencer." Adelina slapped Alexander on the shoulder. Still jumping up and down like a 2 year old, getting her favorite candy.

Nathaniel still hadn't moved. He'd been stunned this whole time, but hearing her name snapped him out of it. "Kara? Are you sure?"

"Yes, isn't that appropriate" Adelina giggled.

"Damn! We could have saved ourselves so much time." Nathaniel replied.

"How so?" Everyone asked at once.

"Don't you all remember the prophecy?" He asked. "Kelmar kept referring to Alexander's chosen one as 'your Kara'. We all assumed he was just saying 'your beloved', but obviously, he was saying her name. Damn!" Nathaniel hit himself in the head.

Adelina cursed "Shit! You're right! Why the hell didn't you tell us that?" She pointed an accusing finger at Kelmar.

"He's no different than an oracle." Alexander snapped. Kelmar just smiled. "They do not tell you anything directly. They can't. It is part of their gift." He stated, while pulling on his coat. Adelina show me where my *Amara* is. It's time I claim her, so I can get back to my responsibilities, and she can begin saving our people."

"Alexander!" everyone yelled simultaneously.

"Alex, she's not one of us, she won't even know what this means." Adelina warned him, hoping he would understand. She knew her brother well enough to know, he wasn't used to waiting for anything. When Alexander wanted something, he expected to obtain it immediately. The beauty of being a prince and the leader of the Supernatural world, or at least that's what humans call it. Adelina silently wondered how Kara would handle their world. Humans now knew Cruetians existed, they call them vampires. Ugh!! We're not vampires! Vampires are *our* criminals. It's why centuries ago we referred to ourselves as Dark-Souls.

29 years ago, when humans discovered their vampire myths were true, they assumed Cruetians were all evil and tried to kill them. They presumed Cruetians didn't have souls. Crazy...no souls... what were they thinking? Ultimately, Cruetians tried to teach them to call them Dark-Souls. It's what Cruetians have been called for millenniums by ancient humans and otherworldly races. Humans still haven't realized the rest of the beings they call supernatural or myth, actually exist, and the Magikos council decided it was better that way. Finding Dark-Souls was an accident, and good people were lost until they could convince humans they weren't evil. Dark-Souls didn't want their allies to go through the same thing. The poor witches had already dealt with humans a few centuries ago.

"She's right!" Nathaniel continued. "This isn't Rome. We have no power here. If you try to force her, you could end up in jail. You're going to have to seduce her. You're going to have to win her over."

"*Kyrios*, this is why *I'm* here. You have to learn patience. We all know patience is not one of your strong points, but if you do not, you could lose her altogether." Kelmar warned.

Alexander chuckled. He was quite amused. "You all think that will be a problem? Have I ever had trouble bedding a woman?"

Adelina punched him in the shoulder as hard as she could.

"Ouch!"

"That's for your stupid, arrogant ego. You're not a prince here... remember? She won't even know you as the great leader you are, the amazing General, or your supposed superiority in bed. To her you're just another average guy, so you better start acting like one and get off your highness horse."

"We need to find out about her." Nathaniel was stating. "Does she have family? What does she like? Dislike?"

They all turned looking at Namorita. Who immediately put her hands up in defeat. "I can't read her yet. I'm not sure why I could see her when Adelina met her, but for one instant I saw her clearly, and knew who she was. That's why I knew she was wearing a red sweater. Sorry guys."

"Well the good thing is, the Cruetian I was meeting at her store is good friends with her. As his prince, I bet he would give you that information." Adelina stated confidently.

"I really don't have time for this." Alexander complained. "You're all wrong. I have never had trouble with women, even when they were unaware of my status in life." He gave Adelina a pointed stare. "I'm told, I'm naturally charismatic, so this shouldn't be a problem."

Kalab burst out laughing. "*Kyrios* has a point. In 800 years, I've never seen him rejected by a woman. No matter *whom* they were."

"Kalab, you need to shut up. You're not helping his ego." Adelina chastised. "The good news is she's not married. I looked at her hand. No ring. So stop acting so conceited, and let's find a way for you to win her over. Nathaniel and I will help, but your ego has to come down a thousand notches. If it doesn't you could end up losing her. She's American, you know. We've lived here for 10 years. By now, you should understand how pigheaded they can be." She poked Alexander in the chest. "Understand? Now let's go! I know she's currently there eating breakfast. Try to remember our advice."

Kelmar knew the time was now to give the prince the prophecy he'd came here with. Like Namorita, he had also seen Adelina with Kara, but he had seen more than just Kara's looks, he had seen her pain, her hurt, her fears, and most of all how lonely she was. If Alexander allowed his normal tendencies to take control, there was no doubt that Kara would run from him. Maybe not in the literal term, but in her mind, and for Kara that was far worse than physically running.

"*Kyrios!*"

As Alexander turned to look at Kelmar, he noticed his eyes glossed over. A sure sign he was about to give a prophecy. Alexander stopped and immediately listened, knowing whatever Kelmar was about to say was very important. *This* was truly why he was here.

> *Patience is a virtue you must learn,*
> *to unite yourself with your chosen one.*
> *Kara is a light with many dark spots,*
> *You must heal the dark, or lose her for eternity.*
> *When she heals, Darkness Falls!*

3

K ara enjoyed having breakfast with her uncle, Chung Yuan. He wasn't really her uncle. She adopted him years ago, or was it him adopting her? It didn't really matter, they adopted each other. He was the first vampire to settle in Colorado, after his people came out of the…closet, so to speak, in 1980. He became friends with her grandparents, and would come in every morning for breakfast. From the time she was two, she would sit on his lap eating her breakfast, listening to his stories about old China, and how tea was discovered. As a child, she was only able to see him when she stayed with her grandparents. Since Kara had her own responsibilities, like school, they hadn't seen each other as much as she would have liked. She had always adored the gentle warrior sitting across from her, even when her school friends warned her how dangerous vampires were. She knew they were just afraid of differences they didn't understand. All prejudices are fueled by fear in one way or another. This man would never harm her, he watched over her, protected her, and loved her everyday of her life. Twice a week her uncle took the time to train her in martial arts, reciting honor codes and ethics, explaining the importance of self-protection.

When Kara took over the tea store from her grandparents, he came by everyday, teaching her everything he knew about tea. He taught her how to blend and create her own unique style of teas; how to properly store tea to keep it fresh; and even how to process live tea plants. He then helped her turn the old storage space into Chinese and Japanese tea rooms, and worked with her brother to redesign the main store, giving it a more modern feel. Uncle Chung is really a great visionary.

They added the "S" shaped tea bar, and changed all the tables from tan oak to a dark red mahogany wood. They decorated everything in black, red, and gold. Naturally! In Asia red and gold are considered lucky colors, and her uncle wanted to give her store as much luck as possible. Besides, red is Kara's favorite color. They even changed the fireplace from stones, to black marble, and made it a gas fireplace. Her uncle said this way he wouldn't have to worry about her chopping wood. Ha! Like any of the men in her life would ever let her chop wood! Sometimes they were too ridiculous for their own good. Way… over protective! They even brought in beautiful red sofas to circle the fireplace. Even her grandparents approved of the new look…once it was done.

"So…Um…Uncle Chung. I've never seen you with another vampire before. Was she your date?" Kara wiggled her eyebrows at him.

Chung had known this was coming, Kara was always too curious for her own good. He had to admit, it was quite flattering having his niece think he was still capable of attracting beautiful women. Kara was a very honest person, and if she thought he still had it, then his immortality must be working out for him. "Kara, I've told you, I am *not* a Vampire. I am a Cruetian." He said disappointedly, frowning at her.

"Yeah! Yeah! Yeah! I know, but the news says it's the same thing." She teased eating a spoonful of her Zhou, a Chinese rice congee that is a popular Chinese breakfast, served with dried pork, eggs, vegetables, and tea. Since they have breakfast almost everyday together, they try to change it up, by serving a different countries breakfast each day of the week.

"They are wrong! Do not believe everything you hear or read in the news, Kara. We are different." Chung scolded. "Vampires are Cruetian criminals. They are Dark-Souls who kill or blood rape humans. Can you understand why we wouldn't want to be called vampires?"

"Fine-Fine-Fine." Kara chanted teasingly. "Sooooo? Was she your date?" She cocked her eyebrow amusingly. "Am I going to have an aunt?"

"No!" Chung said. Not amused. "You know I do not like to associate with my kind. That's why I moved here. Adelina is a researcher, and is trying to understand...um...my people's disease, and our evolution compared to humans. Her brother is a researcher at the university, and is hoping to find a cure."

"Oh! Well that's not very romantic." Kara frowned disappointed. She had really hoped that her uncle was beginning to date. She didn't really know much about his past, or his kind, because he refused to discuss it. But she knew he was lonely, and he was such a great, handsome guy, some woman should steal his heart and make him extremely happy. That woman would naturally have to meet with her approval, of course. For she would never allow him to be hurt.

"It wasn't supposed to be romantic, Kara, it was strictly business."

Alexander stepped into a modernly decorated tea shop. Instantaneously, he was hit with the sweet scent of orchids, jasmine, cherry blossoms, and pure unadulterated femininity that aroused his loins to the point of pain.

Kara!

Alexander glanced around, memorizing the store that was nothing like the traditional establishments he'd frequented in Europe and Asia, but unique in its own way. It was bright and cheery with its modern look, in yet, it had a homey atmosphere. One wall was lined with jars full of different types of tea. Above a sign read 'The Great Wall of Tea'. Amused he smiled. Someone has a great sense of humor.

Sitting at the black counter that wrapped around in an 'S' shape making itself into a bar, were five people enjoying their tea, while an older lady waited on them. In different areas of the store, were shelves full of different types of teapots and tea paraphernalia. A tall young red head was discussing the different tea infusers with customers. Pretty, if you could rid her of all the tattoos and body piercings, but she wasn't small and petite like Adelina had described Kara, and it wasn't the face he'd seen in his dream. Alexander was pretty sure that image was Kara, and she had long blond hair. He was hopeful. He loved a woman's hair teasing his skin. From the description Adelina had given, Kara would be Fae in appearance. He inhaled a deep breath, allowing her scent to infiltrate every pore of his body.

Kara looked up as the front door opened. *Wow! Holy! Shiz-nat! Is that eye candy or what! Damn! I just saturated my panties looking at him. I'm going to need a cold shower...and quick!* This wasn't a man. No! This was a living, breathing, Adonis in the flesh. Just his presence had every woman in the store panting. Add 6'1"of Herculean, hard, sculpted bronze body, clean cut golden blond hair, and those beautiful teal eyes, and you had *Mr. Drop Dead Gorgeous* in the flesh. Combining the black duster that swirled around his long powerful legs, he was definitely, that sexy, mysterious dark stranger that starred in every girl's fantasy. *Oh, Baby! He could slide that tight ass into my bed anytime.*

Alexander's head snapped towards a table in the back corner, near a black marble fireplace, where two people sat eating breakfast. There she was...his *Amara*. He felt an overwhelming pull towards the woman at that table. His dream image in the flesh.

Kara!

Adelina shot Alexander a strange look as he started towards Kara. How had he known *that* woman was Kara? She hadn't described her to him. Had she?

The man's back was to Alexander. All he could make out was long black hair that was pulled back into a ponytail, but the woman sitting across from him was breathtaking. Small, pixie like, Adelina had been right, Kara reminded him of the fairies. He knew without a shadow of a doubt this was his *Amara*. It was this incredibly beautiful woman, creating the electric pull he'd felt the instant he entered this store. Her gold spun hair was a couple shades lighter than his, and seemed to glow like sunlight. She had the most beautiful big brown eyes he'd ever seen. They sparkled like jewels in her soft heart shaped face. Her perfectly formed lips begged him to kiss her. She was wearing jeans and a tight red sweater. Alexander chuckled remembering Namorita's hint earlier. It hugged voluptuous breasts that he knew would overflow his large hands, a tiny waist, and hips he'd love to bend over his lap. Every curve was perfect. She was sexy as hell and his cock stood up to salute her.

This woman with her mesmerizing brown eyes was his chosen

one. Alexander started towards them when the man reached across the table, and folded Kara's hand into his. Alexander growled deep in his chest, as it felt like a dagger just ripped through his heart.

Mine! She is mine!

Adelina saw her brother's temper flare and grabbed his arm. Neither of them knew this couple's relationship. Even if they were intimate, Alexander couldn't go storming over there if he was going to try and win Kara over. Shaking her head, she pulled him back towards her. "She doesn't know who you are, *adelfos.* Calm yourself!"

Alexander paused trying to compose himself, jealousy ripping through every cell of his body, screaming for him to kill the man who dared touch his *Amara.* The jealousy he felt was undeniable. Surprising, but undeniable! The need to rip that man's heart out was as strong as killing his enemy on the battlefield. In yet, Adelina was right, Kara didn't even know he existed. Could she feel the pull between them? Did she know she was created specifically for him? Alexander knew he would have to control his emotions, somehow, someway, until he could explain all this to her.

Adelina must have sensed his fury, because she patted his arm in comfort, letting him know everything would work out. He just hoped she was right. His people needed this woman. *He* might actually need this woman. Now there's a scary thought, a fearless warrior needing a woman? Alexander's dad needed his mom, so maybe warriors do need good women. *Yikes!*

Kara couldn't take her eyes off the very tall, incredibly handsome man that was looking around her store. She was sure a lake of drool had puddled on the table. So completely sensual, he had 'Do Me!' written all over, every inch of those sinewy muscles. His swagger alone breathed danger, excitement, and made every woman around him wet and crazy with need. Kara knew instantly he was not like the men she'd dated. No! They were all boys attempting to be men. This fine male specimen was *all* man. 100%...Grade...A...Male! Kara was knocked out of her fantasy, and swung back into reality when her uncle touched her hand.

As Alexander and Adelina approached the table, they could

hear the conversation as clearly as if they were sitting at the table themselves. Just one of the many benefits of being a Dark-Soul, all their senses were amplified a hundred times over humans, so listening in on private conversations was quite a simple task.

"Do *not* worry about me." Chung scolded.

Kara scowled. "You know I do........"

"I have lived a long time, *bao-bei*, I worry more for you......"

"*bao-bei*?"

Kara looked up to see Uncle Chung's so called business associate standing at their table, accompanied by that very tall, and extremely handsome stud she'd been ogling just minutes before. Her breathing staggered as she looked up and down every inch of his body that she wanted to map with her tongue. A strange sensation enveloped her, like little waves of electricity flashing all over her skin as she looked into the teal depths of his eyes. He smiled knowingly. She jerked her eyes back to Adelina.

Kara had been introduced to Adelina earlier, a beautiful woman, appearing to be in her mid- twenties. Adelina's auburn red curls touched her shoulders in a light caress, and her bright green eyes seemed to study both of them for an intensely long moment. This woman makes every woman in the room take a couple hits on her self-esteem when she walks through. The hottie standing next to her was no exception. Up close he was even more amazing than when she had spied him across the room. He looked like he had just stepped off the front cover of GQ magazine. Clean cut, he wore his beautiful blond hair short, with just enough length at the back of his neck for her fingers to lewdly roam through. His eyes were a brilliant teal, odd but exceptionally breathtaking, she had never seen anything like them. They reminded her of the ocean she had visited in Greece. Worse, when their eyes met, her body shook to her core, sending warmth and moisture pooling between her thighs. She had this incredible urge to wrap her arms around him and kiss him breathless, *or maybe let him kiss me breathless.* He had the most luscious full lips. *Oooooh, they were made for kissing.* Kara's mind slapped herself back into reality.

What the hell are you thinking? He's probably Adelina's fiancé or something. They could even be married. Get a hold of yourself, you stupid lustful girl. It's one thing to fantasize, but this is reality. Get your mind out of his pants!

"Adelina, you came back. Is everything ok?" Chung was asking. "When you rushed out of here, I was worried." He motioned for her to join them, and Adelina sat down next to him in the booth. Kara just smiled. *Business acquaintance, huh? Yeah right!*

"No everything is fine...now." Adelina smiled at Kara, giving her the feeling there was something she was missing in this whole conversation. "There was a mix up, that's all, but we can continue our earlier conversation...Now. If that's ok?"

As often as Chung had told Kara that he had no interest in his own people, he found himself pleasantly surprised to find out that more of his people lived right here in Fort Collins. He had been disappointed when Adelina had left so abruptly. "Absolutely!" He handed her a menu. "I know Kara would be happy to get you breakfast."

Adelina opened the menu acting like she was looking it over, but realized she needed to find out what Kara and Chung's relationship was immediately, before her brother blew a gasket. "Earlier, I hadn't realized Kara was your *bao-bei*. If you would like to do this another time, that would be fine. I completely understand." She questioned him trying not to sound accusatory, or as if she was prying into his personal life, but not sure if she was actually succeeding.

Chung started laughing. "No, now is fine. Your Chinese is outdated Adelina. How old are you? *bao-bei* is used for a child...daughter, son, etc. Not a lover. I've known Kara since she was a baby. I'm friends with her family, and have spent a lot of time with her." He smiled at Kara and patted her hand. "She's my only family. When Kara was two she adopted me as her uncle. So yes, she is my *bao-bei,* she's like a daughter to me." He squeezed Kara's hand.

In that instant the situation caught up to Kara and she lost herself laughing. "You...actually...thought...we...were..." Kara burst out hysterically. She couldn't stop laughing until her stomach hurt so bad that she was actually afraid she'd cracked a rib.

Adelina blushed with embarrassment, but was relieved. It would have been more difficult if they had been a couple, for Chung was a Cruetian and this woman was ultimately to be *his* Princess. Alexander would have demanded Chung stayed away from her, and he wouldn't have had a choice. If Chung had refused a royal demand, it would have made him a traitor. In their world, it would have meant his execution.

Adelina knew Kara was not married, because she didn't wear a ring, and now she knew that Chung and Kara were not involved. Hopefully, Kara was not involved with anyone else either. "I'm sorry. I didn't mean to pry into your personal life."

Alexander was still standing behind the man, as Adelina finally remembered he was there and stood up to introduce him. "Oh, my apology, I brought my brother to meet you." She raised her hand towards Alexander. "This is my brother Dr. Alexander Conti; he heads up the research we've been discussing at the university and works in the local emergency room."

As Chung stood up, turning to shake Alexander's hand, both of their mouths instantly fell open. Kara stifled a chuckle with her hand, but it was funny how they were both gaping at each other like they were long lost lovers. Maybe they were. Maybe that's why her uncle never dated women, maybe he likes men. She could work with that. She'd have to remember to ask him. She could set him up with men, just as easy as she could women.

"Sonofabitch!" Chung started to laugh. "Alexander Valerius Maximus? Commander? General? *Kyrios*? I don't even know what to call you anymore."

"General Chung?" Alexander smacked him on the shoulder. "I thought you were dead? We heard you had been burnt alive and then decapitated."

Kara grimaced at that thought and then gave Adelina her 'Do-you-know-what's-going-on' look. She shook her head, and Kara just shrugged her shoulders.

Until today, Adelina had never met this man, so she had no idea how Alexander knew him. Wait! Did Alexander say General Chung? The…General Chung! One of Alexander's most honored Generals. Surely not! He died centuries ago, a couple days before she was born actually. General Chung's family had been visiting one of the Cruetian families raided by Seth during Fiona's plot to kill Alexander.

Chung laughed. "They tried, but you know me. Never stop fighting until you're completely dead, and I was not. They were so busy with everyone else, they forgot to decapitate me. It took weeks for my body to heal, but it finally did. Of course, you cannot heal the memories or the pain from the loss."

Kara watched her uncle go from laughing and light hearted, to utter sadness in a matter of seconds. She had never seen him so somber. She could actually feel his pain, it was radiating from him. Is this why her uncle never talked about his life? Was it to painful? If someone actually tried to kill him, then naturally he wouldn't want to remember.

"Conti?" Chung raised an inquisitive eyebrow.

"Our family took an Italian surname to blend in with humans, when Roman names became somewhat...outdated."

"Ah! Please...*Kyrios*." Chung motioned for Alexander to have a seat next to Kara. As soon as he sat down, Kara slid as far away from him in the booth as possible. She felt this overwhelming need to touch him, to slide her hand over his tightly muscled thigh, to explore if Alexander's muscles were as taut as they appeared. And his scent... *Oh Baby!* His scent was like a drug. Spicy! Masculine! Dangerous! It reminded her of a forest spring rain with a hint of spicy ginger, cinnamon, and leather. *Damn!* What was she thinking? This is a friend of her uncle's. *Stay away!* Kara reminded herself as she huddled as close to the wall as she could. Attempting to control her urges, she sat on her left hand as Chung continued to talk. "Commander, I was afraid you were dead."

"Why would you think that?" Alexander asked, looking over and smiling at Kara.

Kara about dropped her tea cup as his smile sent heat waves slamming through her body. He had the most beautiful smile she'd ever seen. It was just a hint crooked and made his smile sexy as hell. *With that smile I bet women drop at his feet.* Kara dreamily sighed. *I... most certainly would!*

This was a form of desire she had never experienced before.

She studied him from under her long eyelashes. How could a simple smile cause her body so much havoc? Granted Alexander's drop dead gorgeous, but it's not like she hasn't been around gorgeous men before. Look at Uncle Chung, he's equally as good looking and she never had this reaction to him. Of course, that would be disgusting. He's her uncle. It would be like dating one of her brothers.

Sick! Ew-ew-ew.

"The person who tried to take *my* life was your cousin. That's why I left and hid. Seth bragged how you and your father were already dead, by the hands of your own wife. If I had known you were still alive, I sure wouldn't be here hiding. I have deliberately kept a low profile all this time for that reason. I normally stay away from all of our people. Like Adelina, I will meet on occasion with one of us I don't know for Cruetian news. I do however, stay completely away from the topic of the royal family. I guess that's why I never realized you were still alive. You obviously found the treachery or you wouldn't be." Chung smiled big, reached across and slapped him on the shoulder. "It's so good to see you. You have no idea how long I mourned you and your family's deaths. How have you been and what brings you to Colorado, or for that matter the United States? By now, I would've thought you'd be leading the Cruetian council."

Alexander was never at a loss for words, but sitting here in front of his old friend, he truly didn't know what to say. How many times over the centuries had he wondered about Chung, and what had happened that horrible night? Wondering what he would say to any of those poor families should he ever have the chance? Now he did, and he didn't know where to begin. "General, I am very sorry for what happened to you and your family. I take complete responsibility for my wife and cousin's actions. I cannot express enough the guilt I hold. I know this will never change what happened........."

"Commander...*Kyrios!* I do not hold you responsible. If I had known you were alive, I would've been standing with you all these centuries. Please do not blame yourself for some delusional bastard and his bitch. I know you loved Fiona, I'm sure you were equally hurt and suffered your own pain." Chung soothed Alexander the best way he knew how. He knew his Commander well, and knew Alexander always held himself personally responsible when life was lost. Chung never wanted him to feel guilty over his family. The only one responsible was the traitors themselves.

"General, how long have you been away from our kind?" Alexander asked scooting into the booth a little more. Being such a big man, his shoulders still touched Kara's even with her cowering in the corner.

Damn! That simple touch caused her whole body to stand up and take notice of him. His heat was like the sun and her body a tree reaching out to it. How could her body want someone it didn't even know? Now who's the traitor? *My body!* Kara's mind knew its place, so why couldn't her body. *Ok. Maybe I'm exaggerating a little. I can't stop imaging my tongue all over those luscious muscles. Agh! My mind's a traitor too. Don't they like…decapitate traitors or something?* She had better pull her shit together and quick.

Alexander noticed Kara slide to the corner of the booth. He wasn't sure why she was shying away from him, but he was determined *not* to allow it. He'd slid further in making sure their bodies had no choice but to touch. Alexander was positive Kara felt the same electric jolt he felt with each brush of their skin. It might even be why she withdrew into the corner, but by the gods he wasn't going to allow her to escape him. He spread his legs wide enough that their knees touched, sending another shockwave racing through him. The jolt was like a match lighting a fire, a fire that raged and burned throughout his entire body. The inferno started where they touched, spreading until every inch of his body was consumed by her heat. Watching Kara, he was absolutely positive she was feeling it to.

"800 years. Why?"

"That's why you don't recognize me, and I didn't recognize you. I'm only 800 years old." Adeline chirped in. "So you really are…the *great* General Chung. Alexander speaks very highly of you."

"I can assure you, there is no one greater than your brother as a commanding general. He saved my life on numerous occasions. *General* Alexander has always been a great warrior." He turned towards Alexander "Since you *are* still alive, *Kyrios*, I would like my old job back." Knowing this conversation might disturb Kara, he motioned to the kitchen. "Kara would you please get my guests some breakfast."

The blush spread across her cheeks instantly as Kara comprehended her mistake. Her grandmother would be furious. What kind of hostess was she? She hadn't even offered them a drink. "Sure uncle. Um... Excuse me......" she stuttered.

"Alexander!" The gorgeous man reminded her of his name, as he took her hand and helped her out of the booth, searing her with desire.

"Would your friend like some breakfast as well?" Kara pointed to the tall, dark haired man standing in the far corner, while trying to get her mind out of the gutter.

"Who?" Chung was looking over where Kara pointed. "Is that Kalab? He was just a babe the last time I saw him."

"It is." Alexander waved him over. "He is *now* my personal bodyguard. Kalab was the one who saved our lives. He discovered Fiona pouring the poison into the wine and stopped her." Kara could see the pain enter Alexander's eyes before he continued, "I'm only sorry we didn't notice her treachery before the raids."

It was Uncle Chung who finally answered her with a pat on her cheek. For as long as she could remember, he always patted her cheek when he wanted to show his approval. "Yes, Kara. Please bring breakfast for all of them."

4

As Kara walked to the kitchen, she couldn't ease the desire she felt for that stranger. How could she want someone she didn't even know? It's absolutely crazy. She had never wanted to sleep with anyone. Ever! Not even with her previous boyfriends had she ever been turned on like this. Something was seriously wrong with her, there had to be, there was no other explanation. Every time they brush up against each other, it feels like she's been electrocuted, and not in a bad way. It's like a jumpstart to her body's hormonal desires. She kept picturing Alexander naked in her bed. With her tongue somewhere, anywhere on that amazing body of his. Oh, and that crooked, sexy smile of his. *Damn! Let's not even go there.* When Alexander smiled at her, her heart instantly stopped. Even right now, it's as if she could feel him wrapped around her. *Shit! I am completely and utterly nuts. Obviously, I've been reading way too many romance novels and watching way too many romantic comedies. They're totally screwing with my reality.* But when Kara looked back over her shoulder, all she could think was how much she would like to taste that man. She was actually wondering if he tasted as good as his scent. He'd be delicious. It made her mouth water just thinking about it.

Alexander watched Kara as she made her way to the kitchen. Her walk was graceful, flowing, positively seductive in a way he'd never experienced before, and Alexander had watched a lot of seductive women. He's always loved the way a woman's hips sway. Every woman tells a story with her strut, and Kara's was telling him she was passionate as hell. His groin jolted just watching her. How could he be hard from watching her walk? He's a general…damn it…a commander; he's been trained to control his emotions. In yet, all Alexander wanted to do was locate the nearest bed and claim her as his. He wanted to run after her, explain to her that she belonged to him, and take her to his bed to consummate their bonding. Right…Now! Adelina was right. Kara was devastatingly beautiful. Alexander couldn't have asked the gods for a more ravishing goddess. She was complete perfection wrapped in an exquisite package. If only she wasn't human. Humans couldn't appreciate what it means to be a chosen one, or how special it was to find yours. Kara would never understand. Could he go slow? Try to win her over? Alexander wasn't sure. Patience has never been easy for him. He just hoped he could. Nathaniel and Adelina were correct; he was not used to waiting for anything. When he wanted something, it was always right there, and Kelmar had warned him that he would have to be patient.

"I assume you have warriors in the Middle East?" Chung was asking, until he glanced over and noticed Alexander following Kara's every move. At once, his protective side took over. He loved his Commander and even considered Alexander a brother, but when it came to Kara, she was like his daughter. Chung would not allow her to be a conquest. He would not allow Kara to get hurt, not even for Alexander. "*Kyrios*, Kara is not to become one of your conquests! You are my brother, my commander, my lord, but she is the daughter I never had. I will not let you hurt her. There are plenty of other women for you to bed. Stay…Away…From…Kara! Understand?"

Hearing the threat in Chung's voice, Kalab jumped out of his chair and was instantly standing next to Alexander's side, palming a blade.

Chung couldn't see the blade, but knew it was there all the same. "Kalab, I would never threaten Alexander's life. I was simply warning him away from Kara. I would protect our Commander, just as I am protecting Kara. Please sit down." With the wave of Alexander's hand, Kalab sat back down, keeping a firm eye on Chung.

"It's not that easy……" Adelina started to explain.

"It is that easy!" Chung roared. "You would not want me bedding one of your daughters would you? You would kill me." He accused Alexander, clenching his fists on the table.

Alexander knew he'd better explain the situation to his old friend. Yes, he could demand, as his commander or as his crown prince that Chung back off, but Chung was right. If this was Alexander's daughter and Chung was after her, he would kill him. If Chung actually thought of her as his daughter, then he owed him an explanation. Not that this would be easy for Chung to accept, but Alexander would still try. Besides he loved his old friend, and if they weren't careful, Kalab would kill him for his threats.

"General, I do *not* want to bed her." Alexander smiled slyly. "Ok! Well…actually I do, but it's not what you think. Kara is my chosen one." He confessed looking back towards the kitchen. Alexander was hoping to end this confrontation long before Kara returned. Fighting with her uncle probably wouldn't help his case any.

"What?" Chung looked pissed off and confused at the same time. "What do you mean she's your chosen one?"

"Have you not heard of our curse?" Alexander inquired; looking around to make sure no one was listening to their conversation.

"Of course I have, but she's human. Kara's not one of us."

"*The Phoenix* said she would be human, and Kara holds my mark." Alexander put his right hand on the table, and with a napkin, wiped away the makeup he used to cover the mark each day. He wasn't ashamed of their mark; he covered it, hoping to protect Kara from his enemies. As Alexander wiped away the makeup, there on his hand was the small red heart surrounded by his crown. "For years we have been looking for her. The Phoenix predicted, as my wife, Kara is the balance for humanity and our people. She will be given the powers to find our people's *Amara's*. More importantly our children, Kara's and mine, are destined to be this worlds uniters. Our people and I have put a lot of effort into finding her. I don't want to earn your disrespect, General. I just want to start living my destiny."

Chung was still incredibly confused. How could small, delicate, little Kara be Alexander's *Amara*? She's not strong enough to live in their world. She didn't even believe in fighting. He had been training her in martial arts every week of her life, and Kara still wouldn't spar with anyone but him. She was afraid she'd hurt someone. Their world was full of confrontation. They still carried swords, for gods sake. What was fate thinking? "I thought you were the protector?" Chung asked still not ready to accept what Alexander was telling him. "I thought you were the one to balance and unite?"

"I am...or...I was. When we were cursed, my prophecy changed. Since we can no longer have children without our *Amara*, our kind is becoming extinct. A prophecy revealed that with fear of extinction, our worlds would fight each other for supremacy. Only my chosen one will be given powers of the other races to balance us, and together our children will combine and create peace. There are people even now, my enemies, including my banished cousin looking to kill her. I have to complete the bonding ceremony before they find her." Alexander scrubbed his hand down his face. "General, it's the only way to protect Kara's life. I'm asking for your help in this matter. If you truly love her, you will help me convince her to bond with me immediately. Everyday her life is in danger. Last night alone 19 human females were brutally killed, simply for being born the same year she was. We can only hold them off so long, General. We need your help. I will never order you to do this, but I'm asking for your help as a friend. Yes, if it were my daughter, I would want to protect her as well, but you know I'm a good man. I promise you I will never intentionally hurt her. Chung... she is my chosen one, my *Amara*. You know what that means, Kara is the Cruetian Princess, and will be treated as such. Anything she desires will be hers. Help me?" Alexander pleaded with him. "Help me explain this to her. Help me convince her."

Chung rubbed his forehead over and over, as he digested this new information. Kara belonged to Alexander. Kara is *his* Princess, and she is in danger. "Then my job has changed. As one of your Generals, I demand to stay and protect her." Chung sat up in his seat. "Please, just always remember, Kara is *my* family."

"General, I will never forget she's your daughter, and I would be greatly honored for you to take on that job." Alexander said relieved. "I need her protected at all times. Kara is a treasure to both me and our people. She trusts you. That will make it easier for you to stay close to her. I don't want her to know the danger, unless we absolutely have to tell her. I don't want her to ever be afraid."

"This will not be easy." Chung stated. "Kara is stubborn, independent, and highly intelligent. Nothing gets past her. We should be honest with her. That will be the easiest way. However, I agree with you, we should not tell her about the danger…just yet."

"You know her, as we do not. Of course, we will take your advice." Alexander agreed, relaxing a little in the booth. If Chung was willing to help them, then this could become easier than he'd expected.

"Is Kara involved with someone?" Adelina asked.

"Not at this time, but her sisters are always trying to set her up." Chung answered as Kara walked out with their food.

After setting everything on the table, Kara decided to pull up a chair at the end of the table. She figured it was better to stay away from Alexander, so she could keep her hormones in check. Besides Kara had already explained to herself numerous times while cooking, he was way out of her league. There is no way in this world Alexander would be interested in her. She was absolutely…positively…normal and he was extremely…amazingly …magnificent. Before she could move the chair to the table, Alexander stood up. Taking Kara's hand he guided her back into the booth.

Great! This is just great! Alexander has no idea the torture he's putting me through with my raging, out of control hormones. It's as if I'm some love sick teenager again.

Alexander motioned to Kalab to pull the chair up to the table like Kara had planned to do. Once Kalab sat down, Alexander turned his full attention to Kara. "I apologize that we really didn't get a chance to be properly introduced earlier. When I realized who your uncle was, I'm afraid we got…a little carried away with reminiscing. My name is Dr. Alexander Conti, and it's a great pleasure to finally meet you Kara." He kissed her hand gently, letting his lips linger on her birthmark, before letting it go.

Damn it! There goes that electricity jolt again. Shit! Kara realized she wasn't breathing. *Breathe. Damn it, breathe.* Just like when Alexander touched her the first time, her head started spinning. *Oh my Gosh! His eyes are amazing. It's like looking into…forever.* Kara sighed. *I feel so stupid, I can't even think a coherent sentence when he's looking at me, and his touch...let's not even go there. I will probably never see him again, so it doesn't matter anyway. All thoughts of his touch need to stop now. It's just so invigorating ...amazing...sensual... and he's just plain...sexy. NO! NO! NO! STOP IT! STOP IT NOW! And what the hell did he mean finally. That's really weird.*

Motioning to the other man at the end of the table, Alexander added "and this is Kalab Nottingham."

"Nice to meet you, Kalab." Thankful for the distraction, Kara shoved her hand out towards Kalab to shake his hand, but instead he simply lowered his head and replied "It's an honor, *Kyria!*"

Kara wondered if it would be rude to correct him on the proper pronunciation of her name, but decided it really didn't matter after all. So what if he couldn't pronounce her name, it wasn't like she was going to see him again, and if she does, she could correct him then. Then it would look like he had just forgotten.

"Kara, could I see your left hand, please" Chung asked.

Kara looked confused. Why did he want to see her left hand? He was always trying to be overly protective. He's as bad as the rest of her family. "Why? I didn't burn it or anything. It looks the same as it always does." Kara snapped at him, knowing she shouldn't get so irritated, but unable to help it. Why couldn't they all see her as an adult? She moved out of her family home for this exact reason, and now her uncle treats her like a child. Why? She doesn't look like a child anymore. Does she?

"Kara, this is important!" Chung said sternly. "Put your left hand on the table, please."

Kara had every intent of arguing with him, but by the irritated look on her uncle's face, she went ahead and put her hand on the table without arguing. That did not mean she wouldn't give him shit about it.

"Yeah...right! This is ludicrous. It's just a stupid hand. If it's so damn important, I'll make you a mold." Kara stated sarcastically. "or better yet, I'll cut off my sisters and give it to you."

Adeline started to laugh until Alexander gave her a dirty look to shut her up.

Chung just rolled his eyes at her. "Could you stop being a smart ass for two minutes, and let me see your damn hand."

"You know, you *really* need to learn a little couth, uncle. No wonder you have trouble with women. Right now…I just *really* want to reach out and touch you…in a *really* negative way." Kara ranted as she put her hand on the table.

Alexander, Kalab, and Chung all gasped, when they saw her hand. Alexander's heart started pounding in his chest and his mouth went dry. Kalab let out a sigh of relief, and Chung reached across and patted her cheek. Sure enough, Kara wore Alexander's mark. There was no longer any doubt that she was definitely Alexander's chosen one. Alexander's *Amara*! Their long search was finally over. At last Alexander could relax. He was so relieved, he actually felt like crying, or jumping up and down, like Adelina had done earlier. He truly wasn't sure how to react. What does a person do after waiting 400 years for this angel to come into your life? How can you even begin to decipher so many feelings?

Adelina was pointing to Kara's birthmark, while Chung traced it. Even Chung couldn't believe it was true, but he had seen Alexander's mark with his own eyes, and Kara had a matching one, which could only mean she was without a doubt Alexander's *Amara*. Alexander's chosen one!

"I told you. See." Adelina said with excitement.

"Yeah, I have a birthmark, so what." Kara snapped. Embarrassed over the one thing that every kid in school had been able to tease her about. She'd always had it, and all the other kids used to call it a "*Love Mark*", since part of it resembled a valentine's heart. Even her identical twin didn't have one. "I've tried to cover it up with make up over the years, but even cover up doesn't work, and the doctors say it's too deep to surgically remove it."

"Kara, I know we've all thought this was a birthmark over the years, but I believe we were wrong." Chung tried to explain to her.

"No, Uncle Chung, I've had it since birth. The doctors insist it's a birthmark."

"I know. That's what we all believed, but the doctors could never explain why your twin didn't have one. Could they?" Chung asked.

Shocked, Adelina asked. "She has a twin?"

"Yes, an identical twin." Kara replied. "And no, she doesn't have one, only I do. So what? Are you saying I'm a freak? I already knew that." She sighed. "The doctors say it's strange since we're identical, but it is, what it is. When your parents start having litters, instead of a baby, there's bound to be some weird defects. We should just be happy that it's only a birthmark on me, and not a third eye or something else on one of my sisters."

"She'll have to be protected as well" Alexander said. Worried he looked over at Chung and Kalab.

"No. I think we'll be ok." Chung explained. "Kara demands independence from her twin, so she dyes her hair blonde. Kasi's is their natural color...auburn. Kasi also likes short hair, another reason why Kara's is so long."

Alexander couldn't picture Kara as a brunette. From what he'd seen of her personality, blonde definitely suited her better, and he loved long hair on a woman. He was glad she didn't try to mimic her sister.

"That's a plus." Adelina said. "I still agree with Alexander, however. Kasi should be protected, for now."

"Kalab and Nathaniel are already here." Alexander stated. "I will have Tiberius transferred here as well. Adding Chung and Tiberius to our current staff, we should be ok."

"That sounds like a good plan for......" Chung was saying before Kara rudely interrupted him.

"Ok you guys, stop talking in code. What the hell's going on here? Why is my birthmark all of the sudden, all the rage. Why's it so damn interesting to all of you?" Kara demanded, looking around at the rest of them expecting immediate answers and not one of them had the decency to enlighten her. "Well. I'm waiting."

Chung sighed knowing this was not going to be good. Kara was already agitated, and when she gets upset...let's just say...she tends to close off her ears. "Kara, do you remember what the kids in school used to call your birthmark?"

Embarrassed she turned her head away from Alexander and under her breath rasped. "Uncle!"

"What did they call it, Kara?"

Pissed she spat. "Damn you! You know what they called it. You don't need me to say it."

Chung sat back in the booth with another sigh. "Kara, please calm down. What I'm trying to tell you, is that they weren't far off from their joke." He noticed the other three looking at each other with questioning looks on their faces. "That mark the doctors all call a birthmark, is not a birthmark. It's the mark of a Dark-Soul's chosen one."

Oooookkkkkk! Was this some type of joke, or had her uncle finally went off the deep end. This time it was Kara's turn to sit back and sigh with annoyance. What had come over him? Why were they all acting mysterious, and what the hell did it have to do with her? "Uncle Chung, what the hell are you talking about? A chosen what?"

"You always talk about a soul-mate, correct?" She nodded, as Chung continued. "A chosen one is a soul-mate to my kind, Kara. It's *a soul-mate to a Cruetian, a Dark-Soul.*"

Kara must have sat there in shock for a good couple of minutes, before she finally put all of her thoughts together. She was sure her mouth had instantly fallen to the floor, and decided it was time to snap it shut. No way was her soul-mate a vampire. This kind of stuff only happened in movies. Like on Buffy, and even on T.V. and the movies, it never works out for them. Why would a vampire even want her for a… what did he call them?...a chosen one? Why? From what she could tell, vampire women were gorgeous compared to humans. They obviously had all lost their minds. "You're telling me *my* soul-mate is a vampire. Why would a vampire want me? You all really have lost your minds, haven't you?" She started laughing, but quickly stopped as she realized no one else had joined her.

"No Kara, I haven't lost my mind, and how many times do I have to tell you, we are *not* vampires." Irritated Chung corrected her…again.

"Yeah! Yeah! I know *you're* Cruetians or Dark-Souls. I get it and the news doesn't know what the hell their talking about. Got that to! Got it! *Ok!*" Her hands flew from side to side, expressing her emotions, while she blew off what they were trying to tell her. Kara just couldn't believe they were even remotely serious about this. As if reading her mind......

"Kara this is serious." Chung said in a firm, very irritated voice. "The person that holds that same mark *is* your soul-mate, and that person" He motioned for Alexander to put his hand on the table "*is* Alexander."

Kara's mouth, for the second time in mere minutes, fell open, gaping, as she looked down and saw the same exact mark on Alexander's hand that she had on hers since the day she was born. Kara couldn't stop gawking. It took her a good minute before she realized her mouth was still hanging open and again snapped it shut. She was so confused. Kara had a million questions rolling through her head. Could this be real? Could *her* soul-mate be a vampire? Not that she has a problem with vampires, but she really didn't know much about them. Uncle Chung was great, but he was her uncle, not a potential husband. Do they even marry? Can they have kids? Are humans and vampires compatible? How do they treat their wives? Or is it mates? Most importantly is she dreaming? Because this was definitely not real! It couldn't be! She was obviously hallucinating or dreaming. The best way to check was to pinch herself.

"Ow!" Ok, she was definitely awake.

Chung knew this wasn't going to be easy, but he hadn't anticipated Kara being out and out cynical about it either. This was obviously not good for his Commander's ego. Alexander was a Prince for gods sake. He was not used to rejection in any way, shape, or form. Furthermore, it was offensive for his kind to be called a vampire. How Chung wished Kara would stop listening to those *damn* televisions and listen to him.

Alexander was relieved when Kara finally stopped gawking at their hands and seemed to come to some sort of rational thinking. He had been so afraid of her reaction, he had been holding his breath this entire time, but when she pinched herself, all he could do was laugh. Alexander tried to cover his mouth, but seriously why would she pinch herself?

Rolling his eyes in desperation, Chung asked, "Kara, What are you doing? Why did you pinch yourself?"

Embarrassed she answered, "Checking to see if I'm hallucinating or if this is a dream."

Adelina couldn't help but laugh over the situation. She had sat here and watched these men make complete fools out of themselves. From their reactions, it seemed that they thought Kara would just say *Great. Where do I sign up to be Alexander's Amara?* How stupid are they? Of course, she's scared. Who wouldn't be? She's not from their world. Kara doesn't understand *Amaras* and true mates. How could they expect her to? She was a young human woman. A woman, who is used to being courted, not hit over the head with a club and drug off to their cave. "Kara, what are you thinking?"

"I'm wondering where the candid cameras are." Kara admitted looking around the store's ceiling.

"Candid Cameras? I don't think I understand." Adelina responded following Kara's gaze of the ceiling.

"It's a television show where people play tricks on each other." Chung explained. "It's one of her favorites."

"Nice try, Uncle Chung." Kara chuckled nervously. "How much did you and my family have to pay for the actors and actress? This is so ridiculous. Sometimes I wish you all would just leave me the hell alone."

"Oh!" Adelina acknowledged, "This is not a joke, sweetie, you *are* my brother's *Amara*, Alexander's chosen one. That's why I left so quickly earlier. When I saw your mark, I knew exactly who you were. I was so excited! We've been looking for you for a very long time, and I needed to bring Alexander to you as quickly as possible. As his *Amara*, you're very important in our world, and I couldn't wait to let Alexander know where you were."

"Why then is *his* mark darker than mine?" Kara said in a disbelieving tone. "It looks painted on. Mine is real. See." She started rubbing it and pulling on it. Kara knew it wouldn't change; she'd tried a million times to get rid of it.

"Yours will be also" Alexander explained, "Yours was made lighter, so it wasn't as noticeable while you were young. It was to protect you."

Kara was clearly done with the charade. This was getting way out of hand. "Ok! Uncle Chung, where is my sisters. I'm sure their all laughing their asses off right now."

"This is *not* a joke Kara, and I will prove it to you." With those simple words Alexander cupped Kara's face and kissed her. Neither one of them expected the wave of desire that hit them. The sweet taste of her was more than Alexander could handle, as intense desire rushed through him. Kara was pure heaven. She tasted so sweet, and smelled amazing, like orchids, jasmine, and cherry blossoms. Over his exceptionally long life, Alexander had kissed more women than he could remember, but none of them had ever tasted so sweet. Wanting more, Alexander teased her mouth open with his tongue, deepening their first kiss.

Kara couldn't breathe, as his tongue plunged deep into her mouth, teasing her. *Damn!* She loved the taste of this man. She could actually taste a hint of ginger on her tongue. Yep! Alexander tastes just like his scent. No more wondering. She now had firsthand experience. Kara knew she shouldn't be enjoying this, she didn't even know him, but damn it felt right. His tongue slid against hers, caressing, exploring. She needed more, she wanted all of him, and by God she knew it was wrong. Her mind was telling her to stop him, but her body was flying with need. What was wrong with her? She was actually considering taking him upstairs; stripping him naked, and giving him what she'd never given another man in her life. Kara knew her mind was right. You can't let a man control you. Alexander was obviously arrogant, domineering, and used to taking what he wanted. This is not the type of man Kara wanted. No matter how good he felt, this is wrong. Kara finally gathered her resolve, and as hard as it was, she pulled herself away from him, slapping him as hard as she could, before jumping over the back of the booth and stomping around to the front of the table.

"How dare you?" Kara screamed. "Who do you think you are? I don't even know you, and my lips are not open to the public. They are very private. Thank you very much."

Alexander grabbed her hand. "As our marks show, you are mine." He growled. "So with that logic, your lips are mine as well."

Kara sucked in a deep breath, trying to calm her temper. As Alexander pointed to her birthmark, she noticed, he was right. Her birthmark was darker than it had been before. What the hell was going on? It was clearly closer to the same color as his. Kara threw her shoulders back. That didn't matter. No one treats her this way. She lifted her chin in defiance. It didn't matter why her birthmark just became darker, no man talks to her that way. She would never be a possession. Ever!

"Big mistake!" Chung said under his breath, cringing for Kara's next reaction.

"*Mr. Alpha Male* let me explain something to you. Mark or no mark, Soul-mate or no soul-mate, this" Kara moved her hand in the air over her body. "Is mine. *All* mine. To touch it, you need an invitation, and you have none. I do *not* like arrogant, domineering men. I am *not* small, meek, or a follower. I am a leader, and I demand respect. Not only of my mind, and my abilities, but for my body as well. I will not be a possession. I will not be owned." She turned towards Chung, "If what you say is real, uncle, then you need to teach your Commander how to treat a lady. For if you don't, mark or no mark, it will be on my death bed before he touches me again." With that she turned and stomped away. The last thing Alexander heard was Kara telling her employees not to let anyone in to see her, including her uncle.

"Sorry Alexander, I should have warned you." Chung sighed. "When I said she was independent and stubborn, I truly meant it. Kara also has a pretty good temper. One you just witnessed firsthand. In high school, she had a boyfriend that was domineering. He used their relationship and her feelings for him, to try and make her do things she wasn't ready for. After he broke her heart, it took me a year to make her strong enough to fight for herself, for her own feelings. To stand up to anyone that tried to dominate and control her. Once Kara found her inner strength again, she swore, she would never let another man treat her disrespectfully."

"Shit!" Alexander ran his fingers through his hair. *Ok! That was stupid.* This was why Kelmar said he would need patience. He just acted like that same immature, stupid high school boyfriend of hers.

Ex-boyfriend! "Who hurt her? Where does he live?" Another horrible thought crossed Alexander's mind and sent his anger spiraling. No one would hurt her. No one! Not even him. "Did he…Did he force himself on her?"

"No-No-No!" Chung tsked. "Her brothers would have killed him. No, he cheated on her and Kara caught them. He only bedded the other girl, because Kara had refused him. In Kara's eyes, cheating on her was the same as forcing her. He humiliated her, and Kara's not the forgiving type when it comes to cheating."

"That's horrible!" Adelina spat. "You should kill him Alexander. No woman should have to watch her man with someone else. Chung's right it's humiliating."

"Whoa!" Chung chuckled. "You both need to back down. This is America. You can't just go around killing people here. Trust me. I know. I wanted to kill him myself, but Kara asked me not to. Besides as I said, she has three brothers that will mutilate anyone that hurts her."

"I have to say, I like her brothers." Alexander said approvingly. "Ok, so what do I do now?"

"Apologize first. Then let Kara get to know you." Adelina replied. "It was evident she was enjoying your kiss. Most likely she's embarrassed by that fact. Kara doesn't really know you, and from what the General just told us, she's not a woman to give in to her desires very easily. You two obviously have some serious chemistry going on, and it probably scares the shit out of her."

"Didn't you hear her?" Alexander snapped. "She refuses to see any of us."

"Kara has a bad temper, *Kyrios*. Give her an hour to calm down, and she'll be more reasonable." Chung stated. "I think Adelina is correct. It did take her a little while to pull away from you, so I too believe she enjoyed it. Knowing Kara, she's pissed at herself for savoring it and embarrassed that you know she desired you."

Alexander let out a deep breath and pinched the bridge of his nose. "I hope you both are right. I want to stop the killing of innocent females immediately, and the only way to accomplish that is to make

Kara my wife as soon as possible."

Going into military mode, Chung asked, "What does Seth know about Kara?"

"Only that she's human" Kalab answered "and that she was born in 1986."

Chung reached over and picked up the teapot Kara had sat on the table, pouring everyone a cup. He smiled to himself when he recognized the blend. Kara had created this blend for him a couple years ago. She named it 'Triple Dragon'. It was a very complex and expensive blend. For Kara to serve it to his guests, it showed not only her upmost respect for him, but that she did in fact like them.

"Why have they not followed you here?" Chung asked Alexander.

"When I learned that my *Amara* was human, I became a doctor. I wanted to be able to take care of her properly. As I'm sure you are aware, none of our people have ever bonded with a human. Before our curse, if we fell in love with a human, we changed them. Like my father did with my mother. We would make them Cruetian. Since the curse, no one has had a human for a chosen one. I was unsure if our two kinds were compatible. I assumed the gods originally, had a reason for requiring us to change our loved ones into Cruetians before they could conceive our children. Adelina's *Amara* was a Lycan. They have four children together, but she carried the children. I was afraid a human would be unable to carry a Cruetian child, so I began researching our two kinds. This research gave us a perfect cover when we came here. Seth knew how focused I have been on my research, so we explained to the councils that this was the only place that would grant me access to the proper equipment. We also came 5 years earlier than Kara's legal age to throw them off the trail." Alexander's jaw ticked. "In the last 6 months, human females have been murdered all over Europe. We recently realized they were all born in 1986. It's their common similarity. Seth knows about Kara. We just don't know how he found out. My family and I have taken every precaution to try and keep her safe, but now it's causing innocent deaths."

This new information sucked the air right out of Chung, as if someone had hit him in the gut. He'd never considered the dangers this could cause Kara's health or her life. Thank the gods Alexander had. "*Are* we compatible? Will she be ok carrying your child?"

"Yes. It would seem the gods created us more alike than we thought. The big difference between us is our nourishment. We need blood to survive, where they do not. Other than that, we are just more enhanced than they are. Were stronger, faster, our senses are more refined, but ultimately we are very similar." Alexander reached across covering Chung's hand. "I need your help, *ge-ge*." Using a Chinese term for elder brother out of respect. "I've been planning this day for 400 years. As soon as I knew where and when I was going to find her, I focused my whole existence on this *one* moment. I started my research, honed my armies, and negotiated more alliances, simply to protect her. I have built her a home in our castle, accumulating the finest treasures to offer her, and most important, I have not been with another woman in the last century. It just didn't feel right. As I said, my whole life became centered on finding and caring for her."

Chung rubbed his forehead over and over again thinking. Alexander would make a great husband. He had never doubted that before. He respected this man and trusted him completely, so why did he have a problem with the thought of Kara being with him? Probably, because he couldn't stand the thought of her being with any man. The good thing was he'd never have to watch her die. Kara would be bonded to Alexander's life force, and since he was immortal, so would she. He would never lose her. That in itself was worth his help. "Ok then. I will help you. I love Kara as my own flesh and blood. She truly is the daughter I never had, *Kyrios*, and she couldn't do any better than you. You are my commander, my friend, and my brother. I know you will take good care of her. You have both my blessing and my support."

"Could you tell us about her?" Adelina was asking. "Her likes, dislikes. Her personality. It will help us to understand her."

"Kara comes from a large family. A fact that for some reason embarrasses her."

That statement made Alexander curious "Why?"

"I really don't know. I haven't been able to understand that aspect of her life. All I know is that it does. Kara's a fire cat. You've already experienced her temper, she's feisty, stubborn, and has a spirit like no other woman I've ever met. She won't put up with anyone's crap. In yet, she is as loving and caring as they come. She does tend to be sarcastic sometimes, but she will not intentionally hurt someone else's feelings. Kara has more compassion in her little finger, than most people have in their whole being. Stranger or not, she would help anyone in need, and she's extremely loyal to her family and friends. She has a wild side, but since high school she doesn't let it out much. She's very independent. Kara is the only one of her siblings that has moved off their parent's ranch. She loves all animals, but is partial to dogs, horses, chinchillas, and tigers, but she's allergic to the latter. She holds a degree in political science and music, and is currently attending law school. She took ownership of 'A Tea Utopia' after her grandparents retired, and has become one of the greatest tea blenders, I have ever seen. She enjoys world history, and likes to travel. She's an incredible singer, dancer" Chung chuckled, "and she spars with me." Looking at Alexander he gave him an amused smirk "One thing you might find interesting are her mother's parents. Her grandmother, Lalita is from Greece, and her grandfather, Salvatore is from Italy."

"No shit!" Adelina screeched. "Talk about perfect. Our parents are going to love that last little fact. Where did her father's side originate?"

"England? I believe they are English."

"What about relationships?" Alexander cringed as he asked. He knew he should have let this topic go, but he had this intense need to know. Of course, controlling his jealousy was difficult and was proving to be more challenging by the minute. The idea of Kara in another man's bed caused a murderous rage to rush through his mind. The only man that sweet, little sexy body was going to be under was him.

Chung let out a sigh. "Damn it, Alexander. I was trying to avoid that question. Are you sure you really want to know? If my memory serves me well, you become quite jealous over your women."

"Tell me." Alexander demanded.

"Fine!" Chung leaned back against the booth. "But you need to eat. If you don't finish breakfast that will piss her off more than your kiss did." Alexander nodded and started eating. "Kara doesn't like to date. She has and does, because her family insists on it. They feel she's lonely, so they try to get her to go out. They even set her up on dates, but Kara doesn't enjoy it. She has always believed in soul-mates. Kara believes that God created two people to belong to each other. That these two people are tied together, and when they find each other, their love will last eternally. *Forever love* is what she is waiting for. She has had three serious relationships, the one in high school that I already told you about, a one year and a two year relationship in college. Her longest relationship broke up when he left for the military. He wanted his freedom to explore worldly women; at least that's how he explained it to her. I can assure you Kara doesn't change her mind easily after she's made a decision. That last boyfriend came back last month and asked her to marry him. He confessed that he'd realized she was the best thing that ever happened to him, and he wanted her back. Kara turned him down flat. She informed him that she only gives one chance and he had screwed it up, and that he was obviously not her soul-mate. Even after her family told Kara to really consider his offer, she refused to budge. I have to admit that I am quite shocked, but he's still trying."

Chung saw the tension in Alexander's locked jaw. He knew telling Alexander about Kara's ex-boyfriends was a mistake. Alexander was always too jealous for his own good.

"She sounds like an amazingly, intelligent woman." Adelina said. "Do you think we could try to talk to her again?"

Chung thought about it for a minute "I would suggest Alexander apologizing first. Whatever you say, say it from your heart. Don't try to be high-handed. She'll respect you for your honesty. Then you should try to win over her family. If they like you, they will support your relationship. If they don't…well…let's just say she respects their opinions." Chung sat back with a devious smile on his face. "Better yet, she'll be at Mel's bar tonight. Kara's hosting her best friend's engagement party. I wasn't planning on going, but I do have an invitation. If you want to attend, I'll take you."

"I don't think Alexander should go alone. We should all go."

Adelina stated. "It will be good support for Alexander and it'll keep him from doing something stupid."

"I'll call Becky and let her know that there will be five of us. It's her engagement party. I'm sure she won't mind. Especially, if I tell her it's for Kara. They love each other like sisters." Chung pulled out a card from his brief case. "Here's where they are registered. I've already bought my gift. I was going to send it with Kara, but I'll now take it myself. Make sure you go to one of those places and buy a gift. It's customary. You should also know she has a large family, and they will all be there. Her brothers are very protective of her, so I would *not* piss her off at the party. Ok? I need to get to another meeting, but I'll meet you there at let's say…seven?"

"Thank you, Chung. We'll be there. What should we wear?" Alexander asked.

"It's Casual. Mel's is a country bar. Kara knows the owner, and Becky's fiancé is a farmer, so Kara thought Mel's was best. I'll go in a nice pair of jeans and a dress shirt. Knowing Kara she'll be in a dress. Keep it somewhat casual." Chung stood up and then turned back around. "I'll try to drop by later if you have any other questions."

5

Kara sat in her office looking at her birthmark, or at least what she thought had been a birthmark. When she was younger, she had been constantly teased about this mark. A mark that resembled a heart with something encircling it. Kids had called it a demon's love mark. Kara flipped her hand back and forth, noticing how dark it had become since Alexander kissed her. Coincidence? If she was to believe her uncle, this is the mark of a chosen one. A Soul-Mate to a Dark-Soul. Oh, and it gets even better. Not just any Dark-Soul, but the sexy as hell, Alexander. Kara had no reason not to believe her uncle, he's never lied to her before, and he's always protected and cared for her as if she was his own daughter, but to believe she was chosen for Alexander. That was just unheard of. They were entirely opposite of each other. Alexander was this exceptional male specimen, where she was absolutely average. He was a male chauvinist, and she was an independent feminist. Of course, she had never been so affected by a man before. This attraction was stronger than anything she'd ever felt. Kara couldn't stop fantasizing about him. The memory of his warm masculine scent wrapping around her body in a protective caress, or the taste of his tongue as it glided along hers. The electrical buzz that warmed every cell of her body each time they touched. What if this *is* what a soul-mate feels like? Could this be what her grandparents felt for each other? Is *this* what her parents meant, when they said they immediately knew they were destined for each other? For an hour, she sat pondering her thoughts, before she decided to call her grandmother and ask someone who had firsthand experience.

"Hello!" Sara answered.

"Hey, me-ma!" She had always called her grandma, me-ma. Kara's mom said when she was little; she couldn't say grandma, so she said me-ma. As she grew, they assumed she continued calling them that to show her sisters that Kara's grandmother's belonged to her. For whatever reason, her grandmothers adored it, so it just always stuck. Kara had to agree, she was somewhat possessive of her grandparents. She had always felt a special connection with them, which is why Kara had spent so much time with them as a child.

"Kara? Child what are you doing today? Do you need help with the engagement party? "

Kara let out a deep sigh. Naturally her grandmother would assume her stress was over the party. She hated parties and everyone knew it. Ever since prom, Kara hadn't really enjoyed partying. Most people assumed she'd turned into a prude, thinking herself better than everyone else, but that wasn't the case. Ever since two of her friends were killed after partying hard, she viewed partying as dangerous. She had always loved a good party, and in high school was considered the life of a many, but after that horrible night...How could she participate, knowing it had taken two lives. The most she did these days was sing and dance at Mel's, to satisfy her wild side. "No. The planning is going great. I just had a question for you."

"Go ahead, sweetheart, what's on your mind?"

Kara was never one to beat around the bush, so to speak. She felt the direct approach was always the best approach, even when most people thought she was to blunt. So, Kara did what she did best. She just asked. "When you met grandpa...and you said you immediately knew he was your soul-mate, what exactly did you mean? How did you know? Was it a mental or a physical attraction?"

Sara could hear the stress in her granddaughter's voice, and it worried her. Kara always acted so brave and courageous, but she knew the truth. Kara was an extremely lonely woman, and Sara had no idea how to help her. Kara held her heart open for any man who walked into her life, and so far, all those men had taken it and ripped it apart without a second thought. How Sara wished she could have beaten some sense into them. Instead all that had been accomplished was

Kara pulling further and further into her own secluded world. "We've talked about this on many occasions, sweetie. I told you, it's like your whole body wakes up and takes notice of that one man. Kind of like you were sleeping, waiting for him to come a long and awaken you." Sara chuckled. "I think that's where Sleeping Beauty comes from."

Damn it! That still didn't explain how you were supposed to know. Kara still didn't understand. She needed exact details. Like, would her heart race, would it stop, or would her mind scream 'he's mine'. What was she supposed to look for? "So is it physical, like desire, or is that just lust."

This conversation was making Sara more nervous by the minute. Kara hadn't been interested in men, since Kevin had broken her heart. In fact, they all but had to force her to even consider going out on a date. Kara was such a loving girl, that each time her heart had been broken, she seemed to die and shrivel up a little bit more inside. It had changed her. Kara had become hard and cold to her own passion for life. A true tragedy, considering how vivacious she had been as a teenager, a marvelous life had been spread out before her, and all she had to do was grab a hold of it. Instead Kara boxed herself away from the world. "Yes…and No, Kara. You'll feel desire like you've never felt for another man, but you'll also feel hollow inside…like you're missing something when's he's not around, and when he's around you'll feel whole again. Kara, why do you ask?"

"Don't worry, me-ma. It's nothing. I was just curious, that's all. I'll see you tonight at the party. Love you. Tell grandpa 'hi'."

Sara knew her granddaughter well enough to know something was amiss. She was to level headed to just ask random questions. "Kara, wait! Did you meet someone?"

"Sorry, Me-ma. I have a customer. Gotta go!"

Kara hung up the phone, as quickly as possible, and shrank into her chair. She didn't want to explain her thoughts to her grandmother, and she didn't want to lie to her either, so the best option was to end the conversation. This way she could think about her feelings in private, and hopefully find a way to decipher this whole 'chosen one' business. The first step was to rein in her emotions. She obviously couldn't think logically, if all she was thinking about was Alexander naked. She would have to find a way to get a hold of her emotions, she was already dying to see him again, and that was unacceptable. Of course, it could only be lust. That was always a possibility. It had been awhile since she'd been with a man. That would definitely make more sense, than her...*Stop it! Concentrate, damn it!*

Lust? Duh! That would explain...everything. Stop thinking with your libido and use this brain God gave you. Ok! Exhibit A....That incredibly hot, smoldering, sexy body...mmmm...definitely lust. Alexander's divinely, lick-ably delicious scent. An essence so sublime it drives me absolutely crazy...has to be lust. His kiss? Well, that was... it was...well...definitely earth shattering...I have to admit, it did rock every little point of my entire existence. In fact, it knocked my whole life right off its axis. Lust? Maybe...or maybe not.

Kara smiled to herself.

I've had some pretty amazing kisses before, but not the...assault of hot passion from Alexander's kiss. Maybe, just maybe, it's because I've never kissed a vampire before. It could be. Right? I mean, they are all walking supermodels. Maybe they all make you go weak in the knees. It could be some chemistry thing. Hmmm...I'll have to put a question mark by that one. Then of course there's my mark, or is it Alexander's mark? Doctors say it's a birthmark, but it did become a little darker after our kiss...or was I hallucinating? Am I so desperate for a soul-mate I'd believe anything? There has to be a way to prove if I am Alexander's chosen one. Somehow I need to test my uncle's theory. But how? How do you prove someone is your soul-mate? Obviously I suck at it! I've had three failed relationships to prove that.

Frustrated, Kara leaned back into her chair and closed her eyes. If only she could be 100 percent certain she truly was Alexander's ... what did they call it? *Amara?* Yeah, that was it. If only she could be positively certain she was Alexander's *Amara,* she might be willing to take another chance. Kara just didn't think her heart could survive another heartbreak...but, maybe...

Nathaniel couldn't stop laughing. "She slapped you?" Now he was howling "and you let her? Kalab let her?"

"I would not have let her" Kalab scowled "except our stubborn Commander motioned me back."

Alexander, Kalab, Adelina, and Nathaniel were all sitting around Alexander's office, discussing what had happened with Kara. When Alexander had returned to his office, Nathaniel had been taking a nap on the sofa, giving him a reprieve from discussing the situation. Since then however, Adelina had returned with the gifts she had bought, and the four of them were now going over every instant of their introduction.

"What did you want me to do?" Alexander snapped irritated and clearly embarrassed. He scrubbed his hand over his face. "I'm not really sure if I want her." He admitted. "I don't want another violent, aggressive wife. Nor do I want a disrespectful one. You all know what happened with my last woman." He slammed his palm down on his desk out of frustration. "Kara calls us *vampires* for gods sake."

Alexander's little outburst sobered Nathaniel up quickly. "Are you saying you won't bond with her?"

Alexander slammed his fist into the palm of his hand. He actually wasn't sure what he was saying, or why he was so irritated with the whole situation. He knew this would be difficult. Kara was human for crying out loud and a young one at that. "I'm simply saying, maybe it's not worth it. Last time I married for our people, I married a violent and deceitful woman. We almost *all* lost our lives because of Fiona." Alexander was trying to ignore all of their looks of disbelief as he continued with his explanation. "I don't want to put our family or our people in danger again."

"Alexander, you're going overboard here." Adelina scolded. "You just met her and the first thing you did was become a high-handed barbarian and you kissed her. How did you expect her to react?"

"The mark had already been explained to her. Kara should have understood." Alexander countered. "Besides she calls us vampires. We are *not* vampires." He growled between clenched teeth.

Adelina knew her brother was scared. For the last 800 years, he had blamed himself for the lives lost that night in the raids, and the horrible curse that had been put upon their people, but now it was time he let the guilt go. It was time he allowed himself to love and to be loved. Adelina understood the love an *Amara* brought, the daily satisfaction, and the completeness you felt together. Even now she could feel Walter inside her head, just as he could feel her. There is nothing greater than the *Amara* bond, and finally it was time her brother had his. This was a gift *she* could help give him.

"First" Adelina began "you know humans believe we are vampires. Kara is no different than any other human. It's *our* job to teach her the difference." Alexander started to disagree, but she shook her head and finger to silence him. "Second, you knew she didn't believe what we were saying about the mark, in yet you still decided to kiss her. As far as Kara was concerned you were a complete stranger. Any woman, unless they were a harlot would have hit you. You have to remember, she is not one of us. Kara doesn't understand our customs. Third, I think she really likes you. Did you notice how long she embraced your kiss? She's clearly confused over this whole situation. I think she's trying to justify her feelings. Kara's your *Amara,* Alexander. She'll come around."

Alexander sat there looking between all of them. The three people sitting in this room knew him better than he probably knew himself. Kalab, now one of his Vici Warriors, had become his personal bodyguard the day of Fiona's betrayal. He had been by his side every day for the last 800 years. He was more than just his bodyguard; he was his friend, no different than one of his brothers. Actually, Kalab was closer to him than some of his own brothers. While Nathaniel and Adelina were truly his family, they were also two of his advisors. As Alexander's youngest brother and sister, he had always kept them close. After Fiona's treachery, he had always wanted to protect them from harm. Alexander trained them himself, making sure they knew every fighting, tracking, shadowing, and discipline technique he knew. It was only natural that spending so much time together would create an unbreakable bond between them all.

He let out a resigned sigh. "What would you have me do, Adelina?"

"*adelfos*" Adelina walked over to him laying her hand on his shoulder. "You know how to court a woman. Show her the man you *really* are. I know you are a caring, compassionate, loving, and extremely protective man. Show Kara that side of you. Let her see the man your family knows. Kara seems to be an amazing woman. You'd be a fool to walk away from her." Adelina laughed. "Do you actually even have a choice? Your destiny and hers have already been decided. I don't believe it's up for debate. Do you?"

Alexander pulled Adelina around into his lap like he used to do when she was a child. "You really think Kara is a good woman, *sorella*? I can accept my own fate, but I cannot allow another woman to hurt our people. Ever! No matter what the gods have deemed my fate, I cannot allow it to hurt our race."

Oh, how Adelina missed this side of her brother. If only he could see himself the way his people saw him. He would never doubt himself. His people knew how much he loved them. They knew Alexander always did what he felt was best for them, but when would he look for his own happiness? When would he open himself up to find his own love? "a*delfos*, Kara's not a good woman, she's a great woman. The gods knew who you needed. They knew who our people needed, and they chose well. I know you've been hurt." She brushed his hair off his forehead. "I damn Fiona everyday for what she did to your heart, but you can't punish Kara for Fiona's evil. That's not fair and you know it. Kara's the one for you. I have no doubts. Don't screw this up."

Nathaniel understood what Adelina was doing. Alexander was entirely too hard on himself. Alexander had intently punished himself over the centuries for Fiona's betrayal. Never allowing himself more than a few specks of happiness here and there. It was as if he was too afraid of being happy. Even knowing this, however …the conversation had taken on a much too gloomy feeling. It was time for Nathaniel to liven it up a bit. "Yes, and next time you go to her, I want to be with you." Nathaniel was chuckling again. "I want to meet the woman that had the balls to slap you, especially when they say she's no more than…what?…Five feet tall. I'm sorry I missed it the first time. It had to have been hysterical seeing such a small creature lay into a monster like you."

"Shut up, Nathaniel! You're not helping." Adelina snapped. "Alexander should be happy Kara stands up for herself. Kelmar said she would be strong. You all were probably stupid enough to think he meant physically. I think the prophecy meant she would be mentally strong, and Kara is. I have no doubt Kara will make you an extraordinary wife, and an even more exceptional, and worthy Princess to our people."

"Bravo…Bravo…Bravo!" A deep voice chanted as they heard clapping at the door. They all spun around ducking into their attack crouches, until they recognized who it was.

"Son of a bitch! General Chung? Is that really you?" Nathaniel asked, clearly puzzled by this man's sudden appearance. "We thought you were dead. In fact…centuries dead."

"Sorry" Alexander apologized. "We forgot to tell you Chung is very much alive. That's who Adelina met for breakfast this morning."

"No shit! Where have you been?" Nathaniel strolled over to him, slowly, looking him up and down. "Well, you definitely don't look like a ghost, so I have to assume your death was quite exaggerated."

Chung laughed, strolling into the room, winking in Alexander and Adelina's direction, telling them to stay out of this. "Kid, you're looking pretty good yourself. Last time I saw you, you were still something of a youngling. Although, I can see you haven't grown up much, or are you just a little lax on intelligence?" He cocked an eyebrow. "Antagonizing your brother like you were," Chung teased. "He could wipe this floor with your ass, without straining a muscle."

Nathaniel started laughing. "You and I both know it, but he won't, he enjoys pushing me around too much. Besides, *he* was hit by a girl. What'd you expect me to do? Feel sorry for him?"

Chung hadn't been around the royal family in centuries, but their teasing actually surprised him. He didn't remember his Commander being playful. At least, not unless Alexander was with a woman, attempting to bed her. He had always been so serious, the ultimate

Commander to the end. It was nice to see that he had loosened up over the years, at least with his brother and sister. Chung walked around to the sofa and plopped down smiling. He was enjoying himself more than he thought he would. He had truly missed these people. Not necessarily Dark-Souls in general, but definitely this family. They had always treated him as one of their own. "As your sister said, you haven't met the girl." Chung motioned Nathaniel to take a seat. "I trained her myself."

Nathaniel was still stunned by General Chung's sudden appearance, in yet, he couldn't have been more overjoyed about the situation. Chung obviously wasn't a traitor, or Alexander wouldn't be calm about his unexpected arrival. Clearly Alexander knew he was here. Why he hadn't mentioned it to anyone was clearly beyond Nathaniel, but who was he to question Alexander's motives? Nathaniel sat down in the chair next to Chung to quiz him on Alexander's future mate. "What precisely do you mean you trained her?"

Chung chuckled as he slapped Nathaniel on the shoulder. "Well, it was quite obvious, by the look on your face when I entered, that Alexander hadn't gotten around to telling you that Adelina had found me, which also means, he hadn't told you that Kara's like a daughter to me. I've known Kara since she was a baby. She's very important to me."

"No, they didn't say a word." Nathaniel rubbed the back of his neck. "In fact, it seems like they failed to mention a lot of things." Nathaniel looked over his shoulder giving them both a disapproving frown. "So, what exactly did you teach Kara?"

Kalab came around and sat down at the other end of the couch to join in the conversation. "This is something I believe I would like to know as well. Since Kara will be my Princess, I will ultimately end up protecting her. It will be good to know about her strengths and weaknesses."

Alexander had no idea how the conversation had turned from… Is this woman safe…to…How do we protect her? He was still on the safety question, but Alexander assumed it was important to know Kara's vulnerabilities. He walked around the sofa and slid into the other chair, preparing to learn everything he could about his fated *Amara*. "Go ahead General, tell us about my chosen one."

Chung smiled at the amazed expressions on each of their faces as he looked around the room. He had been talking about Kara and her accomplishments for the last two hours, and couldn't help but be proud of her. As he had relayed to them, Kara was extremely intelligent and exceptionally talented. Chung had taught her numerous styles of martial arts, fencing, kendo, sword and discipline techniques, and she had excelled at all of them. On her own, she was an accomplished musician, including voice, piano, guitar, and many other musical instruments. She enjoyed dancing and in his mind had mastered numerous styles, even though Kara insisted she was strictly a beginner. She volunteered helping disadvantaged children, teaching them horseback riding, music, and dance. The children's favorite was belly dancing. Kara always thought it was because it was so unique, and she might be right about the female students, but Chung knew, normally males didn't want to take a belly dance class. He assumed they were there for the view. You know teenage boys, their hormones run wild, and Kara is quite pretty.

"Ok, I can officially say...I'm highly impressed." Nathaniel shot Alexander an envious look. "You lucky bastard. From what I'm hearing, not only is Kara super-hot, but she'll have moves in bed that most men would kill for. A dancer?...and not just any dancer, but a belly dancer. Damn! If you still don't want her, I'm game."

"Shut up, Nathaniel!" Alexander roared. Nathaniel smirked. That seemed to be a common phrase today.

"Down boys!" Adelina jumped off the couch and stepped in the middle of the two chairs "Nathaniel are you a complete idiot. Do you really want to get your ass kicked?"

"I was just saying......"

"Shut up! No you weren't thinking. You know how jealous Alexander becomes over his women, and this particular woman will become *your* Princess. Get your brain out of the gutter, and show some respect." Adelina lectured him "and for you Alexander. You need to get your head out of your ass. Yes. Fiona screwed you and our people.

We got that. We've all lived it. It's time for you to realize Kara is completely different. You need to give her a chance. Give yourself a chance to learn who she really is. From what you two have always told me, General Chung is one of your toughest commanders. If that's true, and Kara won his heart and earned his respect, then she must be pretty damn special. Both of you need to grow up and stop being so fucking stupid." Adelina flung herself back onto the couch with a loud "humph!"

Chung decided this might be a good time to make a quick exit. They seemed to need a little...family time. "Commander, I know you have a lot on your mind, however, when you have a chance, I would like to discuss Kara's protection with you and Kalab. Adelina has my number." Alexander nodded as Chung stood up and started towards the door. Just before he reached it, he spun around and faced Nathaniel. "If you really want to get to know Kara, you could help me train her tomorrow. I've been her only Martial Arts instructor. She could use fresh blood to spar against. You game?"

Nathaniel looked up startled at the offer, but couldn't refuse a chance to meet this amazing woman on his own, so he jumped at the chance. "Hell Yeah! I'd love to help you out. Can't wait! Just tell me when and where."

"Your sister knows where my dojo is located. Be there at two, that's Kara's private session."

"Nathaniel." Alexander growled. "You had better make damn sure you don't hurt her. Understand? You had best be very careful with her." Alexander didn't need to say it, the "or else" hung in the air, so Nathaniel just nodded his head.

"I'll see you all tonight." Chung shouted as he strolled out the door.

Alexander had felt Kara drift off to sleep earlier, and knew she was currently deeply sleeping. This was the perfect time for his apology. He grabbed his coat. "Kara's sleeping. I think I'll shift to her and leave roses for my apology."

Adelina nodded approvingly "Good idea."

Shocked! Nathaniel asked "You can already feel her? From one kiss, you can trace her energy?"

It had shocked Alexander as well. As Dark-Soul's bond with their *Amara,* they begin to share certain traits with each other. The first to show up is empathy. His kind can sense emotions when they're near a person, but unless you're an empath, you can only sense your *Amara* from a distance and only after the bonding begins. The second is reading their *Amara's* energy signature. For his species, shifting is their primary way of travel. They picture where they want to go, and they shift to that location. They can also shift directly to a person by feeling someone's energy signature. Just like human's fingerprints are unique, so is every being's energy signature. It allows his species to shift directly to a specific person. The only problem is there are only three ways you can feel someone's energy signature. One. They're your bonded *Amara.* Two. You are blood bonded with them. Three. You have that particular ability that allows you to feel energy signatures. Alexander does not have this ability, so the fact that he can sense Kara means their bond is already forming, and they haven't even exchanged blood. "I'm as surprised as you are, but yes I can. So I better deliver the roses before Kara wakes up."

They all nodded in agreement as he shifted to Kara.

Alexander shifted into Kara's office. When he sensed she had fallen asleep, he decided this would be the perfect opportunity to leave his apology. Earlier he'd wanted to shift in beside her and catch her off guard, but Chung had reminded them that humans didn't know about their ability to shift. Alexander had been afraid that she would end up frightened of him. Not an emotion any of them wanted her to feel.

Alexander was shocked at how quickly their connection was being established. He seriously doubted Kara would be able to sense him yet. Since she wasn't a telepath, she wouldn't be used to using her mind in that way, but it would come. Once he had kissed her, the bond had begun to form, it would only get stronger, and with each bonding step, it would grow. It would evolve until they both would be able to read each other's thoughts, know all of each other's memories, feel what the other was feeling, and have complete conversations, all in their minds. In essence they would become one.

Alexander set the bouquet of roses in the middle of Kara's desk and looked around her office. He noticed she really hadn't taken the time to actually decorate it. Everything was for a specific purpose. She had an antique desk in dire need of refurbishing, shoved up against the far wall. On top of it sat stacks of books and papers, a red phone, and a red laptop computer. There were shelves hung above her desk that held more books and an iPod docking station that at this moment held a red iPod in its clutches. Alexander chuckled as he realized the color red held a special place in his *Amara's* heart. Of course, he had noticed the significant amount of red in the store's design, but Alexander hadn't understood that was a part of Kara, until now. Seeing her personal items in red, allowed him one small piece of insight into his mate. Funny, considering his family line was represented by the color red.

He turned around and memorized the rest of the office, a row of filing cabinets was lined along the side wall, and the opposite wall was the only comfort Alexander saw in the office. There was an old Victorian chaise that had been redone in red velvet. Alexander looked down at the peaceful site of Kara sound asleep in her office chair. As a Dark-Soul, his movements were soundless and very precise. Knowing he could pick Kara up without waking her, he gently lifted her out of the chair.

How small and fragile she felt in his arms. Kara was so tiny compared to his people. Not that they didn't have all different sizes, but Alexander couldn't remember ever seeing one of their women this delicate. Kara stirred briefly, rubbing her cheek on his shoulder, before taking a deep breath and letting out the cutest sigh he'd ever heard. Kara's sigh of content was all the motivation his damaged ego needed. Maybe the gods did know what they were doing.

Alexander rubbed his cheek in her hair, breathing in the intoxicating scent of orchids, jasmine and cherry blossoms. Considering everything he had learned about her today, Kara's exotic scent matched an equally exotic woman. How someone so young could have accomplished so much, was beyond him.

He moved to the chaise, and gently laid her down. Then grabbed the quilt off the back and placed it over her, before lightly stroking her hair. It was so silky soft he wanted to wrap himself in it. Feel it across his chest, his thighs, to just bury his face in it, but not today. He refused to scare her with his overwhelming desires.

Instead, Alexander pulled up the office chair Kara had been sleeping in and sat down, committing himself to watching her sleep. Her face was peaceful...soft. Alexander thought back to Fiona, even in her sleep Fiona had worn a frown he realized. How could he have missed that? How could he have missed that one simple fact? Fiona had never been happy. He had seen only what he had wanted to see. Alexander had never opened himself up to the truth. Here he was, a ruthless commander, a general who had conquered numerous armies, and an accomplished negotiator who had been deceived by one insignificant evil woman. If only he had paid better attention.

Alexander looked down at Kara in her peaceful slumber. She had a soft smile on her full luscious lips, as her generous breasts lightly rose and fell with each breath. Damn, how he'd love to cradle them in his hands. Lying there, so delicate and fragile, she was flawless. That scared him more than the thought of her ever becoming evil. How could he ever deserve such perfection? How could he bring such a beautiful soul into his violent world? Yes. Alexander's people needed Kara, but would it be fair to her. Was it right for them to ask her to sacrifice the life she knows, simply to save his race? A people Kara didn't even understand, and most likely wouldn't approve of their culture. Some would say, yes. Forcing her into their lives, their culture, will save an entire race, so yes, sacrificing Kara's happiness would be justifiable. Would she feel the same way? Alexander doubted it, and would he be betraying Kara just as he had been betrayed by Fiona? The most important question had yet to be asked. Could Alexander live with himself if Kara hated him? Once they were fully bonded, Kara would be immortal, just as Alexander is. Could he live eternity knowing and feeling the pain he'd caused her? He needed advice, and there were only two people who could truly understand what he was going through, so Alexander shifted to Italy...to his parents.

Alexander should have shifted directly to his parents, just like he'd done with Kara earlier. However, unlike with Kara, he's unable to sense precisely what they're doing at a specific moment. A fact that as a child had caused him embarrassment on more than one occasion, and is the reason why, unless it's an emergency, he doesn't shift directly to anyone's side. This is why he had to search the entire castle to finally find his parents.

Avitus and Hypatia both looked up at Alexander as he strolled into the library. They hadn't been expecting him, since he'd found his *Amara*. They'd assumed he'd be with Kara establishing their bond.

He looks stressed. Hypatia projected into Avitus's mind.

Yes, akribos, he does. Maybe that is why he is here. He must need our help.

Hypatia moved over opening a space between herself and Avitus for Alexander to sit down. She patted the space "*gios*...come...sit down. We were not expecting to see you so soon after finding Kara. Although I admit, I am glad you did." Hypatia patted the seat again, until Alexander finally sat down, so she could put her arms around him.

It never ceased to amaze him, no matter how old he became, he always enjoyed having his parents arms wrapped around him. Alexander always knew with their arms around him he was home.

"*filius*, how can we help you?" Avitus asked. "We can see something is seriously bothering you. Let us help if we can."

"*patris...matris*, I'm confused about our situation with Kara." Alexander stated grimly. "I'm unsure if I can force her to accept her role as my *Amara*."

Hypatia was stunned. Why would this woman refuse her son? Women everywhere would kill to be in her position. "Kara's turned you down?"

"Not yet." Alexander admitted on a sigh.

"You believe she will?" Avitus said in an amused tone. "I have never seen a woman strong enough to refuse my eldest son."

Alexander explained his concerns, fears, and desires with their current situation. Telling them what he'd learned so far about Kara, and his reservations with forcing her into their society.

"*gios*, you are like your father." Hypatia lectured. "You are analyzing everything. This is not one of your battles. This is your life." She shook her head with disgust. "Males can be so obtuse. There is no strategy. This is not a win or lose situation. You have to allow yourself and Kara time to explore your feelings." Hypatia gave Alexander a sympathetic look. "I think Adelina's correct. You are rushing things. You two have just met, give her some time."

"Your mother's correct. You have already admitted that Kara stirs desires within you that you never felt for Fiona." Avitus smiled. "How do you think I recognized your mother? Some needs and desires are worth fighting for. It is true there is no battle plan, but you do not have to give up. You can fight until you convince her. Follow your heart, Alexander, it will not deceive you." His father assured him. "I believe the real battle you are fighting is within yourself. You are afraid to allow this remarkable woman into your soul…into your heart. You cannot fight your destiny, *filius*. You have to embrace it. Go to Kara… talk to her…just the two of you. Shift her somewhere you can be alone, and explain everything. You are worried about deciding for her then let her decide for herself. You cannot make this decision for Kara, any more than we could make the decision for you."

"I know you're both right." Alexander admitted. "I guess I just needed to hear it." He kissed both of them on the cheeks. "I feel completely out of my realm with Kara. I'm not used to questioning myself or feeling a loss of control, and I'm doing both."

Avitus laughed. "*filius*, a good woman will do that to a man. It sounds like the gods chose well for you. You will come to enjoy and need Kara, just as I do your mother. The gods understand that warriors need strong women at their sides, and as the gods gave me your mother, they have given you Kara. Do not fight your feelings. They are not a weakness; they will become your strength. Now go and claim your *Amara*."

Kara was startled awake by someone yelling and pounding on her office door. "Ker, hey baby girl, you ok in there? You've been in there for hours. Ker, can you hear me? You need to answer me, or I'm going to break down this door. You hear me, Ker."

Kara sat up smiling, rubbing her eyes. *Tasha!* "Hey Tasha, I'm alright. I just fell asleep, nothing to worry about. I'll be out in a few."

"Fine!" Kara smiled at Tasha's irritation. "Next time you decide to take a siesta, leave your damn door unlocked. You had me scared shitless." Tasha hit the door one more time for effect, before she pivoted and stomped away.

Kara knew Tasha was all bark and no bite…well that was true enough for Kara. Tasha did bite, just not her. Tasha was the ultimate biker babe, at a towering height of 5'8", which left Kara red with envy. Tasha consistently worked out, which was shown in her superbly toned muscles. The woman could throw a punch better than most men. Tasha's look intimidated most people. She wore her fire red hair super short, with little wisps that actually kind of spiked. While working she ditched the leathers, and wore jeans and t-shirts, but Tasha couldn't hide all her piercings and tattoos, and that alone made a lot of people nervous. Tasha actually enjoyed her dangerous persona, and used it to her advantage. Most of the time she used it to protect her loved ones, which just happened to include Kara.

Kara looked around confused, how had she ended up on her chaise? She didn't remember lying down. In fact, she was pretty sure, she hadn't planned on taking a nap, and why in the world was her office chair sitting next to the chaise? She would have never moved it there. It was as if someone had been sitting there watching her.

Ok, now you're going insane. No one could have been in here, because your door is locked. Duh!

Kara slowly stood up rubbing the sleep out of her eyes, when she noticed a huge vase of lavender roses in the middle of her desk. How the hell could someone have put them there? Didn't Tasha say her door was locked? That was the only way into the office, there wasn't even any windows.

Kara stood in the middle of her office confused and a little terrified while she tried to come up with a rational explanation. Finally, she snapped her fingers. Got it! Whoever left the flowers, was kind enough to comprehend that she needed her rest. They must have carefully moved her to the chaise and locked the door behind them when they left. That was it. That explained what happened. But who?

She strolled over to the roses and bent down inhaling their invigorating scent, before reaching for the card. She had barely torn open the envelope, when the aroma of spicy spring rain drifted through the air, arousing her body in quite a few alluring ways. Kara closed her eyes and deeply inhaled, allowing her body to absorb the scent it was begging for. Her heart was racing a marathon, but from the outside you wouldn't have known as she calmly opened the card.

Amara,
Perfection deserves perfection.
Please except these sublime roses as my apology.
I'm sorry if I offended you, for that was never my intent.
I hope you will forgive my heart's moment of weakness,
For the meaning of these flowers, is mine as well.
Forever Yours, Alexander

Kara reached out stroking one of the petals, how pleasing and soft it was, truly it was perfection. A lump formed in her throat as tears filled her eyes. *Damn it! I don't cry. What the hell?* She never reacted this way to men's sentiments. Apologies usually just pissed her off. *I don't need a man, and I don't need his damn apology.* She preferred to stay mad when men irritated her. She'd learned the hard way, forgiving a man just gave them permission to do it again. Kara's motto had become, 'if they're stupid enough to get themselves into a situation, than an apology was pointless.' Most of the time, they didn't mean the apology anyway. But something about this apology was different... Alexander's words...or the meaning behind the words? Kara wasn't sure, but for some reason, she was inclined to forgive him. *Damn!* First rule with men, never back down! Be a hard core bitch to the end. If you don't, their domineering side will appear with a vengeance.

Kara knew she couldn't allow him to get in her head this way. She sighed. Oh! How this man ate at her. Just his scent had turned her body inside out. How could she keep her wits about her, when all of the sudden Alexander haunted every aspect of her anatomy. It screamed for him. *Bullshit! My family says I have the strongest will they know. Now it's time I prove it. It's time my mind was stronger than my body.* With that thought her determination roared to life. Kara decided she just wouldn't allow it. She would be firm, hard, unbending, it didn't matter what her body wanted.

She knew presumptuous men, and she understood domineering, arrogant men did not know how to treat women. These men wanted the ditzy little followers, the silly little girls who would swoon at their mere presence. Those women were the complete opposite of Kara. She had made herself strong. Strong and stubborn enough to protect her heart from the cruelty of men. Alexander might be gorgeous, and he might have invaded every cell of her body, but like hell was she going to digress to the passive, submissive school girl she had been in high school. Kara had created herself into a force to be reckoned with, and *by gosh* that was not going to change.

With her new resolve, Kara tossed the card onto her desk and marched herself out of the office, right into another egotistical man's arms. Who at this very moment was staring down at her with the most amusing smile she had ever seen on his cocky lips.

Kara pushed away from him with a slap of her hands on his chest. "*Kevin!* What the hell are you doing here? I thought I told you to stay away from me."

Kevin couldn't help but chuckle at her fury. He always loved her angry. Her cheeks always flushed the most beautiful crimson red, while she'd bite that perfectly shaped seductive bottom lip of hers. Just like she was doing right now! Without thinking, he swooped forward capturing her bottom lip with his teeth, teasing her with his tongue, just like he'd done a thousand times before. He was astonished when he felt Kara's knee connect with his balls, and then his back hit the floor.

Kara stood over Kevin watching him roll around on the floor cursing her in pain. She felt absolutely no remorse over racking the jackass's family jewels. He deserved it. *How dare him?* He actually had the balls to touch her. Why was it so hard for him to understand they were over? Done! Finished! Ended! They would never be together again. Kevin had made sure of that, the day he decided he wanted to audition other women for her position.

There had been a time when Kara had believed in Kevin. A time when she saw them having children and growing old together, a time when her future was very clear and Kevin had been the center of it. Kara had worked her ass off, so she could finish her Bachelor's degree in three years instead of four. So they could graduate together, get married, and she'd be ready to move wherever the military decided to station him.

It had been the perfect plan, until Kevin canceled the wedding. His only explanation was that he wanted to see what worldly women were like. He said he wanted to make sure that Kara was the right woman for him, and the only way to do that was to explore his options. That day, he had successfully ripped out the last piece of her heart that had allowed her to believe in relationships. Then a month ago, he had the cojones to show up and inform her that his exploration was over, and he would definitely like her to marry him. Kara had been proud of herself. She had showed a considerable amount of control. Yes, Kevin walked away with a couple bruises, but he did walk away. Yep! If she did say so, it was excellent control on her part.

"I'll ask you again, Kevin, and then I'm going to call Tasha to throw your despicable ass out of my store. What the hell are you doing here?"

Kevin was finally catching his breath as he scooted up against the wall. He couldn't understand how she could still be so hateful, and why she was unable to forgive him. The only thing he had done, since the day he'd returned, was attempt to prove his love for her. The same reason he had come here today. "Kara, I'm sorry I bit your lip, and

I'm sorry I tried to kiss you. I couldn't help myself. Even if you don't believe it, I do actually love you, and God knows how much I miss you."

Kara was tired of his groveling, and she was tired of men thinking her lips were open to the public. That was the second time today someone had assumed her lips were fair game. "Kevin, save the apologies. I've had enough of those today. Just tell me why you're here."

"I think you might be in danger." He said as he looked around nervously. "I was over at Java-House, when I overheard three men discussing your birthmark. They were saying something about needing to take you out before you're able to mate. I know it sounds weird, but that's what they said. They didn't seem to know your name, or where you live, but they knew you were here in Fort Collins and they're looking for you." Hesitantly, Kevin reached down, and took Kara's left hand, rubbing his finger across her birthmark "I knew it was you, because they describe your birthmark perfectly. I didn't come here to fight with you, Kara. I just didn't want to see you get hurt. I thought I should warn you about them. Maybe you could get one of your brothers to stay with you for a couple of nights." When Kara pulled her hand away, Kevin had a sly smile on his face. "You know I'd offer to stay with you myself, but I'm still hoping you'll change your mind. Seeing how you want kids, I'd better protect my manhood from your temper."

Kara felt like a complete heel. She had overreacted again, hurting Kevin before knowing the real reason he was there. Here he was trying to protect her and she had laid him out across the floor. She reached down, helped him up, and then helped him into her office onto her chaise. She grabbed a couple bags of ice and sat down next to him. "I'm *really* sorry, Kevin. I shouldn't have jumped to conclusions. I know it's not a valid excuse, but you know my temper sometimes gets the best of me. I truly do appreciate you taking the time to warn me."

With that one sentence, Kevin saw the opportunity he had been hoping for. "How about a dance at Becky's engagement party tonight and we can call it even?"

Shiz-nat! She had walked right into that one. Kara forced herself to smile, not showing any of the irritation she was feeling at that moment, and replied "Sure…Why not? *One* dance!"

6

Stupid! Stupid! Stupid! Stupid!

Kara said over and over again in her mind. Why had she agreed to host Becky and Alan's engagement party? *I hate parties! I hate them with a homicidal passion! All get-together's do, is allow my insanely large family a place to embarrass me, even when it has nothing to do with them.* Kara yelled at herself disgustedly.

She looked around as guests arrived for her best friend's engagement party. Kara knew she was exaggerating, her whole family wasn't actually here, but all of her immediate family was, and that was bad enough. It was like walking around with your own personal entourage. She looked around again remembering what her Me-ma, Lalita, always says 'Take deep breaths. Calm your temper before it controls you.' Breathe in slowly...breathe out slowly. In...slowly...Out...slowly. In...out...in...out...in...out. Kara concentrated on breathing until she started to calm down.

She ran her finger slowly around the top of her Champaign glass. *I can do this. I can do this. Think positive and anything is possible.* Kara had always considered her grandparents to be her sanity in a completely insane family. She had spent a lot of time with them when she was little. Kara loved her paternal grandparent's tea store, and always thought it fun to hang out and mix teas with them, and her maternal grandparents she always traveled with. It gave her some release from her freakishly large family. She sometimes missed being a child, spending her days with them and their wisdom. Of course, Kara knew her grandmother was always right. Kara would be the ultimate host. She would do this, it's only for a few hours and Becky Dando is her best friend, plus Kara was Becky's maid of honor, it's her job. *Of course, Becky is also a part of my family. Hence...why all my family is at her party. Yes! I owe her, and if it means being miserable at a few parties, so be it. Stop being a coward! Straighten up, and start being the hostess you're supposed to be tonight. Do this for Becky.*

Kara looked around the bar...again, but didn't see any dark handsome strangers lurking about. *Pity!* She did notice everyone was beginning to have fun. Obviously Kara wasn't as bad a hostess as she thought she was. She laughed to herself. No, she wasn't a bad hostess, just a disgruntled one. It made her feel a little bit better. She caught a glimpse of her brother, Trey, and his fiancée, Tanya, dancing in the middle of the crowd. Kara couldn't help but smile. Tanya has been her sister, Kali's, best friend since college. Then last year...who knew... after years of flirting, Trey fell head over heels for her. *Freaked us all out!* Kali's still not happy sharing Tanya with Trey, but she'll get over it...someday. As they moved, clearing a view of the entry, Kara's heart stopped.

Walking in a group, as if on cue, was her Uncle Chung, Adelina, Kalab, a man that looked similar to Adelina, and of course, the most beautiful man she'd ever seen. That animalistic swagger of his left Kara aroused with desires she shouldn't feel...but did. Alexander was an airbrushed *Mr. GQ*, one of those guys you never see in person, because they don't really exist. In yet, there he was! Right...here... in Mel's Bar. If possible he appealed to Kara more now, than he did this morning. *Damn it!* He was magnificent, scrumptious, the kind of man you just wanted to jump, and then deal with the consequences later. Alexander's body screamed *TOUCH ME!* and Kara's whole body stood up and took notice. Her heart was saying...run to him. He's your soul-mate, go to him. Her mind was saying...How could he be? He's not even human. He's not even from this time. Kara didn't know how old Alexander was, but as a vampire...or Dark-Soul, he'd have lived a very, very long life. Naturally, Kara's heart was persistent. *You felt it when you touched. You felt it in his eyes. Alexander is your soul-mate.* Intense desire invaded her. Shaking every bone in her body so strongly, she might have knocked the earth out of alignment. Kara pictured her hands twisting themselves around his silky blonde hair, tracing those full scrumptious lips, and roaming all that tanned......

"Uh...hum!" Kara jumped as she heard someone clear their throat, jarring her out of her fantasy. *Shiz-nat! If I had to be here, couldn't they at least leave me alone to live out my fantasies?*

Kara turned around to see the bartender looking over her. He was obviously new to Mel's, because she had no idea who he was. He wasn't a pleasant looking man at all, big, muscular, rugged. Definitely dangerous! He had that bad boy image going on, and his face kind of reminded Kara of those pug dogs, like someone had gotten mad at him and smashed it. He had short curly blond hair, and very pretty blue eyes, except when he was looking at you, they just seemed really angry.

"Yes?" Kara asked.

"Do you think you could order another drink?" He scowled. "I mean, I don't mind you sitting at the bar, but I need to make a little money tonight. You've been sulking in that same drink for well over an hour."

He did have a point. She had been sitting there with the same champagne that she and Becky had used to toast each other, after they finished the party preparations, and that had been well over an hour ago.

"I'm sorry. Go ahead and give me another one. This one's hot anyway."

"I'd be happy to buy that for you." Kara looked up into a cowboy's dark eyes she didn't recognize. He looked like he spent most of his time in a bottle. His pot belly was as big as his hips. It seemed he had no idea what good hygiene meant. He wasn't wearing a cowboy hat, but he should have, to cover his nasty greasy hair.

Great, just what I need. Ugh! This is why I hate bars. Guys are always hitting on you. Thinking if a girls alone, she obviously needs a man. Completely absurd!

Kara watched him wink at a table where two more equally disgusting cowboys sat watching them.

Oh! So that's what this is. A game is it? Assholes!

"Sorry. Not interested!"

He smirked. "You shouldn't blow me off so quickly. I could be the man of your dreams."

Idiot! Can't you take a hint? Kara acted like she was considering his offer. "Well...let me think...that's not too difficult...because the man of my dreams is definitely, nowhere...in this bar." *Well maybe he is, but you're not him.*

"Fine lady...whatever! I'm sitting at that table." He pointed to the other two guys, "If you change your mind."

Sitting there Kara had been hit on three times in less than an hour. What was the world coming to? Such *desperation.* She knew men didn't like to be turned down, it hurt their egos, but she has her own rules. Rules like: she never picks up men in bars, their drunk, obnoxious, and only looking for one thing, a good time in the sack. Not Kara's idea of a relationship.

Sitting there Kara thought, *Becky always tells me I need to lighten up and have some fun. She says my idea of a man is pure fantasy and doesn't exist. That I will end up alone, like some old cat lady, if I keep up my nonsense. You know...maybe she's right...but I was raised in a house where relationships are sacred. Both sets of my grandparents have been married for over sixty years and my parents almost thirty. I've watched their love get stronger every day of my life, and even though my family infuriates me sometimes, the love they show each other is very real, and that's the type of love I want. I won't settle for less. If I never find it...Well...then I guess Becky will be right, and I'll be that lonely cat lady...actually it would be a lonely dog lady. Well, not really alone, my whole family lives in a ninety mile radius. Being alone is a sacrifice I'm willing to chance, to wait for the right man.*

Alexander followed Chung to a table in the center of the bar that was near the dance floor. As they sat down, he introduced all of them to Kara's grandparents and parents. Alexander was sitting between one of her grandmothers and Chung. He was pleasantly surprised how friendly they all were. They had completely accepted Chung into their family, and that gave Alexander hope for himself, because he knew it would be easier for Kara to accept him, if her family did, so he laid on the charm.

Kara continued looking around Mel's bar, enjoying the nostalgia of it. It's the oldest bar in Fort Collins. Mel, the owner is a childhood friend of her grandpa Earl. They could have went to Denver, to one of the modern clubs, but most of the permanent residents in Fort Collins think of themselves as small town folks, and Mel's definitely has that feeling about it. It kind of makes you feel like you've stepped back into the old west. With the wrap around old wood bar, the dim lighting, and the oak tables, it gives you that old west, small town feeling.

Since Alan grew up in a small town, Kara knew he would appreciate Mel's. She hoped it would make him feel more at home. Across the room from the bar was a small dance floor, right in front of a small stage, and they had a wonderful band that played every night. The only thing really modern about the whole bar was the karaoke set up next to the stage.

Kara found Becky and Alan arm in arm, strolling table to table, chatting with their guests. Seeing that Becky was happy, Kara couldn't help searching for *Mr. GQ*. Of course, his table was surrounded by women. You wouldn't expect anything less. This was a man who could have his choice of anyone of them. Alexander was way out of Kara's league. Men like him always went for Becky's type…and why shouldn't they…perfection should be with perfection…but damn he's hot…what she wouldn't give to have one night with all that lush tanned skin, of course according to her uncle she could have more than one night. If only she could believe that. As she was salivating over his delicious body, Kara realized Alexander was sitting with her family.

Shit! What the hell is Alexander doing?

Instantly, Alexander captured Kara's staring gaze. It seemed very deliberate. *As if I had called his name, and he had looked up to answer me.* She didn't want Alexander knowing she'd been salivating over him.

Smiling at her, Alexander held her gaze for a couple of extremely awkward minutes, as if he was searching her for something. It was actually kind of ire, in yet, his sparkling eyes sent sizzling desire throughout her entire body. Shocked by the pulsating cravings running through her mind, Kara forced herself to turn away and go out the back door to clear her head.

Alexander laughed to himself. Truly Kara felt attracted to him, as strongly as he felt the pull to her. Chung's right. She's stubborn. He would buy his time, get to know her family, let them get to know him, and then try to apologize to her. Kara couldn't hide forever, and that's when Alexander would pounce. Like the predator he was catching his prey.

"Hi, Chung!" Becky walked up and kissed his cheek, "this is my fiancé, Alan. I'm so glad you came." In a quieter voice she asked, "Does Kara know you're here yet? Who is this dream guy you're trying to set her up with?"

"Let me introduce you. Alexander, meet Kara's best friend and hopefully your ally, Becky" motioning his hands between them "and her fiancé, Alan." Chung then turned and said "This is Kalab and Alexander's sister and brother, Adelina and Nathaniel."

"Pleasure to meet you all." Becky took Alexander's hand.

"Actually, the pleasures ours." He kissed her knuckles. "Congratulations on your engagement, and thank you for allowing us to celebrate the occasion with you."

Becky blushed. "Alan go mingle, I need to speak to Alexander for a few minutes." Alan nodded and headed towards his friends. Becky turned to everyone at the table "Hey everyone, where's Kara?"

A man walking up to table answered, "She's at the bar hiding. Where do you think she is? She's afraid we're going to embarrass her tonight." He started laughing, "Do you want me grab her?"

"No, Trey!" Becky yelled. Then realizing others might be listening, she said quieter "This man" holding Alexander's hand up "claims to be Kara's soul-mate. Of course in true Kara fashion, she slapped him, and now refuses to talk to him."

"Dude, are you *crazy*." Trey laughed. "My sister's a Tigress. She's cute, but when you get too close, she'll bite your head off." He warned. "Why do you think Kara lives by herself?"

"Stop that Trey." The elderly lady, with her short curly gray hair, and the same signature brown eyes as Kara's, sitting next to Alexander snapped.

"Sorry, Grandma Sara"

"That's not true about my Kara." Sara patted Alexander's arm. "She's just very independent, that's why she lives alone. You must be the gentleman she called me about today." She scrutinized him up and down before asking, "I'd be very interested in knowing what makes *you* think you're my *granddaughter's* soul-mate."

"Mom?" Melody, Kara's mother looked questionly at her mother-in-law. "Kara called you today? About...him?" she asked. Alexander could see where Kara's beauty originated from. Her mother had the same flawless peach complexion and high cheek bones, but with dark auburn hair and green eyes.

"Yes...she did."

Melody sat forward, resting her elbows on the table, cradling her chin in her laced fingers. "This is serious then. Kara must feel something, if she called you."

A woman, whom Alexander assumed was Kasi, since she looked identical to Kara other than her short auburn hair, walked up and asked "What's up with my twin?"

"Hey Kasi, this is Alexander. He claims to be your twin's soul-mate." Becky answered.

"No shit! Are you sure you're not mine, we look alike you know. As gorgeous as you are, I'll be your soul-mate." Kasi laughed.

"Kasi!" Kara's family all yelled in horror.

"Sorry, sorry, just kidding." she laughed again, throwing her hands up in mock surrender.

"Trey...Kasi! Keep the rest of the family away from here, and not a word of this to anyone." Kara's father, Edward, demanded pinning Chung with those same dark brown eyes that Kara had inherited. "Ok, Chung. *Please* explain this to us."

Chung, Alexander, and his family spent the next half hour explaining the mark on Alexander and Kara's hands, and what a Dark-Soul's *Amara*, a chosen one was. Everyone sat there stunned for at least five minutes in silence. Finally, Grandmother Lalita spoke.

"Until today, I had forgotten this, but when I took Kara to Greece that summer when she was ten. A fortune-teller stopped us on the street and pointed to her birthmark, calling her a chosen one. I asked her what she meant, she said that our Kara was important to the world and her mark meant she had a special soul-mate. I don't always believe these things, you know, but if it's not real, it's a hell of a coincidence."

"Well" Edward leaned back in his chair with his arms behind his head. "You all know, my daughter will never accept her fate, unless she thinks it's her decision. Kara's so damned independent and stubborn; we'll all have to help her see her true destiny."

"That's what I was trying to tell Alexander this afternoon." Chung sat forward over the table. "Do you have a plan?"

Edward contemplated, rubbing his chin. "Ok! First we need to keep her siblings out of this. You know Kara will become defensive if we all get involved. Second, we need to understand this *Amara* situation a little more. So let's put our heads together to plan this through."

Alexander was completely amazed. He'd never seen a family so accepting of his kind. They quizzed him on how he would care for Kara; his thoughts on women and careers; his occupation; how he'd protect her; etc., but not once did they worry about him being a different species. Every question was simply to make sure Kara would have a safe and decent life. From the conversation Kara's grandmother Sara had with her today, it would seem that Kara's feeling their connection as well. Both families sat there trying to plan away for Kara to accept her situation as Alexander's chosen one.

⌇

"Are you OK?"

Kara turned glaring as Adelina sat down next to her. She really didn't know Adelina very well and wasn't in the mood to have a discussion, or a conversation for that matter.

"I saw those guys harassing you earlier." Adelina explained, pointing to the table of cowboys. "Alexander will have a coronary if he thought they were bothering you."

Kara laughed sarcastically. "Yeah right! He doesn't even know me.

Why would he give a shit? Besides can vamps…I mean…can Dark-souls even have coronaries."

Adelina tried not to laugh, but a chuckle still escaped her lips. "Technically? No. But when it comes to you, my brother will."

Kara completely turned to face Adelina. "Why?"

Adelina pointed to Kara's mark. "We explained that today. Your mark proves you're his *Amara*. Alexander protects what's his, and he would die before allowing you to get hurt."

Kara sat there a moment absorbing what Adelina was saying. "Does Alexander have someone else?"

Adelina let out the breath she'd been holding. If Kara was worried about another woman in Alexander's life, there was surely hope for them. Kara might even be jealous. This was a better sign than she'd hoped. Adelina couldn't be more pleased with this revelation. She wouldn't tell her about Catherine or Fiona. She'd let Alexander explain them to her, but she wouldn't lie to Kara either. "Since Alexander found out about you, he hasn't *really* been with another woman."

"That's been like…What?…about ten hours." Kara said sarcastically.

Adelina chuckled, "I really like you. No! Emotionally it's been centuries. We came here 10 years ago looking for you, but Alexander hasn't slept with a woman in a century. You need to understand, you've been in every waking thought he's had for decades. You have nothing to worry about, Kara. Alexander would never hurt you, you're his *Amara,* and our people take that very seriously."

Kara looked at Adelina with a deep sadness in her eyes. The dullness in Kara's eyes broke Adelina's heart. To see the same pain in her that she saw daily in Alexander…ate at her soul. It wasn't right for two loving people to hurt so badly.

"Are you sure?" Kara whispered.

Adelina took her hand. "I know you're probably still in shock over everything you've learned today, but someday I believe you'll be my sister-in-law. I'll never lie to you. I can promise you, Alexander won't hurt you."

Kara was amazed how comforting Adelina's touch was. She did seem to truly care. Kara squeezed her hand in return. "Thank you! I think I just need a little…alone time to gather my thoughts. That's all."

Adelina released her hand "No problem." Shoving her business card into Kara's hand, "Here's my card if you ever want to talk. Your special Kara, don't forget that." Then she turned and left, leaving Kara sitting alone at the bar.

Kara sighed just before she looked over recognizing that Cassidy, one of Becky's guests, was extremely high and about to cause a scene. *Damn! Tonight's never going to end.* Kara slid off the bar stool, grabbing Tanya as she headed towards Cassidy. "Hey Cass, why don't you come with us." Kara pulled Cassidy towards the back door.

Cassidy pulled free. "I'm happy right here."

"Cassidy, we just want to talk to you" Tanya interjected. Motioning to Kara to grab Cassidy's other arm.

Cassidy jerked free latching onto Kara's hair. "Bitch, I'm not going anywhere with you. I'm having fun, right here."

Kara twisted around, clasping Cassidy's wrist behind her back, freeing her hair from her grip, and roughly pushed her out the back door. Relieved to have her outside where she couldn't make a scene. Kara pushed her towards the parking lot.

"Bitch, what are you doing?" Cassidy yelled. "I told you, I was having fun."

"Keeping you from ruining Becky's party." Kara spat. "You're high! I don't need the cops to show up and ruin Becky's party. Tanya will take you home."

"Stupid Bitch, I'm not going anywhere. I'm having fun." Cassidy began trying to fight them as Tanya got a grip around her neck and yanked Cassidy towards her car. "I've got her. Go back inside and let Trey know I'm taking care of Cassidy tonight."

"Thanks" Kara turned around to find Becky standing behind her.

She gave Becky a weak smile "Sorry, I just didn't want Cassidy ruining your party. She's high again."

"It's a bar, Ker. A fight is bound to happen." Becky shrugged her shoulders. "Besides, you know I love a good brawl. I'm just surprised your brothers didn't handle her for you."

Kara couldn't say anything, her temper was still blazing. She just laughed and rolled her eyes at Becky. Besides, her brothers would never hurt a girl. Even in self-defense.

Becky put her arm around Kara's shoulder walking her back into the bar. "Do me a favor?"

"Sure...anything! Tonight's all about you, babe. What do you want?" Kara asked.

"First...*please* try to have some fun. We've already been here 2 hours and you're still hiding out. Did you see the buff God sitting with your family?" Becky said teasingly.

Kara gave her that *'Duh'* smart ass look.

"No, I'm dead." Kara said sarcastically. "Of course I saw him. Way out of my league and you know it. If you were still on the market, you might have a chance. Me...never!"

Becky rolled her eyes and huffed. "You don't give yourself enough credit. Go flaunt your twins in front of any man, and you'd be surprised what you can catch. But the buff God, I think you've already hooked"

Now it was Kara's turn to roll her eyes. "Yeah, right! Besides if my breasts are all that interests him, I wouldn't want him anyway."

Becky snorted. "Yeah, oooookkkkk! I doubt if even you would continue saving yourself, if Alexander was lying naked in your bed."

Kara punched her shoulder, as they both cracked up laughing.

"Hey you two what's so funny?" Kami interrupted as she and her new boyfriend Ted approached them.

Kami met Ted last year at college, but they just started dating last month. He's a Texas boy, born and raised on his family's ranch outside of Dallas. You'd never catch him without his cowboy hat and boots. He's a shitkicker through and through, right down to his bow legs.

"Becky, if you want to make it to your wedding alive, I would *drop* this subject while Ted's around." Kara warned with a pointed stare.

"Ooo, this has to be good" Kami purred. "Ted, could you go get us some beers...please." She pushed him towards the bar.

"I was just telling your sister" Becky winked at Kami "that if that gorgeous blonde Adonis ended up in her bed, even she would spread her thighs for him."

"You mean the hot-hot-hottie, sitting with our parents?" Kami asked. Becky nodded. "Oh, yeah! He's so do-able! Your right, even Kara couldn't be a prude with all that lean muscle in her bed." Kami smiled wickedly. "You know Becky; you just might have found the way to de-virginize Kara."

They winked at each other. "Should we?"

"I have my key I could give him." Kami joked.

"Oh, No you two don't." Kara grabbed both of their arms, as they started laughing. "You two stay out of my sex life."

"What sex life? You're a virgin, Kara" they both laughed.

Kara frowned. "Becky, didn't you have another favor to ask me?"

"Right!" Becky slid her arm through Kara's. "Sing for Alan and me?"

"What? No way! Not here. Not with all my family here." Kara protested. "Uh-Uh! They'll cause a scene."

"Good luck Becky, I think I'll stay out of this one and go find Ted." Kami elbowed her and then departed towards the bar.

"Come on Kara…please, you know I love hearing you sing." Becky had a huge smile on her face. "Please!" she begged. "Remember when we were in high school and we used to go to karaoke every weekend? *Please* for old times' sake? Sing for Alan and me, something we can dance to. I always love when you sing a good ballad. Please-Please-Please, and you did say anything."

Shiz-nat! Becky always traps me with my own words. I know better than to allow it, in yet, I still let her do it. Kara felt defeated, knowing Becky would never let this go, since she'd promised.

"Fine, I'll do it!" Kara let out a deep sigh of resignation. "What do you want me to sing?" Becky squealed with delight hugging Kara.

"Any love ballad. Your choice, and our old high school karaoke song, 'I'm Crazy' for old times' sake." Becky was jumping up and down, clapping her hands together like a little kid. How could Kara say no to that, besides Becky was right, she did love to sing.

In high school Kara was definitely more of a party girl. She went to all the school parties and hung out here singing karaoke with her friends. It truly was fun, and she had a blast. She had felt free then, no responsibilities, no concerns, nothing except her own self-gratification.

It was a different time, a time when her only worry was school, friends, and parties. Then in one single moment everything changed. Alcohol took two of her friends away from her on prom night, and Kara has never been the same since. When she started college, she became the responsible one. With four girls starting college at the same time, Kara knew money would be tight, so she decided to pay her own way. She didn't need or want the party life, she just wanted the career. Her grandparents owned a tea store in town, on North College, and they wanted to retire. Kara agreed to take it over, so she could pay for her education. The only promise she had to make was to keep it open and running the same way it's been for the last 30 years. Kara's family even remodeled the upstairs apartment for her. With such a large extended family, they pretty much have every career covered, Electrician, Carpenter, Plumber, you name it and they have it. So it was easy and cost effective to do. Her Brother, Trey is an architect, so he designed a beautiful two bedroom modern apartment, with a beautiful garden on the roof. Her sister Kami is an interior designer, so she decorated it in Kara's favorite color red, adding white and black.

Kara's thoughts were interrupted as Becky pulled her towards the stage. "Sing us a great ballad Ker." Then she was gone. Becky and Alan stood on the dance floor waiting for her to begin.

Nathaniel nudged Alexander's arm. "Kara's singing."

"Oh good!" Kasi smiled proudly. "My twins the best. Not one of us are anywhere near the vocalist Kara is, but she'd never admit it."

Alexander couldn't believe it. Not only was his *Amara* strong, intelligent, and beautiful, but she had a list of other talents. How could he be so lucky?

"I've heard Kara has numerous talents, do you share them?" Alexander asked Kasi. It was astonishing how much they looked alike. Other than Kasi's dark auburn hair cut short, they were truly identical. Of course, the main difference for Alexander was the chosen mark on Kara's hand.

Kasi started laughing, "Not as many. My twin's talents are astronomical, but don't tell her I said so. She spends a lot of time learning, whereas I prefer to have fun. Did you know she Belly dances?" He shook his head frowning. Alexander wasn't sure he liked his *Amara* being provocative. "That's my favorite. I'll see if Becky and I can get her to belly dance, but you'll have to pay attention, because usually when Kara realizes that she's belly dancing in a crowd…she stops…completely embarrassed. We all love making her blush." Kasi laughed.

"Alexander, I told you your *Amara* is quite talented." Chung added, sensing his Commander's discomfort.

"Don't forget she has the tongue of a goddess." Lalita joked.

"Excuse me?" Nathaniel choked, shocked by Kara's grandmother's statement. Although, he shouldn't have been, Lalita is Greek. Being half himself, Nathaniel's well aware how open Greeks are about sex. It takes a lot to embarrass them.

"Her palate is like no one's we've ever encountered. Right, Chung?" Sara explained.

"That's correct. In 4000 years, I've never met anyone who could blend teas the way Kara can." Chung admitted. "She has exquisite taste."

"Well, brother" Embarrassed as he realized what they were actually talking about, Nathaniel hit Alexander on the arm. "It seems like you hit the jackpot."

If only Alexander knew how to win Kara's heart. Truly that's all he wanted. Alexander was blindly happy that Kara was so talented. A woman who would prove to be his equal, but was he worthy of her. Could he earn her love? As he watched her talk to the elderly woman on stage, he understood why her family and friends loved her so much, why they protected her, and what a treasure Kara truly was.

Kara looked over at the older lady sitting behind the karaoke machine. Nancy was Mel's wife and a true sweetheart; although she always seemed to have an angry look in her eyes. No…maybe not angry, maybe just a 'hard life' look. Kara knew from listening to her grandparents talk, that Mel and Nancy had tough times until they had paid off their bar.

"Hi, Nancy. Do you have the female version of 'True Love'?" Kara asked.

"Yes, I do sweetie. Is that what you'll be singing?"

"Yes, that one first, and then 'I'm Crazy'."

Nancy nodded and motioned to the microphone. As the song began, the words lit up on the giant flat screen on the back wall, above the bar. *"Just you and I...understand why...As I look in your eyes...I feel true love...Sometimes we fight...Sometimes we cry...but in the heat of the night...We know true love"* It was actually a really cool system, not like the ones in high school where the small TV was on the stage, and you would have to turn to it and squint your eyes to see the words. This was a really big flat screen and it was directly over the bar, so it looked like you were looking at the audience, not the screen. Of course for this song, Kara didn't need to read the words. She loved this song, and knew every word by heart. So to make it more personal, she looked down at Alan and Becky.

Becky shot her a big smile, and Kara knew she'd chosen a song Becky approved of. Singing came naturally for Kara. She never understood why, it just did. She has a great vocal range, at least that's what her choir teachers always said. She could go from low Alto to high Soprano without any problem, and can hold a note for a really long time. Good diaphragm her teachers used to compliment. Kara sang with all her heart giving the song all the emotion a good ballad should have. When the song ended, she noticed the whole bar had become silent and was either watching her or dancing. There was a sudden loud applause and a lot of whistles. Of course, half the bar *was* her family, so what did she expect. Kara raised her hands for silence. She was used to crowds, and knew how to handle them. "This next song is for my best friend Becky, a song we both thought we understood in high school, but we've learned not everything is so black and white."

Alexander saw Kara wink at Becky before the music started, and was shocked by the possessive jealousy that burned within him. Kara's voice was truly the voice of a goddess, and he wanted Kara singing to him with that passion, for that wink to be directed at him, and most of all he wanted her affections.

As the music started, Kara couldn't help but move to it as she began singing. *"All my friends think I'm crazy...going out of my mind...*

They say I'm making a mistake...but I'm binding my time ...They say forgiveness is a virtue that I need to learn...but they haven't been with you." As the song ended, she heard someone yell "Another one. Sing another."

Kara bowed gracefully "Thank you! But tonight is all about my best friend Becky Dando and her fiancé Alan Gregmore... Congratulations on your engagement." She pointed to both of them, and smiled before turning around.

Kevin jumped up on stage. "That's exactly why Kara and I are going to sing a duet for them. Nancy please put in 'The Right Combination'."

Alexander could feel Kara's fury. She didn't want to sing with this man, and Alexander wanted to kick his ass. "Who is that?" He growled, gritting his teeth.

"Kevin" Everyone answered.

"Kara's ex-fiancé. The one that won't give up." Chung filled in the blanks.

At the end of the song, Kara furiously flew off the stage. She wanted to escape, before Kevin had a chance to stop her. How dare he put her in that position? They hadn't sung together since they had broken-up. She had never wanted to sing with him again. He knew that. It was too personal.

Alexander wanted to knock the smug smirk off Kevin's face. He'd pursued enough women in his life to recognize the look of a chase, and like hell was Kevin going to capture Kara. *Kara is mine!*

Alan pulled Kara to a stop, as she stomped away from the stage. "Oh, no you don't. You're going to dance at least once tonight, and that's going to be now...with me."

"You know you really don't need to patronize me Alan. I'll be fine. Besides if I really want to dance, all my brothers are here."

"Becky says you love to dance, and since there are obviously so many losers here tonight, I'll claim your first dance. Besides your brothers want you out there, they just didn't want to fight with you to get you on the dance floor, so I'm the guinea pig." Alan confessed.

"Lucky you! You're not afraid of my wrath?" Kara joked, punching him in the shoulder.

"Nah, you're not so scary." He teased back. "As long as I keep your hands above my waist." That seemed to ease Kara's tension, and they both laughed.

"By the way, Thanks for saving me from Kevin just now. I didn't want to talk to him."

"No problem! I can't stand guys who make us all look out to be jerks; guys like him should be beat."

Kara laughed as Alan pulled her into an amazing quick step. No wonder Becky enjoyed going dancing with him; he truly did know how to dance, or at least the quick step. For the next 30 minutes, Kara was passed between Alan, her brothers, and her dad, before she could escape the dance floor. Just as she thought she was safe, Becky pulled her back to dance the electric slide.

"Hey, I'm tired." Kara complained.

Becky shook her head. "Oh, no you don't. You're going to have fun tonight, if I have to handcuff you to me."

Kara ended up dancing every line dance known to man. She knew this was part of some scheme that Becky and her sisters had conjured up, but she was having fun, so she wouldn't complain. As another line dance finished, 'Whenever, Wherever', began to play, and she couldn't help but use her belly dancing moves. Kara just couldn't help but feel the music…she loved it.

Alexander couldn't take his eyes off Kara; she was having so much fun. It was infectious. His only regret was he wasn't out there with her, but he assured himself that would never happen again. As the music changed, Kasi got his attention, giving him the thumbs up sign. This must be the song Kara liked belly dancing to. Alexander, Nathaniel, Kalab and Adelina moved towards the dance floor so that could get a better view. They had been warned to try and stay out of Kara's site, or she'd become embarrassed and stop. As Kara's hips started to move, Alexander's cocked jerked in response. He hardened instantly, as all his blood raced to his groin. Damn, how he wanted his hands on those luscious hips. Kara's hips were mesmerizing, it took his entire warrior training to stand his ground and not run to her.

"Damn! Alexander." Nathaniel gawked. "Look at her hips move,

I've been in the presence of professional belly dancers, and she's right there, *adelfos*."

"Shut up!" Alexander punched Nathaniel's arm. "That's my wife, you're drooling over."

"Not yet she's not." Nathaniel wagged his eyebrows. Alexander shot him a deadly warning. "Hey!" He raised his hands in surrender. "You know I'm just kidding."

"If I were you, I wouldn't tease about Kara." Adelina sternly interjected.

Kara admitted that she was having fun, and thanked all of them before going back to her stool at the bar. She sat down and asked the bartender for a glass of Moscato this time. Kara isn't much of a drinker anymore, which is why she still hadn't finished one full glass. Waking up on your front lawn, with a really bad hangover, and no idea what happened the night before, was no longer her idea of fun.

7

K ara sipped on her wine, waiting for the time she could go home. She was hit on a few more times in the next hour; she thanked them all and said no. Kara was just thinking that she would be able to leave, when she realized the three obnoxious, drunk cowboys that she had turned down earlier had surrounded her.

"So you think it's ok to embarrass us?" Kara looked up into dangerous eyes, completely cold and unfeeling. She gasped with fear. "Turning us down and then dancing with another guy. We don't think so. No one embarrasses us, and no filly turns us down." Two of them grabbed her arms. "You need to learn your place, little girl." Kara looked around, but couldn't get anyone's attention. She started to yell, but one of them put their hand over her mouth. Kara bit down hard, as he jerked back, slapping her. "Bitch" he roared. She didn't think anyone could see what was happening. The bartender had left to restock, and they had her backed into a dark corner of the bar. They were all so big; Kara didn't think anyone could see her around them.

Shit! Stupid! Why did I sit at the end of the bar near the corner? Stupid! Stupid! Stupid!"

Then, out of nowhere, she heard the most magical voice she'd ever heard. Low and husky, the voice sent Kara's body aching with desire. Alexander's voice was Strong, Confident, and completely mesmerizing, but very dangerous…almost lethal.

"I believe the lady told you '*NO*'!"

They all spun around facing him. That strong, beautiful voice, the voice of her savior. Kara tried to look around them, or through them, to see Alexander. She wanted to tell him to find her brothers, but she couldn't see anything. Just like before, they had blocked her view completely. The laughter burst out of all their chests at the exact same moment. It seemed like Kara was wrong, even with the lethal, dangerous edge in Alexander's voice, they didn't seem threatened by him.

"Are you talking to us?" They howled.

"I suggest…you let…the lady…go. No! Means No! True Gentlemen understand that…they never force themselves on a lady." Alexander's voice was harsh and deadly, it sounded like he was spitting every word out between his teeth.

"Whatever!" They all burst into hysterics again. "Who the hell do you think you are? Her guardian angel? I *suggest* you leave us alone, or the paramedics will be scraping your dumb ass off the floor."

It happened so quickly, Kara didn't even see it. The leader of the group was face down on the floor, with his arms behind his back, and a foot, wearing some pretty expensive black boots, was holding them in place. The cowboy that had been standing next to him was in a choke hold, and the other one was backing away quickly, with his hands in the air, palms facing her rescuer.

"I suggest you *leave* her alone!" Alexander threatened in that same deadly tone. "Ladies deserve to be treated with respect and dignity."

Alexander pushed the cowboy he had in the choke hold away. Pushing him so hard; he ended up ten feet away knocking over two bar stools and crashing into the counter, before slumping to the floor. Alexander stepped down hard on the leader's hands, he was still holding in place with his foot. "I hope I've made myself perfectly clear." He stepped down harder, as Kara heard something snap. Then in one very elegant step, Alexander was standing directly in front of her, releasing his hold on the stupid cowboy.

Kara saw the cowboy trying to get up off the floor, he was moaning and it sounded like cursing at the same time. He didn't even turn back around to say anything else to either one of them, he seemed too afraid. He ran for the exit, stumbling over what seemed to be nothing on the floor.

She looked up into Alexander's cold coal black eyes. He was

definitely Mr. GQ in the flesh. Standing this close to him Kara couldn't think straight. Her body was reacting to him in ways she couldn't even begin to explain. Kara thought he was talking to her, but she couldn't hear anything he was saying. Kara's mind was racing trying to control her urges to touch him. She tried to concentrate on Alexander's mouth moving, but those amazingly perfect satin lips, had her completely entranced. She tried to understand what he was saying, but she couldn't make it out. All she could think about was kissing those very tempting lips. Kara looked back into Alexander's eyes, trying to get herself to focus. What the...his eyes were slowly changing colors. Freaked out, she finally pulled herself together. How can his eyes change color? That's really freaky. Now that Kara was a little bit afraid, she was able to understand that Alexander was trying to get her to sit down on the bar stool. The same bar stool she had been sitting on all evening.

"Are you alright?" Alexander was asking.

Kara still hadn't caught her breath yet. She wasn't sure if she couldn't speak because of fear, from the previous situation, or because Alexander was mouthwatering breathless. She didn't know how to describe him. Words like handsome...beautiful... exotic...just didn't come close to describing how drop dead gorgeous he was. There were truly no words in the English dictionary to describe his radiance. At 6'1" he was very tall. Of course, to Kara everyone's tall. He had a perfectly proportioned body, a body that you only see on billboards, or magazines, but never in real life. He had long elegant legs, wide broad shoulders, a tight firm butt, which she was dying to touch, powerfully muscled thighs, flat rock hard abs, and muscles flexing over every inch of his lean cougar like frame. The black pull over sweater he wore, outlined every muscle in perfect detail, and each of those sculpted muscles screamed '*Touch me*'!

He had a noble quality about his face that aired somewhat of a royal expression about it. He had high cheek bones, a square jaw line, and a straight nose. His face was masculine, elegant, and dangerous all at the same time. His perfectly luscious full lips, begged to be kissed, and his eyes sucked the breath right out of her, melting Kara right to the floor. His eyes were now a brilliant ocean teal that seemed to sparkle with amusement as she gazed over his entire body. His hair was a golden blond, extremely clean cut. He wore his hair short, reminding Kara of Jessie's hairstyle on *Full House*, short on the sides, longer on top, but swept back on top of his head, with just a few wispy strands falling on his forehead.

Alexander had a beautiful tan skin tone, which Kara couldn't tell if it was natural or from tanning. It seemed to have an exotic luminescent quality to it. Then it hit her! Alexander's eyes change color because he's a vampire. She'd heard their eyes could change color, but she'd been around Uncle Chung for years and had never seen his eyes change.

"Your eyes change colors?" Kara asked Alexander.

He smiled at her. "You noticed that, did you? Yes, they do. Our eyes change color with intense emotion. When we're extremely angry, our eyes turn jet black. I'm sorry if they scared you."

"They don't scare me, I was just surprised. I hadn't…expected that."

"Are you sure you're alright? You were looking a little confused a minute ago." Alexander said with an amused expression on his face.

"You're enjoying this, aren't you?" Kara accused him.

"I have no idea what you're talking about" He claimed with an innocent face.

"If I were you, and you truly believe that I'm your…chosen one, I would stop lying to me and fess up. We both know you are aware of how you are scrambling my brains, and you obviously think it's funny."

Alexander grinned realizing he'd been caught. "Actually, I don't think it's funny. I'm delighted that I cause such a strong reaction in you, considering you do the exact same thing to me." He confessed "by the way…nice dancing" he winked at her. Kara felt the heat rise and cover every inch of her face. "Furthermore, I'll never lie to you. I cherish you in ways I don't think you can comprehend."

"How can you…cherish me? You don't even know me?" she pointed out.

"Kara, may I have your hand?" Alexander held out his hand to her, and she slowly put hers into his. "Do you not feel complete when we touch?" He asked. "You make me feel whole Kara; this is why I cherish you. You were meant for me…as I was meant for you…together we're one."

Kara turned their hands over so she could see Alexander's mark. His mark was still darker than hers, she still wasn't sure this wasn't all a joke. Granted he was right, the chemistry between them was incredible, but was Alexander *really* her soul-mate.

I can't allow my libido to encourage my mind. Even if he's the most scrumptious eye candy I've ever seen.

Kara rubbed Alexander's mark with her thumb to see if it would come off.

Alexander was highly amused. "What are you doing?"

"Seeing…if your mark will rub off." She said matter of fact. "I'm still not convinced this isn't some kind of joke."

"It is *not* a joke, Kara, and mine will not rub off any more than yours will. I can prove to you this is real, if you'll let me."

"How?" She asked suspicious of what he wanted.

"Let me kiss you again." Kara immediately started shaking her head. Oh, No, he's not. We've already tried this once, and she wasn't sure she could control herself if they touched again. "Kara, once I kiss you again, your mark will become as dark as mine. That should prove that this is not a joke. Correct?"

"You already kissed me once today, and mine's not as dark as yours." Kara protested.

"You pulled away too quickly. I *barely* kissed you. Let me *really* kiss you. I can prove what I'm saying is the truth." Alexander could still see Kara was skeptical, but she was considering his offer. "Shouldn't you give yourself the chance to know the truth?"

Kara knew if she answered him, she would chicken out. Since Alexander was sitting on the stool next to her, all she had to do was stand up and she could reach his lips. So that's exactly what she did, leaning forward until their lips touched.

As soon as Alexander understood what Kara was doing, he wrapped his arms around her waist to steady her. Her lips were so soft, so gentle on his, she was truly amazing. He let her control it briefly, before he gave into his own desires. He pulled her between his thighs locking her against him. Using his tongue, Alexander parted her lips and just like this afternoon Kara tasted sweet and heavenly. Alexander had never had a woman taste so good.

Kara couldn't breathe with Alexander's tongue sliding against hers. His tongue was demanding, invasive. She should be angry that he took control of their kiss, but she couldn't remember why. Kara wrapped her arms around his neck, allowing Alexander to pull her closer, molding their bodies together. She could feel every one of his muscles tighten against her. It made her ache for more of him, and when he pulled away, she wanted to scream.

In a rough voice, Alexander declared, "Give it five minutes then look at your hand. If you believe me, come find me. If not I'll understand."

He stood up and left. Leaving Kara more confused than ever. There was no denying the connection between them. She felt closer to Alexander after one day, then she'd ever felt with Kevin after two years.

Waiting was the longest five minutes of Kara's life, but it was quite obvious that Alexander was telling the truth when the time was up. Her mark was now as dark as his, and just as defined. She could now tell that the ring around the heart was actually a crown. She was excited and scared at the same time. She didn't want to miss her chance for true love, but Alexander's a vampire, and she didn't really know much about them. If anything, however, Kara was logical and rational, part of the reason for her going to law school. After taking a few minutes to analyze their predicament, she decided it would be best to understand the situation better. Looking around the room, she found Alexander at her family's table and headed that way.

Kara's father slapped the table. "What did I say? Play on her analytical half and it always works. She's on her way over here. Now that we have them talking, I think us old folks should bow out." Edward committed. He stood up and grabbed Kara into a hug as she approached the table. "Hey sweetie, great job, you sang beautifully tonight. We were just leaving to take your grandparents home."

Kara kissed her dad's cheek and then made her way to her mom and grandparents to tell them goodbye. She started to sit down across from Alexander, when he pulled the chair out next to him. "My lady" he held it out. Hesitantly Kara went around and sat down next to him.

"Ok, I'll admit the evidence is overwhelming." Kara confessed.

Kalab, Adelina, Nathaniel, and Chung all started laughing.

"Told you it would come down to evidence." Chung said between laughs.

"UNCLE!" Kara spat. "Someday you're going to need my services and you'll appreciate my evidence skills."

"*bao-bei*, you know we all love your analytical skills, don't take offense to us admiring them." Chung reached across and patted her cheek.

"Then let me admire your warrior skills, uncle, as you practice on my nosy family." Kara glowered back.

Alexander decided if he was going to have a conversation with her, he would have to interrupt their bantering. "Kara, as you were saying, the evidence is unquestionable?"

"Yes, that's correct. I believe I need to" Kara glanced around, becoming self-conscious about how many people were listening to their conversation "learn more about you and your people." Looking at Nathaniel, Kara held out her hand, "you must be...Alexander's brother?"

Nathaniel took Kara's hand, kissing her knuckles. "Pleasure to finally meet you, Kara. I'm his youngest brother, Nathaniel."

"Pleased to meet you." She looked back over at Alexander. "If you'll excuse me, I need some fresh air. Then I think we need to talk... without the audience." She tipped her head towards the table.

Kara definitely needed some fresh air, her breathing was staggered, and her heart was racing. This made no sense. Every time she got near Alexander her whole body...no her whole being just came unglued!

Get outside. Get some fresh air. You know better than to hope. He can't truly be interested in you. Look at him, he's gorgeous. Then look at you, you're pretty at best. Normal! Absolutely 100% Average! Pull yourself together and get outside.

Kara headed for the exit, but she hadn't gotten halfway to the door, when she felt big burly arms around her waist.

"Hey beautiful, don't you owe me a dance?"

Kara couldn't believe it. She knew that voice. She turned around and her mouth fell open. Standing in front of her was Steven Malroy. Steven had been Kara's boyfriend senior year of high school. At the time she actually thought they'd end up together. Until the horrible night of prom, true to male form, Steven got drunk and Kara caught him cheating on her in the teachers' bathroom with Stella. Worse, Kara and Stella hated each other.

For the last 2 months of high school, Steven begged her to forgive him, but Kara couldn't do it. He'd betrayed her. A betrayal Kara could never forgive. She knew that if a person couldn't trust the person who was supposed to be their soul-mate, then they shouldn't be with them. Steven had left immediately following graduation, and she had never seen him since. She had heard through friends that he was doing well, living somewhere in California, married with a child.

"Oh...My...Gosh! Look at you! How have you been?" Kara shrieked.

"Wow!! Blonde, huh? Never thought of you that way. I almost didn't recognize you, but you look...marvelous." Then he gave her one of those out-the-car-window-whistles.

Kara just laughed. "Marvelous! That's a new one for you, must be a California thing. I wouldn't do that whistle though, my brothers are here."

Steven grimaced. "All of them?"

She nodded. "All of them!"

Steven had been a football player in high school. The typical all muscle, all American, completely handsome, high school football quarterback. Sandy brown hair and dark brown eyes, 6'2", and 100% lean muscle. Even after four years, he hadn't really changed much. He was a little tanner than he used to be, probably from the rays in California, but he was still the same old Steven, and Steven always was able to make Kara laugh, so she figured, what the hell. "Didn't you say something about dancing?" Kara eagerly asked.

"You bet I did. I can't wait to put my arms around you. You *really* look amazing." He wagged his eyebrows.

"Hey!" She laughed, punching his arm. "This isn't pick up where you left off. I'm not that kind of girl. Besides aren't you married?" Kara corrected him.

"Somethin like that" he said under his breath.

Steven pulled Kara to the dance floor and they began to sway. He told her he was moving back to Fort Collins, and that they should get together sometime. Kara tried to find out about his wife and child, but he wouldn't discuss them. He told her that if she agreed to dinner some evening, he would tell her all about them. Kara agreed, but she wasn't really excited about going to dinner with him, he seemed to be talking like they were going to be a couple again, and they both knew that wasn't true, and it never would be. By the third dance, Steven was pawing all over her, and it was all she could do to keep his hands off her butt. *Once a cheater, always a cheater. His poor wife.* All of the sudden she realized letting Steven dance with her was a really bad idea. As much as Kara had fun with Steven in high school, she really didn't need this kind of juvenile drama right now, besides she just met Alexander and needed to pursue that relationship at the moment.

Kara was about to tell him she needed to leave, when someone tapped Steven's shoulder, and the most beautiful voice in the world asked "May I cut in?"

Steven looked completely startled, and seemed a little scared when he glanced around and saw Alexander. Kara didn't really understand his reaction, but he pulled himself together and murmured "Oh…um… sure…I guess…Is that ok with you Kara?"

She nodded, and an instant later she was dancing with Alexander. He held her so close that his whole, amazingly, drop dead gorgeous body was plastered against hers. Kara hadn't realized that she'd stopped breathing, until Alexander chuckled and whispered in her ear, "Breathing is always a good idea while you're dancing." She laughed and inhaled a long deep breath.

"I guess I forgot that." she murmured.

You know! Alexander whispering in her ear did nothing but stir the already blazing fire running through every one of her veins. Kara was completely incoherent at this point. She couldn't think. She couldn't even create a full sentence if her life depended on it. All she could do was let him twirl her around the dance floor, while she blushed.

"I hope you didn't mind me cutting in? I thought you looked a little...uneasy, and personally I didn't like the way he was rubbing all over you." Kara wasn't sure what she heard in Alexander's voice. Was he being protective or possessive? Normally it would have pissed her off, but with Alexander, she actually liked it.

Damn! He wants to talk while were dancing. Kara tried to collect all the thoughts that were running rampid in her head into some type of coherency, but when she spoke she was still stumbling. "Um...yeah. He *was* getting a little...frisky."

"So I saw, and you call that a little. I thought you were going to get some fresh air, and then we were going to talk." He spun her out and brought her back against him.

"That was the plan, until Steven stopped me. I haven't seen him since high school."

"Well, since I have you on the dance floor, where it's proper to have our bodies pressed together, let's not waste this precious time together. We can talk later."

Alexander looked down and smiled that wicked, crooked smile that she was beginning to adore. The most gorgeous smile Kara had ever seen. He pulled her even closer to his body, which Kara didn't think was possible, and continued to twirl her around the dance floor. If it had been any other guy in that bar, she would have immediately pulled away and kneed him in the groin. It wasn't like he had his hands anywhere they shouldn't be, one was on her waist pulling her closer to him, and the other was holding her other hand. It just felt so...intimate. It felt more intimate than when Steven had his hands all over her butt, and she hated that. Every cell in Kara's body was responding to Alexander's soft, confident touch, his smooth voice, his sweet breath, his rock hard body, and yes, his mesmerizingly beautiful, brilliant teal eyes.

Kara felt the heat saturating her, and what felt like an electrical current running all over her skin. All she could think about at that very moment was how much she wanted Alexander's mouth on hers. She wanted to feel the warmth of his lips moving against hers, and she wanted to dance her tongue over his and taste him completely. Kara couldn't remember ever wanting something so much in her life.

Alexander kept Kara's eyes locked on his for four wonderful songs. He twirled her around the dance floor, with the technique of a professional ballroom dancer. Never releasing her from his strong hold, the same hold that had Kara plastered to his body. Alexander never said anything; it was as if he could see everything she was feeling by just looking into her deep golden-brown eyes. Then just as suddenly as he had cut in, he had her off the dance floor, and headed for the bar.

"Um…Hold on a moment." She pulled him to a stop. "I need to use the restroom. I'll meet you at the bar."

"What would you like, and I'll order it?" he asked.

"Plum wine"

"Really?" Alexander looked shocked.

"Yes. It's delicious. I love Japan, and after high school graduation I toured the country, and fell in love with it…and plum wine." Kara flashed a brilliant smile. "I'll be right back."

Kara had started out of the bathroom, heading for Alexander, when Carla grabbed her arm and pulled her back inside.

"What the hell was that?" She demanded. "What are you doing with that hot blond?"

"Dancing…duh!" Kara answered irritated. "What's your problem Carla?"

Carla was Kevin's sister, and when Kevin and her had been engaged, pretty close friends, but when he entered the military, everything changed. Immediately, Kevin had wanted his freedom. He said he felt it was better for them to date other people since they would be far apart. He thought it wouldn't be fair for them to be tied down. Then last month he came home and asked her to marry him. It wasn't that Kara had been seeing anyone, but she hadn't really missed him, and that told her that Kevin wasn't her soul-mate. Ever since she turned him down, his family has treated her like the plague. Which is why Kara had no idea why Carla was even talking to her?

"Kara, do you realize he's a vampire?" Carla tapped her foot in irritation.

That took Kara completely by surprise. Carla actually sounded angry. *Why would she be angry? Shouldn't I be happy? I realize Alexander isn't her brother, but can't she just let me be happy?*

Angry she snapped. "I know he's a vampire. So what?"

"What do you mean? So what? Kara, I love you, you know that… but a vampire? What are you thinking? You know they're not safe. Steven just reminded me there predators…human predators. We don't want you hurt, and Steven says they're really quite dangerous. He says he saw a lot of them in California, and that people tend to get hurt around them. I just want you to be careful." Carla ranted.

Kara wasn't sure why she felt so irritated, but she did. She was actually really pissed off at Steven for saying that. She actually felt the need to defend Alexander and his kind.

"Carla, you know they've walked amongst us for centuries. I'm not saying that some of them aren't dangerous, but not all of them are. Just like humans, we have the good and the bad. Besides, you have nothing to worry about. He's very nice, and he's one of Uncle Chung's oldest friends. Alexander saw those cowboys trying to ruff me up, and he stepped in. Then when he saw I was uncomfortable with Steven groping me, he stepped in…again. He's extremely kind." she explained to Carla.

"Oh! Well…I guess…that's different then! I didn't realize the vampire was such a damn Good Samaritan. Maybe we should all offer our blood to him in thanks. Sorry for jumping to conclusions." Carla spat sarcastically.

Kara wasn't sure why, but Carla actually seemed concerned about her. Naturally, that didn't make sense since Carla had admittedly been pissed at her for turning down Kevin's proposal. Why was Carla listening to Steven's prejudices anyway? That angered her. It was so like Steven to judge people before he knew them. Who does he think he is? She should go right over and give him a piece of her mind, but Kara didn't want to make a scene at Becky's engagement party.

"Never mind, Carla. I don't know why you give a shit anyway. I'm not changing my mind about about your brother. It's over between us."

Carla grabbed Kara and kissed her cheek "Kara, I still love you. I know it's been difficult between us. I do believe you belong with my brother, but I don't want you hurt. You danced with Steven?"

"Yeah! Not interested! Besides he's married…remember."

"What!" Carla gaped. "You can't be serious. Kara, I thought you'd be happy he was back. Even Kevin thought you'd be ecstatic. We all assumed you'd never gotten over him. That's why I called him about Becky's wedding. I mean…I know you and Kevin were together for a couple of years, but you didn't even…well…you know. I just thought maybe you'd never gotten over Steven."

"Carla, Thank you for your concern, but I don't want Steven. I never did after prom night. I've never been able to forgive him for that, and it made me open my eyes to who he really is as a person, and I don't like him. I don't know what I'm looking for exactly, but the man that only thinks about himself, sex, and getting drunk, is not my kind of man. I'm sorry. Besides, Steven has a lot of baggage. I don't need that."

"Wow! Kara, you might actually end up alone. I don't want that for you." Carla wrapped her arms around Kara again, and gave her a big hug. "Seriously we have to get you out more. I don't want you to be lonely. You're someone's Angel, even if it's not Kevin's. We just have to find him." Carla hugged her tighter.

"Don't worry about me." Kara tried to put on a smile, but she was sure it looked strained. "At least Becky is getting her happy ending. That's good enough for me. Besides, I'll never be alone. Just walk out that door and everyone out there is connected to me somehow." Kara laughed, hugged Carla again, and headed for Alexander.

Kara was stunning wearing a short red sweater dress that outlined every one of her curves. It took every ounce of control for Alexander not to push her up against the bar, and take her right there in front of everyone. He wanted nothing more than to be inside that amazingly lithe body, to claim her as his own, but he knew that would be the biggest mistake of his life. Kara didn't approve of aggressive men, so instead he reached over gently, and rubbed her cheek.

Kara was discussing the differences in plum wine, and how good they really were. Alexander agreed, "You're right. It's delicious. I've just never seen anyone outside of Asia drink it, and I've never seen an American bar stock it."

Kara gave him a flirting smile. A smile that melted him instantly and made him hard enough to pound nails. Not that Alexander hadn't had an erection since the first moment he'd laid eyes on her. He had the feeling he was going to become very intimate with cold showers.

"Shh! Mel keeps a small amount as my personal stash." she confided. "He'd agree with you, I'm the only one who drinks it, just like the Ice Wine and Moscato I make him keep on hand."

Alexander took her hand, guiding her to a small table in a dark corner. "Interesting, you have very exquisite taste." Rubbing the back of her hand, he asked. "What would you like to discuss?"

Kara couldn't understand her apprehension. Alexander stirred feelings inside her she'd never known. This is what she had waited for her whole life. In yet, now she was terrified of it. What was her problem? Finding her soul-mate was what she'd wanted, it was her dream. What Alexander said was obviously true, her attraction for him was more than just physical; she could feel him in every cell of her body. Maybe she was just scared, because she really didn't know him very well. Kara decided she would start with the basics.

"First of all, how old are you?"

This was the one question that Alexander was hoping she wouldn't ask quite yet. He was afraid that she'd bolt for the door just as soon as she realized how old he really was. He knew from experience that humans had a hard time viewing life in centuries instead of years. He also knew he couldn't hide it from her, but he really wished he could put it off just a little while longer. Preparing himself for the worst, he took a deep breath and slowly let it out.

"I'm 2309 years old. I was born in 301 BC in Rome. My mother is Macedonian or what you would consider an ancient Greek, and my father is Roman."

"Shiz-nat!" Kara's mind was racing with questions…like…What

that time was like? Where had he lived? Did they really wear togas? *Damn, he'd look sexy in a toga.* But Kara knew she first needed to understand him, not how he lived before. "and you're a doctor? a human doctor?"

"Yes, among other things." Alexander admitted. He was relieved that she seemed to accept his age and parentage. Most woman of his kind was appalled that he was both Greek and Roman, since they had been brutal enemies. In fact, most of the woman of his kind had lived during that time, and held a grudge for one side or the other.

"What other things?" Kara asked suspiciously, eyeing him like she was trying to rip away his skin to see inside him.

Alexander sucked in a deep breath and exhaled forcefully. "I'll have to tell you this sooner or later. Naturally, I was hoping it would be later, after you got to know me."

"You're a criminal. Shit!" Kara jumped up, planning to bolt for the exit. "I knew this was too good to be true." Alexander grabbed her arm before she could run away from him, and pushed her back into her chair. Irritated, but somewhat amused that Kara would even consider him a criminal, Alexander prepared himself for her to lash out.

In shock, Kara looked up at him ready to hit him, how dare he push her into the chair. She was not about to be man handled by anyone, especially not a pompous ass criminal. As Kara started to take a swing at him, she saw the most unbelievable look on his face. Alexander had an amused smile on his face, and one eyebrow cocked, as if he was daring her to hit him. It stopped her cold. Why wasn't he trying to stop her? It made no sense. What he did next completely confused her. Alexander bent down lightly kissing her cheek, then her jaw, and then kissed a trail to her ear. Kara had never known torture until that moment; his lips on her skin made her dizzy with desire, but she knew she could not succumb to her passion.

"No, Kara I'm not a criminal, or anything else evil, although some humans would consider my kind so. I'm part of my people's ruling party, as well as the Commanding General of all our forces. I'm also a business man, a researcher, and yes, a doctor. Most importantly I'm your chosen one, but above all these things; I hold a more important destiny. I am the protector of all moral beings."

With Alexander whispering in her ear, it sent Kara over the edge. She twined her fingers in his hair, turning his head until her lips could take possession of his. The instant their lips touched, all Kara's worries disappeared, and a sense of contentment that all things were right in the world filled her heart.

Alexander was in complete shock, not only had Kara initiated a kiss, but her kiss was more passionate than he'd ever imagined. Alexander was needy in ways he didn't understand. What this woman stirred inside him, he'd never thought possible. He wanted her...no he needed her, with every cell of his existence. Needing more, he pulled her into his lap, and deepened their kiss. He loved the feel of Kara's tongue exploring his mouth. He loved her sweet taste, but most of all Alexander loved her passion for him. He could feel it, she might not be willing to admit it, but he could feel it within her.

Kara took a deep breath and sighed, as she pulled back from their kiss. "Ok, you're not a criminal or an evil man. This is good. I could never be with someone that was either of those. Most of your jobs I understand, although you have quite a few. You must be a very busy man." Kara giggled "You said you're part of the ruling party. What office do you hold? and what do you mean protector of all beings."

"Kara...I'm...I'm the Cruetian crown prince. That's the position I hold in the ruling party. I hold a seat on the council, and if my father ever dies...I would be King."

"Shit-Shit-Shit!" Kara ranted. "I didn't think I was worthy of you when I thought you could be a model in GQ. Now you're telling me you're a prince. I can't compete with that. I'm not the right type of person for you. I'm not royalty material...trust me...that's like *Cinderella*, or some fairy tale shit. Alexander we come from two really different worlds, and I'm not talking about the fact that I'm human and you're a vamp...I mean a Dark-Soul. I'm talking about that you are royalty, for God sake. I know they say God doesn't make mistakes, but one of his angels must have put your mark on the wrong girl."

Kara was completely hysterical, when Alexander cupped her face with both hands making her look at him. "Kara, my mark was not put on the wrong girl. You were made specifically for me. We complete each other, you're my other half. You make me whole. You're a princess just the way you are, but you're more than that, you're strong willed, compassionate, and you're pure. Once our ceremony is complete, you will be even more than you are now." Alexander rubbed his knuckles down Kara's cheek. "The answer to your second question. Before my birth a prophet revealed I would become the protector of all moral beings. I've been negotiating and fighting wars my whole life protecting this world. That's my most important job. Your destiny is similar. The prophecy states that my *Amara*...that would be you, will be strong enough to bring balance. Balance to me, and balance to the world. Once we complete the ceremony that will bind us together as husband and wife for eternity, certain powers will be bestowed upon you, helping you complete *your* destiny. Kara you *are* my *Amara*, and I can't wait to make you my wife." He gently traced her lips.

Kara was overwhelmed, completely speechless. Could she be this person? She'd never thought of herself as strong or special in anyway. Could this really be her destiny? *No Way! There's no way I'm some sort of superhero. They're wrong. I'm extremely average. Nothing special here.*

Alexander's heart broke at the sadness expressed in Kara's eyes. "You're wrong. I'll only disappoint you. I'm not some type of superhero. I can't save the world."

Alexander instantly realized his mistake. Humans can't fathom one person making a difference in the world, even when they do everyday. "Kara, I'm not wrong. You have to have faith in your destiny. You have to have faith in the higher powers knowing what they're doing. Trust me. You won't be alone in this; I'll always be there to help you. I promise."

"What happens when your family finds out I'm nothing special? Do they even know I'm human?"

"Yes, they know you're human. The prophecy told us that, just like it told me to find you her in Fort Collins, and your wrong. You're very special. You just don't realize it yet. There is no mistake. You bare my mark, you *are* my *Amara*."

Kara was so confused. She hated feeling lost. She needed control of her life, and here she was unsure of everything.

Alexander felt her despair. "Kara, my family and I have searched the last 400 years for you. Kelmar located you and the time you would reach majority. I came here 10 years ago waiting for you to turn 18 years old. My family has searched everyday for the last 10 years to locate you without success until today. Our devotion is endless. We're not wrong about who you are."

Kara looked down playing with her fingers. "Where's your parents?"

"Italy. My parents live near Rome." Alexander felt how nervous she was. He wished he could reassure her, but only Kara could make herself accept the facts he'd told her.

"So, why do *you* live in Fort Collins, instead of near your family?"

"I love my people and needed to research differences between our people. It's why I became a doctor in the first place. CSU allows me to do research, as well as practice medicine. It was a win-win situation for both of us. The school gets credit for my research, and I get to help my people."

Kara sighed folding her hands in her lap. "I'd be lying if I told you I wasn't afraid. I'm afraid of not being worthy of you. I'm afraid of what your people will think when you marry someone who isn't beautiful enough to be royalty. I'm afraid of what your family will think of me, but most of all I'm afraid of losing myself. Will I be allowed to finish my education, have my career, continue blending teas…continue being me? I'm not perfect, Alexander."

He snorted. "Neither am I." He kissed her forehead. "You'll never be *allowed* to do anything. You're not my slave or servant. You're my wife, and we are equal in every way. You'll never need to ask permission to do anything. I would hope you would discuss matters with me because you want to, but you would never have to. I'm not a barbarian, Kara, I'm a man who will treasure you, care for you, and protect you forever. You're extremely beautiful. I cannot keep my eyes off you. I burn inside for you with a rage I've never had for another woman, and I can assure you my family will love you. You are more than worthy for me, my family, and my people. Never doubt yourself, Kara, and I will never ask you to give up the things that are important to you."

Alexander saw a small hint of a smile, sucking his breath in sharply, he gave Kara an appreciated once over "Baby, you're enough to drive even a god mad with desire."

Kara giggled but was amazed at his sincerity. He truly believed what he said; she just wished she could believe it too.

As Kara drove home, she started thinking about her day and how your life can change in an instant. Maybe Alexander was her soul-mate. There was no doubt in her mind that there was a special connection between them. She could still feel his last kiss as he kissed her goodbye. That delicious sweet, spicy smell of cinnamon, ginger and male masculinity still circled around her, and she already felt like a part of her was missing. Alexander very well could be the man she'd been waiting for her whole life. She started laughing thinking back to all those conversations with her friends, where they told her how crazy she was to even consider a happily ever after. They always said soul-mates didn't exist. "You're setting yourself up to fail, because you've set your standards to high." Kara never believed them, how could her standards be too high. All she wanted was someone to want her as much as she wanted him. Someone who desired her as much as she desired him, a man who would love her unconditionally, no matter what she looked like when she became old, and someone who would respect her and appreciate her intelligence and her little quirks, and most importantly someone who would let her treat him that way as well. Kara always told her friends, she wanted someone who would treat her like his princess, even though she wasn't one. "It's a fairytale. That's all it is, those man don't exist, find a real man or you'll end up alone Kara." That's what they always said, in yet, she might have just found her fairytale, for Alexander didn't just want to treat her as a princess, he wanted to make her one.

8

Kara awoke with a renewed determination. Last night had been incredible. Alexander was more than she'd anticipated. With a great personality; he's charming, funny, intelligent, he'd been the perfect gentleman. Although…she swooned inside…he's absolutely the hero type. He reminded her of Brad as Achilles, except Alexander was taller, and radiantly more handsome. He's also a phenomenal dancer, a major plus in Kara's book.

After last night, Kara was beginning to believe that Alexander might actually be the man she'd waited her whole life for. She was finally coming to terms with her feelings; he just might really be her soul-mate. It was time she stopped being afraid and explored the idea fully. Next time she saw him, she'd let herself go. Whatever happened between them would happen. No more trying to hide her emotions, or keep her desire in check. She would let it out. *Yeah, right!* If only she could keep her resolve. It was easier said than done.

Even if he is, I'm not going to throw myself at him. He's much too arrogant for his own good. He's definitely used to ordering people around and getting what he wants. If he wants me, he'll have to work to get me. Otherwise he'll never respect me. Yep! That's what he'll have to do.

Kara rolled out of bed. Stumbling to the window, she looked out. Ugh! Colorado weather changes so fast. Yesterday it was 70 degrees. Today it's a gloomy gray with thick clouds. You couldn't even see the sun through the clouds and the pouring rain. Kara walked over to her T.V. and turned it on. Grabbing the controller, she jumped back under her covers. She had a little while before she had to meet Uncle Chung downstairs for breakfast, so she flipped the channels until she found a news channel and listened to the weather report. Ugh! REALLY? Only 40 degrees today.

Kara flipped the T.V. off, sliding off the bed. She made her way to the closet pulling out a pair of jeans and a black V neck sweater, opening a drawer she grabbed a matching lacy black bra and panty set. Kara always prided herself in matching everything she wore, even if no one else was going to see them.

Kara took a long hot shower, contemplating how to approach her uncle for more information about Alexander. She knew he was a doctor and he was here doing research for his people. They had talked a lot about his research and her college degrees, but Alexander avoided anything about his past, or about Dark-Soul's in general, other than his roles in their society. *A prince! How am I supposed to deal with that?* She wanted more information, and hopefully her uncle would enlighten her.

Kara always enjoyed hot showers, but today she was anxious. She cut it off sooner than she normally would have, then she brushed her teeth twice. Alexander had promised to drop by later, and she wanted fresh breath in case he tried to kiss her again. Oh, the thought of that kiss made her weak in the knees. That man knew how to kiss. Truly, his tongue should be illegal. The most he had done last night was kiss her, but she could see the flaming desire in his sea green eyes. He'd been such a good boy, no roaming hands, he had even asked before kissing her. Today maybe she'd give him the full invitation.

She took extra time blow drying her hair and then using hot rollers to make small curls. Once she removed the curlers, she pulled it half up into a clip, curling the ends into big curls and letting it stream down her back. Kara's hair hit the lower part of her back. She'd always thought of her hair as one of her best features, and intended to show it off. She loves long hair and is very proud of hers. It's always made her feel very sexual in some way. Kara never truly understood why, she just feels sexier with long hair. She grew up thinking men preferred long hair, and enjoys that it's one of her assets. After applying her makeup, she grabbed an umbrella, gym bag, her purse and headed downstairs to her store to meet Uncle Chung.

Alexander had been sitting at Kara's tea bar for a little over two hours, waiting for her to arrive. He shouldn't have been so eager this morning. He had already drank so much tea, he felt like he was going to float away. Chung had reminded him last night that he has breakfast with Kara every morning, and offered to stay away today, giving them more time to get to know each other. Alexander knew how much Chung enjoyed his daily breakfast ritual with Kara, and understood the sacrifice he was making allowing him to have this time alone with her. He truly appreciated it.

Alexander knew they didn't meet until 9:00am, but he had been so excited, not that he would ever admit it, that he had ended up arriving just before 7:00am, hoping that maybe she would already be here. She was not, so he had to wait. Not a bad thing by any means, because he had learned a lot. He now knew Kara's employees pretty well, and knew that Mable had been with the company since its beginning's a little over 30 years ago, and that Tasha was a single mom that Kara had helped off the streets. Again, he was shocked at her compassion for others. Most American women her age are extremely selfish. He had certainly misjudged her.

Kara felt someone watching her. She looked around, but didn't see anyone. Kevin must have scared her more than she'd thought. When he told her about the three men looking for her, she blew it off, thinking it was Alexander and his friends. They'd already admitted that they had been looking for her, but after last night's attack. *They were just drunk horny men. That's all! Stop being such a wuss.*

Kara stood at back door, admiring her grandparent's building, an old solid red brick building two stories tall. She loved this building, not only did it house the tea store, but she lived on the second floor overlooking the older part of College Avenue.

The store opens at 6 am, but she never went down until 9 am, when she meets Uncle Chung for breakfast. It gives her time to walk in the park…well, most days anyway. She doesn't when it's raining or snowing. Kara employs two employees, Mable and Tasha. Mable is older, and reminds Kara of her grandma. Mable is in her 60's with curly gray, silvery hair. She's plump and round, wears thick glasses, and is always wearing the typical grandma flower dresses and aprons. She's a great employee, and a good friend. She's really like another grandmother to Kara, and watches over her as such. Tasha on the other hand is in her mid-20's. Being a red head, she has a steaming temper, which Kara loves when she has a rude male customer that won't take "No" for an answer, and ultimately needs to leave. Tasha handles it every time. Tasha's very tall, which makes men squirm, because she's usually looking them directly in the eyes or down on them. She has short spiky hair, and numerous tattoos, and she relishes in the biker seen.

"Good Morning, Mable...Tasha." Kara yelled. "Did UPS get here yet? I should have a shipment from China today. I'll blend after my dance classes." She continued yelling as she walked in through the back door, shaking the water off her umbrella.

Alexander sat up when he heard Kara's voice. Her voice aroused every inch of his body. He looked at his watch 8:55, right on time.

"Hi, Sweetie! How are you feeling today? Mable yelled back.

"I feel fine. I just needed a little 'me' time yesterday, that's all. Nothing serious. Thank you both for helping out. I owe you guys big time, just let me know what I can do for you, Ok." Kara was working her way through the kitchen, towards her office to stow her stuff.

"Don't worry about it. You know we love you. We're just glad you're feeling better. I wished I knew who made you so upset yesterday, I'd go and show them what a biker babe is made of." Tasha threatened.

Hearing Tasha's threat made Alexander cringe. Had Kara been that upset over his kiss?

"Then to allow Kevin to slip through the back" Tasha gritted her teeth "I'm really sorry about that. That dumb prick should have taken my last warning. Next time I'll make earrings out of his balls." Tasha slammed her fist into the bar. "Don't you worry about what he said, baby girl. No one's going to touch you. I'll move back in if I need to."

Alexander could hear the concern in Mable's voice as she talked to Kara in the back. "UPS hasn't gotten here yet. Are you sure you're feeling better? If Kevin heard correctly or not, the idea of someone looking for you scares us all, Kara. No matter what their reasoning is, it's very unsettling. We have the store under control, take another day off, we'll be ok. You've been under a lot of pressure lately with Becky's wedding, Kevin, and now this."

Alexander reached over the bar and grabbed Tasha's arm. "What did Kevin say to Kara?"

"Let go of my fucking arm!" Tasha jerked away.

"I'm sorry, Tasha. I didn't mean to offend you. I just want to help. What did Kevin say to Kara?" He asked urgently.

Tasha gave Alexander the once over. "I don't normally trust men, but you were with Chung, and I do trust him." She leaned forward whispering, "I screwed up yesterday. Somehow Kevin got in the back. He said he'd overheard three men talking about Kara's birthmark, and how they had to find and eliminate her before she mated. Weird huh? Kara doesn't believe it. It does sound pretty far-fetched, but I'm not willing to take any chances."

At that moment, Mable came out of the kitchen, remembering Alexander. "Oh! By the way. You have a guest out here. He's been waiting a while." She yelled back into the kitchen, before turning to Alexander and mouthing "Sorry!"

What? Who could be here? Mable would never announce Uncle Chung as a guest. For that matter she never tells Kara he's here. Most of her regulars know she doesn't come in until 9 am, besides they know it's her breakfast time. Mable and Tasha made sure of that, no one's allowed to disturb her. They claim they at least know she has eaten one full meal everyday. They're both so damn motherly. Could the health department be here for an inspection? No! They wouldn't wait. They'd just do the inspection. If someone waited, it was obviously important.

Kara dropped her bags on the desk as she noticed the beautiful bouquet of pink and coral roses. Opening the card, she caught her breath.

Seek the meaning of these Roses.
For they represent my feelings.
Alexander

Kara didn't understand what Alexander meant. What meaning other than romance did roses have? She should really tend to her waiting customer, but she was dying to solve this riddle. Kara sat down at her computer clicking on internet explorer. She typed into the search engine: *meanings of roses*. Numerous websites popped up. She clicked on the first site and sure enough it had a list of what each color rose meant. Lavender: Love at first site. The roses Alexander left yesterday were lavender. Today's roses were coral and pink. Coral: Desire. Pink: Beautiful. She continued to glance over the other colors. Yellow with Red Tips: Falling in Love. Red: Love. Red and white together: Unity. Kara clicked on numerous sites, and sure enough they all had the same lists. She started laughing. How old fashioned. Alexander expresses his feelings with roses, how truly romantic. Not that she was complaining. It's just the men she knew would never do this. It's…quite…refreshing.

Kara placed her umbrella in its stand next to the door. After removing her jacket, she headed towards the front of the store to meet her guest. Her office is in the small rear corner of the store, in the back of the kitchen. It's nothing spectacular, just a few pictures of tea plantations, a calendar, and a big erase board to keep track of shipments. From her office she's unable to see the front, which is great when she doesn't want to be bothered, but like today, it'd be useful to know who was out front waiting for her. Like her mom says, "Can't have your cake and eat it too."

She stepped out of the kitchen, directly into the tea bar and right smack into Alexander's amazingly, sparkling teal eyes. Her heart stopped. Her breathing stopped. Butterflies swarmed her stomach. Alexander's here! He'd promised to drop by, Kara just hadn't expected first thing. Wow! Alexander's perfectly sublime body was sitting at *her* tea bar.

"Good morning" Alexander shot her a huge smile. The same gorgeous smile that had haunted her dreams. The same gorgeous smile that melts her right to the ground. She grabbed the counter for support. Damn, her legs were like mush. Of course, an action Alexander hadn't missed. He tried to stifle his laugh, but a chuckle still escaped. Kara could tell he was amused by her reaction. *Shit!* Didn't she tell herself she wasn't going to advertise his effect on her? In yet, within minutes, she already had. She wondered if he actually realized the enormous power he has over her. *This is crazy! Insane! I've never felt this way before. Could this be some effect that Vampires have on humans? No, that doesn't really make any sense. I've touched other male vampires, and they've never had this effect on me.* Kara needed to gain control over her raging hormones and quick.

"Good morning" She finally answered. "I'm sorry I kept you waiting. I just didn't realize you'd be here this early. Did you need to speak with Uncle Chung?" That's when Kara noticed he wasn't sitting at their normal table. That's odd. Uncle Chung's never late, and he never misses breakfast. She hoped he was ok.

Alexander sensed her distress "Kara, are you ok?"

"Um…I need to call Uncle Chung. He's never late. I need to check on him, and make sure he's ok. Excuse me." She began to turn away, when she felt a strong hand grab her arm. She looked down to see Alexander's hand stopping her.

"Kara, he's fine."

"How do you know?" She asked very confused, staring into his eyes, looking for answers. Answers she wasn't sure she wanted. Had Alexander sent him away? Was that why he was here, to tell her Uncle Chung wouldn't be coming back. Uncle Chung had mentioned he was getting his old job back. Kara guessed that meant re-enlisting in the vamp…Dark-Soul's military. Why did she always forget they hated being called vampires? It didn't make sense to her. Personally she thought vampires were kind of cool. Look at her uncle. He's lived along time, and seen some really cool things. It couldn't be all that bad. Vampires…Dark-Souls…Cruetians…or whatever they preferred to be called, she was sure it was an awesome life.

"Your uncle thought we should have breakfast together, if that's ok with you. He said he'll see you later at practice."

Kara wasn't sure what she saw in his eyes. Fear? No. Alexander wouldn't be afraid. Anticipation…need…desire? Maybe. That would make more sense. In yet, it looked like…all of those…why …why would he fear her? She couldn't really hurt him…could she? He was some great general, for God's sake; at least that's what they said yesterday. What could he be afraid of?

"I would like that." She said slowly, curiously. This man was definitely an enigma. If she was his *Amara*, she'd have to get to know him better. It's what Kara knew she wanted last night, a chance to understand him...to understand their situation.

"Perfect! Cause I'm really hungry." He smiled, relaxing a little.

Alexander was relieved when she had agreed to breakfast, it proved he'd made some headway last night. Chung had assured him he had, stating that he knew his little girl well. Alexander still didn't feel comfortable with Kara and Chung's relationship. He knew he would have to accept it, or he'd never gain Kara's trust, but he didn't like it. He didn't want any other men around her, not even someone she viewed as her uncle. "May I?" He held out his hand, and an instant surge of pride hit him when Kara instantly accepted it.

Kara almost moaned when she felt his hand wrap around hers. It felt so right. At first touch, that electrical jolt, she'd come to associate with Alexander, ran through her body enveloping her in a blanket of warmth. A sense of rightness surged through her, as he helped her around the bar; guiding her to the table they had sat at yesterday. Instead of sitting across from each other, Alexander motioned her inside the booth again and sat next to her. Just like yesterday, their thighs were touching, giving way to an intense desire that Kara wasn't sure she could control, or that she really wanted to control, now that she'd had time to think about everything. *No! No! No! I have to play hard to get. Alexander will never respect me if I don't.* Could she do it?

"Is this Ok?" Alexander asked. After last night, he needed Kara's touch so badly. He didn't even understand why he needed it. He just did. Every part of his body ached for her. He ached in ways he never knew existed, and would give up everything if she would just touch him. Of course, he would never admit that to her. He was a prince, the Imperator, Commander of the great Cruetian army. Alexander didn't need anyone. Except, after holding Kara in his arms last night, it felt so right, he felt so complete...he knew he needed this woman, even if he wasn't willing to admit it...yet.

"Are you sure we shouldn't sit across from each other?" Kara asked. Hoping he would say no.

"I would prefer sitting next to you if you don't mind. I've waited 400 years to find you. Call me a little possessive, but I really don't want you far away from me." Damn! Why did he just say that? Hadn't he just reminded himself, not to admit how much he wanted her, in yet, in less than a minute, he did just that. *Idiot!*

"So" Kara started "you don't view us as an obligation? You know the whole *Amara* thing. You don't view it as an obligation?" Alexander was so big and tall, she had to look up to see into his beautiful eyes.

"An obligation?" He asked. "If you're asking if finding you was an obligation, than yes it was. I do have an obligation to my people, and my *Amara* is destined to help them." Alexander saw disappointment flash across Kara's face, before she got control of her emotions. Oh!! Shit! He misunderstood. "But if you're asking if I desire you, that answer is yes as well. Kara, I could not be happier that you were chosen for me." He reached out and brushed her hair away from her face, cupping her cheek, he tilted her chin so he could look in her big beautiful brown eyes. "Don't you feel our connection? Every time I touch you. Every time you touch me. Every time I hear your voice. Don't you feel it? We were meant for each other. You believe in soul-mates, and I believe in my chosen one, my *Amara*. Don't you think they're the same thing?" He saw a bit of happiness creep back into her features.

"I want to. I really do. I'm just so confused. You've had 400 years to get used to this, and I've had a day. To answer your question… yes…I feel it to. It's like you complete me somehow, and I didn't even know I wasn't whole." Kara laughed. The sound slammed into him like a hurricane, stirring all kinds of interesting things in his body. Still cupping Kara's face, it would be so easy to kiss her, but he didn't want to anger her. Alexander's cravings were running rampid. If he could kiss her, just one kiss, he could get a hold on his desires and focus.

Kara saw passion fill his eyes. It wasn't imaginary. Alexander wanted her, and damn if she didn't want him. She felt his eagerness to embrace her, but he pulled back, desperately trying to control himself.

It shouldn't surprise her after how she'd reacted yesterday, but today she felt different. She shouldn't hunger for him, but she did. Following her heart, Kara pulled his lips down to hers, wrapping her arms around his neck.

Alexander was stunned by Kara's actions. Last night, she had allowed his kiss out of curiosity. Nothing more. Each time Kara had kissed him, he understood it was only experimentation. He'd brushed her lips with his a few times, begging for an invitation that never came. Last night, he hadn't been sure she'd ever let him kiss her again, but again, like last night, she had pulled him to her. This was an invitation. Today, he could feel the intensity of her passion as soon as their lips touched. Alexander moaned. Kara was truly decadent; her sweetness flowed out of her, enveloping him, leaving him in a trance. He pulled her onto his lap, making it easier to take control of their kiss.

Kara was lost in his lips when Alexander pulled her onto his lap. His tongue dived deeper into her mouth, searching, deviling, learning and mapping every inch of her. She moaned as she laced her fingers through his soft silken hair. She was surprised at how satiny it felt. It was soft like silk swaddled around her hands. Alexander's tongue was magic as it brushed against hers over and over again. Kara had completely lost herself in this kiss. The world could implode around them and she wouldn't care. This was heaven.

"Uh-hum" Tasha cleared her throat, making both of them look up.

Tasha stood with their breakfast in her hands. She had two large trays. A traditional Japanese breakfast. It consisted of rice with eggs, miso soup, fish, and small dishes of a variety of Japanese pickles, and naturally today's tea, Genmai. Everyday Chung and Kara had a different type of breakfast, today was Japanese. Kara hadn't actually considered that until Tasha brought their food over. Did Alexander eat Japanese food?

"Would you two like breakfast, or are you having each other instead?" Tasha chuckled, winking at Kara.

Kara stuck her tongue out teasingly. "We'll take our food. Thank you very much."

Tasha laughed again. "Only if you're sure. You two looked a little

…busy. I could probably find someone else to eat this delicious food."

Kara pointed to the table, as Tasha sat the trays down, and poured the tea for them.

"Thank you!" Alexander said as Kara blushed and slid off his lap. Kara tried to pull herself together and act like this was all perfectly normal. Which she was having a hard time doing, when her body was demanding she crawl right back into Alexander's lap.

After Tasha left, still chuckling to herself, Alexander reached over and gently kissed Kara's cheek, whispering "Thank you" in her ear.

Kara jumped. Not only at him saying thank you, but at the way her body responded to his breath on her ear. It was like a very intimate caress. Like Kara was completely naked, and Alexander had just ran his hands all over her.

She looked up at him "For?"

"Kissing me." Alexander admitted with somewhat of a shy grin. "I wasn't sure kissing would be permitted today. I didn't want to offend you again, and I was unsure how to approach the subject, after yesterday."

So Kara had been right. He had been afraid. "You're welcome" she teased "but I should actually be thanking you. I haven't been able to stop thinking about yesterday." With her confession, she blushed a bright crimson red.

"You're really great for a man's ego." He teased draping his arm around her shoulders, then with a smug smile he added. "You know practice makes perfect." Realizing Kara might misinterpret that as him being a player, he added "Only with you, of course."

"Well, I'm positive in…2309 years; I'm not the first to tell you that."

"You're the only woman I've ever tried to make feel that way."

"Don't lie to me." Kara snapped. "That is rule number one. I will not be with someone who lies. Ever."

"Kara, I'm not lying." Alexander took her hand, "I've never tried to make women want me. You're the first. Most of the time, I have to push women away. I've never found one that I had a yearning for until I found you." Kara started to speak, as he put his fingers to her mouth.

"It's not because you're my *Amara*. Well, maybe it is. Maybe that's why my body reacts this way to you. I don't know. What I know is my whole being; mind, body, and soul adore you, and I have never felt this way before."

Kara looked up at him with tears in her eyes. "Alexander, it won't last. Look at you and then look at me. Men like you deserve supermodels, not average country girls."

"Why would you think that?"

"That's the body men are attracted to." she pointed out. "Every guy wants a supermodel. It's just that most aren't good-looking enough to capture one, so they have to settle for average. You are. You will never have to settle. It's just a matter of time before you realize that, and then I'd......"

Alexander pulled Kara out of the booth, swinging her up into his arms, he marched to her office, kicking the door closed behind them. Releasing everything but her hand, Kara slid down his body. "Feel my appetite for you." Using Kara's hand he cupped himself. Alexander bit his tongue, as Kara moved her hand up his length.

Oh! Baby! Kara bit her bottom lip. *Gorgeous and well endowed. Oh, he's definitely aroused.* Alexander was as stiff as a board. "That doesn't prove anything, except that you want to get laid. Guys get a hard on...what...every time a female passes by them."

"Damn, Kara, you can be vile." Alexander stalked forward until Kara hit the wall behind her. "The men of your past were obviously assholes for you to have this much distrust. Yes, some cocks stand up for anything that walks. Let me assure you, mine doesn't. It's been over 100 years since I bedded a woman, and in 2300 years, I've never had a constant hard on, until I met you." He captured her lips with his. "Feel my heart." Kara placed her hand on his chest, Alexander mirrored her movements. "Feel how fast our hearts are beating. If my desire's fake, then so is yours."

Alexander felt Kara's smile on his lips, and knew he'd succeeded, even before she wrapped her leg around him. "You win, Alexander. Point taken!"

"Good! There's plenty of other ways I'd prefer to convince you of my sincerity, and it's not in words." He lifted her up, thrilled when she wrapped her tight little legs around his waist. "For the record, I like my women with soft curves, not skin and bones like human supermodels. It disgusts me. If I wanted hard muscles, I'd swing a different way, and find me a good warrior." Alexander stifled Kara's laugh and officially ended their conversation when his lips took possession of hers.

9

A lexander stood alone in his atrium, listening to some country singer singing 'True Love', while overlooking the stream that snaked its way through the mountains encasing his ranch. His home was actually more of a fortress than a ranch. As prince of the Dark-Souls and leader of the supernatural world, his father always insisted on complete safety. Not that Alexander couldn't defend himself; he's considered one of the most ruthless commanders in history. Not just among the supernatural world, but among humans as well. Alexander was a revered General, the son of a Roman father, and a Greek mother, who had fought over the centuries on both sides to ignite balance. His skills are lethal and deadly, but his show of compassion honorable. It's been said that he followed his grandfather, who was one of the greatest commanders in Greek history.

Alexander is a respected warrior, so why his parents thought he needed a fortress to hide behind was beyond him, but out of respect he always obeyed. Now he understood why his home was so important. If only he could get Kara to agree to stay here. He'd built his home on a large meadow in the middle of the Rocky Mountains, miles outside of Fort Collins. For a person to find it would be a miracle, unless they knew exactly where it was. If anyone did happen across it, all they would see is a beautiful mansion in the middle of nowhere. They wouldn't have any idea the security it held, or the danger they'd be in if they entered it. For no one is able to enter or exit his home without Alexander's expressed permission.

Alexander felt his sister's presence, long before she wrapped her arms around his waist to hug him. He was always amazed at how comforting his baby sister could be. When Adelina was younger, she'd always run up behind him, gripping him in a bear hug, when he returned from battle. Just like she was now, except Adelina was so small then, she'd be hugging his knees. Alexander laughed at the memory, how much he valued that hug. He missed her innocence, but as a woman she was a formable ally. Of all people, Adelina had seen his wife for what she was, long before Kalab discovered Fiona's treachery. Where Alexander is blind, Adelina sees, and together it's saved them and their family numerous times.

"Isn't that the song Kara sung?"

"Yes, it's soothing, but I think she sings it better." He admitted.

"Ahhh. Spoken like a true mate. Xander, why do you worry so? Kara has a pure heart. This I am sure." Adelina whispered. As a child she had nicknamed him Xander, and only called him that when she wanted him to know she was talking as his sister.

Alexander laughed. "Yes, *sorella*. Kara is everything you promised me she'd be. I feel complete when I'm with her, and I now understand how Walter completes you." He turned and kissed her cheek. "I'm glad you stopped me from making a mistake with Catherine, and forced me to find my *Amara*."

Adelina hated her brother looking so sad. He'd finally found his *Amara,* this should be the happiest time of his life, in yet, it wasn't. That she couldn't understand.

"Xander, do you remember when I found Walter? Even though we were forbidden to love each other, I couldn't hide my happiness. I don't understand how you can be so sad after finding Kara."

Alexander tried to smile for her, but Adelina knew it was fake. It didn't light up his face.

"I'm worried she won't accept me. She already holds my heart in her hands, and she doesn't even know it. Walter understood what your mark meant. He never needed an explanation. Even though you were supposed to be enemies, you two immediately went through the betrothal ceremony. Your only fight was with the families. Kara doesn't live in our world. Even now, after she understands our mark, she hasn't committed to me, and I can't ask her to. I will *not* force her into our lives. She has to decide this on her own." He took a deep breath and worriedly sighed. "I guess I'm afraid I won't be enough for her."

Alexander was shocked when Adelina doubled over with laughter. Here he was bearing his soul to her, letting her know his most intimate fears, and she thinks it's hysterical?

"Thanks a lot sis, I love you to. You sure know how to slap a man's pride."

"You...Silly...Man." Adelina said between laughs. "You're the catch of a lifetime. Kara knows that. She's already head over heels in love with you. She just hasn't admitted it yet. All you need to do is continue spending time with her, and she'll be yours for eternity." Still laughing, she hit him on the shoulder, as she started walking away. "I can't believe this is what you're worried about. A man who has lived thousands of years and still doesn't understand women...unbelievable."

Adelina was probably right. There was no doubt Kara was equally attracted to him. Alexander could hear her heart speed up when he was near, he could smell her arousal, and anytime they touch, her heart stops for a brief second. Yes, there was definitely chemistry between them. He thought about the night before. After a few dances, they had left Mel's and ended up back at her store blending teas. Kara had been so excited to show him her passion. He never knew blending tea could be such an art form, but watching Kara blend just the right amount of oil and tea leaves to create what she considered the perfect taste, was incredible. She positively glowed. Alexander loved Kara's passion, and wished that he could have just laid her across the floor and sampled it himself, tracing every soft curve of her delicious body. He had imagined himself inside her, claiming her as his own, reciting his oath, and drinking her blood to fulfill the first step of their unbreakable bond. As passionate as Kara was in life, she would make a fabulous lover. Alexander wasn't sure how much longer he could control himself before he'd have to bed her. Last night he settled on her laughter to warm him, but his body burned for her, and that fire needed to be sated...and soon.

Alexander heard his Vici Warriors arriving in the parlor. He'd called a meeting after Kara had left for her volunteer work. She gave free dance classes to disadvantaged children. Alexander would have loved to watch, but Kevin's revelation scared him. Could Seth's assassins already be here? If so, why hasn't any of his Vici noticed them? Alexander made his way to the parlor, wanting to get this meeting over with, so he could return to Kara.

He walked into his office to find Adelina, Chung, Kalab, and Nathaniel waiting for him. As soon as he walked through the door, they all stood out of respect. This was not a social gathering, this was a military meeting, and they all acted as such. Alexander walked around his large antique cherry desk, and sat down in his high back red leather chair. He motioned with his hands for them to all sit.

"General Chung, I cannot tell you how pleased I am to find you are alive and well. Are you certain you want to re-enlist, taking back your position?" He asked.

Chung stood walking around the desk and knelt in front of Alexander. "Commander, I would never have left if I knew you still breathed. It is my honor to serve you. I pledge you my life, *Kyrios.*"

Nathaniel handed a sword to Alexander. Alexander stood before Chung with the sword laid in both of his palms. "I accept your life into my service." Then he laid the sword in front of Chung.

Chung stood picking up the sword with both hands "Thank you, *Kyrios.* What is my first duty, Commander?"

Alexander sat back down and motioned for the others to do the same.

"We need to protect Kara. My first instinct was to send for ten of our Elite warriors, but it would only raise suspicion, and they would be followed here. As much as I would like to have her guarded around the clock, I believe it would be better to utilize our Vici warriors. Adelina's brought Walter here. It won't look suspicious since he's her husband. That will give us one more warrior. I'll meet you all in the parlor for final assignments."

Alexander watched as they left his office. He looked over today's reports discovering a disturbing change. No women were killed last night. Not that Alexander wasn't happy, he hated innocents dying, but that would mean Seth thinks he knows where Kara is. This changes everything.

Alexander strided into the parlor, "I apologize for calling you all here on such short notice. I see you're all aware General Chung is alive and well, and it sounds like Adelina has updated you on my status with Kara. She's the reason for the current situation and it needs to be addressed immediately." Alexander began reciting everything Tasha had relayed to him in complete detail. "Kevin never mentioned what the three men looked like, but they described Kara's mark perfectly. If this information is correct, our enemies are right here in Fort Collins."

Namorita was the first to respond, knowing Alexander needed some assurances. "I don't think we've missed them, Commander. I've been all over this town, and I haven't sensed anyone." Everyone knew as a Lunarian, Namorita had very special powers. No one knew what her powers were, but she had the uncanny ability to sense danger.

"Maybe these men aren't otherworldly" Nathaniel popped up. "They might be humans."

"True." Alexander agreed. "Except not one single woman was killed last night, the first time in six months. I have to assume Seth believes he knows where she is."

"*Kyrios!*" Alexander looked up at his brother. Tiberius was only 4 years younger than him, and at 6'3", every bit as intimidating as Alexander. When Tiberius turned 16, he'd followed Alexander into the Roman army, and they've been fighting together ever since. With his dirty blond hair and deep blue eyes, Tiberius and Alexander resembled each other, more than most of their siblings. "We should focus our attentions on protecting your *Amara*. If we're watching her no one will be able to get to her, even if we don't know who *they* are."

"True" Namorita agreed, "But there are enough of us for both jobs. Protecting Kara and looking for her hunters."

"I agree. Since they already know she's here, there's no reason to patrol Europe. You can move some of us here." Dante, one of Alexander's youngest brothers spoke up. Normally, he was quite during meetings, but protecting his brother's *Amara* was important, and Dante wanted to make sure they utilized every warrior they had.

Alexander looked over at Dante. Even though Dante was 1032 years old, all Alexander saw was the black haired, blue eyed toddler that used to hide in their parents villa. Alexander loved his siblings. As the oldest, he always felt responsible for them. Lately though, they all seem to be taking care of him.

"I agree with your assessments. Until Kara and I are blood bonded, her protection is paramount. I'd like to report" Alexander looked at Adelina, "I'm making progress. I at least haven't annoyed her today." Everyone laughed. "Kara is unaware of this danger, and I want to keep it that way. I don't want her to be afraid."

"How did it go today with her?" Nathaniel asked. "How long before you think she'll bond with you?"

"It went better than we could expect, for a human that doesn't understand the meaning of a chosen one. We have General Chung to thank for that. She trusts him explicitly. I answered some of her questions about me, but she will definitely have many more before she'll bond with me. I want all of you to be honest with her. She asked me to give her time to get to know me, and that's the least I can do. This has to be difficult for her. Her life has been completely turned upside down, but she's dealing with it admirably."

"Will she agree to the betrothal ceremony with you? Adelina asked. "That will at least allow her to call you if she's in trouble."

"She's allowing me to kiss her, from what we heard from General Chung and her family, that's a miracle in itself. I will not push her any further. Kara is my *Amara*, and we will protect her until she is willing to perform the bonding rituals." Alexander looked around the room. "I will spend as much time with her as possible, allowing her to get to know me. Hopefully, I'm worthy of her affections. Chung, how many times a week do you have breakfast with Kara?"

"I'm there every morning. Kara is there most mornings, but never on Sunday's." Chung answered.

"I want anyone available to meet for breakfast at Kara's." Alexander continued. "The more she's around our people, the sooner she'll accept my family. Namorita put two teams together, one for Denver and one for here. Find the hunters. Adelina, Walter, put a team together to patrol

Denver. Tiberius your team will protect Kara. Dante yours will protect her identical twin. Kalab's always with me, so he'll be in charge of communication. I'll work on getting Kara into this house." He looked around, "Any questions?"

"Only One." Kalab laughed. "You entering the pool?"

"What's the bet?"

Everyone chuckled. "How soon you'll bed her?"

Alexander heard more laughter as he looked over at Chung. "You allowed this?"

Chung started laughing. "Not that I'm thrilled with the idea of you bedding my little girl, but it's obviously going to happen. Kara has a great sense of humor, I figure she wouldn't mind. I know her better than anyone, so I might as well clean these fools out."

Alexander cocked an amused eyebrow, as he studied the board. Chung was the furthest out, at six months. Tiberius was the earliest, betting a week from now. They can't be serious. This is his *Amara*. There's no way he's waiting that long, to wrap those tight little thighs around his hips. "You've forgotten my charm, General. My bet's before the weeks out."

Chung laughed like he knew a secret. "We'll see. I know my *bao-bei*. Now we better go or we'll be late for Kara's lesson."

⟨⟩

Chung shifted them into his dojo. It was a large room, divided by a hard wood floor. One side was mats, the other tatami.

"Kara's studio is upstairs, by the music it sounds like she's still teaching. I'll shift us up there." Chung announced.

They arrived in the doorway of a traditional dance studio, wood floors, surrounded by mirrored walls, and lined with ballet bars. A group of teenagers were impatiently waiting on the floor. An Indian song began to play as Kara made her appearance wearing a turquoise and silver bedlah.

Nathaniel covered his mouth, stifling a laugh at the stunned look on

Alexander's face. Teasing him, "Hm-Hm-Hm! Look at those curves, your one lucky......"

"Shut up, Nathaniel! What the hell is she doing?" Alexander growled.

Chung clapped him on the shoulder. "Kara teaches Belly Dancing. What do you think she is doing?"

Kara felt a familiar buzz flash across her skin. Smiling, she glanced around finding the four men standing in the doorway. She seductively danced her way over, leading Chung and Nathaniel further into the room. "Class, we have guests. Give me a second and I'll demonstrate the Isis Wings." She made her way back to Alexander and Kalab; taking their hands she escorted them to Chung's side.

Alexander was astonished. Kara was showing more skin than cloth, coupled with her professionally sensuous moves, it was no wonder every male was panting uncontrollably. When she opened the Isis wings, it just added to the whole allure. By the end of the dance, Alexander was as hard as a rock. It wouldn't surprise him, if every male needed a little more room in their pants.

Alexander watched a teenage boy approach Kara. "Can I feel your last move? I didn't get it."

"Absolutely!" Kara put the boy's hands on her hips.

"No!" Menacingly, Alexander moved quickly to Kara's side. At the same time, the boy jumped back.

Kara was baffled by Alexander's outburst. Is he jealous of a teenage boy? "It's Ok." She assured him. "It's how they learn. Come here Andy." She moved her hips allowing Andy to feel the motions. "Got it?"

"Got it!" Andy spied the giant standing next to Kara and timidly backed away. "Thanks Kara."

A few more students required the 'hands on' demonstration, which had Alexander cringing every time a male touched her succulent hips. Finally the class dissipated, leaving him and Kara alone, since Chung had taken the others downstairs, preparing for Kara's lesson.

Kara was pleased by the dazed expression on Alexander's face. Turning in a slow circle she asked, "You like?"

Alexander was speechless. He continued imagining his tongue teasing the jewel dangling from her sweet navel. Oh, yes! Alexander liked. "Too Much." His voice was low and husky.

Kara was thrilled with his fierce stare that lit her body on fire. She swayed closer, turning away from him. She reached behind her, placing his hands on her hips, as she continued rotating them. "Private lesson?"

Alexander knew if Kara didn't stop moving, he'd have her naked and on the floor. He leaned into her ear whispering, "All right my little temptress, I don't think you're ready to saturate the fire you're igniting. So unless you want to be pressed up against that wall, we should probably end this demonstration."

Before Alexander comprehended what she was doing, Kara had turned, wrapped her arms around his neck, and captured his bottom lip with a playful tug of her teeth. Oh, how this woman brought him to life. He scooped her up, taking control of the kiss, and carried her over to a corner table, freeing his hands to explore all her delectable exposed flesh.

Kara lost herself in the heady feeling of Alexander's tongue teasing hers. She felt his hand gliding up her inner thigh. *Oh, Thank God for skirts!* While his other hand worked its way under her top.

Alexander relished in Kara's silky skin as his hand slowly made its way to her radiant heat. The satin protecting his treasure was already damp. He pushed it aside, feeling heaven for the first time. Alexander swallowed Kara's murmurs as he toyed with her clit. She was so hot and wet, and from her reactions, he could put her over the edge in a heartbeat.

Alexander guided Kara down onto the table, suckling her breasts, before laving a path down to that cute little navel, that's been driving him wild. He dipped his tongue inside, playing with the jewel, as he slid a finger inside her, reveling in her sexy little moans.

Kara didn't know why she was allowing this, with men she always took things slow, but like hell was she going to let Alexander stop. Kara was immersed in sensations she'd never felt before. Any second…*Oh, God, Yes! Don't let him stooooop.* Her whole body ignited with tiny spasms. Alexander jerked her to him, swallowing every one of Kara's passionate screams, before laying her head, panting on his shoulder. No one had ever given her such an intense orgasm. Kara heard the smugness in Alexander's chuckle, and knew he was pleased with himself. Not that she wasn't pleased with him, but did men always have to let it go to their heads.

Knowing Kara's euphoria was from his touch, Alexander felt like he was the King of the world.

"Uh…um! Do I need to hose you both down? Kara, we have practice. Now!" Kara looked up in time to see her uncle's backside stomp away. *Crap! How much had he seen?*

Alexander still had his hand between her legs as Kara announced they should go. He held her tight, removing his hand; he looked deep in her eyes, as he sucked her release off his fingers. "Delicious! I'm branded for life." Playfully he nipped her ear sighing. "Let's go."

Alexander left Kara to change and shifted back to the Dojo.

"*Kyrios*" Chung dropped to one knee out of respect. "Forgive my anger."

Alexander knew this relationship was hard on his General, he just hoped it wouldn't cause too much friction. Alexander had just found his old friend, and he had no intention of alienating him. "There's nothing to forgive. Kara's your child, I understand that. Be assured it wasn't what you thought. I will take her somewhere special for that."

Alexander was happy to see Chung stand up smiling. "I'd appreciate that. Kara deserves happiness, but also respect."

"What do I deserve, uncle?" Kara walked in wearing a black dance unitard, a shock considering they were all wearing a traditional Gi.

"New sparring partners." Chung pointed to the others. "You know Kalab, and you're *very* familiar with Alexander" he flashed Kara a we'll-talk-later look "You met his brother, Nathaniel, last night."

Brothers? Even last night she'd had a hard time imagining them as brothers, Nathaniel didn't look like Alexander. They were about the same height, but Nathaniel had jet black hair with sky blue eyes. Well, maybe there was some family resemblance.

Why did Uncle Chung want her sparring with them? She only

sparred with her uncle, no one else. Ever! "I only spar with you!"

"Not today!" Kara started to protest, "As your *sensei*, you will obey my instructions. You will spar with all of us. Understand?" Chung was leaving no room for discussion. It was time Kara learned to fight others. If she was in danger, she needed to fight people she couldn't anticipate.

"Fine!" Kara pouted. "If I hurt them it's not my fault."

"Highly unlikely" Nathaniel laughed, with the others joining in.

Kara stood up straight, pushing her shoulders back, her chin out. "We'll see. Free arts today, *Uncle!*"

They all gave Chung a quizzical expression. "I've taught her many forms of martial arts. Free art means she can use any of them."

Kalab nodded, "Good, let's see what you've got."

Alexander was impressed at the precision and flow of Kara's moves. She was as graceful as a dancer, but with the attack of a warrior. Not as good with swords, but she could throw a weapon with accuracy. Kara was fast and had strength in her kicks, she'd even knocked Kalab back a few steps. Of course, Alexander hated seeing Kara attacked, and attacking her himself felt treacherous, but the more she knew, the better they could protect her.

Kara was exhausted. Her private lesson usually only lasted an hour, but today they'd been going at it for three. Not that she was complaining, she'd actually learned a lot. As Kara drank her water, watching the four men wield their swords, she realized, she'd been sparring with actual warriors. What she does for fun and exercise, these poor men have done to survive. Sadness washed over her, as she looked around at these four strong and powerful men, and realized what they've had to endure to survive. Maybe while they're here, she could show them a little fun, a bright spot in their lives.

Kara cleared her throat to get their attentions. "Guys! I'm adult enough to admit when I was wrong. I learned a lot sparring with all of you. Thank you! To show my appreciation, if you're all free tonight, I'm meeting some friends at Mel's; you're welcome to join us. Drinks are on me. We're meeting around 7 pm, but you can drop by whenever. I gotta get, so I'm presentable. Hope to see you there." Kara ran over and kissed them all on their cheeks and was out the door in a flash.

Chung snickered, "Well, gentleman, you've just had your first hit and run by Kara, or at least that's what her family calls it. She's always running from one thing to the next. Never giving anyone time to have a discussion or answer her for that matter."

"Shit!" Kalab growled, "Kara just left without protection."

They all four cursed, before Chung raised his hand to calm them, "I'll shift you all outside her apartment. That's where she's headed. We'll catch her there."

10

ara couldn't believe she'd invited all of them to Mel's. What was
she thinking? Oh! Well that was easy, she'd been thinking of all
those strong, mouth-watering, ropes of muscles that were begging to
be mapped by her tongue. Kara couldn't get their little diversion out of
her head. If only Uncle Chung hadn't disturbed them, she might have
gotten Alexander out of his shirt...or possibly even more. Hopefully
more! Kara's basic motivation... ask them all and conceivably
Alexander would show.

Kara checked herself in the mirror, before going inside. She had
used every last minute to shine, making sure her makeup was flawless,
her outfit sublime, and big blonde curls streamed down her back. She
looked and felt incredible. Anticipating this would be enough, to ignite
those burning flames in one Dark-Soul's eyes, she strutted into Mel's.
Now let's hope perfection himself strolls through the door.

Kara noticed Becky and Alan had grabbed tables near the dance
floor, but she wasn't ready to confront her best friend. Becky is Kara's
rock of stability, her sanity break from her largely insane family. As
an only child, Becky enjoyed Kara's obnoxious family, and Becky's
family always enjoyed having Kara stay with them when she needed a
little peace. Becky always tried to make Kara feel special.

Kara once told Becky "You never realize how lost you can get,
until you have nine siblings." Since kindergarten, they've been best
friends, sharing each other's families, being each other's support, and
keeping each other's secrets. Kara viewed Becky as hers, something of
her own, that she didn't have to share with her sisters. It isn't that Kara
doesn't love her family. They just sometimes get on her nerves. Which

seems to happen a lot.

Kara sat down at the bar, ordering an ice wine, watching her best friend. At 5'7" and the perfect size 2, Becky could easily grace any runway. With her shoulder length black hair, that's never out of place, and soft baby blues, that males fall into, Becky's always a picture of perfection. Too bad Kara couldn't claim the same. No, Kara's always considered herself height challenged. At 5'2", *everyone* is taller than she is. Kara's always been envious of Becky's height. Becky just laughs and scolds her. "You know Ker, you should stop bitching. You're blessed on top, which is more important to guys than your height, but if you want to complain, we can fix both our flaws. My flaw is tiny tits. I'll trade you 2 1/2" of my height, for half your D cup. That will make us even. We'll both be 5'4 ½" tall with B cups. What daya say?"

Kara smiled at the memories. *If Becky only understood how horrible it is to be top heavy. It's much easier to add padding, then to try to take something away. Even taping them down doesn't work. I would gladly give her some of mine, even without getting any taller, if only they didn't have to cut me. Most people don't understand, boobs truly just get in the way. I've been told, all my life by girls how my breasts are a blessing...trust me...they're not a blessing...they're a horrible curse.*

"They sure are happy together aren't they?" The bartender, Chuck, sat down Kara's wine. Reminding her of the buff biker guys Tasha hangs with, he had more piercings and tattoos than Tasha did.

"Yes, they are." Not that Kara understood what Becky saw in Alan. Not that Alan isn't cute, with his cropped black hair, hazel eyes, and big husky build; he's definitely one hot cowboy. He's even a great guy. He's just not the kind of man Kara would have chosen for her best friend. Alan's simple, with simple tastes. He dreams of owning a dairy farm like his father, and Becky's one of those girls that could truly be a model, traveling the world, visiting exotic places, and up until she met Alan, that was Becky's dream. Kara just couldn't picture Becky milking cows.

"Wow! Look at you. You're lookin hot!" Steven licked his finger touching Kara's arm "Sizzelin! Steamin! Smokin! And the blonde? Extremely sexy!"

Kara rolled her eyes. She definitely didn't need this tonight. "Hi, Steven. I was surprised to see you last night. When did you get back in town, and where's your wife?"

"A couple weeks ago. You hadn't heard?" Steven wrapped his arms around Kara's waist. "Lucky you, I'm a free man again. Wife's divorcing me." He whispered in her ear, kissing the sensual spot behind it.

Kara instantly pulled away, not wanting to give him any ideas. Kara swore Steven's only talent was pissing her off. "Steven, if you touch me again, you won't be walking out of here with your family jewels. Kapish?" Kara pushed his hands off her.

Steven positioned himself on the stool next to Kara's, blocking any escape. "Come on Baby. You don't still play hard to get, do you? You looked happy to see me last night."

"Back...off...Steven!"

Alexander walked into Mel's instantly feeling Kara's anger. He still had to be a couple blocks in proximity to feel her, but their bond was getting stronger. He glanced around, spotting her at the bar being harassed by a-soon-to-be-dead man. Alexander started towards her with Nathaniel, Adelina, Chung, and Kalab in tow, when a guy reached out and stopped him.

"What are you doing?"

"She needs help." Alexander jerked away, as Chung stepped in front of him.

"Wait! This is Darrius, another one of Kara's brothers. If she were in danger, he'd already be there." Chung slapped Darrius's shoulder, introducing him to everyone. "Where's the rest of the family?"

Darrius pointed across the half circle, where Trent, Kami, Alan, and Becky stood. "That's all of us tonight. Steven's with those three guys," he pointed to a table, where the same three big cowboys that attacked Kara yesterday were watching Steven and Kara. "We're just making sure they don't interfere." Darrius held out his hand to Alexander, "Appreciate your concern, but you don't know my sister. You'll just piss her off if you interfere. Best thing you can do is enjoy the show. Besides" he gave Chung a knowing look "she deserves this confrontation. We've waited a long time for her to lose her cool with this asshole."

Alexander started to question that comment, when Steven placed his hand on Kara's thigh. That's when Alexander recognized the jerk from the night before. He was the same person who had groped Kara on the dance floor. Something didn't seem right. Steven was with the same guys he'd protected Kara from last night.

"Come on Kara, you don't want to be like that." Steven stuttered, groping Kara's thigh. He was clearly already drunk.

"Dumbass! I was serious when I said to keep your paws off me." She slapped Steven's hands away, "you know my brothers don't take kindly to me being groped by animals. They tend to mount them on their walls."

Steven was all too aware of Kara's *brothers*. They'd knocked him on his butt a few times. "Come on baby! Just one dance, it won't kill you. Your brothers won't mind. Trust me." He pulled her off the stool so hard, she stumbled into arms. Immediately Steven's arms went around her waist again.

Darrius laughed. "Poor guy just made a *huge* mistake."

"Come on, Kara. You've been sittin here all by yourself. I can tell you're lonely."

"Steven, go home. You're drunk."

Steven wagged his eyebrows, and twisted Kara's hair. "Blonde. Very beautiful. You know what I've discovered since I've been gone. I really like blondes."

Kara jerked away. "You know I'm not a real Blonde, so I'm obviously *not* your type."

Kara was furious. She hadn't realized everyone in the bar was watching them. "You were once, and I was yours. Come on Kara. Don't you owe me? You never put out, not even after a year. You definitely owe me for being a tease that long." Steven whispered in her ear, "Baby, we don't need to dance. I just need payment for my wasted senior year."

Who the hell does he think he is? Damn, Kara hated arrogant pricks. Kara's blood boiled, she jumped up poking Steven in his chest, at the same time yelling at him. "No, you did not! You stupid! Arrogant! Jackass! Who the hell do you think you are? God's gift to women! You did not just insinuate I'm a whore. If I were you, I'd run away. Now! I'd run back to California as fast as you can, cause you're a dead man walking."

Alexander pushed forward, but Chung shook his head. "He called her a whore!" Alexander growled through clenched teeth. Flinching his fists.

Darrius was right, Kara was a fireball, but it was taking all of Alexander's control not to go and beat the living shit out of that asshole.

Kara noticed out of her peripheral vision, Steven's friends were doubled over in laughter. The same dirt-bags that tried to hurt her last night. How dare they think this is funny? This is exactly why she'd dumped Steven, he's a pig.

Steven still hadn't taken the hint. He grabbed Kara around the waist, pulling her onto his lap.

"You're as feisty as always."

Kara was livid. She's always had a really bad temper, and now she couldn't control it, not that she had been controlling it much before. Kara reached down between her legs, grabbing Steven's balls, and squeezing as hard as she could, she used her nails to grip his nuts so she wouldn't lose her hold.

Alexander was surprised. He wanted to applaud Kara's move, but was still shocked silent. She didn't seem intimidated at all. She had used the male weakness against Steven, and he was begging for mercy. Everyone was laughing.

"That's my sis." Darrius said proudly.

"He won't be using that for a while." Nathaniel roared laughing.

"Told you Kara can handle herself." Darrius bragged, motioning to Trent and Alan to move towards Kara. "We should stop her, before she damages him for life."

Steven was doubled over Kara, grinding his teeth, as she twisted her wrist just a little, until he winced. "This is what happens when I get close to a man's balls." She whispered in his ear. "Do you really want me this close again?"

It seemed to take all Steven's energy just to shake his head, but he managed.

Steven was turning blue, as Kara looked into his eyes. "Do we have an understanding?"

He nodded and squeaked, "Yes!"

"Good!" She let him go and slid off his lap. "By the way. Welcome home."

"Hey what's going on?" Kara turned around and saw Becky standing behind her with Alan pushing his way between Kara and this disgusting parasite. Behind them stood Trent, Darrius, and... Alexander? "Steven and I had a little misunderstanding. He was under the impression, since we dated, I owe him a piece of ass."

Trent grabbed Steven off the stool. "Boy, you called my sister a whore?"

"Trent, I didn't mean it like that. Really, I didn't." Steven groveled.

Trent pushed Steven into Darrius. "I should beat the shit out of you, but seeing your shit faced, I'm going to assume you've lost all common sense. Consider this a freebee. You're just lucky Trey's not here, he wasn't done knockin the shit out you for hurting Kara the last time. Stay...away...from...her."

Darrius pushed him towards Alan. "Next time you won't be so lucky."

Like a pinball machine, Alan pushed him towards his friends. Watching him stumble over two tables.

Becky was laughing as Steven fell backwards over a table. "Did you see his face? Girl, you had a death grip on him. Poor guys not going to be doing anyone, unless it's an ice sculpture for weeks."

Steven stood up snarling, "Kara, you're such a stupid bitch, you'll pay for that." He began stomping away very angry.

When out of know where Alexander had Steven by his throat. No one saw him move. "If you value your life, you'll never call her a bitch again." Alexander hastily released his grip, pushing Steven towards an exit.

Kara was still stunned and pissed off. What the hell had come over Steven? At least in high school, he might have hated her saying *'No'*, but Steven never got this pushy, and where the hell did Alexander go?

"Hey Ker, you ok?"

Kara turned to see her sister, Kasi behind her. "Yes, I'm just *really* pissed off."

Kara's other sister, Kami had joined them and they were all hovering around Kara. "You know we'll all beat the shit out of him, if you want us to." Kasi declared.

Kara did her signature eye roll. "Like that's going to solve anything."

"Oh! Baby! He is soooooooo hot and he's walking this way. I'm going to see if I can snag this one." Kami interrupted with her eyes glossed over.

"I'll flip you for him." Kasi replied jokingly.

Becky and Kara couldn't see who they were talking about, since their backs were to the door. Knowing these two, it's some burly cowboy or decked out biker, but probably a cowboy, since they frequented Mel's more than bikers. Kara rolled her eyes at her sisters; they were such hounds, always sniffing out the next tomcat.

"Would you two stop drooling, it's so demeaning to a person. How would you like guys doing that to you?" Kara scolded them.

"Oh! He can drool over us all he wants, but all we get to do is dream, since he thinks he's already taken. Too bad it's not a mutual relationship." They both giggled, high-fiveing each other.

That made no sense to Kara. She really hated when people treated others like a piece meat.

Alexander stepped behind Kara, wrapping his arms around her. "Hey gorgeous, without me loosing anything important, can I have a dance." Alexander chuckled, as he lightly kissed Kara's neck. "You ok?"

Kara couldn't believe it. Was this who her sisters were talking about? She'd kill them!

Kara had never heard Alexander speak so seductively, but that low decadent voice of his, she'd know anywhere. She looked up into the most beautiful eyes, she'd ever seen. They were lighter tonight than the last time she saw them, almost a green. "Alexander?" She choked out, trying not to show the excitement that was raging through her body.

ANN MARIE KAZUTOMI

Kara's heart was racing, her adrenaline pumping, but the instant Alexander's arms had wrapped around her, calm enveloped her. She was safe. In this Dark-Soul's arms, she was safe. She gazed up at him smiling, "I am now." With a scorching kiss Alexander made her forget all about Steven. Kara heard her family's questions surround her, but she was lost in the heat of Alexander's tongue dancing with hers. At this moment, Kara didn't care what anyone thought.

"Who is that?" Trent asked.

"Chung, what the hell's Alexander doing?" Darrius demanded.

"Um…Kara should explain." Chung dodged their questions.

"Excuse me!" Kara heard anger in Trent's voice, as she broke away from Alexander in time to see everyone's questioning stare.

Darrius used his best Ricky imitation, "Kara, you got some splannin to do."

"No! She has more than *splannin* to do." Becky stomped forward. "In eighteen years we've never kept secrets from each other. Yesterday you wanted nothing to do with him, and today you're all over him? What gives?"

"Excuse me…Alexander? I think we all need to talk with you." Kami insisted.

"Why?" Kara asked terrified. They already knew Alexander from the engagement party, why did they want to talk to him. Kara's family has a tendency to embarrass her in every situation, and she had no intention of them doing it with Alexander.

"It seems something has changed since yesterday, and we want to know what?" Kasi answered.

Great! Just great! This is going to be bad. Kara could already feel it.

Alexander looked at Kara with an amused smile that told her he knew her family was making her feel uncomfortable, and replied, "It would be an honor to have all of your company this evening."

"Fine!" Kara snapped, motioning between them, "What do you want to know?"

Darrius tsked at her. "Oh, Sis! It's not going to be that easy."

Kara let out a resigned laugh, throwing her hands up to surrender.

"OK! Fine! Could we at least sit down before you interrogate us?"

"Interrogate? This is going to be more of an inquisition" Darrius laughed, as Trent poked her. "I'm following you, so don't try to escape."

"My lady" Holding out his hand for her, Alexander cocked an eyebrow and gave Kara an amused smile. He was delighted at Kara's public show of affection. After her altercation with Steven, he hadn't been sure if he'd be allowed to touch her.

Kara slipped her hand into his. *Oh Man!* Just holding Alexander's hand made her hot all over. Knowing she was obviously bright red, and that her sisters were *loving* every minute of this, she decided they would have to play along with the interrogation...or inquisition... whatever her family wanted to call it.

Alexander followed Kara, not saying a word. Curious about what Kara's explanation would be. He pulled out a chair for her and sat down beside her.

After everyone else sat down, Kara began. "I know some of you met Alexander last night, but let me just introduce everyone." She began with Alexander next to her and went around the tables. "This is Dr. Alexander Conti; his brother, Nathaniel; his sister, Adelina; Kalab; and you all know Uncle Chung. That's my best friend Becky Dando and her fiancé Alan Gregmore; my brother's Trent and Darrius; and my sister's Kami and Kasi. Now......"

"Hey, what about us?"

Kara cursed under her breath. "You've got to be joking!" Kami held the shittiest grin on her face. "Bitch!"

"You're just lucky I couldn't get a hold of Trey and Tanya." Kami crooned.

"Great!" she spat. "These are my other sisters Kali, Daphne, Dahlia, and Arabella." Kara pointedly starred at each of her siblings. "Not that it's any of your business, but I just recently met Alexander."

"You want to try again, little sis?" Trent chastised. "We all saw you lip locked......"

"And the Kara I know doesn't go from zero to hero" Becky snapped her fingers "like that, nor does she keep secrets from her best friend."

"Alexander, we know you spoke with the older generation of our household, and they seem to approve of your intentions, but they refuse to tell us anything." Trent stated in a matter of fact tone.

"What?" Kara looked at Alexander, "What does he mean?"

"Kara, you know I sat with your family yesterday."

"Yes, you did. So, what's your intention with our sister?" Kami tried to look aggressive, but wasn't pulling it off very well.

"Kami" Kara yelled. Horrified at how direct she was being, and the fact that it was none of her business.

"Sis, First of all, you would never let someone call you *gorgeous* without hurting his privates unless you're head over heels for him, and he obviously knew that by his statement. Second, you look a little too comfortable with him after just meeting him. So what gives?" Kasi chimed in. "I know my twin and I know something is up. I can sense it."

Kara knew she'd turned another three shades of red on top of the blazing cheeks she already had. How dare they? Who do they think they are...she would never...ok...maybe she would...But that's different. Kara didn't pick up loser guys at bars. She's not like her sisters, and she didn't need their...nosy protection.

"Really?" Alexander was eyeing them both. "So you're telling me she's head over heels for me." He asked using their terminology. "Oh Crap!" Kara's irritation started flowing. "Fine you three nosy brats. Since we're all connected supposedly, why don't you just read my mind, instead of embarrassing the crap out of me all the time."

"Very funny Kara, just because we're quads doesn't allow us to read each other's minds, you know that. It's more sensing your feelings, and we all know you're excited. And yes Alexander, we can guarantee you're here with her approval. We can feel it." Kasi snorted.

"I'm sure he can sense that as well since he's a vampire. I understand your people can sense human emotions?" Becky chimed in, looking at Alexander questionably.

"I thought they didn't like being called vampires?" Kami asked. "You prefer Dark-Souls...or something like that, right?"

Kara couldn't believe what Becky had just asked. What is her problem? Alexander just nodded to Kami, while he rubbed his thumb on the back on Kara's hand. "That's correct, Kami. I'm not a vampire. I'm a Cruetian, or humans call us Dark-Souls."

"Personally, I just think you're steamin hot. He's so hot, you could steam ice right off his ass! Where'd you meet him, sis, cause I'm going there."

Kara's mouth fell open, as laughter circled the table, the same time Kasi slapped Arabella on the back of the head. "You're only sixteen little girl, you better not be melting ice off any one's ass. Although she has a point, Ker. I need to go where you two met."

Kara heard more chuckles around the table, as she threw her hands in the air. "I'm done! I will not embarrass Alexander by having this conversation."

Alexander caught Kara's hand, "I honestly don't mind." He glanced around the table, "It's a pleasure meeting more of your family." He looked around at Kara's siblings, "I met your parents, grandparents, Kasi, and Trey last night."

Frustrated Kara pulled away, slamming her chair back. "Then you explain it to them!" she yelled, while stomping away.

"Where the hell were we?" Trent asked.

"Dad wanted privacy. He didn't want to scare Kara away." Kasi explained.

"Don't worry, she'll be back." Daphne assured him. "She's actually the one embarrassed." They all laughed. "It's why she hates having nine siblings plus Becky. She thinks we're all crazy and way too nosy for our own good."

"She'll get over it, she always does." Kasi laughed.

"With that said. Let the interrogation begin!" Darrius chuckled.

"So explain the difference between vampires and you." Kami and Kasi said in unison.

"Ok, but what I tell you here is not human knowledge, and we'd like to keep it that way. You can't speak of this to others. If you do we'll deny everything." Alexander looked around the table at all their nodding heads. "Technically we're the same species, but vampires are our criminals. They violate humans in what we call 'Blood Raping'. It means they drain a human's blood until their dead. We both drink blood, but Dark-Souls can eat food. Vampires become dependent on human blood and stop eating food altogether. Dark-Souls can be out in the daylight, and we don't need permission to enter a human's home. Vampires can do neither one of those things." He smiled at them. "Those are the main differences. You can understand why it would be offensive for a Dark-Soul to be called a vampire. It's like saying you're a felon."

Everyone agreed and began talking at once. Alexander could understand why Kara wouldn't like this. He even had trouble keeping track of the conversations, and as a Dark-Soul he could process information quicker than humans could.

Irritation flowed through Kara, lashing out at anyone who got in her way. Why had she asked Alexander here? *Oh! Yeah! Some alone time! So much for that!* Kara had no intention on analyzing their relationship with her family, when she hadn't deciphered it herself.

If only her parents had understood the meaning of birth control, but nooooooooo, they had to go off and have ten kids. That's right *ten*! Three boys and seven girls. You would think after their second pregnancy they would have gotten fixed, but not Kara's parents. Her mom wanted to have what she called 'A normal pregnancy', a *single* child pregnancy. "I want to know what other mom's feel when they care for only one child and not a litter." Stupid, considering how fertile Kara's family is. Multi-births are hereditary in three out of her four grandparents.

Her parent's first pregnancy ended with Kara's older twin brothers, Trent and Trey. Identical twins, except a scar Trey received on his chin during a high school fight, they're handsome with brown eyes, and short brown hair. Two years older than Kara, at 5'11" these farm boys are all brute force, and very protective of their baby sisters.

Next came quadruplets, Kami, Kali, Kasi, and of course Kara. Since human eggs can't split four ways, they're actually two sets of identical twins. Kami and Kali received the athletic muscular bodies, and the 5'5" height that Kara envies, as well as, the naturally tan skin, another trait she wished she'd received. She hates tanning. Although the darker skin tone does enhance their raven black hair, and brown eyes.

Kara and Kasi are petite, with pixie type bodies. Their grandmother, Lalita, says it's the body of a Greek Goddess, but at only 5'2", they're really short, everyone towers over them. Kara can't imagine a Goddess being short. Petite maybe…Short…No way. Kara will admit they were blessed with all the right curves, and big beautiful brown eyes. A trait their grandmother Sara insists was the first thing people saw when they were babies. Their natural hair color is a dark auburn brown, but Kara dyes hers blonde to showcase her own individuality.

The third pregnancy was a miracle, or so the doctors said. 5 years after the quads, Kara's parents had triplets. Daphne, Dahlia, and Darrius, none being twins. Daphne and Dahlia are complete opposites. Where Daphne is tall at 5'6" with black hair and blue eyes, Dahlia's shorter at 5'4" with light auburn hair and brown eyes. Darrius was the unique one. The only one of Kara's family that ended up with blond hair and green eyes, he's also very tall at 6'3", even towering over his older brothers.

Then finally, thank God, her mother received her wish with her fourth and final pregnancy. Arabella was born a year after the triplets. She is definitely the baby and coddled by the complete family. Standing at 5'5", she reminds Kara of a gymnast. Arabella has beautiful long curly red hair and ocean blue eyes. She's the envy of her siblings, for not sharing her birthday with anyone else.

What was I thinking, bringing Alexander here? I knew my family would show up. My family's a complete freak of nature. No one should have this many kids, and if no one's noticed, my stupid parents thought it was cute to keep each pregnancy's names in the same letter of the alphabet. Again, another stupid idea, your tongue gets tied just trying to yell them all out. It's the ultimate tongue twister.

Luckily they wised up after Arabella. Kara's parents stopped being crazy and both took the plunge to get fixed. None of the family felt safe with just one of them committing, so they both went under the knife. Double protection, always the safer bet, at least that's what Kara thought.

Kara needed time to calm down, and the best thing for her was singing. Singing and dancing always calmed her down and helped her think things through. She found Nancy at the bar.

"Hi, Nancy. Ok if I sing tonight?"

"Of course, sweetie." Nancy was shaking her head and finger at Kara. "You should know by now that you never have to ask."

Nancy and Kara started walking, straightening chairs as they made their way to the stage. "We just wished we could convince you to do this more often. What happened this time? The only time you do this anymore is to release your anxiety."

Alexander noticed Kara and Nancy whispering, but he could hear them as if they were sitting at the table. A benefit of being a Cruetian, their eyesight and hearing were a hundred times more powerful than any humans.

"Thank you, Nancy." Kara hugged her, allowing Nancy to comfort her. "It's nothing really. As always, I'm trying to escape my crazy family, and I'm trying to sort through some feelings and stray emotions. I just need to analyze my current feelings for someone. That's all. I really don't want to discuss it. K?"

Nancy pulled away from her, "Kara" she said sternly "if this is about a boy, remember to follow your heart, not your mind. You tend to over analyze things. Follow your heart for a change."

"I've done that how many times...three...and look where it got me." Kara turned away, not wanting Nancy to see her tears. Even after all these years. It still hurt. Three times! Three times Kara had thought she would marry, and three times they turned out to be asses. Complete creeps! She didn't know if she could do it again. Could she even trust herself to make a good decision? She looked down at her birthmark... no Alexander's mark, and rubbed it over and over again.

Alexander's heart stopped, as he saw Kara rubbing his mark on her hand. He swore he could feel the caress on his own mark. Was she thinking about him? The conversation between her and Nancy sure sounded like it, but he didn't want to hope, until he was sure. Could she just be afraid? If so, he would ease her fears. He would never hurt her. How could he prove that to her? He needs to find away.

Alexander watched Nancy touch Kara's chin and pull it around to face her. "Sweetie, to find *Mr. Right*, we all have a few heartbreaks along the way. It's what makes us stronger. It's that pain that allows you to recognize him, when he strolls into your life. Don't be afraid of love, and never give up on it. You're special, Sweetie. Just wait, *Mr. Right* will show up and sweep you off your feet." Nancy winked at Kara. "Now, the stage is all yours."

She really hoped Nancy was correct. Did Mr. Right actually exist? Kara always believed he did. Every time she'd been hurt, Kara just told herself he was not her soul-mate. Her soul-mate would not be that cruel. Her soul-mate would not play with her feelings so callously. Now Alexander had walked into her life. She laughed. No crashed into her life. He had thrown this whole *Amara* thing on her. Could a chosen one be the same as a soul-mate? Kara was beginning to think so.

Without thinking, she put the first CD in and began to sing. She was halfway through the song before Kara realized what she'd chosen. 'You make me weak'. She laughed. That was the understatement of the year, and it was completely true. Every time Alexander was near, she became weak. Kara entirely lost all control of her mind, body, and soul. Those alluring teal eyes ate her up inside, filling her with a refreshing desire she'd never experienced before. She threw the next CD in and began to sing.

"How do I know if this time it's true love?...How do I know if it's real?... How do I know if it'll last, or if it's simply another thrill?"

Could she be in love? Kara had learned very young that her mind spoke to her through song. Nancy had been right, sometimes she allowed doubt to interfere with her rational thought process...or for that matter...she allowed rational thought to interfere with her hearts desires. Singing always seemed to clarify everything. It seemed to put everything into perspective. If Kara was to listen this time...Alexander *is* her soul-mate.

Damn! Why did my family have to show up tonight? I didn't need the third degree. I have too many things to figure out on my own.

Alexander froze when Kara began singing. She had the voice of an angel. Comforting, soothing, it wrapped around you and held you, caressing you, and easing all your pain. He was hypnotized by her. The passion in Kara's voice was captivating. You could hear her sadness in sad songs, and her excitement in happy songs. She had the range of an opera singer, but easily adapted to different musical styles. She gracefully encompassed the stage, moving, swaying, and dancing to the music, dazzling Alexander even more. Proudly he thought. *That's my woman. Kara is mine!*

He was even more astonished when Kara began singing Japanese love songs, *in* Japanese. 'I'll Fall in Love' and 'I Can't Stop My Love For You'. Training in Japan for many years, he understood what she was singing, but doubted anyone other than Chung did. "Kara speaks Japanese?"

"Some." Kasi smiled. "Her second serious boyfriend was Japanese."

Chung looked amused, "Naturally Kara knows some Chinese, Greek, Italian, and Spanish. She picks up languages very quickly."

"Naturally?" Alexander's eyebrows rose quizzically. "Spanish? The other languages make sense, but do you have family from Spain as well."

"No." Darrius snorted. "High School Class. It's America's favorite second language"

Alexander had sat watching Kara for over an hour, when Nancy brought them another beer. "Kara sings her true feelings you know."

"Pardon me?" Alexander glanced up at Nancy confused. "What did you say?"

"Kara always sings about what's on her mind. She finds that songs help her express her feelings." Nancy smiled knowingly, before turning to leave.

Alexander tried to think about what Nancy had just said. Was she accurate about Kara's songs…Alexander's heart skipped a beat. Could it be? Was Nancy correct? Looking around the table he asked, "Is that true? Does Kara honestly sing about her feelings?"

Daphne smiled in embarrassment. "Yes, that's true, unless it's a requested song. I'd say by my big sister's selections, you've made quite an impact."

Chung downed his beer, "I'm really glad you're able to see this side of Kara, few people do and realize she's not just singing, she's expressing herself. Amazing, isn't she?"

Alexander could barely nod. He was going over every song Kara had sung in his head. Every song was about love at first site, learning to trust someone, or most importantly, discovering you love someone.

Damn! He had almost given up on her. He'd been so angry after Kara slapped him, he'd almost walked away. As much as Kara was scared of this relationship, so was he. Funny, it seemed they were afraid for the same reasons. She had been hurt by numerous men, and he had been deceived by his first wife. Alexander's first wife had caused him centuries of fear. Fear of all women. Not just Kara, but *all* women. He didn't trust them. The only exception was his mother and sisters. Every other woman he'd ever come in contact with he'd refused to trust...except Catherine, but they've known each other for centuries. His fear had almost cost him this extraordinary woman.

"Thank you...thank you for enlightening me. Kara's an extremely complicated woman."

"Commander, you have no idea." Chung answered amusingly. "I can assure you, you'll never get bored."

"That's an understatement!" Trent laughed as everyone joined in.

Kara felt better, and was ready to end her set, when Nancy brought up a request. 'When you Fall'. A beautiful song that she enjoyed singing.

"I know you've been hurt before...and refuse to trust in love...you built walls around yourself...built so high that no one can ever reach you...but that was before...there's no reason now...If you can take a leap of faith...and trust me somehow...I can promise never to hurt you...If you're ever going to fall...just take the first step... and fall into my arms...for I will never hurt you.....if you are ever willing to trust me...I promise to catch you when you fall"

As Kara finished singing, Alexander stepped onto the dance floor. He walked to the stage, stopping just below her with his arms outstretched.

Oh, Shiz-nat! He requested this song. For me? What the hell did my family tell him. He's asking me to take a chance...on him. He's asking for my trust, to literally fall into his arms. Can I do this? Everyone says to follow my heart. Can I risk the pain? Can I not?

Alexander stood waiting, unsure how Kara would respond. As a prince, he'd never known rejection, and he really didn't want his first experience to be with Kara. Smiling impishly, Kara stood there for a few minutes letting Alexander brood, before the little tease finally jumped off the stage into his arms.

Alexander caught her with such ease it amazed her. He immediately captured her lips. "Trust me, Kara. I promise you'll never regret it. I'll never hurt you." She searched his eyes, but saw only sincerity looking back at her. He honestly meant what he was saying. Kara wanted to believe him. She could so easily loose herself to him forever.

"I'm sorry I made you feel uncomfortable with your family." Alexander apologized brushing her hair back from her face. He loved touching her soft silky hair; it sent fire and need through him, equivalent only to her touch.

"That's really sweet, but it wasn't you. I have a very large family, and we're all very outspoken. They tend to embarrass me. I know you've already spoken to most of them, but now that they know we're seeing each other, the questions will become much more personal. Ultimately, I should be apologizing to you for what I'm about to subject you to."

Alexander started laughing, "I think I can handle them. I've looked into the greatest commanders eyes that have ever graced history. I'm sure I can handle a few questions. So, you're Quadruplets? I thought you were a twin."

Kara cringed, "I am. Kasi is my identical twin, but Kami and Kali are also identical twins, and all together we make quadruplets."

Alexander cherished these moments of alone time together. He'd noticed Kara was a lot more open and affectionate when they were alone, and he loved her touch. His body ached for her in ways he didn't understand, and in all the centuries he'd lived, no other woman made him ache with desire to the point he could not concentrate. He'd always been in control of every aspect of his life. Kara ripped right through that tight nit resolve he had, and created massive chaos throughout his whole body. It was completely driving him crazy. Kara would be able to torture Alexander in ways no other commander could, just by withholding her touch, her smile, and her mouth. That amazingly seductive mouth of hers. *Oh, yes. If Kara tortured me, I would cave.*

"Did your mother take fertility drugs?" He asked.

She laughed. "Gosh No! Lord help us all if she did. My family is just a freak of nature. We're just naturally fertile, three of my grandparents have multiple births in their families."

Alexander cupped Kara's face lifting it so she could meet his eyes, "Your sisters tell me I'm here with your approval. That you're…head over heels for me…is that true?"

Kara's heart stopped. Damn! Why did he have to ask a question she didn't want to answer? Smiling she brushed Alexander's cheek. "Let's just say, I'm *really* glad you found me. Give me a couple minutes to breathe. Ok? I'll meet you at the table."

It wasn't exactly what Alexander had hoped for, but he could live with that. Kara hadn't rejected him. Yet!

11

K ara headed for the back door needing a little fresh air. She stomped out, as steel arms encircled her, slapping a hand over her mouth. Kara kicked as hard as she could. She heard someone scream and groan towards the ground, and knew she'd impacted someone's family jewels. She bit down hard, tasting her attacker's blood. He squealed "Bitch" releasing her, slapping her hard enough she ended up on the ground.

Kara felt the blood escape from her mouth, and somewhere on her head, she felt it oozing through her hair. Someone grabbed her again, and pushed her against a car. He was standing on her feet so she couldn't try to kick again. Kara swung trying to punch him, but someone twisted her arm around until she screamed in pain, while someone else held her other arm. He slapped her again, so hard she felt like a rag doll.

Kara felt blood flowing from her nose. She tried to scream, choking on blood. He dropped her to the ground, laughing. "Not so tuff when you're not around a lot of people to save you, are you?" He kicked her as hard as he could. She began to crawl under the car. "Oh, no you don't!" They grabbed her pulling her out by her legs; the rocks ripped her dress cutting into her skin. She kicked out, landing a strong kick, and knocking the asshole back. Unfortunately, she was losing strength, and she couldn't see, her eyes were swollen shut. "Stop playing with her!" Kara heard another man shout. "Let's get her home" he laughed "then we'll play with her. I bet that tight little ass will put out for all of us, before we deliver her." They dropped her, kicking her one last time before everything went dark.

Kara must have passed out, because she was riding in the back of a truck when she awoke. Sitting up, excruciating pain shot through her body. She was extremely dizzy, but she had to see where they were taking her. She fought open one eye, long enough to realize she hadn't been out long. They were only a few blocks from the bar. She tried to see inside the cab, so she could identify her captors, but the window held a heavy tint. She could hear numerous people talking, but their voices were garbled. She had thought that she recognized their voices earlier, but none of them sounded familiar now.

Kara scanned her situation for an escape. There was no rear gate, so she decided her only option was to roll off the back of the truck. Would she live through it? She wasn't sure, but it sure the hell beat, being raped by these men. Weak and in severe pain, she tried to move. She'd lost a lot of blood, and her arm was broken, but slowly she moved to the back of the truck, making sure she didn't attract her assailants' attention. She waited for them to turn a corner, hoping it would throw her towards the sidewalk, the last thing she needed was to be hit by another car. Half way through their turn, Kara prayed and rolled off the back of the truck, rolling over and over, until the last thing she remembered was landing in the gutter.

As Alexander returned to the table, he found himself facing nine pairs of demanding eyes. He knew he had to stay and answer their questions. He should send Kalab to watch over Kara, but he didn't want to tip anyone off to the danger she was in. If her family thought he brought danger, they'd make this very difficult.

Chung spoke first, "*Kyrios,* please put your right hand on the table." Alexander complied, as Chung began explaining what the mark meant to a Dark-Soul, and that Kara's mark, on her left hand, meant she was Alexander's *Amara.* When Chung finished, they all began talking at once, until Trent raised his hand to silence them. Alexander was aware that Trent was Trey's twin and was the oldest, and that he needed him as an ally.

"So" Trent rubbed the back of his neck. "You think you're my little sister's soul-mate?"

Alexander sat forward, "No. I know I am. For a Dark-Soul there's never any doubt. Our identical marks prove it."

Trent sat back, crossing his arms over his chest. "So what does this mean for Kara? How does……"

"Dark-Souls?"

"Yes. How do Dark-Souls treat these *Amaras*?"

First rule in negotiations, match your opponent, so Alexander mimicked Trent, sitting back and crossing his arms over his chest. "My people will treasure her. Kara will never want for anything, and will be treated as royalty."

Not satisfied with Alexander's answer, Trent snorted. "What about you? Doesn't Dark-Soul's live a very long time? How long before you get tired of her, finding someone else, and hurting her?"

Alexander respected Trent's candidness, "That won't happen. Hence…Soul-Mate! A Dark-Soul's *Amara* is the only one they'll ever want. Proven by the fact I've had centuries to…test the waters so to speak, and in all that time, no one has ever aroused me the way Kara does. I've been waiting 400 years for her, and searching 400 before that, the one thing I can promise all of you is I'll never intentionally hurt her."

"Fair enough!"

"No, it's not!" Becky interrupted. "Kara's had enough heartache. I need more information before I'm willing to put my stamp of approval on you. Last night I helped you, thinking you would date her. I never dreamed Kara would fall so fast, that's not her M.O. You don't just walk in here, swinging that mark around, and expect us to accept you without questions. I don't think so. I want proof. I think the families should have dinner. If you want to be our brother-in-law, then we should get to know your family." Becky glanced at Trent, who nodded. "Does your family live here?"

"No. They live in Italy actually. I do have a few siblings here, and friends I consider family."

Becky smiled, "Good, bring them all." Winking at Kara's sisters, she exclaimed, "Ladies, get your questions ready."

"Does Kara believe you're her soul-mate?" They all focused on Alan, who'd been quite this whole time.

"In the beginning...No. She thought it was a joke." Alexander admitted. "Now, I'm not sure."

"Well at least you're not a liar. Kara would never accept this at face value." Darrius frowned. "If what you're telling us is true, and I hope it is for Kara's sake. She's been alone far too long. If this is real, I wish you luck. My big sister is very stubborn. It'll take a lot to convince her."

"The fates determined centuries ago that Kara was mine. I believe they'll show her the way, just as they guided me to her. I thank all of you for your concern. I'm happy to see my *Amara* is loved this much. It says a lot about her character."

"Do *you* love her?" Everyone glanced down the table, as Dahlia spoke for the first time.

"Excuse me?"

"I asked if...*you* love Kara." Dahlia demanded. "It sounds like you're capable of providing for her, maybe even devoted to her, but if my older sister accepts you, it will be with unconditional love. That's the only type of love Kara knows how to give, she'll give you her heart and soul, and she'll deserve the same."

Adelina moved to sit next to Dahlia. "That's what happened in Kara's other relationships, isn't it? She gave 100% of herself and they left." Dahlia nodded. "My brother's been equally hurt. Just as Kara is afraid to love again, so is Alexander, but I can assure you, just like Kara's, his love is unconditional. We have to help them both overcome their fears."

"Promise?" Dahlia asked. "I don't want Kara hurt again."

"That I can guarantee. Alexander would never hurt her. He needs her, as much as she needs him. Will you help me...help them?" Dahlia nodded.

Alexander was truly enjoying himself. Kara's family was intelligent and willing to consider their relationship. They had interrogated Alexander and his family, asking everything from basic questions to very personal ones. He had tried to answer all of them as truthfully as possible. There was still some things he felt was better left unexplained; the fact that he was the Cruetian crown prince, his ex-wife, the curse, and of course, the danger Kara might be in.

They were equally willing to answer his questions. He had learned that Kara had nine siblings, and not only was she an identical twin, but part of quadruplets. He now knew the asshole hitting on her earlier, was Kara's high school ex-boyfriend, Steven, and the pain he'd caused her. Kara loved all animals, but especially dogs, horses, chinchillas and tigers, even though she was allergic to the latter, and she loved nature, movies, traveling, and exploring different countries foods. A girl from his own heart, he appreciated good food as well.

Alexander suddenly had a horrible feeling Kara was in trouble. He tried to connect to her, but the bond wasn't strong enough. He glanced over the crowd, unable to locate her. "Find Kara! Now!" Nathaniel, Adelina, and Chung knocked over their chairs, as they jumped up. "You also Kalab. I'll be fine. She's in trouble, I can feel it."

Kalab was gone by the time Kara's family understood what had just happened. "What do you mean she's in trouble?"

"I don't know, Trent. Dark-Souls have a bond with their *Amara's*. Kara's and mine is…just forming, but I can sense her feelings. Earlier when she left she was angry. Then when she sang, she was calm. She was feeling anxious when she went for air, and then for a few minutes, I couldn't feel her. I assumed she had moved out of our range. Just now I felt extreme pain, and then she went blank to me. If I'm wrong, I'm sorry, but I can't take the chance she's hurt." Alexander shoved his hand through his hair in frustration.

"What do you mean, you can feel……"

Trent was cut off when Alexander's warriors all appeared. "Kara's car is in the parking lot, but she's not here."

Alexander jumped up at the same moment Kara's brothers did. "Stay here!" Trent demanded to his sisters. "Alan watch them, I'll keep in contact."

Alexander and his warriors were already out the front doors, when Trent and Darrius caught up to them.

"Kara would not leave her car." Darrius advised.

"We know. She's been taken." Nathaniel countered.

"What? How do you know?"

Alexander didn't have time for twenty questions. "Nathaniel, explain it. Adelina go back to the girls. Trent, Kalab, come with me." He walked them around a corner, "Trent, I can get to Kara. Now! Right, Now! There are things about my people humans don't know. I can't chance you telling anyone, but I appreciate your concern for your sister. Can you keep our secrets to yourself?"

"Just get me to my sister." Trent barked. "I swear, I'll never say a word. Please, just get me to Kara."

Kara heard sirens in the distance. She wanted to yell, let them know she needed help, but nothing came out. Maybe, just maybe if she was lucky, someone had seen her and called for help.

There was darkness all around her, she couldn't break through it. Kara realized the ambulance was near, she tried to move, nothing happened. Certainly she was still alive. You can't be in this much pain and be dead. Could you? *That's just stupid. You're not dead.* Again, she tried to look around, to get her bearings, but everything seemed really foggy, and she couldn't see anything.

Kara could hear the paramedics talking to someone, or maybe to each other, she wasn't sure. "Hurry, get the stretcher!" A man yelled. "Ma'am, can you hear me?" *Yes, please help me.* "She's unresponsive." *Why can't they hear me?* Kara tried again, still nothing came out. She tried to shake her head, to move any part of her body, but the darkness was overwhelming. It continued to push the voices farther away, until there was nothing at all.

Trent couldn't believe what he was seeing. One minute they were behind Mel's, and the next they were standing on a street corner next to an ambulance.

One of the paramedics spotted Alexander running towards them. "Hey, what's the Assistant Medical Director doing here?" He asked the other paramedic who was arriving with the stretcher. "Not sure."

"Hey, Dr. Conti. What's up?" The medic asked him as he neared.

Alexander recognized the medics. "Hi, guys! Move aside so I can look at her."

"You know we can't let you touch her." One of them scowled. "As much as I think the laws are ridiculous, we can't let a vampire doc treat without patient permission, and she's unconscious. I hate the prejudice, but it's the law."

Alexander knew that stupid law, he knew it all too well, and so did Trent. It stated that vampire doctors couldn't treat humans without permission from the individual, or their guardian prior to treatment. It also stated a human doctor would be on call at all times, in case the human refused treatment from a vampire. Personally, Trent always thought the law was absurd. It was created by people who feared anyone different from themselves…Prejudice people. You would think after all the wars fought over people's differences, that we would've learned our lesson by now, and stopped making the same mistakes over and over again. Kara had never feared the unknown or differences in people. She'd actually embraced it, and would have no problem with a vampire doctor, and she needed help, a doctor is a doctor. Vampire or not!

Trent stepped forward, "That's my sister, Kara Spencer, and Dr. Conti's Fiancée. Kara wouldn't want anyone else touching her except him." The paramedics looked at each other in disbelief. "They even have matching…um…tattoos on their hands."

The medic kneeling over Kara viewed their marks. "He's telling the truth."

"Well, all be damned!" The other medic whistled teasingly, "Vamp doc, Good for you, she's hot. Which hospital……"

Alexander sharply cut him off. "I'll take her home."

"You know the injuries are too severe. We have to transport her to a trauma center." The medic argued.

"I'll handle it!" Alexander demanded. "She's *my* fiancée. I will handle her care. You can go back into service."

Exasperated, the medics gave each other a what-are-we-supposed-to-do look. "You're the Assistant Medical Director, but you'll take the heat if……"

Alexander didn't give them a chance to argue. He scooped Kara off the stretcher, and carried her around the corner to a parking lot. "Kalab, make sure they leave. Then bring Namorita to me at the house." He cupped Kalab's shoulder, and Kalab saw the worry in his eyes. "Hurry!"

Again, one minute they were in a parking lot, and the next they were in a bedroom like nothing Trent had ever seen before. There was an oversized four poster bed, with red velvet drapes that were tied with gold ropes at each corner, and gold sheers enclosed the bed itself. There was a large triangle, glass fireplace separating three attached rooms. Trent couldn't tell what the other rooms were, but large arches led into both. There was three smaller arches connected to the room as well, and it was completely adorned with antiques.

Alexander laid Kara on their bed. He'd had it hand carved for his *Amara*, just after Kelmar told him where to find her. This was clearly not how he'd pictured her in it. He reached in a drawer, removing a dagger, and gently cut away her clothes.

"Where are we?" Trent asked.

"My home."

Alexander ran to his closet, grabbing what looked like a medical kit. He unzipped the bag and grabbed handfuls of packets, throwing them at Trent. "That's sterile gauze and here's saline. Carefully, clean her wounds." Trent watched as Alexander opened another drawer that seemed to hold different types of medical equipment. Alexander grabbed a stethoscope, as he went to work diagnosing Kara's wounds.

Kara had been worked over pretty badly. With a broken arm, broken ribs, a shattered pelvis, a punctured lung, and internal bleeding, there was no wonder why she was unconscious.

Alexander couldn't believe it. His worst fears were coming true. Kara lay swollen, bruised, beaten, and broken. All Alexander wanted to do was kill the bastard who had done this. Luckily, the beating was not going to be life threatening, he'd sent for one of his best healers. Namorita would be able to heal Kara's injuries in about a day, instead of Kara staying in a human hospital for weeks. If only they had completed the first stage of bonding. Kara would still have been mortal, but her body would have healed itself, and once they are fully blood bonded, she will be immortal. How Alexander wished he could speed things up. The good news…it's not one of his enemies. If it was…Kara would be dead. The bad news…he'd failed her. Alexander hadn't even protected her from some weak humans. What kind of man couldn't protect his woman from the weakest species on earth? He wasn't worthy of her. If he couldn't protect her, he didn't deserve her.

Slamming his fist down, Alexander grimaced at the sight of Kara. They'd cleaned her wounds, but the trauma was extensive. Her face was so swollen, even if she wasn't unconscious, her eyes couldn't open. Alexander's fury shook him. He clenched his teeth, trying to control his temper. He would have the bastard's head.

Alexander sat on the edge of the bed, being very careful not to move her, he lifted Kara's left hand and kissed their mark. "I'm sorry I was unable to protect you, love, but I promise you the person who did this will pay. Whoever he was will pay with his life." The guilt Alexander felt overwhelmed him. How could he have allowed this to happen to her? At least he knew she wasn't suffering right now. Kara was completely unconscious.

Trent had let Alexander work, but he didn't understand why they hadn't taken Kara to a hospital. "How is she?"

"Not Good."

Ok, Trent was getting tired of Alexander's short answers. "Why didn't we go to the hospital?"

Alexander heard the irritation in Trent's voice. He understood Trent deserved an explanation, but Kara was so badly hurt, she was all he could concentrate on. "Trent, trust me. Kara's in really bad shape. She'll be in pain for weeks at the hospital. Please…just let me help her. I can't stand for her to be in pain. You don't understand, I can feel every bit of her pain, like it's my own. I don't want her to hurt. Ok?"

Trent could see Alexander's sincerity. He only wanted to help Kara. "OK!"

"Did you really mean you'd kill him?" Trent asked.

"*Kyrios*, where is she?"

Alexander was thankful for the interruption. He would kill the person who hurt Kara, but he wasn't sure how Trent would view that revelation.

Trent turned around to see a beautiful woman, with the strangest black eyes stroll into the room. "This is one of my Generals." Alexander indicated. "Namorita, this is Kara's brother, Trent."

"Pleasure." Namorita shook Trent's hand. "Now both of you, out!" Alexander balked. "Commander! That means you too. *Kyria's* in good hands. Mine."

"Kara." Trent corrected, "Her name is Kara."

Namorita smiled at Alexander, as if they knew something Trent didn't. "Out! If you want me to heal her, move it!"

They walked through one of the big arches into a very large sitting room. One wall held four flat screens, with two large sectional sofa's surrounding them. Alexander walked over to the wet bar. "What can I get you?"

"Whatever you're having is fine." Trent plopped down, clearly exhausted. "Alexander we need to talk."

"I warned you, there are some thing's humans aren't aware of about my people."

"That's not what I mean. What was the look between you and Namorita? There's something you're not telling me."

Alexander handed Trent a scotch and sank down next to him. "Namorita knew Kara's name, she just thought it was funny, you corrected her."

"She pronounced it wrong."

"Actually...*Kyria* will be your sister's title after we are bonded." Alexander downed his drink, as Kalab walked in.

"I don't understand." Trent admitted. "What title?"

"You're right. I haven't been upfront about everything." Alexander studied Trent. So far, he hadn't panicked, not with the shifting, or with Namorita healing Kara. Would he keep this secret until Alexander was ready to tell Kara's family everything? "I'm afraid Kara is somewhat overwhelmed by who I am in my world. If I tell you, I ask you not to reveal my secrets to your family, until I'm ready."

Trent nodded, eager for Alexander to continue. "I hold three very important titles. First, I am the Commanding General for both the Cruetian and Magikos military; Second, I am the Imperator of the Magikos Council; Third, I am the Cruetian crown prince. I mentioned these to Kara, but she panicked, so I focused on my role as a human doctor. She needs time to adjust to everything before I go into details."

Trent's jaw dropped as he registered what Alexander had just shared with him. "Are you saying...if my baby sister was born to be your wife...then she will......"

"Be a princess? Yes. Kara is destined to be the Cruetian Crown Princess. *Kyria* is her royal title, just as mine is *Kyrios*. She will also hold the title *Imperatess*, equivalent to Queen, of the Magikos Alliance, a council of otherworldly beings."

Trent leaned back and looked around, "This isn't the whole house, is it?"

Alexander amusingly grinned. "Not even close. These are my private chambers. I'll have someone give you a tour of my ranch."

Trent snorted, running his fingers through his hair. "Ok, I see why you're nervous. Kara might very well be apprehensive. For now, I'll keep my mouth shut, but you have to tell her everything. Kara has to know what she's getting into." Trent rubbed his forehead, "My sister, a princess?" he laughed.

Alexander slapped his shoulder. "Don't you worry. Kara and I have lots of things we need to settle, just as soon as she's healed."

Kalab took that moment to speak up "*Kyrios*, everyone's in the atrium. They want their orders."

"I want her attackers found." He growled. "Take Tiberius and Walter and track them down." Alexander raised his hand to pause Kalab's argument. "I promise to stay at the ranch until you return. You know I'm safe here."

Kalab nodded and left. "Is Kalab, like *your* bodyguard?" Trent asked.

"Yes, he is. He's been my personal bodyguard for 800 years."

"Shit! That's a long time."

"Tell me about it." Alexander laughed, but immediately leaped off the couch as Namorita appeared in the doorway.

"*Kyrios*, you need a fairy."

"A fairy? Are you serious?" Trent said in disbelief. "They exist?"

"Yes, I'm very serious, and yes, most of your myths do. My own grandmother is a Celtic God." Namorita scolded, before focusing on Alexander "I've healed Kara's exterior wounds. She's no longer losing blood, but I'm not a strong enough healer to mend her internal injuries. Kara briefly woke up, but I put her back under. It's better if *Kyria* stays unconscious until she's healed. I know Tanya's in town. I can bring her here."

Alexander crooked an eyebrow. "I wasn't aware the Magusian princess is in town. Definitely bring her here."

"Tanya doesn't know you're here either, she's playing human. As a human, she is keeping a low profile with otherworldly races." With a flash Namorita was gone.

"What the hell was that? We didn't flash. Did we?" Trent looked confused.

"Namorita is Lunarian. They don't shift like Cruetians do. As Namorita said, her relatives are gods, so they travel the same way the gods do, they flash."

Trent pinched his nose. "Obviously, I have a lot to learn." His laugh was stressed, but Alexander appreciated Trent's acceptance. Alexander liked Trent, and his acceptance would make Kara's easier.

Trent and Alexander had been sitting next to Kara for a half hour when a cool breeze encompassed the room and a tiny woman, with long platinum hair, and grayish-blue eyes appeared.

"Tanya?"

"Shit!" Tanya started to mist, but it was too late, Trent had already recognized her. "Trent? What are you doing here?"

"Tanya? You're a…Shit!…Does Trey know?"

Now Alexander was the one confused. How did Trent know Tanya? "You two know each other?"

Trent gasped. "Hell, yeah! Tanya is Trey's fiancée."

"You're his what? Alexander said in disbelief. "Does he know you're Magusian? A fairy?"

Tanya stomped her foot. "No, Alexander, he doesn't, but before we're married he will."

Alexander loved Tanya. After the Magikos council tried to force them to marry, they'd become good friends. She'd become like a baby sister to him.

"Tanya!"

"Don't Tanya me, Alexander." She pouted. "We'll discuss this later. First, who needs healed? Namorita said there was an attack."

"It's Kara." Trent pulled Tanya towards Alexander's bed.

Tanya was horrified seeing Kara's broken body. "Kara was attacked? By Who?" She shook her head, "Why?"

"We don't know." Trent answered. "But you need to tell Trey that dick Steven's causing trouble again."

"You don't honestly think Steven hurt Kara, do you? Trey says he's scared of you three." Tanya placed her hand on Kara's head.

"How's *Kyria*?" Adelina shifted into the room.

Tanya cocked an amused eyebrow, as realization hit. "Kara's your *Amara?*"

Alexander nodded. "Yes, she is. Please help her."

Tanya slyly grinned, "Don't worry. I will. Two important men in my life need her." She winked at Alexander, "You and my *Adora*, Trey."

Alexander choked on the water he'd just swallowed. "Trey's your *Adora*?" Tanya nodded.

"Are you sure?"

Tanya lifted her hair, and sure enough behind her ear was the golden fairy wing. "Son of a Bitch. He is."

"Well, now. This is interesting." Adelina chirped. "Two Magikos soul-mates in one family."

Tanya spent a long time working on Kara, mending all her crushed and broken bones, but there was one thing she couldn't heal. "Alexander you need to give her blood. There's extensive damage to her uterus. If I heal it, it'll scar. She'll never have children. The only way to heal it properly is for Kara to rejuvenate."

"That's the first step to bonding." Alexander declared. "I haven't discussed that with her."

"It's just the first step." Adelina reminded him. "Kara could still change her mind."

"The bonding will get stronger, what if she doesn't understand?" Alexander never wanted to deceive Kara, and he felt this was dishonest.

Trent spoke up, "Kara's understanding. She's actually very logical, besides she wants children. If this is her only chance, she'd want you to help her."

Any other time, it would thrill Alexander knowing Kara wanted children, but right now, he just hoped she'd understand what he's about to do.

"Why don't I take Trent home, so you can have some privacy?" Tanya offered, giving a pointed stare for Adelina to leave. "I'll bring him back tomorrow."

"Thank you."

Alexander walked into his bed chamber, bless Tanya, she had changed the bedding. Kara appeared peaceful, but as he leaned over her, deep brown eyes starred back at him.

Alexander could tell Kara was still out of it, when she choked out. "You found me."

She reached up touching his cheek. "I knew you would."

Alexander closed his eyes savoring her touch and her heart felt words. He was mentally drained from worrying about her injuries and if she would ever accept him, but her touch gave him more hope than he's had in centuries.

"Kara" he gently stroked her cheek "I cannot live without you, and I cannot stand to see you hurt. I'm sorry if that scares you, but it's the truth." He braced himself for her reply, he wasn't sure if it was too soon to show her his feelings or not. Dealing with human emotions was exhausting.

If Kara was a Cruetian, as soon as their marks were exposed she would have submitted to the ceremonies, and she would already be his wife, but she's not, so he has to play it her way. He has to be patient. Not easy for a man who is used to commanding and getting his way.

Kara couldn't believe what Alexander had just confessed. She knew her mind was fuzzy, but she also knew what she had heard. Kara was sure that as such a powerful and extremely sexy man, in all the centuries Alexander has lived, he's never needed a woman. They've probably always fell at his feet. The fact that he wanted her, took her breath away. How could she turn him down? No matter how much pain she was in, she needed him to.

"Kiss me Alexander. I need you to."

Alexander's head swam with those words. Did he just imagine them, or had Kara really spoken them, but when he looked down at her he knew the truth. Kara's sparkling eyes spoke volumes, Alexander could see the longing, the same desire he felt for her, she felt for him. With that simple knowledge his heart flew, and when his lips gently took hers, her passion overwhelmed him. Alexander loved the taste of this woman, Kara's sweetness was beyond imagination, and for the first time since Alexander had met Kara, the kiss was not just passion and desire, but full of real emotion. Not that he was complaining. He loved kissing her, but this kiss was something more. He could feel tenderness, acceptance, and most of all warmth. A heat washed through him like nothing he's ever felt in his entire existence.

Kara could no longer fight her feelings for Alexander, as he kissed her she knew there was no denying that she loved this man in ways she didn't even know existed. Yes, Alexander was dangerous, she was sure he could be cruel, and he was extremely arrogant and domineering. For God's sake, Alexander was a commander, a General of armies, of course he's ruthless, he had to be, but he was also hers, and with her he'd always been kind, gentle, and caring. Yes, he was a vamp... Dark-Soul, so he drank blood. No one's perfect. If that's his only fault, she could live with that. At this moment, Kara decided she would give 100% of herself to him, and then she would see where this would lead. No more holding back. Ever!

Kara let out a small whimper, as Alexander left her lips. Alexander knew she was in pain, and he knew what he had to do. He looked into her eyes, "Sleep, Kara, sleep and heal."

As soon as she was back in a deep sleep, using his canines, he cut his wrist and put it to Kara's mouth, letting his blood slide down her throat. This definitely wasn't how Alexander had envisioned their first bonding, but there was no doubt Kara needed his blood. He lightly caressed her neck, whispering his bonding vow in her ear. Then Alexander bit Kara's neck.

Instantly, he jerked back in horror. He had never tasted blood so intensely sweet. Blood he'd forbidden himself from ever tasting.

gods, Kara's a virgin! How could that be? She's been in three serious relationships. Alexander's head was swimming with this new revelation. He'd never taken a virgin human. His father had told him about virgin blood, and how his kind used to kill for it. Even during his lifetime, humans would sacrifice their virgins, to his people for protection. He had always refused to take them. He'd never wanted to harm a human, and now lying beneath him, was without a doubt a very virgin human. Alexander was so worried about breaking his oath; he wasn't even considering Kara's feelings. Centuries ago, he made an oath to himself; he would never feed from a virgin. It would take away their innocence, and he would never harm them that way. How would Kara feel about him violating hers?

Shit! What kind of a monster am I taking her blood? The kind that's saving your future children. gods help me, if Kara doesn't understand.

12

Kara whimpered most of the night, as Alexander's blood began the blood bond, and her body started regenerating itself. Since, this was the first time a human and Cruetian had ever began the bonding process, Alexander was unsure how quickly she would actually heal, so he still hooked her up to an IV to keep her from dehydration. He knew it would take at least twenty-four hours before she was completely healed. Needing to feel Kara alive and well, he moved an armchair next to their bed, intent on staying near her during her recovery. Alexander sat for hours listening to Kara's shallow breaths, tiny uncomfortable moans, and the drip from the IV. Watching Kara's slow methodical healing, Alexander tried to inundate her with his strength.

Just after sunrise, Alexander felt tension in the air, as Tanya, Trent, and Trey misted into his bed-chamber. He immediately recognized Trey; who looked identical to Trent, except for a small scar on his chin. Trey briefly greeted Alexander before asking a million questions. By Trey's knowledgeable questions, Alexander realized instantly that Tanya had told him the truth about herself. Noticing the dark circles under their eyes, it had obviously been a long night for them as well. Again, he was amazed at the love Trey bestowed upon Kara. Alexander answered all Trey's questions, before excusing himself to have breakfast. It had been a good forty-eight hours since he had fed, and he was in dire need of blood.

As Alexander walked into his office with a glass of blood, he realized he hadn't looked at any reports in two days. He sat down at his desk determined to go through them, but for the first time in his existence, he was having trouble concentrating on his duties. Kara had invaded his mind and he couldn't dispel her. Not that he really wanted too; the memory of her kisses, of her touch was still hot in his mind. The problem was his body wanted more. Just thinking about her made him stiff and drove him mad with desire. Alexander was constantly pulling at his pants to make more room. Good thing he was usually wearing his duster, otherwise everyone would get an eye full. An embarrassing situation, he didn't want to have to explain. If only he could bed her, maybe it would ease his insanity, but now more than ever he couldn't. She would need time for the pain to ease, before he could really touch her, and then he would still have to be careful not to hurt her. Even though she was regenerating, it would still take time for the pain to subside. As much as he longed to be with her, he could wait. At least now he could hold her, she had proved that with her display of affection.

Kara slowly regained consciousness, feeling like she'd been run over by a freight train. Her body ached all over, even slight movements were painful. It took a few minutes, before the horrors of the night before washed over her. *Shiz-nat! Did I get away? Did they come back and find me? Am I in a hospital?* Kara gradually opened her eyes, looking down her body, examining it for trauma, but finding nothing. *What the hell? I'm not crazy. I was attacked. I remember. I was severely injured. What the hell is going on?* Then she vaguely remembered the night before. Alexander had been here. He'd found her. She started breathing easier. She was safe. Alexander had helped her. He'd kissed her, and made it better.

Kara smiled to herself. Gosh that man could kiss. She could very easily get used to those lips. She laughed to herself, looking down at their chosen mark. According to Alexander, she's his, and he's hers. The Ultimate Fairytale. Could it really be this easy? She sure hoped so; she was tired of losing in love. She was no stranger to dating, but she'd only had three serious relationships, and they all turned out to be disappointments.

Kara gazed around her strange surroundings. She was spread out completely naked in a gigantic mahogany four poster bed. She felt like *Snow White*, waiting for her prince, with the gold sheers draped around her. She could see shadows on the other side of them, but couldn't make out who it was. She spotted an IV hanging above the bed, but other than that, she was definitely not in a hospital. Kara was in a large and very elegant bedroom. Who's she had no idea and Why? She trembled with that thought. If her captors had found her instead of Alexander… her body shook again, not wanting to consider that possibility.

"She's awake." That sounded like Tanya, but Kara still couldn't make her out.

"Kara?" That was absolutely Trent.

The sheers were tied back as Tanya, Trey and Trent ended up standing over her, with big grins on their faces. Kara looked around the strange room at all the beautiful flowers. She was undeniably loved by her family, but she wanted someone of her own. Was that too much to ask? She stopped at three large rose bouquets on a stand near a flat-screen. Her family normally didn't send roses. Those had to be from Alexander. They were beautiful all three different colors, purple, orange, and yellow with red tips.

"How do you feel?" Trey asked.

"Beat up!" She croaked.

Tanya handed her a bottle of water. "Do you remember what happened last night?"

Kara drank half the bottle before responding. "Duh! I was jumped!" She snapped. "Four…or maybe five men? Kara shrugged and grimaced with pain. "Never saw their faces, and I didn't recognize their voices either, so don't ask." She glanced around the enormous room, beautifully decorated with antiques. "Where am I?"

"Alexander's." Tanya confided. "There are a few things we should tell you before he returns." Tanya glanced at Trent.

"You think we should tell her?" Trent grimaced.

"I think Alexander's beating himself up over it. We should take responsibility for our part in the decision." Tanya countered.

"You're right. It's only fair." Trent sighed. "Kara, listen carefully. "OK?" Kara nodded, clearly confused by how they were acting. "We encouraged Alexander to initiate your bonding."

"YOU WHAT?" Kara screeched.

"Kara, calm down and let them explain." Trey scolded.

Tanya and Trent described everything that had happened after Kara left Mel's. How Alexander had found her, brought her to his home, took care of her. They explained how devastating her injuries had been, and why Alexander insisted on Kara being healed by two Magikos beings, one of which was Tanya.

"You actually expect me to believe you're a fairy?" Kara asked sarcastically. "We've been friends for years. What! You all of the sudden grew wings?"

"Tanya told me last night." Trey frowned, clearly disturbed by the revelation. "I can assure you, it's true."

"Please, Kara, let us finish. This is important" Tanya pleaded.

"Fine! Fine! Whatever." Kara waved her hand for them to continue.

They reiterated how severe her injuries were, explaining that Alexander had no choice except begin their bonding process, or Kara wouldn't have been able to conceive children. They went on and on, elaborating on every detail.

"Alexander saved your life." Trent concluded.

Kara's head was swimming with all the information. Ultimately, he had saved her, and she was extremely grateful for that. She just wasn't sure about this bonding thing.

"That's just great! So now what? I'm going to run around drinking people's blood."

Tanya rolled her eyes. "No, silly! That's a myth. Dark-Souls aren't contagious. You were already destined to become Alexander's *Amara*. He simply began the process, giving you some of his healing powers."

"Soooo...Like...I'm immortal?"

"Not yet!" Everyone turned to see Alexander standing in the doorway. Kara's breath caught in her throat. He was such a handsome site for her sore eyes.

"Let's leave these two to this discussion. Shall we." Tanya pushed the other two towards the door.

As soon as they left Alexander sat down next to Kara on the bed. "You should be resting."

"I was under the impression you've already healed me, doctor."

She pushed herself up leaning against the headboard. "Is that a service you provide all your patients?" She said teasingly.

Alexander released a sigh of relief, when he saw the mischief in her eyes. "You've been awake longer than I thought." He accused. "Or Tanya talks faster than I remember. I have never, nor would I ever give anyone else the gift I gave you, Kara. That gift of myself is reserved exclusively for you."

Kara didn't believe him. He was lying. "I watched a documentary about your people. They said you all share blood during sex."

"True. Taking blood for my species can be a very erotic act, and I have taken blood from many of my partners, however, I've never allowed them to take mine."

"Isn't that a little selfish" Kara accused. "Taking their blood, but not giving yours."

"When my people share their blood, it gives the recipient certain powers over them. Empathy! Telepathy! Tracking! Depending on how much blood was given. I have ingested each of my general's blood. This allows me to reach out to them. I can enter their minds, but they can't enter mine, since they've never had my blood. If two of my people share their blood, they become fully bonded. This allows them to become one person."

"I don't understand."

"Fully Bonded *Amaras* can see through each other's eyes, converse without speaking, know each other's feelings, they literally become one." Alexander sat back, allowing Kara time to digest the information.

"I guess when Dark-Souls say 'Get out of my head', they really mean it." She chuckled, "so you're connected to every human you've taken blood from?"

Alexander snorted. Needing Kara's touch he snatched her hand off the bed. "No! The only *human* I can be connected to, is you. Cruetians can only have a connection with other Dark-Souls, or to their *Amaras*. If they want to be bonded to another species, they must become fully bonded."

Kara was intrigued at how complex this whole bonding thing was. "How do you become fully bonded?"

Alexander rubbed Kara's mark, basking in the waves of electricity flowing through them. He wasn't even sure if Kara had noticed it. "You go through an elaborate ceremony." He winked with an amused sparkle in his eyes. "One you wouldn't have to host, but I believe would thoroughly enjoy."

Great! That's just freaking great! Someone must have told Alexander she didn't like hosting parties. It makes her very nervous. Kara's always been confident and strong in everything else in her life, but when it came to hosting parties, she hated it. It meant her entire family would show up, and 99% of the time, they'd embarrass her.

Alexander was still wearing that amused smile, until Kara spoke. Then it turned into a deep frown. "Why don't you explain this whole ceremony thing?"

"Alright! While you take a bath."

"No!" Kara spatted. "I don't do ultimatums."

Alexander reached over pulling her into his arms. Kara punched him, while trying to wiggle free, all it felt like was little butterfly wings hitting his chest. "I said *NO*! Put me down."

Alexander ended Kara's anger quite effectively, claiming her mouth in a fiery hot kiss. "I promise I'll answer every one of your questions while you're soaking in a bath." He whispered in her ear, his hot breath sending tremors rushing through her still aching body. "I can feel your muscles are in agony, they need to soak while you're healing." He removed the IV.

Alexander was right. Kara just didn't want to admit it, but she felt sticky and nasty. She could really use a nice hot bath.

Alexander cradled her close, craving the warmth she kindled inside him, as he carried her into his bath-chamber. Kara's eyes opened wide in disbelief, as she gasped at the enticing site. Everything was covered in beautiful white marble with blue veins running wildly throughout. Attached was the same glass fireplace from Alexander's room, keeping the bathroom nice and toasty. In the middle was a large circular bath built into the floor, surrounded by a huge glass shower on one wall, and two bright blue sinks on the other.

Alexander was elated over Kara's enthusiasm for his home. He had designed it specifically for her. He gently lowered her into the tub, already filled with hot water and herbal oils from the Stregians, to help her body heal. He quickly stripped, sliding in behind her.

"Oh, no you don't! Uh-uh! What the hell are you doing?" She demanded.

"I'm being a *proper* mate." Alexander raised an eyebrow, daring her to contradict him. "Taking care of my *Amara*." He gently kissed a path up her neck. "As much as I want to bask inside your delicious wet heat, you're still healing. I will *never* hurt you, so this won't be intimate." Amusement flashed across his face. "Or at least neither one of us will have an orgasm. Intimate? We'll see."

Kara wanted to object, but forgot why she should, when Alexander removed a hot towel from a container next to the tub. He laid it across the back of Kara's shoulders, before pulling her back against his chest.

Alexander slowly soaped down the front of Kara's body, enjoying the feel of her soft skin gliding under his hands. He cupped her full voluptuous breasts, soaping them, while admiring how they overflowed in his very large hands, eager to make his way to the dark auburn curls between her legs. The absolute proof that Kara dyed her hair blonde.

Kara leaned back on his shoulder, closing her eyes, in maximum overload from his meticulous exploration of her torso, as he made his way down, soaping her inner thighs, then gently the folds between her legs, it was so stimulating, a moan escaped her lips. *Not intimate, my ass!* Kara's body might be in pain, but it was also on fire. Flames ignited everywhere Alexander touched.

Alexander felt both of their arousals building, and knew they both needed to think about something else. "You asked about the blood bonding ceremony."

"Blood Bonding!" *Ewe!* "That's what it's called?" Kara asked thankful for the distraction.

"Yes! There are actually three ceremonies. You exchange blood in all three, hence...blood bonding. Each one must be performed to become fully bonded. The first step is the Acceptance ceremony. The Dark-Soul accepts their *Amara* with a vow and a gift of themselves, their blood. This begins the bonding process, allowing their *Amara* self-healing powers, and an empathy connection between them. The second step is the Betrothal Ceremony. The couple must share themselves with each other intimately, consummating their relationship in a very specific ceremony, commencing their telepathy connection." Alexander smiled. "It's also when the male betroths the female with an engagement ring. The final step is the joining ceremony. This ceremony is basically a very special wedding. They will establish an eternal union as husband and wife. Their life forces will be bound together, unlocking the ability to act as one. It also bestows certain powers on the *Amara*, and allows the Dark-Soul to produce children. This last ceremony has to be done in Italy."

Kara's head was spinning. She had so many questions she didn't know where to begin. "Tanya said we performed the first ceremony. What was your vow?" She whispered. "I don't remember."

Kara nervously played with his fingers. Alexander turned her across his lap, lifting her chin so their eyes met. "*I, Alexander Valerius Maximus, a Dark-Soul, the crown prince of the Cruetian people, claim you, Kara Spencer, as my Amara. As my acceptance, I give my most precious treasure a part of myself, my most valued asset.*"

Kara heard the candor in Alexander's voice and it melted some of her fears. He meant every word. Alexander accepted her just the way she was. He wanted her.

"Is there an English translation for the word '*Amara*'?

"Cruetians have lived for millenniums, and have lived within many human cultures. We tend to use many languages as our own. Some words keep the same meaning as humans used them. Some words we've adapted their meanings to fit our purpose. In Cruetian, *Amara* means: chosen one. In German and Greek it means: eternal. In Sanskrit and Hindu: immortal. African: paradise. Spanish: imperishable, and in Italian *Amata* or *Amato* means beloved and *Amara* is a form of the Latin word amarantus meaning everlasting and beloved. Cruetians chose the word *Amara* because it fits our Chosen one's perfectly. An eternal steadfast immortal beloved."

Alexander wasn't sure why Kara was crying, but they seemed to be happy tears, as he kissed them away.

Kara composed herself, ready to learn more about this incredible man holding her. She reached up and stroked his cheek. It was rough with a day's worth of stubble that tickled her hand. "You can't father children?"

"My people cannot conceive or father children, until we are bound to our *Amara*. A curse my dead wife's mother, and the Goddess Cerridwen, enacted upon my people out of misguided revenge." Alexander admitted between gritted teeth.

Kara's eyes widened with shock. "You were married?"

"Not by choice. I was arrogant. In the thirteenth century my only concern was fulfilling my destiny." He scrubbed his hand down his face. "Which I believed was to create the Magikos Alliance."

Kara smiled, "Tanya told me about Magikos, it's kind of like NATO, but for otherworldly races. Right?"

"Yes"

"A worthy destiny."

"I thought so, but to establish the Alliance, I had to agree to an arranged marriage with Fiona, a Stregian princess. Fiona was a witch, and I underestimated her powers. Fiona made it clear she never loved me. I put my whole family in danger when I made her my wife. For two years Fiona plotted with my cousin to kill my family and steal our Crown. When Kalab discovered her treachery......"

When Alexander said they feel each other, Kara never anticipated he meant literally, but she could feel his pain. "I'm really sorry, Alexander. That's horrible. I can't imagine anyone doing that to you." She reached up and cupped his cheek. "What did you do?"

He really didn't want to discuss Fiona with Kara, but sooner or later he'd have to. Alexander snorted. "Alright, Kara. I'll tell you about Fiona. Please try to keep in mind we come from different cultures and it was a different time. Punishment was delivered differently than it is today. Remember that when you judge my actions."

"Agreed." Not that Kara could imagine anything she'd judge him poorly about.

"I carried out Cruetian law. I executed Fiona myself, causing the curse." Alexander explained in a monotone voice. No emotion. No feeling. At that moment, the Commander Kara had heard about was revealed. She heard no feeling in his voice, just cold hard facts. "The curse was designed to cause our extinction, but the Goddess Hecate protected us. She changed the curse by allowing us an *Amara*. Hecate canceled out our extinction, by making Cruetians more Magikos than we had ever been. You see every Magikos race has to find their chosen one, their one true mate, to complete themselves. Dark-Souls have to find their *Amaras* to procreate, where Fairies have to find their *Adoras* to gain all their powers. Every Magikos being was created this way, except Dark-Souls, until the curse. Up until then, we were able to choose who our spouses would be, and turn them into Cruetians. Now the only way Dark-Souls can produce children is finding their *Amara*." His pain was obvious as Alexander gazed into Kara's eyes. "It doesn't stop the pain we endure trying to find them."

That bitch! How could Fiona hurt him? I've waited years to find such a man. Honorable. Caring. How could she be so heartless? How could she even consider destroying him? Kara had never met Fiona, but she hated her.

Kara wanted to reassure Alexander that his search for his *Amara* was over, but she still wasn't sure. Oh, God, Yes she wanted him, but she needed a little more time. So instead, she changed the subject. "I thought Tanya said witches were part of Magikos."

Alexander stroked her hair, feeling her uncertainties, hoping to the gods that he could trust this woman, and that she wouldn't turn out like Fiona. Kara felt different; she desired Alexander's touch, where Fiona never had. Fiona had always been cold.

"Yes, it's true we are allies again. In the Sixteenth century, humans became ruthless, burning people they believed to be witches. Cruetians were asked to ally against the humans. At that time, humans were aware of otherworldly beings walking among them. Humans were afraid of us, but they knew we existed, and for the most part, they ignored us. When humans started to attack, out of fear of the unknown, witches were hit the hardest. Fiona's mother, Miander, had been burned at the stake, and the new Stregian Queen asked for our protection." He traced their mark, "I agreed in exchange for my mark being raised on my *Amara's* hand."

"Alexander, you allied with some heartless race to find *me*?" Kara screeched. "Why didn't you make them remove the curse?"

Alexander smiled, pleased that Kara was already thinking about his people, she was thinking like the crown princess she was. "Naturally, that was the first thing I asked for. Unfortunately, Miander was dead; assuring the curse could never be lifted." Alexander felt Kara's concern for his people, melting his heart even more for this fragile woman. "Let's dry you off, and put you to bed. You still need your rest. We'll talk more when you're healed."

Alexander lifted her out of the tub, carefully toweling her off, before dressing her in a red silk nightgown.

"It's beautiful." Kara caressed the silk. "I've never felt anything so exquisite."

"I'm pleased you like it." He brushed his lips across hers, laying her beneath soft Egyptian cotton, which she realized had to be expensive.

Kara tried to pull Alexander down with her, but due to sheer weakness, had no effect. "Hold me, Alexander. Please." She didn't understand why she needed his arms around her, but she did. Kara wanted to feel his strength wrapped around her, his power encompassing her, and his warmth encircling her.

At first Alexander was shocked, then overjoyed by her request. She was still pale, a little weak, but he knew she was healing rapidly, and there was nothing he wanted more than to spoon up behind Kara, cradling her to his body.

Kara traced the triple arrows tattoo on Alexander's wrist. "You have such exotic tattoos. They're beautiful."

"The arrows your tracing is the Cruetian royal seal. Three arrows for the original three Titan protectors, with laurel leaves tying them together. My arrow heads are gold, and the feathers are green, red, and blue proving that I'm the crown prince. Each color arrow represents one of the protectors. Red is my father's line, blue the Egyptian line, and green is the Asian line." Alexander gently kissed Kara's neck.

"Do your other tattoos have meanings?"

"Yes." Alexander loved Kara's caress. "The circled seven point star, on my left upper arm, is the Magikos seal."

"What's the letters mean?"

"You saw them? You're more observant than I thought. In each point is one roman letter spelling out '*Magikos*'. Again, mine is colorful representing the many different otherworldly races. The dragon and phoenix on my back were gifts from those beings. It's a type of magic that bestows telepathic ability between us, and the laurel leaves band around my right bicep is proof I'm a General."

Kara pulled his arms tighter around her, needing to feel secure in his embrace. "They're beautiful. Such intricate colorful detail. There truly a work of art."

Alexander held Kara close, savoring the sensation of their bodies intertwined together. In 2000 years, he'd never encountered such comfort. Kara had a calming effect on his nerves, she alleviated his anxieties, relaxing him to the point he thought he might actually begin to trust her. *Was that possible? Could I trust a woman, or more importantly...Kara?* It sure felt like it, as Alexander fell asleep for the first time in 800 years next to a woman.

13

Kara awoke with steel bands encircling her, and pressed up against a rock hard body. She smiled, feeling Alexander's hot breath teasing the back of her neck, as she was inundated by his heady masculine scent. Surprised he was still holding her; Kara glided her hands over Alexander's sinewy arms, appreciating the protection she felt. Damn, if this didn't feel perfect, having him wrapped around her. Kara had never felt so content in her entire life. *Is this what a soulmate feels like?* She gently rolled onto her back, viewing Alexander's peaceful slumber, which sent butterflies soaring through her belly. How sweet he looked, a masterpiece chiseled to perfection. Kara giggled as Alexander lightly snored. *Oh, sweet heavens. My fantasy, butt naked in the flesh!* Kara brushed his hair away, lightly tracing his gorgeous features. Earlier in the bath, she'd been too embarrassed to really look over all of Alexander's assets, but now, she couldn't help herself as she wiggled out of his embrace, sat up, and lifted the sheets to thoroughly examine him. *Oh, Baby! There's nothing small about this man. Just look at that scrumptious bod.* Kara refused to look away, engraving every inch of Alexander's sublime physique into her mind. She couldn't keep her eyes off his naked body. If she thought he was a walking GQ cover fully dressed, Alexander was a vision of pure perfection naked.

"I'm glad you approve." Alexander chuckled with amusement, watching Kara jump out of her skin. Alexander had awoken the minute Kara touched him. Enjoying her admiring exploration, he hadn't wanted to disturb her; until Kara's feelings had turned to legitimate appreciation, and then he couldn't help himself.

Shit! Kara dropped the sheet, feeling her cheeks burning bright red. "Ooooooh!" She was dragged down onto her back, with Alexander laughing over her, with amusement sparkling in his eyes.

"*topolina*, there's nothing to be embarrassed about." Kara burst into flames, as Alexander's slow worshiping gaze traveled over her body, while he licked his lips. "I'm very partial to these delicious curves myself."

Alexander's kiss warmed Kara from the inside out, making her hot, wet, and needy all at the same time. How could a man, she'd just met, have such an effect on her whole being. *Soul-mate!* Kara pushed the thought aside, not wanting to analyze or ruin this moment.

Alexander couldn't breathe as Kara wrapped her tiny legs around his waist, positioning his swollen cock in perfect position of her enticingly wet heat. The little temptress began seductively rubbing against him, his scrotum tightening to the point of pain. Alexander could smell Kara's arousal, feel her heat radiating off her, and see untapped desire filling her eyes. A war raged inside him.

Damn it! Take her. I want Kara more than I've ever wanted another woman. She's mine, take her! NO! I can't. She's a virgin. Kara needs to know everything. Only then can she freely give me this precious gift.

As extremely difficult as it was, Alexander pushed away, sitting on the edge of the bed. "Kara, I can't......"

Kara flew up, gasping, trying to understand what she'd possibly done wrong. "You don't want me? I thought you said......"

Alexander couldn't believe what he was hearing. She actually thought he didn't want her? He reached out cupping her face, rubbing his thumb over her cheek. "gods, no, love! All I want is your beautiful little body wrapped around mine."

Kara was clearly confused, as Alexander's rejection stung. "Then why'd you stop?"

Stammering for an explanation, Alexander tried to get a hold of his thoughts. "You're...you're...You're a virgin!"

"So!" Kara rolled her eyes. "You'd think an ancient would appreciate that fact, didn't you guys, like...what...marry virgins. Hold it! How did you know that?" She demanded, as she felt the heat of her blush hit her cheeks.

"Your blood...it is pure. A virgin's blood tastes much different from other women. Why didn't you tell me?"

Embarrassed and humiliated Kara snapped, "What's to tell, it's not like I go around announcing it. Wearing a big sign, '*Virgin*'! Technically, yes. I'm a virgin. I've never felt a man inside me." She pushed him out of the way and jumped off the bed. "Is that what you want to hear? I'm sure you think I can't please you because I'm so naïve, but I don't consider myself innocent, Alexander. I've had oral sex on numerous occasions, and I know how to please a man in that aspect."

Alexander felt like an ass. What a selfish bastard he was being. He hadn't anticipated her feeling inadequate. "I'm sorry, Kara. I didn't mean to upset or embarrass you. If Chung hadn't interrupted us...Well, let's just say...you wouldn't be a virgin right now." He reached out seizing her around the waist and pulling her onto his lap. "Don't you think I should have known? I could have hurt you."

Kara refused to look at him. She was already hurt enough, she didn't need to see Alexander's disappointment. As usual every male is the same. "I decided a long time ago, that I would only allow one man inside me." She whispered. "That man would be my soul-mate. You see, I've watched my grandparent's love and my parent's. They're all soul-mates, and that's the kind of love I want. I knew someday I would find him, and when I did, he would be the only one to have all of me." Alexander reached out and turned her to face him. His heart ached knowing he had hurt her, but more than that, he relished in the knowledge that Kara might believe he was her soul-mate.

Kara glared up at Alexander with tears in her eyes. "You believe I'm your soul-mate?" He held her face.

"I honestly don't know, Alexander. I know I've never wanted this type of intimacy with another man, and I've never felt so complete, as I do in your arms, but honestly, I just don't know. I need time."

Alexander understood. He'd been avoiding the same feelings. He could easily loose himself in Kara, and he didn't want to think what that meant. "In yet, you're willing to give yourself to me?"

What Kara saw in his eyes scared her, he looked so confused. *If he believes I'm his Amara, shouldn't he want me?* "I was under the impression you believe I'm your *Amara*. Has that changed?"

"Never!" Alexander's eyes pierced hers.

"In that case...you're the man I've been saving myself for...sooooo" She bit her lower lip, "Yes, if you want me!"

"Oh, Kara." Alexander was breathless, embracing Kara in a kiss so gentle, so passionate, it sent fire scorching through every inch of her body, melting her into his, until she couldn't tell where he began and she ended. "I want and desire nothing more than you, and yes, baby, ancients love virgins. I love that fact about you. To be your first, would be a great honor, what an incredible gift for an *Amara* to give their Dark-Soul. Do you understand the amazing gift you'd be giving me? Am I even worthy of such a gift?"

"Alexander" she purred in his ear. "Stop asking questions, and just take what's yours." She kissed his neck. "I would never give myself to an unworthy man."

"Not now, love. Soon! You're healing!" Alexander's cock twitched in anticipation as Kara turned straddling him. Stiff and swollen, he couldn't concentrate as she rubbed erotically against him. "Kara, seriously you're still healing." He gasped. "Besides we need to have an important discussion first."

Kara refused to stop. Healing? Maybe, but she felt marvelous. Alexander continued stroking her hair, very gently, pulling her closer to him. "Oh, my little temptress, you have no idea what you're playing with. It's been a century since I've been with anyone."

"I'm not a tease, Alexander. I want you, and you said you want me, now is as good a time as any." She reached down cupping him, "Besides I don't want to stop." She seductively sucked her finger, before tracing his lips. "From where my hand is, neither do you. I want to continue...I need to continue." Kara admitted.

Alexander knew he should insist on talking first, but with Kara rubbing up and down his shaft, nothing was going to stop him from having his own piece of heaven. Alexander kissed her passionately, urgently. Wanting more, his tongue immediately parted Kara's lips and darted in, ravishing anything it touched. Kara moaned at the intensity of his probing. She relished in his tongue dancing with hers, and savored his exotic taste. *Oh, God! This is what I wanted. I've waited my entire life for this. This is what I needed from him.* Alexander's tongue danced around Kara's mouth, filling every cell in her body with a searing heat. She ran her fingers through his silky soft hair, while Alexander's hands roamed her entire body, stroking everywhere he could reach.

Never breaking their kiss, he laid her back onto the bed. He continued exploring down her shoulder, across her ribs, over her shapely hips, and down her exquisite thighs, he loved Kara's softness, and relished in tracing every one of her enticing curves.

Alexander's hand was like satin touching Kara's skin. His fingers glided up her inner thighs, moving leisurely over her hips, igniting a fire between her legs that demanded his attention. She squirmed under him, pushing her hips upwards toward him, offering herself to him, begging him to take her.

Needing to catch her breath, Kara gasped for air breaking their kiss, but Alexander's lips never left her skin. His soft, warm lips moved across her throat, leaving a trail of tiny kisses, while his hands continued teasing her body.

He growled in approval as he tasted her breast, tormenting one nipple and then the other, while enjoying Kara squirming under him. gods, she is perfect in every way imaginable. A true goddess. Wanting to view her passion flushed body, Alexander rolled over on his elbow to admire her. Keeping one hand splayed across her stomach.

"What's wrong?" A pang of fear hit Kara.

"You're absolutely exquisite, more beautiful than I ever imagined," he gave Kara a wicked grin "and trust me, I have a really good imagination." Alexander winked at her, easing her fears, as his hand glided down her stomach. "Even I couldn't have imagined anyone so perfect. I've been dreaming of you for 400 years, wondering what you would feel like, how you'd taste, imagining your delicious scent. Oh, baby, nothing could've prepared me for you. Magnificent! Alluring... Delicious... Perfection."

Kara giggled. "You're hallucinating, but *I* like it." Alexander arched a quizzical brow. Kara felt the heat of her blush enter her cheeks, "I'm flattered, but we both know my body isn't remarkable in any way……" Alexander stopped her by putting a finger upon her mouth.

"Oh, baby. You're so wrong. Your body is magnificent. It tempts me in every possible way a woman can tease a man. It begs me to possess you, to take you in every possible manner, to completely dominate you, until I'm all you think of. It creates a desire inside me that is insatiable." Kara inhaled deeply at his touch. It was like satin caressing her skin, as his finger gently made a path from her neck, down between her breasts, to her stomach. "Trust me. I have lived for centuries, and this mind, and this body is the only one that has ever held this type of attraction for me."

Kara rolled over pinning Alexander under her. She stroked his steel muscled chest, loving the feel of his firm muscles coiling under her touch. Alexander growled, as her soft blonde curls brushed over his skin, while she slowly laved his chest, working her way down to his navel, tracing the light dusting of golden hair from his navel down. Kara looked up Alexander's body to see him watching her. She smiled seductively, glazing her nails over his tight sack, before cupping him firmly with both hands. The sight of him so large, and fully aroused, made Kara ache for release.

Alexander moaned in pleasure as Kara wrapped her little pixie hands around his hard, swollen shaft, lightly stroking him from tip to hilt and back, reveling in the pleasure of his groans.

Alexander couldn't help watching her. Like a cat, she crawled up his body and straddled him. Her naked body rubbing against his, sent his blood boiling, and when she straddled him, it took all his years' worth of training, to maintain his control from driving himself deep inside her.

Kara could feel his erection on her butt cheek, it made her wet with anticipation. She teased his lips with her tongue, before Alexander captured them in a passionate invasion. Kara pulled away breathless, as much as she enjoyed the fire Alexander burned inside her, she wanted to prove she was no innocent. Using her tongue to trace every rippling muscle back down his chest, she continued onto his stomach. Each time he let out a soft moan of pleasure, the satisfaction it brought Kara, encouraged her on. She slowly slid her body down so she could kneel between his thighs. Kara drug her nails up his thighs, then ever so gently across his groin, enjoying him squirm momentarily. Catching his gaze, she bent down and took him into her mouth. Damn, he was mouthwatering. Using her tongue, she massaged the sensitive spot just underneath the tip of his head. Alexander growled in sheer pleasure as Kara continued to stroke him. Damn she knew how to drive a man wild. She hadn't been exaggerating when she said she wasn't naïve. This woman knew how to pleasure a man. Each moan that ripped from his throat encouraged her on. She wanted to please him. She wanted to be the one giving him pleasure. She wanted to be the one to take him over the edge to heaven and drop him back to earth.

Breathing heavily Alexander rasped, "Stop! I won't be able to last much longer." Kara looked up catching his eyes. She gave him the most smug little smile he'd ever seen. Yes, Kara might be a virgin, but she definitely knew how to pleasure a man.

"Did you change your mind?" Kara asked seductively.

"No!" Alexander rasped for air. "But this is *your* first time, it should be very memorable. I want to make *you* squirm in ecstasy."

Such a noble thought. Kara had never been with a man that considered her pleasures over his own. The few she'd been with were very selfish when it came to sex, well, not just sex, they were selfish period. In yet, for the first time in her life, Kara didn't feel resentful, she was content watching Alexander squirm under her touch. Seeing him enjoy each of her caresses, gave her a sense of gratification she never knew existed. Ignoring his request, she bent down and took him back into her mouth, gliding her tongue slowly, gently over the tip of his cock. Kara was elated when he moaned. It came from deep inside his chest, and shook his entire body.

Alexander jerked in response, as Kara's talented tongue teased him. It was unconceivable to him, why she hadn't taken his warning. He wasn't joking. He truly wouldn't last much longer. Stopping her, he pulled her up his body. Kissing her so deeply, so passionately, her resolve shattered, as she melted into his arms.

Alexander sucked in a sharp breath at the site of her plump pink nipples, as he rolled her beneath him. They were so taut and firm rubbing against his chest. How did he get to be so lucky? To have this magnificent woman created for him. His chosen one! His *Amara*! "My turn." He winked, reaching down and fondling her breasts. How perfectly they sat in his large hands. As Alexander gently teased one, he licked a hot path around her other nipple, before taking it in between his teeth, pulling on it gently, before letting his tongue focus on her taunt bud.

Kara arched her back, as waves of chills rippled through her. She was delirious from Alexander's touch. Her sole focus was on the white hot desire fueling the fire that was racing through her veins.

Alexander was still savoring the taste of her, as he turned his attention to her other breast that was eagerly awaiting his attention. Kara's scent of Orchids, Jasmine, and Cherry Blossoms saturated every cell in his body, pushing his arousal to the point of pain, but he wouldn't rush her first time. No. He wanted to show her what she had to look forward to as his *Amara*. Bonding with him meant forever, for eternity, he didn't want her to have any regrets.

Kara let Alexander take complete control of her body, as his tongue traced every curve, from her heated breasts to her aching thighs, leaving a blazing trail of bliss in its aftermath. It made her delirious with need.

Alexander reveled in Kara's passionate moans of pleasure. It urged him lower, encouraging him to take the part of her that no other man had ever been allowed to breech. Demanding him to take what was rightfully his. Commanding him to prove his manhood. To show her that she'd never need another man, but him. He would always be enough to please her. He reached the molten lava between Kara's thighs. *Damn!* Her heat was scorching, and wet, sooo wet that he almost came at just the thought of how she'd feel, once he buried himself deep inside her.

Control was lost to Kara as she begged Alexander to take her. The burning ache at her core was causing her to go insane.

Alexander's lips curled into a smug smirk, as he looked up and saw the glossy overcast look in Kara's eyes. Teasing her clit, he slid two fingers inside her.

It wasn't enough, she begged for more. Every move, every touch was as if Alexander knew every erogenous zone of her body. Kara tried to grip his head, his back, anything to hold on to while her body arched and squirmed in delight. Every time she was close to exploding in ecstasy, he would turn his attention to another part of her body, prolonging the sensations, enjoying her pleasure, and relishing in the fact that he was the cause of her need. His tongue replaced his fingers an instant before she screamed out his name. Kara's orgasm was so strong, her teeth chattered as her whole body shook. He licked away every bit of her release, before crawling back up her body. "You're amazing" she crooned, smiling.

"Baby, you haven't felt anything yet." Kara laughed at his playful tone. "But before I make you scream my name again" He kissed her tenderly; pulling back to gaze into her eyes. "I need you to know, I'll never hurt you. You're my *Amara*, the woman I've waited centuries for. I know that scares you. I just want you to know, I appreciate, and I will cherish the gift you're about to give me."

Seizing her lips, Alexander invaded her mouth, taking full possession with his tongue, in a fiery hot kiss. Kara had never felt a kiss so possessive. It was hard and soft all at the same time, and left her wanting more.

He slowly skimmed his hand up the inside of her thigh, finding Kara dripping wet. "gods, Kara, your drenching my hand." He breathed against her lips. After 400 years of waiting, he wanted to savor her, learn every nuance of her body, but Alexander was aware, for a virgin, as wet as Kara was, the time was now.

"Kara...Baby, if you want me inside you, the time is now."

Kara felt tremors of anticipation flow through him, as he positioned himself between her thighs, his tip nestled at the edge of her opening. Kara closed her eyes, sliding her hands down his spine, appreciating the thick ropes of powerful muscles, and enjoying the little tremors that racked his body. "Alexander, please."

Alexander held Kara tight, needing her close to him, needing to claim her as his own. He loved hearing his name slide off her tongue, but he wanted more. He wanted all of her. "Kara, open your eyes. I want to experience the passion of your first time, our first time... together."

The moment Kara gazed into Alexander's striking teal eyes, using a single forceful thrust, he plunged deep inside her. Alexander witnessed the instant he penetrated her hymen. Kara gasped at the stinging pain, as the pain flashed in her eyes, then passion instantaneously resurfaced.

He didn't move. He loved feeling Kara's tight moist heat sheathed around him. It was all he could do to hold still. He knew the first time could be painful, and he didn't want to hurt her anymore then was necessary. He needed to allow Kara's tight little body time to adjust to his abundant size. She was so tight, it was like Alexander's scabbard cradling his sword, and they fit together just as perfectly. He stroked her hair. "How are you feeling? Is it terribly painful?" Kara shook her head, biting her tongue. He kissed her tenderly. "I'm sorry, love. I promise I'll never hurt you again."

Kara savored his concern, but she felt incredible. Yes, she was overwhelmed by the feeling of his invasion. He filled her so completely, but this is what she'd dreamed of. This is what she'd waited for. Alexander inside her was a dream come true. This feeling of completeness satisfied her. Alexander was tender, caring, and concerned for her needs. Everyone had been wrong. *Mr. Right* does exist and Kara held him in her arms. She cupped his face, "I'm perfect!" She smiled lovingly up at him, "I've waited my entire life to give myself to my soul-mate." She kissed him gently, "and I just did. It doesn't get any more perfect than that." Kara's words sent Alexander soaring.

He growled from the pure ecstasy of finally being inside his *Amara*. He slowly moved, watching her for any sign of pain, when there was none, he pushed himself deeper, intensifying Kara's need for him. Neither one could look away from the other. They were enjoying each other's pleasure.

Alexander sucked in a breath, as she wrapped those tiny dancer legs around his waist, raising her hips, taking him all the way to his hilt. Alexander cherished each of Kara's little purrs, as he thrust deep inside her. Watching Kara's passion flushed face, he could feel her getting closer to her climax.

The frenzy building in Kara's body was more than she could stand, she needed more of Alexander. She reached down and grabbed his obscenely tight ass; a hard thrust was his reaction, sending her screaming with ecstasy.

Alexander caught Kara screaming his name in a steamy kiss, thrusting harder to increase the intensity of her pleasure, until he joined her howling with his own release. Not wanting to hurt her, Alexander rolled with Kara draping her over him, before collapsing himself.

Still trying to catch her breath, Kara exclaimed. "That was extraordinary!" She kissed his chest. "It was so much more than I ever fantasized, and *trust* me; I have great fantasies, too."

Alexander laughed, "You know, you're really great for the male ego." He rolled pinning her under him. "Baby, I assure you we're just getting started."

Alexander pressed his weight firmly against Kara, letting her feel his rather impressive erection. She blushed bright red, fumbling over her words. "I didn't think men were able to…um…revive themselves so quickly."

Alexander nuzzled her neck, nibbling on her earlobe. "Sweetheart, I'm not human. There's many things I can do for you that a human male can't." Alexander was pleased how Kara's body quivered from his touch. Unlike Fiona, Kara seemed truly attracted to him. Hopefully, the differences between Fiona and Kara would be night and day. Only then could he honestly trust her.

Kara watched Alexander nibble his way down playing with her belly-button ring. She moaned as his tongue dipped into her navel. "If you like that, you're going to love this." He took her ravenously into his mouth, using his tongue mercilessly on her clit.

Alexander pulled her against his body. His arms were magnificent, all muscle, they were like a steel cage wrapped around protecting her. Kara loved how strong and masculine he was. She always felt protected when she was in his embrace.

Kara couldn't process the many sensations flowing through her body. She'd had more orgasms than was probably healthy. Alexander was insatiable. It would take a long time for Kara to sate his century of drought. But Damn, if she didn't want to be his rain.

Alexander laid in perfect bliss holding his *Amara* in his arms, after releasing his eager seed inside her three times. As he had watched Kara passionately orgasm over and over again, he had relished in the awareness that he had created her desire. That he had been able to give her this extreme pleasure.

Listening to his sated mate lightly snore, while Kara clutched him to herself. He breathed in her intoxicating floral scent, allowing it to saturate every inch of his body. This is what Alexander had waited centuries for. This was his heaven. Kara was his utopia.

Please don't become Fiona. Don't betray me.

14

Alexander awoke the next morning, utterly satisfied. Still cradling Kara in a tight embrace, he was shocked he had slept so long. Carefully slipping out of bed, he silently dressed, and shifted downstairs. Kara needed nourishment to continue healing, and he had business to handle. He had a new club opening tonight, as well as troops that needed his leadership. More importantly, it was time to bring Kara's family to his home. Alexander wanted them to understand that he was more than capable of taking care of her, and they needed to see her. See that she was ok. Kara's family hadn't been happy staying away, when they knew she was hurt, but since Trey, Tanya and Trent had seen her, they agreed to wait. It was time Alexander trusted them. He'd decided to invite them to his ranch for lunch.

So far they've all kept their promises, let's just hope bringing them here isn't a mistake.

Alexander made his way to the kitchen, surprised to see Trey, Trent, and Tanya had already arrived and was having breakfast with his generals.

"How's my sister?" Trey inquired.

"Wonderful!" Fervor ripped from his throat, before Alexander realized what he'd said. He coughed into his fist trying to cover his mistake, composing his voice into a more business tone. "Kara's healing wonderfully."

Chung's head snapped up, he was shocked at hearing that satisfied tone in Alexander's voice. Chung prayed he'd imagined it, but seeing the contented look on his Commander's face...Chung knew. As unwanted as that tone of voice was, Chung knew. Alexander had bedded Kara. *My baby's no longer innocent.* Instantly Chung was in front of Alexander yelling.

"NO, YOU DIDN'T! YOU STUPID *PUTALLO*!" Alexander knew how angry Chung was, when he used the worse insult of the Cruetian language.

Kalab jumped forward, but Alexander motioned him back, as everyone in the room was all of the sudden at attention. "Back off, Kalab. This is a personal matter between the General and me."

Chung spat. "How could you, *Kyrios*? She's healing?"

Alexander heard Trey's urgency. "What the hell is going on? What did he do to Kara?"

Alexander squared off with Chung, never leaving his glare. "I've done nothing to your sister. Kara is healing rapidly. In fact, I came down to invite your family here for lunch. I think she would enjoy the company. Go with Nathaniel, he'll make the arrangements." Chung growled with disgust. "General, this is *not* the place to discuss this." Alexander threw his hand out. "Everyone out!"

"Are you afraid of her family finding out?" Chung roared.

Alexander snarled. "General!" Taking a deep breath to calm his temper, Alexander gritted his teeth. "I...will not...embarrass her. If Kara wants her family to know, she'll tell them. I did *not* hurt her. It was a mutual decision. Kara is...quite pleased."

Chung spat the next words in his Commander's face. He was so disgusted with Alexander, what would possess him to take Kara when she's healing. "Kara...is...hurt!"

At that moment Alexander understood Chung's fury. He wasn't angry because Alexander had deflowered her. He was concerned for her health. Alexander stepped back, standing down. "General, I assure you, I wouldn't have accepted her advances if it would have hurt her. Kara is quite healthy and is currently sleeping peacefully in my bed. You're more than welcome to go and check on her."

Alexander saw Kalab back off as soon as Chung stepped away from him. "Kalab, this is a private conversation." Kalab nodded, understanding his Commander's orders. He would mention this to no one. "Ask Adelina to shift to Italy and bring back breakfast. I want

Kara to have an Italian breakfast."

"*Kyrios*, I'm sorry." Chung scrubbed his hand over his face. "I thought I'd come to terms with you and Kara, but the image of...the rage shot through me so quickly I couldn't control myself."

Alexander cupped Chung's shoulder. "We knew this wasn't going to be easy." Alexander sighed. "You know me as somewhat of a womanizer. You still consider Kara as one of my conquests, but I can assure you she's not. Kara makes me feel......" He stopped when he saw Chung's eyes flash black. "I don't want to set off your fury. Let's just say...I'll never want another woman."

Adelina shifted into the kitchen, holding a tray of Italian pastries, glancing between the two of them. "You two OK?"

"We are." Alexander assured her. "Put two cappuccinos on the tray."

"Make one tea. Kara doesn't drink coffee." Chung explained. "She doesn't like the taste at all. She won't even eat Tiramisu, because she can taste the coffee in it."

"Really?" Alexander raised a curious eyebrow. "An American who doesn't drink coffee. That's interesting."

⚬∞∞⚬

Kara awoke feeling incredible. Looking up through the huge skylights, she saw a beautiful clear blue sky that was dusted with fluffy white clouds. Truly a perfect day! Alexander making love to her was more than she had ever anticipated. Not counting her realizations from last night. Kara no longer had any doubts. Alexander was absolutely her soul-mate. She *was* his *Amara*.

Kara stretched, only to cringe. She was still sore, and the pain in her ribs could still knock her on her butt. Frowning, she noticed Alexander was no longer beside her. Remembering the intricate wood carvings on the headboard, she turned to study them. Alexander had said that he'd had three beds made for them centuries ago. One bed for each stage of their bonding, and this was the 1st bed. Alexander assured Kara he'd never taken another woman to any of their beds; they'd been reserved exclusively for her, and he had been the only one to sleep in them until now. Kara didn't know why, but as she traced the beautiful birds and flowers carved into the headboard, she was pleased with that knowledge.

Wanting to learn more about Alexander, Kara slid off the bed. She walked across to an all glass wall that overlooked a beautiful river, surrounded by the Rocky Mountains. Kara wanted to go out onto the balcony, but couldn't find the door. Content looking around the room, she viewed numerous paintings, statues, and tapestries, which she was sure, were all originals.

Why wouldn't they be? Living 2300 years, he probably knew each and every artist personally. She giggled.

She discovered the romantic fireplace was attached to the huge bathroom she'd bathed in, and an incredible sitting room. Kara made her way to the two smaller arches. The first one was a large walk-in closet, full of designer brands. One side was definitely Alexander's clothes. The other side was…women's clothes? A surge of jealously flashed through Kara's body. *Did Alexander lie to me? Does he entertain women here?* Not wanting to ruin her small piece of euphoria, she pushed those thoughts aside. She'd deal with them later.

Kara's breath caught in her throat as she entered the next room. It was like a museum. She walked around admiring all the swords, daggers, shields, and armor from every century the last 2000 years. Some cultures she recognized, some she didn't. *Could these be Alexander's? Had he actually used these?*

Kara's heart skipped a beat as she felt Alexander watching her. Her body fluttered in anticipation, as she turned around observing him, standing there in all his glory. She had the intense need to be in his arms.

"Shouldn't you be resting?" He gave her an amused smile, catching her out of bed red handed.

Damn! His smile shook her to her core. Instantly, he was behind her, pulling her up against him to stabilize her from falling. At least that's what Alexander told himself. In reality, he knew he would use any excuse to hold her. Even though it made him rock hard, he'd gotten used to the cold showers. Hopefully after last night, he'd no longer have a need for those.

When you're immortal you don't plan on dying, so you have to make your heaven right here on earth, and Kara was Alexander's. There was nothing better than Kara's body molded against his. It was as close to heaven as Alexander would ever come.

"Were these yours?" Kara pointed around the room.

Alexander nuzzled her neck. "Yes, do you like them?"

She let out a breathless sigh. "They all look pretty sexy. I'm sure I'll have fantasies with you wearing them."

He chuckled amusingly. "I bet I could make those fantasies come true. Does my lady have any particular preference?"

"That one!" She pointed.

"Ahh! My Roman Centurion armor. Red. Of course. I'll keep that in mind." He nibbled her ear, kissing a path down her neck.

Kara closed her eyes as Alexander held her. His arm placed just under her breasts, had her body instantly standing up and taking notice of him. Kara's hormones were working overtime. Every inch of her body was on fire, begging her to take Alexander inside her. Kara knew she should pull away; she didn't want to give him the wrong idea. *Like you're easy. He knows you're not. Duh! You were a virgin.* Kara turned around wrapping her arms around his neck.

Alexander held his breath as Kara turned in his arms, wrapping her arms around him. He dropped his arms to her waist, giving her support since she was still weak.

Kara entwined her fingers through his silky blond hair, pulling Alexander down to reach his soft luscious lips. Lips that drove her wild. Alexander picked her up, making it easier for her to reach him. Their tongues were sliding and dancing along each other's, reminding them of last night's coupling, and all the passion they had shared.

Alexander scooped her up, never breaking their kiss. He carried her to his sitting room, gently settling her on the couch. "What's on the tray?" Kara asked inquisitively.

Alexander placed the tray in front of her, before sitting down beside her. "Breakfast. You're hungry…are you not?"

"Famished." She admitted looking over the pastries. "They look delicious. What are they?"

"Bomboloni and Brioches" Alexander smiled. "An Italian breakfast."

"Oooooooooooo" Kara squealed in delight, kissing his cheek. "Thank you. My first Italian breakfast."

Alexander laughed at her enthusiasm. "If it's this easy to please you, I'll serve you breakfast from a different country everyday."

"Cheeky Dark-Soul!" Kara flashed him a wicked smile. "You won't get off that easy."

Alexander pulled her into his lap, licking crème off her lips from the Bomboloni. She moaned from his wet caress. "Baby, I…*get off* every time you touch me." Alexander whispered, as he moved Kara's hand to cover his cock.

Kara jumped at his double entendre. *Oh-my-god! I think I just creamed my panties. I can play this game with a little innuendo of my own.* "I…um…feel your *point*. I think I could relieve your discomfort."

Alexander cocked an amused eyebrow. "What did you have in mind, my lady?" He asked in that deep seductive voice she loved. Kara's laughter was infectious as Alexander fell back onto the couch pulling her with him.

"I like this." Kara kissed him playfully. First on his lips, then she worked her way over to his ear. "Of course, you brought all that yummy food. We should eat it; otherwise I might end up eating… you." She teased nipping his ear.

Alexander had never seen Kara so carefree…so wanton. She'd changed, and he wasn't sure why, but he was enjoying it. With Kara's last nip on his ear, Alexander could no longer control himself. He moaned from the sensations that ran down his spine, and buried his face in Kara's hair before nuzzling her neck. "What has come over you?" He breathed in her ear. "Don't get me wrong, I'm enjoying it, but what changed?"

Kara pulled back studying Alexander's curious gaze while tracing his sweet lips. "Since the first time we met, I've been fighting my attraction towards you. It scared me. Even though I've waited my whole life for my soul-mate, this relationship truly scared me, but yesterday, I decided I will no longer fight my feelings for you. I'm going to embrace them, and give our relationship a fighting chance."

The word 'scared' froze Alexander, just before the dread set in. Is she afraid of him and his kind? If she is then he wouldn't be able to change that. He is who he is. "Why are you afraid of me, Kara?"

Kara looked away as the one question left his lips that she never wanted to answer. *How am I going to explain to a warrior, that I'm a total coward? How can I explain to Alexander, that as much as I dream about my soul-mate, I'm afraid of being hurt in another relationship. He'll never understand.*

Alexander turned Kara's face back to his. When he saw the agony and fear in her eyes, he choked, afraid of what she would say, but knowing he had to know. "Why are you afraid of me, Kara? I need to know."

Understanding she couldn't get out of this explanation, she took a deep breath and cupped his face with both hands. "First. You need to understand I'm not afraid of *you,* Alexander. You've been nothing but kind to me. You're funny, sweet, *extremely sexy*...how could I not be attracted to you."

"I don't understand......" Kara stopped him by placing her finger over his mouth.

"Please it's hard enough to admit this...Just let me finish...then you can say anything you like. Ok?" Alexander nodded, making the imaginary zipper on his lips and handed her the key. Kara smiled at his kindness. "See, it's those sweet things you do, that's pushing me to stop hiding my feelings." She took another deep breath, and slowly let it out.

Alexander was amazed at how sad and cautious Kara looked. "Ok." She began again. "It's not *you* I'm afraid of. It's the relationship. I wouldn't call myself overly experienced with relationships, but I'm not under experienced either. I've dated some, but I was always looking for my soul-mate. That one person who could give me what my grandparents and parents have. Three times I thought I'd found it, and all three times I've had my heart ripped apart. What *scares* me…is the intense feelings I feel when I'm around you. They make a mockery of the feelings I had in my other relationships. I knew if I got to close to you…this time …it could……" Kara straightened up. "You know…it doesn't matter. I've decided I can't ignore my feelings. I have to follow them and see where they lead. I have to take this chance, so the rest really doesn't matter."

Alexander was stunned and relieved at the same time. He was relieved that this had nothing to do with him being a Cruetian, but he was shocked at the depth of her pain. These men had hurt her deeply. It set off a fury that only his enemies on the battlefield had ever seen. He wanted their blood for hurting Kara. More than that he wanted to reassure her, this relationship would be different. If Kara was a Cruetian, she'd know he could never hurt his *Amara*, his chosen one, but she's not. She's human, so Alexander would need to prove it to her. "Kara, what did these men do to hurt you, to make you afraid of relationships?"

She looked down clearly embarrassed. "The first one cheated on me, because I refused to sleep with him. The second one chose his family over me. His family didn't want him marrying an American. They thought I was beneath him, and the third joined the military." Kara snarled, spitting out her next words. "He decided he wanted his freedom, so he could *sample* the women of the world." She caught his gaze. "You see, I'm not good enough for you. I couldn't even hold onto three, very average human men, so how am I supposed to be enough for you. Look at you." She waived her hands up and down his body. "You're perfect. You're drop dead gorgeous. You should have someone who is equivalent to you, someone who can hold your attention. Otherwise, just like all men you'll stray." Kara started to move off him, but Alexander quickly pulled her back.

"You're wrong! You're extremely beautiful, and absolutely my equal. I'm flattered you think I'm perfect, but I'm far from it. I will *not* lie to you, Kara. I have lived 2300 years. I've slept with numerous women. I've also been married, and had long term relationships. The one thing I can assure you, is that even during war, when I was away from home, I've never strayed. Not even when history allowed it. These three men you speak of…were complete idiots. They had no idea what a treasure they had. I guarantee you I'll never hurt you that way. I will never take you for granted, nor will I ever stray. You're more than enough for me, and if you ever accept my hand, I would be extremely honored, and would never deceive you. This I can swear to you, Kara." With great fervor he added, "I will *not* hurt you."

Alexander was determined to let Kara feel his sincerity. As he embraced her, he kissed her with a passion that left Kara limp in his arms. How this man could kiss. Kara forgot every objection she had, as Alexander slid his hand under her nightgown and pulled her closer to him. His hands on her skin, built a fire deep inside her that begged for release. She wanted this man like she'd never wanted another. No. She needed this man like she's never needed another. It was obvious that with every stroke of his hand, with every movement of his tongue, he set her blood boiling. At this very moment, Kara didn't need air, food, or even water to live. She needed Alexander. She could feel his stiff bulge, as she reached down and cupped him gently. He moaned so deep it reverberated through her, giving her a sense of satisfaction.

Alexander jumped from the intense desire that slammed into him, when Kara stroked him. How could that intensify? His whole body has been hot and bothered since the day he met her, just thinking about her gives him an erection. In yet, when she touched him, that need increased tenfold. Oh! How he wanted inside her again, but he couldn't take her right now. Kara was still hurt, and she needed her rest.

Alexander took her hand and kissed it. "Kara…Love, I only have so much control. As much as I enjoy what you're doing, we can't do this right now. You're still hurt, and you need your rest. We have to wait. It's been too soon since last night." Damn! He really hated saying those words.

She chuckled. "Always a doctor" she kissed his cheek. "Alright Dr. Conti, I'll try to be good, even though it won't be easy." Kara gently traced Alexander's bottom lip. "You drive me crazy, but I'll try to behave myself. Should we……" but before Kara could finish her thought someone cleared their throat.

"Uh-hum......"

Alexander sat up, setting Kara on the couch. "This better be important, Nathaniel." He growled.

Kara looked up to see Nathaniel hovering in the doorway. "Kara's family is downstairs. Just thought you might want to know. They're waiting for you to...release her." Nathaniel chuckled amusingly. "I mean as her doctor, of course."

"Shut up, Nathaniel!" Alexander snapped, glaring at him. "We'll be right out. Leave us."

Alexander's breath caught in his throat, when he saw the adoring look in Kara's eyes. "You brought my family here? I thought you said this place was secret."

He ran the back of his knuckles over her cheek. That look alone was worth risking the location of his home. "I knew you'd want to see them, and they were worried about you."

Kara reached over, gently kissing his soft lips. They were really the only soft place on Alexander's hard warrior body. "Thank you! How can I ever repay your kindness?"

Alexander chuckled and winked at her. In a very seductive voice he purred, "I'm sure we can think of something...later."

Normally, such an arrogant statement would have pissed her off, but not coming from Alexander. All it did was lead to anticipation, and a burning in her body that demanded *his* attention. Kara's heart leaped out of her chest, pounding so fast that even she could hear it, so she knew he could. With that thought she blushed. Alexander chuckled again and kissed her hand.

"I'll go down and greet your family. Take a bath, it'll relieve the soreness. One side of the walk-in closet is yours. Adelina and I bought you a wardrobe; hopefully you can find something you like to wear." Alexander cocked his head, as if he was listening to something. "Lunch will be served at noon, so you have about an hour. If you need anything, don't hesitate to call." He pointed to an intercom system. "Any questions?"

Irritated, Kara crossed her arms over her chest, pushing up her breasts in an offering that was driving Alexander insane. "You know I don't like being bossed around. I'm not one of your generals, *Commander*. But…I'm feeling generous today, so I'm going to forgive your demanding tone…this time."

Alexander had anticipated Kara's reply, and it amused him more than he thought it would.

Kara realized that Alexander had an amused smile on his gorgeous face. His gaze locked with hers for what seemed like forever, before he finally spoke. "I'll go give your family a tour." He brushed his lips against hers, and headed for the door.

Alexander stood outside the door, pulling himself together. He needed to catch his breath before facing anyone. He knew he shouldn't have irritated Kara, but he loved the reddish glow of her cheeks, the sparkle in her eyes, and how her voice became an octave lower, it made his body yearn for her. She was seductive as hell, and she didn't even know it. He laughed as he went to find her family.

15

Kara sat on a bench in City Park overlooking the lake. She always enjoyed being outdoors, especially on such a beautifully warm day like today. After a successful lunch with her family, she had decided she needed a little time alone to contemplate everything she's learned in the last two days, before having to meet Becky and her bridal party for their gown fittings at a local boutique.

Alexander had finally given her a tour of his estate, which was quite impressive and then offered to let her use his car, but when he took her to his amazingly huge garage, every car there was at least a quarter million dollars. She couldn't even fathom driving one of them. Alexander just laughed at her, and told her to get in a car she'd never even heard of, and that's saying something, since she's sort of a car buff. A hobby she picked up living with her brothers. She had to admit, the car, or should she call it an...*automobile,* was exotic. A Pagani Roadster F, which Alexander had explained is an Italian company and they only make...like twenty cars a year. Definitely an *automobile* fit for his whole 'I'm-sexy-as-hell' persona. Alexander joked that the fates had made him buy it. Pointing out that the Pagani had a black exterior with a red leather interior. Both our favorite colors combined together.

Lunch had been spectacular. He had brought in an Italian chef that cooked the most amazing dishes she had ever tasted. Her family, which only consisted of her parents and grandparents today, even refrained from embarrassing her. It was wonderful, and led to some pretty interesting conversations. Most of the conversations she had found fascinating. Although, she wasn't thrilled to find out that Alexander had paid her employees a bonus to care for her store while she's away.

He's obviously quite wealthy, but she didn't want to impose on his generosity.

Kara had learned some intriguing facts about vampires. Like the reason vampires can't go out into the sun and Dark-Souls can, is because of their eyes. When a vampire drinks a human dry, it creates a red ring around the vampire's iris, causing blindness to light. They won't burst into flames or anything, but they can't see, which leaves them vulnerable. Most things are simply myth, like garlic, holy water, crosses, wooden stakes; none of those will protect a human from a vampire, and Alexander admitted that they didn't want to scare humans, so the Cruetians let us believe our little fantasies of protection. He said the best protection for humans, is that once they become a vampire, they can't go into a home without an invitation. This is thanks to how the Goddess Hecate changed the Cruetian curse.

Kara noticed the three cowboys who had attacked her at Mel's, lurking around some trees, and she became nervous. She jumped up and began running the two blocks to the gown fitting.

Why are they following me? What do they want? Could these be the guys who beat me up?

She slowed down long enough to pull on her jacket, instantly she picked up the sweet, spicy scent that was powerfully masculine and all Alexander. It enveloped her. Oh! Kara inhaled deeply. It must be lingering from his earlier embrace. It left her aching to run back to him, but gave her a feeling of being protected, and gave her more confidence as she slowed to a walk.

Kara and Becky were quite pleased. The gown fittings were proceeding without any difficulty. Everyone had shown up on time. Becky never was one for the traditional look, so the bridesmaid gowns were straight from the bodice down, tight enough to show every curve, and left little if anything to the imagination. Becky's gown was of course, white and strapless, with a long elegant train. She chose to ignore the veil and go with a simple tiara instead. The bridesmaid gowns were a lovely peach color that Becky insisted enhanced Kara's skin tone, and since she was her maid of honor, the dress should match her and the rest of the bridesmaid's would have to live with it. Not that it really mattered, because all the bridesmaids were her sisters, except Carla, so their skin tones were somewhat similar to hers. Unlike Becky's strapless gown, the bridesmaid gowns had halters, which Becky explained made Kara's breasts look fabulous, showing just enough cleavage without giving it all away. Kara had tried to convince her that no one was going to be looking at her, with Becky wearing that amazing wedding gown. So the bridesmaid gowns really didn't matter, but Becky disagreed.

Waving her arm like she was waving a wand, Becky stated. "In that dress, you might just come back a married woman yourself, or at least I'm hoping you'll no longer be a virgin after my wedding."

Kara's mouth fell open. *No she did not. She did not just say that with everyone at the fitting.* All of her sisters and both of their moms were there, not to mention Kevin's sister, Carla. *What the hell is she thinking saying that out loud?* They were all laughing so hard at her expression, before Kara finally found enough sense to shut her gaping mouth. "I can't believe you just said that. Here…in public…in front of our moms." She squealed horrified.

"It's not like we don't all know. This *is* a small town, Kara, and besides that's nothing to be ashamed about. Both your grandmothers say it's an endearing quality that someday a man will appreciate about you." Melody, Kara's mom replied.

"Good, because I think Kara likes the fact that she's still *"technically"* a virgin. Even though I don't know if you can actually consider her that with everything else she's done." Kali tried to hold back her smile and grimace, but it didn't work. She was now laughing as hard as everyone else.

"Oh yeah! Miss I'll-do-anything-oral-as-long-as-you-don't-stick-me." Kami howled. As soon as it slipped off her tongue, everyone burst into hysterics.

Kali was laughing so hard, she had tears streaming down her face when she replied looking at Becky. "Well, *Mrs. Experience.* If you don't mind Kara bringing a date to your wedding, you might just get your wish. She just might be willing to give up her virgin status."

"Dr. Conti?" Melody asked.

"The vampire?" Carla quizzed.

Becky instantly stopped laughing and frowned at Carla's comment. Now that everyone had stopped laughing, they noticed the little old sales lady had been staring at them in disbelief with her mouth gaping open. When she realized they'd noticed her, her mouth popped shut and she turned on her heels and went back to the front of the store. Kara was still chuckling at the sales lady's expression when Becky grabbed her arm and made her sit down on a couch.

"Have you found him? The man you're always claiming you're saving yourself for, or have you finally come to your senses?" Everyone waited patiently for her answer.

Kara sighed, knowing she was going to have to explain Alexander to them sooner or later. She wasn't sure exactly why she hadn't discussed her feelings about him. They probably knew. How could they not? But, she was worried about what they would think, and about them being judgmental. She didn't know how they would feel about the situation, so like a coward; she had been avoiding this discussion with her family, dismissing their prying little comments. Comments like… *You look like you're glowing, or if you float any higher, I'm going to attach a string to you and pull you around like a balloon.* Kara just hadn't had the guts to tell them she thought she was unconditionally in love with Alexander. It didn't help either, that most of her friends made no qualms about the fact that she should be with Steven. *Gross!* She couldn't even stand to be around him. He's such a male chauvinistic pig!

When Kara had first arrived at the fitting, Carla had made a point to tell her that her brothers had knocked Steven around a bit, and it had opened Steven's eyes to his treatment of women. *My ass! I don't care how much my brothers beat the shit out of Steven; he'll never learn how to treat a woman.* Steven just doesn't want to die, and he knows after the prom situation, her brothers would kill him for her.

Kara smiled remembering Alexander's comment when he dropped her off at the park. "Hey gorgeous, I can't be away from those scrumptious curves all day, so I'll pick you up in a couple hours, OK?" She loved when he talked to her that way. He could be so proper, so elegant, and then other times he could be just downright sexy. She loved it.

Kara finally caved. "Ok! Yes, I'm serious about Alexander…very serious. He might actually be my soul-mate." She cringed, waiting for their attack. "Are you all happy now?"

"No shit! I was wondering when you were going to eventually tell your so called best friend." Pouted Becky, "It's not like we're all blind, you know."

"How about her family?" Kasi complained taking off the dress she'd been trying on. "I'm her twin, for God's sake and she didn't even confide in me, bee-atch"

"Girls stop!" Melody stepped in. "I knew when Kara was ready to tell us she would."

Kara patted the couch motioning for Becky to sit next to her. "Come on Becky, you know it's not like that. I was having trouble facing it myself. I was afraid of being hurt again…I didn't mean to hurt your feelings."

Facing her family, "and for all of you, I just didn't know how you would react."

"Why? Because he's a vampire…a doctor…or because you seem pretty serious about him?" Melody asked.

"Mom….."

"You're dating the vampire doc?" Carla interrupted in horror. "Are you serious? Can they even…you know…have a…well… relationship? I mean…like sex…you know…with humans."

Angry Kara snapped back. "See. This is why I didn't tell anyone."

Becky put her arm around Kara's shoulders. "Kara, you're my best friend. You're like a sister to me. I don't care who you're with, I just want you to be happy. I remember how you were with Steven in high school. Well, before he became an ass." Becky gave a pointed look to Carla, "I'm sure Carla was hoping that he had grown up enough that he could make you happy again. We all know when Kevin left, it tore your heart out, and you've never quite been the same. We just wanted you to start having fun again, that's all."

"You know Kevin did come back and ask her to marry him." Carla said defensively. "This time, she's the one that turned him down."

"Shut up, Carla." Becky yelled. "He canceled their wedding and ripped her heart out, and then he had the nerve to change his mind. What'd you expect her to do? Jump his bones and forgive him. We all know she's not capable of that type of forgiveness."

Kara stood by listening to them argue. Her worst fear had been dissolved, they were supporting her and Alexander, and it was more than she had dreamed possible. "You really just want me to be happy? I was afraid you were going to be judgmental, that's why I was afraid to tell you. You really are part of my family, Becky, and your acceptance means a lot to me."

"You know" Daphne walked over to her. "They can have children, so that must mean they can have sex." Kara blushed.

Kara thought back over the last couple of days with Alexander. She remembered how their kisses had become so steamy that her body had become hot and bothered in all kinds of places. She remembered his soft lips on her breasts, his hands sliding down her waist, her hips, down to her thighs…then it hit her. She remembered him saying that they can only have kids with their *Amaras*. Did that include a human *Amara*? They were obviously capable of having great sex, but did their anatomy work the same way as a humans for reproduction. For the first time in Kara's life her body was jumping up and down saying *take me, take me now!* And she didn't even know if their species were compatible. She'd asked Alexander about sex at Mel's, but why hadn't she asked about children? She wanted children, and as a crown prince he'd need an heir.

Kara could pinpoint the exact moment she had thought about sex with him. They were in one of their flaming kisses, when she had startled Alexander by pulling away abruptly.

She remembered the hurt and confusion in his eyes as he asked, "Is something wrong?"

"No…but I was curious…about……" Kara had stuttered.

"What are you curious about?"

"Are you capable of physical relationships? I mean the way humans think of……"

Alexander chuckled and when Kara looked up he had a very amused smile on his face.

"Ah! You want to know if Dark-Souls are capable of having sexual relations with humans...or more to the point...if you and I are capable at having a sexual relationship."

Kara had felt the heat swarm her face as she choked out, "Yes!"

"Kara...Love, when you are ready, that will *not* be a problem."

Kara was ripped back to reality when Becky's mom spoke. She hadn't realized it, but this whole time, Charlene had been leaning against a wall listening to the conversation, but she hadn't said a word. Not one word. This has to be a record for her, because Charlene never shuts up.

"How do you know that?" Charlene asked. Unlike her daughter's thin tall frame, Charlene was a beautiful, dark hair, blue eyed, voluptuous woman. German through and through, she believes a skinny girl is unhealthy. A fact she constantly let her skinny daughter and Kara know.

"I go to school with a few vampires, I mean Dark-Souls. They explained that even though Dark-Souls only have to renew their diplomas, their children still have to get their first educations the same way we do. The Dark-Souls that go to my school are all my age. They are Dark-Soul's children, or as they call themselves, Cruetian children. They really hate the word vampire. They told me that their people have always been called Dark-Souls by humans, but their species is called Cruetians. It comes from the word Cruentos, meaning blood thirsty. I think it was Latin or Ancient Greek. I forgot which one."

"I had no idea." Charlene said in amazement.

Confirming what her sister was saying, Kara replied, "Yes, she's right. Alexander's no different than a human male."

"Really? Have you?" Becky asked, but turned around and answered her own question, "No, you haven't, because if you had...I know you would have told me that. That's something you couldn't keep from me."

Kara blushed then faked a laugh. She wasn't ready for everyone to know she'd slept with Alexander. She didn't want them making a big deal about her losing her virginity. It was already their favorite topic. "Yeah, you're right. When I do finally allow a guy to have *all* of me, you'll be the first to know…right after him, of course. I wouldn't want to deal with the wrath of Becky."

Becky was still fidgeting with her wedding gown while they all gossiped over Kara's love life.

"Well Ker, if he makes you happy, then he's ok with me. You should bring him to the wedding. He seems like a good guy. Look at everything he's already done for you." Becky turned on her suddenly. "Hey! Is he a good kisser?"

Kara giggled, *"OH! YEAH!* You have no idea. His tongue should be *illegal.* In fact, it probably is in some countries." Then they were all laughing hysterically again.

"All right then. Ladies, I still have a lot to do today, so let's wrap this up. Kara is Alexander going to come to your birthday party? That'll give everyone time to get to know him better." Melody insisted.

"Um…You all actually already know him." She reminded them. "You met him at Mel's and dad and you had lunch with us today. Besides Alexander has friends coming in town, I don't think he can leave them alone. They're from out of the country."

Becky punched her shoulder. "You're lucky that I know you're still healing, or I would punch you so hard, it would leave a bruise. You know what we're talking about. You're serious about him. This changes everything, he has to come."

Kara hated when they ganged up on her. She had hoped to keep Alexander away from them, at least for a little while. Obviously, that's not going to happen. Maybe she could at least lessen the shock for him by keeping it to her immediate family and Becky. Hopefully that would lessen the chance of her embarrassment. Her family had become pro's at embarrassing her.

She let out an 'I-surrender' sigh. "Ok, I'll ask him, but no promises. Like I said, he has friends coming into town. Just one favor? Could we please keep it to immediate family and Becky?"

"Can't do that, it's a birthday party…remember." Melody chastised.

"Of course she won't keep Bob and I away, we're her second

parents. That makes us immediate family." Charlene scolded her, wagging a finger in Kara's direction.

"Dammit, you guys! I really do like him. Could you all *try* to behave? No twenty questions. Please?" Kara begged.

Becky put her arm around her. "Don't worry everyone; we're meeting him at a new club in Denver tonight. If Kara doesn't ask him, I will."

Kara rolled her eyes in defeat. "Sometimes I wish I lived in Antarctica. At least then I'd only have to hear your voices and read your letters."

"What club are you going to?" Carla stepped out of the dressing room, hanging her dress on the hanger.

"Club Nouveau in Denver." Kali answered.

Carla smiled. "Do you mind if my friends and I meet you there? It's supposed to be better than the one here in town, and that one's awesome. I can't even imagine what this new one's going to be like."

"Of course not. Your one of my bridesmaids, come along." Becky agreed before Kara could ask who she was planning on bringing. She hoped Carla wouldn't be stupid enough to bring Steven with her, or if she did it would be as Carla's date.

As they were all leaving in separate directions, Arabella hugged Kara. "You know you love me. You'd miss me in Antarctica, and we'd all miss you. Don't worry about the party, everyone there loves you with all their heart. We would never hurt you, Ker. If your Alexander can't see how much we love and adore you, even when we embarrass you sometimes, or when we ask him embarrassing personal questions, then he's not that right man for you. We only ask those questions to protect you, and he should understand that." She kissed Kara's cheek before getting into the passenger side of her mom's Maxima.

Kara waved goodbye as they drove away. She knew Arabella was right. Her family's only crime *was* loving her too much. The funny thing is that she does the exact same thing with each of them. What she calls…embarrassing, when Kara does it to one of them, she calls it…protection.

Kara realized she'd missed a call as she went back in to meet Becky.

It was Alexander asking her to meet him at the club. Something had come up and he had to be there early, and since he couldn't reach her, the only option was for her to meet him there.

Two hours later Kara was getting into her parents Suburban to make the drive to Denver. She was so excited she couldn't sit still. In a little over an hour she would be with Alexander. The day had gone by so slowly, it seemed like an eternity since she last saw him, since he last kissed her, but she was heading his way, and she would be in his strong, protective arms soon enough.

"Damn, girl. You're sizzelin." Kali teased. "When was the last time you really dressed up? Alexander's eyes are going to pop out of his head. I bet he's never seen you look that hot."

It was true, Kara hadn't really dressed up since Kevin had left her, but today she spent the entire two hours getting ready. She curled her long blonde hair, and put the sides up, so all the curls hung down her back in wringlets. She wore a black mini dress that cut down the front to show off just enough cleavage, to hopefully make Alexander wild with desire, and to make herself feel sexy. She even wore a matching lacy red bra and thong ensemble. She accented the outfit with a wide, blood red belt, to show off her tiny waist, five inch blood red stilettos and blood red jewelry. She even took the time to redo her makeup into what she liked to call, 'Clubbin makeup'. Kara couldn't disagree with Kali, because when she looked into the mirror, she honestly felt hot and sexy.

"I don't know." Becky countered from the backseat. "She's been doing things with Alexander that's out of character for the *prude* Kara. He might actually know our old *wild* Kara."

"That'll be the day" Kami chimed in from the far backseat. "Kevin didn't even know the *wild* Kara."

"You all might be wrong......" Alan started to say as he received a hostile stare from five women, ready to take him down if he had a stupid comment.

"Wrong!" Becky snapped. "Who's wrong?"

Alan held his hands up to surrender. "I was just going to point out that when you find the right person your ideals change. That's all."

Kasi snorted. "My twin finding *Mr. Right? Mr. Right* is a fairytale to her, he doesn't exist. Kara is looking for the perfect man, and we all know there is no such thing as *the perfect man,* only *the flawed man.*"

"Jee, thanks Kas. I love you to." Alan said in a martyred tone.

Becky laughed taking his hand, "You already know all your faults, sweetheart. I've pointed them out to you on many occasions, but don't worry, I still love you." She bent across him and gave him a passionate kiss.

Kara spent the entire hour listening to them discuss her love life… or lack thereof, as if she wasn't there, but she didn't care, for every mile Kali drove, she was closer to Alexander, and that was all that mattered to her.

16

Thank God for GPS, it took them right to their destination. They pulled up in front of a beautiful glass three story building. As Kara marveled at the architecture, she wondered what type of glass had been used to create such a magnificent structure. It was obviously glass, but you couldn't see inside, the glass simply sparkled like crystal. Above the double glass doors was a giant pink and blue neon sign '*Club Nouveau*'. The valet came around and opened her door; he looked about her age, somewhere in his mid-twenties. He took her hand and helped her out, continuing around the Suburban to help everyone else.

"I need your name for the valet tag." He stated to Kali, waiting with a pen and pad in his hand.

"Kali…K.A.L.I." She spelled her name as he wrote it on the tab. "Spencer." His head jerked up.

"Are you related to Miss Kara Spencer?" He asked urgently.

"You know my sister?" Kali asked suspiciously. Especially since Kara was standing right next to her.

"No." He replied. "Which one of you is Miss Kara Spencer?" He glanced around at the group.

Becky mouthed to Kasi, "*Miss Kara Spencer?*" as Kasi shrugged, not understanding what this valet wanted, or how he knew Kara's name.

"I'm Kara Spencer." Kara stepped forward holding out her hand to shake his.

Refusing her hand he bowed low and deep. "Miss Kara, it's an honor. Please have your group follow me."

Confused, everyone followed. Kara could hear them whispering amongst themselves, trying to figure out what was going on. She hadn't told them that Alexander's family owned *Club Nouveau*. She didn't think it was anybody's business, of course, she hadn't anticipated his staff knowing who she was either.

He guided them through a side door, where two security guards sat. They were both huge, like the wrestlers you see on T.V. One of them had a crew cut, while the other was bald, but both looked incredibly mean. No one was getting through these two, unless they allowed them onto the premises.

"This is Miss Kara Spencer." He waved his hand over her, "and her companions."

The bald security guard came forward bowing. "My pleasure, Miss Kara. I'm Henry. If you and your companions would wait here for a moment, I'll get Magnus."

As soon as he left, Kasi grabbed Kara's arm and spun her around. "Ok, Missy. What the hell is going on? Oh, and don't tell me you don't know."

"Their treating you like some sort of celebrity. Fess up!" Kami stood tapping her foot waiting.

Kara guiltily sighed. "Alright! I didn't think it was my place to tell you, but Alexander and his family own this club. I didn't know that until this afternoon when I told him we were coming here. I'm sorry guys. I can assure you, I didn't know he was going to make such a big deal out of this. I wasn't trying to embarrass anyone."

"Sorry? This is great." Kami hugged her, as Henry came back with a very tall, dark, and handsome man. He was definitely a Dark-Soul. He had that same 'walking-GQ-cover-model' image that Kara had come to accept from Cruetian men. He was a good three inches taller than Alexander, with long jet black hair that was pulled back into a pony tail and deep blue eyes. Henry pointed to Kara as Magnus walked towards her.

Taken her hand, he kissed her knuckles. "Miss Kara, it's an honor ta meet *Kyrios's Amara*." He put her hand in the crook of his arm, motioning to everyone else, "please follow me. General Alexander is anxiously awaitin yer arrival."

They walked into a large bustling modern club. 'Let's Dance' was echoing around the dance floor. A large round stage stood in the center of a glass dance floor that was flashing neon colors underneath it. The side wall was a long crystal bar, with the same neon lights flashing at its base. There were small tables surrounding the dance floor, and large booths further away near the glass walls. At the back of the dance floor was a double stair case that lead upstairs, where glass balconies hung over the dance floor. Kara assumed those were private suites. Magnus led them up the stairs to the second floor.

The second floor was darker than the main floor. Another crystal bar, like the one downstairs, lined the back wall, but there was no dance floor on this level, just doors to the rooms that Kara had seen downstairs. He led her to the one of the doors on the right. As he opened the door, she was amazed at how large the suite actually was. The balconies she had seen downstairs were actually private dance floors for each suite. The rest of the suite was furnished with comfortable couches, chairs and small tables.

As she entered the room she recognized most of the people inside. Nathaniel and Kalab sat in chairs against the far wall, across from them sat Uncle Chung, Kelmar, and Namorita, both of whom Kara had met at lunch today. Near the private dance floor Adelina sat with a man she didn't recognize. He was equally as impressive as the rest of the men in the room. He was muscular with reddish-golden hair and an unusual yellow eye color. His eyes were pretty, in a weird kind of way. At the back wall were two small couches that Alexander and another man that she didn't know sat talking.

"*Kyrios,* yer lady has arrived." Magnus bowed.

'*Your lady?*' Kami mouthed to Kali. Who in turn whispered in Becky's ear, "Kara definitely has some explaining to do."

Before Kara could blink, Alexander jumped up and had his arms around her. He bent down brushing his lips against hers sending a wave of electricity crawling all over her body. "Thank you, Magnus." he breathed against Kara's lips.

Alexander couldn't get over just how good Kara felt in his arms.

All day he'd felt empty, now with her here, he felt whole again. Her simple touch, soothed him in ways he couldn't understand, pulling at his heart, demanding him to keep her near.

That simple touch of their lips was not nearly enough for Kara as she took his lips passionately. Alexander was pleased at her aggressive kiss. She was demanding, unyielding, and she set his body on fire. When Kara finally pulled back she enjoyed seeing the glossy look in *his* eyes.

"Uh-hum......" Alexander and Kara looked over at the Becky. "Hi, Alexander." Amused she smiled at them, "I know you two seem to have trouble keeping your hands off each other," there was chuckles around the room "but...we just wanted to say thank you for welcoming all of us to your club. We're all going down to the dance floor while you two," Becky swung her hand between Alexander and Kara, "get each other out of your systems. Then we'll come back and socialize. See you in a little while, Ker."

Kara bit her bottom lip as she looked up at Alexander. "Sorry." She said timidly as her family left the suite.

"Personally, I enjoy the fact that you missed me." He brushed a stray hair away from her face, grazing his eyes up and down her body with approval, awakening hormones she never knew existed until this moment. "You're radiantly beautiful. So much so, I'm not going to be able to keep my eyes off you. You're absolutely stunning, and...I missed you to."

His words sent Kara soaring as she smiled up at him. Alexander took her hand, and guided her to a couch, pulling her down beside him.

Kara looked around the room acknowledging each of them. "Hi, Nathaniel. Why is a hot bod like you up here, instead of downstairs grinding with all the babes?" She teased.

"Duty!"

"Oh, that sucks. Good to see you again Kalab...Namorita... Kelmar." She nodded her head to each of them, which they returned with similar jerks of their heads.

"Hi, Adelina. It's good to see you again. I don't think I've met your fox."

"Wolf!" The man holding her corrected.

"Excuse me?" Kara asked. "I've never heard a cute guy referred to as a wolf. Fox...yes. Wolf...No. Never heard it, but if you prefer being called a wolf, who am I to argue." Everyone laughed.

"Sweetheart, Walter is a Lycan." Alexander stated as if that should explain everything.

"A what?" Kara looked for clarification.

"A Lycan...A Werewolf...Walter is a Werewolf." Her mouth dropped to the floor, as she stared at Walter with disbelief in her eyes.

"Well, that was smart, Alexander." Adelina came and sat down next to her. "She probably didn't know Werewolves actually existed until now." Adelina took Kara's hand, "Kara? Kara, look at me."

Kara finally pulled herself together long enough to look at Adelina, and stuttered. "So...he...like...really turns into...a wolf?"

Adelina nodded her head. "Yes, he can, but just like my people; a lot of what humans believe about Werewolves is myth. He will not hurt a human, unless he is provoked. He's a good man, Kara. I should know he's been my husband for over 300 years."

Kara was trying to deal with the fear that was running rampid through her body. Adelina had just assured her that he wouldn't hurt a human, and she really had no choice but to trust her, but...a Werewolf. Chills went up and down her spine. Walter was Alexander's brother-in-law, and someday Kara hoped to be a part of this family, so she had better get used to these types of unusual circumstances.

Alexander wasn't sure what to do. Had he scared Kara to the point he could lose her? She hadn't run off...yet, but she hadn't moved for a few minutes either. So far everyone in the room was holding their breath to see what she would do. Kara was the future of his people, and every person in that room knew that. Fear struck him as she stood up. Is she leaving? If she is, what should he do to stop her? Damn, he hated feeling so helpless, and completely out of his element. Alexander stood up to follow her.

Kara could sense the fear in the room, and knew they were all waiting for her to make the next move. She could see the fear and uncertainty in Alexander's eyes. Wanting to comfort him, she reached over and touched his arm. "It's ok." She smiled, and before he could say anything, she walked over to Walter, who immediately stood up as she approached. Kara gasped as he came to his full height. He was easily seven feet tall, and was a giant compared to her.

"Pleased to meet you, Walter." Kara's voice slightly trembled as she held out her hand to him in a friendly gesture. Walter grabbed her hand and shook it. "The pleasure's all mine, Kara." She glanced around the room, and jokingly said. "You can all breathe now; I have no intention of freaking out."

Kara walked over to her uncle and sat down on his lap. "You could have warned me, you know." He just laughed and hugged her, then kissed her cheek.

"Chung!" The unknown man yelled jumping up. Just before he lunged, Alexander grabbed him and pushed him back into the couch. "Alexander! He's *touching* your *Amara*."

"Chung is her uncle." Alexander tried to explain to this unknown man, who was extremely agitated. Personally, Kara felt it wasn't any of his business. Who did he think he was interfering in her life?

"What are you talking about?" He demanded.

"I don't think it's any of your business." Kara snapped. "Who the hell is he?" She snarled at Alexander.

"Kara, meet my brother. Tiberius." Alexander said rubbing his forehead. "Tiberius, my extremely stubborn, independent, and strong willed *Amara*, Kara." Giving Kara a warning look, which she just rolled her eyes at. "Kara, allow me to explain this to my brother, please." Alexander turned back to Tiberius. "I found General Chung *with* Kara. Chung's a friend of her grandparents, and helped raise Kara. He sort of adopted her, or as he likes to say she adopted him as her uncle. One more thing you should know, Kara tends to be very affectionate with her friends and family."

"Sorry for jumping to conclusions, Chung." Turning towards Kara he extended his hand, "I'm Tiberius, the second born son in our family. It's a pleasure to finally meet you. Hopefully, there are no hard feelings?"

Kara gladly shook his hand. "Never! Anytime you're working with different cultures there's bound to be misunderstandings."

Tiberius laughed. "You're absolutely right."

Kara heard the door open and Becky, Alan, Carla, and Steven strolled into the room. *Shit!* She had been afraid of this. She knew she should have stopped Becky from inviting Carla, or demanded she not invite Steven to come along with her.

"Hey Ker, look who came to wish you a Happy Birthday?" Becky said irritated.

"Birthday?" Alexander asked. Kara waived him off to thank her new guests. "Thank you, but you didn't need to come all the way here to tell me that."

"We didn't mind." Carla looked around at everyone smiling. "Did we Steven? Besides he wanted to see you."

Kara cringed. "Why? I thought the two of you are together, the way you talked about him all day today."

Carla laughed. "Hell...No! Be serious, Kara. In fact, I'm headed back down stairs to find me some hot guy now. See you later."

Becky gave Kara an apologetic look, as they all sat down. Steven grabbed the seat next to Kara, moving a little closer than she felt comfortable with. She heard Alexander growl, and knew this could get out of hand. She looked over at Alexander giving him a warning look to stay out of it, but he didn't look ready to comply.

Alexander couldn't believe this idiot had the guts to show up here. Kara's brothers had made it clear to him to stay away from her, in yet here he sat, almost on top of her. Tiberius watched exasperation pass between Alexander and Chung, and moved towards his brother.

Tiberius lowered his voice approaching Alexander. "What's going on?"

Alexander raised his hand in a gesture to wait. Although personally he didn't want to, he wanted to throw Steven over the balcony. And what were they all talking about...Kara's birthday?

"Hey Kara, up for a little dirty dancing?" Steven joked, knowing it would not only get a rise out of Kara, but hopefully her vampire boyfriend. He would love nothing more than to kill a vampire. "I owe you a dance for your birthday...remember?"

Irritated Kara spat. "Do you think you could try and *remember* to keep your hands off my ass?"

Becky winked at Kara, letting her know that she would handle this. "Leave her alone Steven. You know she's not interested in you, after you practically molested her on the dance floor last time."

"Maybe she just needs a real *man* to loosen her up."

Alexander fisted his hands together to keep from choking him. Steven didn't seem to notice that he was about to die, as he continued. "I guarantee one night with me, and all her inhibitions would disappear. She'd be a completely *new* woman." Smiling sarcastically, Steven started chuckling. Not a sweet chuckle, but a sarcastic chuckle, a chuckle that ate on each of Kara's nerves. "Most women enjoy me touching them, but you always were a little strange." Steven leaned over putting his hand on Kara's thigh, simultaneously leaning in to kiss her. Chung lunged for Alexander, as Alexander lunged for Steven. Chung grabbed him and pushed him back.

As soon as Steven touched her, fury ran through her body, and Kara instantly jerked away. How dare he touch her, with his arrogant, disgusting hands? Who the hell does he think he is? Did he learn nothing the other night, or is he into the whole pain thing?

Kara slapped Steven as hard as she could across his face. "I'm obviously not your type of woman then. Personally, I prefer my men to have a little respect. Feeling me up in public is not my idea of a good time."

Again, Kara was furious. Steven hadn't changed a bit. He was the same whore dog that he'd been in high school. You'd think after five years he'd have grown up some, and learned to treat women with some small amount of dignity. But, NOOOOOOOOOOOOOO! Here they were now in their mid-20's and he was still acting like a hormonal raged teenager. This was the exact reason they had broken up on prom night, he didn't know how to keep his junk in his pants. When Kara had refused to screw him, she had caught him in the bathroom with Stella. Worse, when she had found them, all they both could do was laugh, and Stella cooed, "Someone has to take care of him, if you won't." Kara was so angry, that in one graceful swing of her arms, she grabbed Stella's dress and Steven's clothes off the floor, and ran as fast as she could, ripping the clothes in her hands, while ignoring their screams. She then ran directly to the principal, throwing him their clothes. "You should check out your bathrooms!" She had shouted and bee-lined it for the exit. That night she realized how horrible and selfish men could truly be. Steven and Kara had planned their lives together, they had already been accepted to a college together in California, and were talking about marriage. It was pretty much assumed by everyone that their lives were already planned out, in yet there she sat, in her grandparent's roof top garden, by herself, understanding for the first time how cruel men could be. All of the sudden she had no future. Everything she had planned for was over…gone…vanished, in Steven's one selfish moment of passion, he had ruined it all.

The month before graduation, he tried to apologize. At first he was angry. He couldn't believe Kara had embarrassed him so completely. The principal, Dr. Davenport made an example out of Steven and Stella, so all 459 students of the student body knew of their humiliation and shame. Dr. Davenport even touched on it in the school newsletter that went home to the parents. He had hoped that by humiliating them, no one would ever attempt to disgrace the high school prom again. Of course, Stella's parents were horrified, which Kara thought was hysterical. Every time she saw Stella, she broke out in laughter. It wasn't really nice, but after Stella's statement to Kara while banging her boyfriend, she didn't really care about being nice.

"You know Kara; you always were such a tease. In yet, you'll let freaks touch you."

Pissed off Kara spat. "Kiss my ass, Steven!"

"Oh, baby! Don't make offers you're not willing to follow through on." Steven laughed a loud obnoxious laugh that just made Kara want to slap that smirk off his disgusting face.

Kara slapped Steven's hand away and stared him down. "I told you Becky, he's a pig. He hasn't learned anything, and if he keeps it up I'll let my brothers' stuff and mount him for their wall."

Steven grabbed Kara's breast. "To bed you and make you scream, I'll take on your brothers," then looking at Alan, "and anyone else who wants to get in my way."

Alexander was done allowing Kara to handle Steven. He understood Kara treasured her independence, but this was out of hand. It was time Steven feared him. Alexander moved forward, at the same instant Kara lost her temper. She jumped up off the couch and without another thought took a swing at Steven's face. All she could think about was knocking that arrogant smile right off Steven's stupid face. But, before her hand connected, another hand grabbed her wrist, and Alexander's arm wrapped around her waist pulling her back into him. She was about to elbow him when his masculine exotic smell enveloped her. The rightness of his touch and his smell, so distinctly Alexander, washed away all her anger.

"Sweetheart, remember what you told me. He's not worth it." Alexander made a point for everyone to hear, then glaring directly at Steven with charcoal black eyes, which Kara had come to realize only, happens when Alexander was very angry. "Real *men*, don't need to prove anything to a lady, and they definitely don't need to force themselves upon one." In a cold voice that was so threatening it could have frozen over hell, he continued, "I suggest you show *my* lady a little more respect, or the issues you have with her will end up being between you and me, and I can assure you next time I won't be talking."

"*Your* woman?" Steven laughed. "Kara has never allowed herself to be possessed by anyone."

"Yes! *My* lady! Or if you understand it better, *my* woman!" Alexander snarled. "If you ever touch Kara again…if you ever so much as look at her without respect…let's just say…you'll never see the light of day. Understand?"

Steven and Alexander stared at each other for what seemed like an eternity. Kara knew Alexander was pissed, and that he wouldn't back down, his eyes were pitch black. "Chung…Tiberius …escort him downstairs. Let security know he's not allowed near Kara or upstairs. If he so much as tries…just throw him out of the club."

Chung motioned towards the door, and they followed Steven out of the room.

"Are you ok, love?" Alexander looked very concerned over Kara's wellbeing.

"I am now." She smiled and wrapped her arms around his neck, biting his lower lip, and teasing him just a little. "I really have missed you today. Thanks for stepping in, but I could have handled him." She bit his lower lip again. "He's really not dangerous; he's just a jerk, but thank you anyway." She gave him another teasing bite, and his lips were on hers, hot and aggressively his tongue dived into her mouth, probing, tasting, sliding rhythmically along her tongue. God he tasted good. Kara melted into him, forgetting where she was or why she was there. He truly knew how to kiss a girl.

"Uh-hum." Becky interrupted them...again, and was laughing. "You two really *can't* stop yourselves can you? Did you invite him to my wedding?"

It took Kara a couple of minutes to pull herself out of that mind boggling kiss, but when she finally did, she noticed everyone in the room staring at them. She could feel the heat rising in her cheeks, and knew in a matter of seconds she would be bright red, but she didn't care. Alexander was worth it. She started giggling.

"No. I hadn't had a chance yet, but I think you just did." Kara was still giggling when she answered Becky.

"Then am I to assume you haven't asked him about Sunday?" Becky asked.

"Becky!" Kara warned.

"Sunday?" Alexander and Alan said at the same time.

"You're going to try and chicken out aren't you?" Becky accused. "Alexander, since I'm part of Kara's family, we would like to invite you to the Quads birthday party Sunday. This will also give Kara's family a chance to get to know you better, and let you get to know us. You're more than welcome to bring any or all of your family and friends. Will you come?"

Angry Kara snapped, "And you all want to know why I don't bring people home."

Alexander kissed Kara's cheek, before looking back over at Becky. "Thank you, I would be delighted to attend the birthday party. You can plan on all us being there."

"Um...Becky. Kara doesn't look so happy; maybe we should go

downstairs and let her cool off." Alan observed.

Becky just laughed at him and patted his cheek. "No baby. Give her a minute. Alexander can't keep his hands off her, and as soon as he kisses her again, Miss Bee-atch will melt back into my best friend. Just watch!" She pointed at them.

Kara just glared at both of them. It's too bad you couldn't choose your own family, because right now she needed a new one. One that wasn't so nosy. She really wanted to wring her best friend's neck. Of all people, Becky should understand her, but instead she was becoming as bad as her family with embarrassing her. At least everyone else in the room didn't seem to be paying them any attention. They were all involved with their own conversations.

Kara squinted her eyes at Becky, "You're such a damn comedian, aren't you? Sometimes I just want to choke you."

"Good. That makes me family, because you always want to choke them."

"Ugh!" Kara groaned.

Alan pulled at Becky. "Let's go Babe." Becky started to protest, but Alan continued to pull her off the couch. "Seriously. Kara needs a moment...without you."

Once they had left, Alexander felt the need to confront Kara about what had just transpired between her and Becky. He didn't understand why she was so upset, and upset was stating it mildly. She was right down pissed.

"Kara?" Something in Alexander's voice made her look up. He sounded...angry...no...sad? As soon as she saw the hurt in his face, she realized she'd done something that had hurt him.

"Alexander, what's wrong?" She reached up and cupped his cheek.

Her compassion soothed him more than it should. Alexander was a fighter, a warrior, a commander, nothing should soften him. He laughed at that thought. Kara made the rest of his anatomy rock hard, except she softened his heart, who would have thought.

"You don't want me to meet the rest of your family? Are you ashamed of us?"

Damn my selfishness! I was only thinking of my feelings not his.

If only she could learn to think before opening her big mouth. Kara hadn't meant to hurt Alexander. Of course she wasn't ashamed of him. She was embarrassed by her family. He had no idea how ridiculous they act when they all get together. She reached over and entwined their fingers together.

"Alexander, I'm not embarrassed about us, or ashamed of you. I'm embarrassed about my family."

"I don't understand."

Kara glanced around making sure no one else was listening. "Do you remember I told you my family is a freak of nature?"

"Yes"

"I didn't just mean it because of all the multiple births. They are truly freaky. My family is very large, and with that comes absolutely no privacy. Since there is so many of us, even when you're trying to hide something, someone finds out and then the whole family knows. Worse! They have no shame in discussing it and asking you about it, which is actually really embarrassing. I just didn't want to subject you to my family's craziness. Trust me; you think they've asked personal questions so far. That's nothing. They'll ask you things that will embarrass both of us."

Alexander sighed and pulled her closer to him. His arms around her felt so good, she thought she'd burst with pride. This magnificent man was hers. "I have to admit that's a relief. I was afraid you had changed your mind about us."

"You can't get rid of me that easy." She smiled, tracing his lips she added. "From the first time you kissed me I was a gonner."

"Love, don't worry about your family. You never have to worry about being embarrassed in front of me. I can't even imagine anything they could say that would embarrass either one of us."

Kara snorted. "Then you don't know my family. Let me explain." She recited their earlier discussion at the bridal salon in complete detail, except them teasing her about being a virgin. That was still very personal, and she wasn't sure how Alexander would feel about her acting like she was still a virgin. It was actually quite amusing to see his eyes widen a couple of times in shock over what they'd asked about

Cruetian sex. "Now do you understand?" Kara teased him. "They have no problem asking us anything."

"I guess I see your point. I can't believe your family discusses sex in public. I thought it was a taboo subject in this century." He said in disbelief. "Not that it bothers me. I come from a time when we were very open about sex."

"Nothing is off limits to them. They won't repeat it to strangers, but what's worse, they'll discuss it at home with the rest of the family. In fact, I'm sure we're the topic at the dinner table tonight. My ears have been burning all evening." She quietly laughed, as Alexander joined in.

"Do not worry, Kara. I can hold my own with your family. It'll be fun, besides I can't miss your birthday." He winked at her. "I cannot believe you were actually hiding that from me. It does explain a lot about your personality...May 21st...you're on the cusp of Gemini and Taurus." Alexander pondered that thought.

Fun! Alexander thinks being with my family will be...fun! If only he knew.

Kara admired Alexander as he went about handling the business at the club, dealing with political issues, as well as troop movements with his Generals. From what she could gather Alexander was working hard to stabilize the Middle East, by using the Cruetian army, to stop terrorist attacks. Kara was proud of her man. He was a true leader, in every sense of the word. Alexander was kind and compassionate, but he was also ruthless when he needed to be. She began to understand, just how much control it had required to restrain himself from hurting Steven earlier. What warmed her heart was the knowledge that the only reason he *had* restrained himself, was his promise to her. Alexander preferred being in the private suite upstairs, but had moved to a large downstairs booth after he had finished his business. He wanted Kara near her family. Kelmar, Namorita, and Chung had left to relay his orders, and the rest had followed them downstairs.

"She's precious, Xander." Adelina was saying. As soon as Kara had stepped onto the dance floor, they had started talking about her nonstop.

"Damn! The way her body moves while she's dancing…I bet she's great in bed. You're one lucky bastard!" Tiberius teased, until he saw the look on his big brother's face. "Hey!" He threw his hands up, "I was joking. You know I would never touch your woman." Adelina hit Tiberius's arm. "Nathaniel already made that comment. It was a mistake."

"My *Amara naked* should not be in any of my generals minds." Alexander growled. "If they want to live."

Tiberius nodded. "Understood, Commander."

Kara strolled up a little while later, and Alexander got up so she could slide in next to him. She noticed he always liked to be on the outside of the booth. Not that it really bothered her; she just thought it was interesting. She went back to listening to their conversation, finding it intriguing how much their world was similar to hers. They talked about their family and friends, and what they were currently doing, but mostly they talked about Alexander's research. Kara learned that his research was funded by the Federal government through CSU, the same university she had received her bachelor's degree at, and that his research was very important to him. She also ascertained that the only reason he worked at the hospital, was to ease human fears about Cruetians. Overall, this man Kara sat next to was an incredibly decent person.

"Nathaniel, it's obvious why none of the women are coming over to Alexander tonight. Look at Kara's hand." Adelina said jokingly.

"I'm sorry, what?" Kara asked, as she had been so deep in thought, all she had heard was her name, and nothing Adelina had actually said.

Alexander pulled her tighter. "Nothing Love, their just teasing me." Then whispering in Kara's ear, he murmured, "I happen to enjoy your hand right where it is."

Nathaniel looked under the table and started laughing. "Yep, that explains it. I just thought after 2300 years he was finally losing his touch with women…or maybe his mojo. When have we ever been able to sit for an hour without him having to turn a woman away?" They laughed. "I have to admit *adelfos*, if an *Amara* gets that possessive after a couple of days, I'm game. I hate having to work so hard to get someone to care. In this century it seems to take forever. It's like some game to the women of this century. How long can they make the poor sap grovel, until they give him their affections?" Nathaniel sighed. "It's just wrong."

"Do you remember when you could buy your wife from her father? That was so much easier than trying to win the heart of a woman now." Tiberius pointed a finger at Alexander, "Only you could get that lucky in this century, *adelfos*."

"I don't know about women in previous centuries, but I think women today are afraid to give men their hearts, because most of them are scum. They'll stomp all over their hearts. Obviously, the men from your century must have had more respect for women. That is probably why the women of that century were able to give themselves so freely." Kara explained very bluntly.

"I really do like her, Xander." Adelina smiled. "She has more spunk than most of our women."

"Kara might actually have a point; men in this century do seem very selfish." Alexander admitted. "Even when we bought wives, the men had to satisfy them. The men today don't seem to care." He rubbed Kara's arm. "Keep looking *fratellino*, you'll find your *Amara*. Remember it took me 800 years and it took Adelina 300. Just don't give up. It's worth the wait." Alexander lectured.

"Shit, Alexander. I didn't know she was here or I would have warned you." Adelina was saying as a gorgeous, 5'10", strawberry blonde runway model walked up to their table.

"Alexander, I haven't seen you in weeks. I thought you'd forgotten about me." She slid in next to him, almost sitting on his lap. Alexander pulled away from her, and scooted closer to Kara. She didn't take the hint. She ran her finger down his chest seductively. "Let me take you upstairs, and refresh your memory." She gave him a seductive smile. "You look a little hungry. Let me quench your appetite...all of them." She reached over and started rubbing his thigh.

Kara grabbed her wrist, removing the slut's hand from him, as rage and jealousy washed through her. "I wouldn't touch him again." Kara spat. "I tend to be a little possessive, and I don't share."

She lashed out, but before she could touch Kara, Alexander caught her claws. "Sorry Catherine not interested." He gave her a warning glare to back off. "I would like to introduce you to…my Kara."

"*Your* Kara?" Catherine looked Kara up and down. "You're not serious, Alexander. Look at her, she's…human. Do not insult me!"

Alexander knew this was going to be bad. They had been together off and on for centuries, right up until the night, a century ago, when he made the decision to be celibate until he found his *Amara*. He hadn't wanted any attachments when he found her. In yet, here stood Catherine. Even after 100 years, and numerous rejections, she still tried to claim him. He'd explained his feelings a million times to her, and Catherine just didn't seem to get it.

Alexander had actually believed Catherine was destined to be his mate at one point in history. Until just like his wife she'd betrayed him. He always knew she was power hungry, it was the one thing that always held him back from taking her as his mate, his wife. He had been blessed with good intuition and it served him well where Catherine was concerned, but right now, he needed to have patience with her, or she would hurt Kara. That he had no doubt about. "Catherine, I'm not trying to insult you. We've had this discussion before. Kara means a great deal to me, and yes, I'm aware she's human."

"Stop trying to make me jealous, Alexander." Catherine purred. "First," she ran her finger up his arm "you don't need to. I'm yours anytime you want me, and second" she stroked his bottom lip, "she's obviously unable, or unwilling to take care of you, since I see no marks on her. She's obviously not *that* important to you, so stop playing with me." She lightly smacked his cheek. "You and I both know we're meant for each other."

"Excuse me! Catherine, is it?" Everyone suddenly froze, as they watched Kara lean forward with determination, clearly unaware of the dangerous situation. A Dark-Soul could snap a human's neck instantly. They were much faster and stronger than humans, and when it comes to Alexander, Catherine wouldn't think twice about it. "Alexander's correct. He's mine! He'll no longer be needing any of your services."

"I'm not a whore, bitch. Alexander and I have been together for centuries." Catherine hit the table…hard. "If you think you can just swoop in and take him from me, you should probably reconsider your plan. I'm not a weak little human, and I can crush you like a twig, so I would think twice about wanting *my* man." Catherine dismissed Kara with her hand. "Besides you have no idea how to satisfy him, and I have been satisfying him for over a millennium."

"I am *not* your man, Catherine. Yes, we had a history together. We have been each other's companion in times of need, but I never took you for my mate. You are *not* my wife." Alexander pointed out. "Kara is correct. She is mine!" He turned and smiled at Kara, "and I am hers, Catherine." He said sternly. "She's my *Amara*. I've finally found her."

With that last statement Catherine whirled around and slapped him. She hit him so hard, his lip started bleeding. Kara heard a growl rip from his throat. She felt how pissed Alexander was, but she was so furious, and with her temper raging out of control Kara wasn't thinking straight. How dare Catherine touch him, after she just explicitly told her not to? How dare Catherine hurt him? Kara jumped half way over the table when Adelina grabbed her from behind and pulled her back down, holding Kara between her and her husband, Walter.

Catherine smirked. "Good thing you stopped her Addie. I would've drained her right here. Once that little bitch is dead, the spell she has on your brother will disappear. We all know an *Amara* cannot be human. A chosen one is designed to meet all her man's needs, and we know humans are to…Fragile…too weak to satisfy our kind. They're incapable of it. They're nice and soft once in a while, but as an *Amara* they would never survive." Catherine slid into the booth next to Alexander, rubbing his cheek. "Besides your father would never grant her the ceremony. We all know he will not grant any woman Alexander's hand unless she bears his mark." Catherine grabbed Alexander's right hand and pointed it at Kara, "Sorry human, you two are doomed by daddy dearest himself." She dropped Alexander's hand. "But do not worry little girl, I'll have no reason to hurt you as long as you stay away from him." She gave Kara a menacing smile.

Kara tapped her long manicured fingernail on the glass table. "Catherine-Catherine-Catherine." She tsked. "That's where you're…

so wrong." Kara held up her left hand, "I will definitely have daddy's approval, where you obviously didn't."

Catherine shook with fury, "What kind of trickery is this?" She demanded. "A human would never carry one of our marks. I will kill you for your treachery, little girl. You should stay far away from Alexander. It's the only way you'll keep your life."

In a move so quick, Kara never saw it, Alexander pushed Catherine out of the booth throwing her into Tiberius, who instantly held her squirming body. Alexander was growling in her face. "If you try to go anywhere near Kara, I will kill you myself. Stay…away…from…her, Catherine! Kara is my chosen one, and I will protect her with my life." Alexander pulled Kara across the table. "Adelina, deal with Catherine before I kill her. I'm barely in control right now, and I need to calm down." He looked around the table at each of them. "I don't want to see her when I return." He wrapped his arms around Kara's waist, and in one final definitive statement to Catherine, he pulled Kara into a very hot, sultry, aggressive kiss. It didn't last long, just long enough for him to make a point. Alexander scooped Kara up into his arms and carried her up to the third floor. She had a ton of questions she wanted to ask him, but they could wait. He was just too angry right now.

17

Kara was stunned at what she saw on the third floor. There was no bar, no dance floor, just eight double doors down a long hallway. Alexander carried her to the last door on the right, before standing her on the floor. He searched in his pocket and came out with a key, which he used to unlock the door before swinging them open to reveal a beautiful suite. Everything was white and decorated in midnight blue and gold. The entry had a beautiful crystal chandelier, a floor of white marble and it was decorated in various pieces of art. A small round table sat under the chandelier, holding a beautiful floral boutique.

"Who lives here?" She asked, as he picked her up again, and cradled her in his arms.

"We keep these apartments for our guests. Right now this one's not being used." Alexander carried Kara through a gold archway into a very large bedroom. The floor was covered in a lush white carpet, and just like the entry, various pieces of art hung on two of the walls. The other two walls were the same type of glass the building was made out of. Kara was sure that just like downstairs no one could see into these floor to ceiling windows. Looking out one set of windows was a glittering view of downtown Denver, while the other set of windows was a majestic view of the Rocky Mountains. In the center of the room was a king size, four poster bed. At each post, midnight blue velvet curtains were tied with gold ropes. There was thin white gauze encasing every side of the bed.

Alexander carried her over to the bed, moving aside the fabric, he gently laid her down. He removed her heels, and then walking around to the other side of the bed, he removed his shoes and joined her.

Kara smiled, as she looked over at him lying next to her. Alexander lying next to her was like her own little utopia, and she intended to enjoy it. He seemed to be shying away from her, but Kara understood he was trying to calm down; maybe she could help quiet his fury.

Alexander was furious with Catherine, but having Kara so close to him in bed, eased a lot of his temper. He wanted so desperately to reach over and pull her near him. He had no doubt, that if he could make love to her, if he could just be inside her, all would be right in his world, but he didn't want to rush her. Kara had just seen him angry… very angry, and most people were terrified of him after seeing him that way. He had no idea what she thought of him right now, so he laid down on his back, with his hands behind his head, and his eyes closed, and kept as much room between them as he could muster.

Kara moved closer to him, molding her body around his. She laid her head on his chest, and draped her arm across his stomach. Alexander moaned deep in his chest, from her touch. She instantly knew it pleased him. It didn't matter what Catherine had said, she would be able to please him…she knew she could. Catherine was wrong and Kara would prove it.

She pulled herself up his body, so she could reach his neck. Slowly, methodically she placed gentle little kisses along his neck, working her way up to his chin.

"What are you doing?" Alexander murmured wrapping one arm around her, letting his hand settle on her lower back. Kara felt so good to him, as he reveled in her soft kisses.

"Getting closer to what's mine." She teased while she continued placing small kisses over his chin. "Or did you change your mind about me." Kara brushed her lips gently over his, anticipating his response, when it didn't come she asked. "Don't you want me this close? Is Catherine right? Am I unable to fulfill your needs?" Not that she understood what those needs were.

"Love, I want to be inside you right now, but you just saw me out of control, aren't you afraid of me?" Alexander hated himself for asking that. He needed Kara, in ways he'd never needed a woman. How stupid he was to push her away, but she'd hate him afterwards if she didn't come to terms with what she just saw, and he wouldn't risk that chance. Alexander had to let Kara completely understand everything about him and his people, before allowing himself to claim her as his.

Kara wasn't sure why Alexander was pulling away from her. She knew he wanted her. She felt his passion every time he touched her. It had to be something Catherine had said. "What did Catherine mean by feed you?"

Alexander winced at Kara's question. He could kill Catherine for saying that in front of her. "You don't need to concern yourself with that. Catherine doesn't know when to keep her mouth shut."

"Alexander, tell me." Kara demanded. She could feel his hesitation, his reluctance in answering her. So she continued, "Alexander, we both know I have a lot to learn about you and your people. I also understand there are still some things you're afraid to tell me, but if I'm your *Amara*, I have to know. I have to know everything about you. The good and the bad. All of it. I think now would be a good time to start. Beginning with what Catherine said." Kara could feel the indecision in Alexander, a battle was waging inside him, and she wasn't sure which side would win.

Alexander knew she was right, but what if Kara wasn't ready to handle the reality of his people. Would she push him away? He couldn't imagine being without her. In just a few days, she had wrapped his life around hers, if he lost her now, it would tear him apart. He gently pulled her up his body, until he could look directly into her big beautiful brown eyes. Eyes that had reached in and somehow stolen his heart.

Kara looked deep into Alexander's brilliant teal eyes. They seemed to sparkle with anticipation, but also with confusion and fear.

"What's wrong?" She asked caressing his cheek.

"I'm not sure you're ready for these explanations. It might be too much, too soon." He answered her as honest as he could.

"No, Alexander. You must tell me. I need to know. I've accepted our relationship. I've accepted who you are. I have to know."

"Do you? Have you really accepted us? Are you ready to be my chosen one?" Alexander searched her eyes for his answers.

"I'm here aren't I?" She reached out, tracing his soft lips; they were begging her, tempting her to explore them with her own. "Alexander, I'm not the type of girl that plays with guy's feelings; or my own for that matter. You heard what my sisters said, and it's true. I've never been just the dating type. I dated with the sole purpose of finding my soul-mate. I take men and relationships very seriously. I wouldn't be here if I wasn't ready and willing to take the next step...no, that's not what I mean. What I mean is that...I'm ready to commit to a relationship with you."

The confusion and fear seemed to fade away from his eyes, leaving only anticipation and tenderness. Alexander closed his eyes. Could she really be ready? Was she actually accepting him?

Alexander seemed to relax with her touch. That knowledge had Kara continuing to trace the lines on his face, caressing his cheeks, enticing him to explain. She knew they needed to understand each other if this relationship was going to work, and she really wanted this relationship to work. She still didn't understand all her feelings for him, but she knew she was beginning to love him. She felt in her heart that Alexander was her soul-mate, and that's all that mattered. The rest they'll work through together.

"I'm sure you're aware my kind needs human blood to survive." Alexander stated. "It's what gives us our strength and our nourishment. We can eat food for pleasure, and our bodies will extract any nourishment available from that food, but ultimately there is very little our bodies gain from actual food consumption other than the enjoyment of it. We need *human* blood to survive. In today's society, most of us tend to drink from blood banks. Since your governments know what we are, they've made blood available for us to buy. This blood sustains us, but feeding from another person is still the preferred choice amongst my kind."

"So that's why vampires attack humans? Do Dark-Soul's attack humans?"

"Some, but my kind does not condone that behavior. Now that humans know we exist, we want to earn their trust, live in harmony with them, so now, we actually track vampires who feed on humans, and...lets just say we prosecute them. It's why we do not like the term vampire. As I explained today at lunch, they are our criminals. They are the ones who still attack and kill humans. Dark-Souls might feed off humans, but we never kill them. We would never drain a human. That's what makes a vampire versus a Dark-Soul; the vampire drains the human, killing them."

"So...you never drink from humans?"

Alexander laughed. "No that's not true, if it's consensual we do, but our laws are very explicit. We can no longer force a human. Human blood, from a living source is the sweetest blood in the universe. It's a delicacy to my people. Like drugs can become addictive to humans, live human blood, can become an addiction for us. It's why some Dark-Souls become vampires." Alexander watched for Kara's reaction, and the horror he expected to see in her eyes. She actually appeared to be handling it alright; she nodded her head in understanding, so he continued. "Kara you need to understand, feeding for my people, can be an extremely erotic experience. It actually enhances the orgasm, and is why we feed from each other even though we don't gain nourishment from it. We enjoy sexual pleasure as much as humans do...maybe more."

"Really? So for you it's...what...like multiple orgasms...extreme ecstasy?...but what is it for me...If you bite me...is there pain?"

"Kara, I could never hurt you." He tucked a strand of hair behind her ear. "Feeding from someone only hurts them if they fight us. That would never happen to you, my love. I would never feed from you without your permission. Now you understand why we changed our laws. For centuries my kind has taken the blood they needed ruthlessly, but now to live with humans, my people need to become more civilized."

Kara now understood his fear. He was afraid she'd condemn him, that she would be disgusted with him for wanting...needing human blood. How silly he was. Every culture has their quirks, their own ideas of right and wrong. We are all different in some way. His was actually trying to live peacefully with humans. How could she be disgusted by that? "Alexander, feed from me. Make love to me, and feed from me."

Alexander opened his eyes and stared dumb founded at Kara.

Was she serious? How could she be so accepting over this? Did she understand that their bond would become stronger if they did this?

Kara watched Alexander as he seemed to study her, trying to determine what she really wanted.

"Kara, are you sure...are you really ready for this? It's different for us then it was for Catherine and me, you're my chosen one. When we do this...each time we make love, and especially when I feed from you, it'll strengthen our bond."

Kara straddled him, feeling all those lean hard muscles under her. Alexander's breath caught in his throat as he looked up at her, sitting on his stomach, the moist silk of her thong teasing his navel. Alexander was so hard for her his body was in a frenzy. Slowly she unbuttoned his shirt, rubbing her hands over his chest, stroking each of his muscles as they flexed under her touch. Using her tongue, Kara began mapping every line of his chest and neck.

Alexander groaned at the sensation, as her tongue laved his skin. As Kara's tongue reached his lips, she slowly traced them seductively. She was just beginning to make her second tour of his lips, when in one sweeping motion he rolled her beneath him. He loved the feel of her delicate, soft body under him, and desperately wanted to strip off her clothes and drive himself deep inside her. He felt his control withering, and needed to make sure she understood the ramifications of feeding from her. Alexander needed Kara's confirmation, that she was positive she wanted this, because after it's done, there's no going back. You don't break a bond.

"Kara, are you truly sure? I can wait." Alexander said through ragged breaths.

Kara couldn't think straight as she answered him. His steel hard body pressed against her started an urgency for Alexander she'd never felt before. "I'm sure. I want you, Alexander. I *want* to take care of you...all of you."

Kara's words ate at his very being. They excited him in a way he never thought was impossible. His life was one of complete control, in yet, around her, he was completely out of control. He kissed her hard and possessively until Kara was breathless. He laved and kissed down her neck, around her collarbone, and up to her ear, savoring the taste of her. "You're absolutely sure?" He whispered. His breath in Kara's ear sent shivers down her spine, awaking every hormone in her now extremely sensitive body.

"Yes!" She choked, wishing he'd stop asking that question. This is what she wanted.

He moved his tongue over her earlobe, gently biting it, before his tongue continued a burning trail along her neck, evolving into little sexy patterns that were so erotic; she couldn't stop moaning with pleasure. Just when she thought it couldn't get any better, she felt a slight sting followed by pure erotic pleasure that sent her over the edge. They were connected. Kara could feel it. She didn't know how to describe it, but it was like they were one person, and the only person in the universe. It felt like their cells had melted together, and somehow Kara felt like she was in his mind.

Kara felt relief...satisfaction...hunger...passion...desire... all wound up into one small package. It was all a very stimulating sensation. Alexander reached down releasing his pants, and shoved them off. He pushed up her dress, moving aside the small patch of silk that was hiding her dark curls, before plunging deep inside her.

Kara screamed at the intense orgasm that hit her, knocking her whole body into earthquake size tremors. Alexander was pounding frantically into her, his balls slapping against her, searching for his own release. She'd unleashed the animal inside him, and she loved it. This primal sex had her head spinning, dizzy with pleasure, and all she could do was hold on for the ride. When another set of tremors racked her body, Alexander growled her name with his own release.

As he collapsed on top of her, Kara held him tight delighting in the spasms shaking his body. Trying to catch her breath, she closed her eyes, reveling in the most sensual sensations she'd ever felt.

"Oh, No, you don't." He rumbled. "Don't you dare shut those sexy brown eyes of yours." Kissing the crook of her neck, he continued. "Baby, we've just barely started." He rolled over pulling her on top of him, holding her like she was his life line.

Kara giggled. "Oooo, you're a voracious Dark-Soul, aren't you?"

"Starved!"

Kara's breath caught as she saw the true hunger in his eyes. She slid off the bed, pulling his pants completely off.

Alexander watched as she finished undressing him. During the heat of the moment, he'd only had time to push his pants down to his knees. Her blood had sent him over the edge, and he couldn't get inside her fast enough. Kara's blood was so sweet, if he didn't know better, he'd swear it was sweeter now than when she was a virgin.

Still a little shy, Kara turned away from him as she released her belt, gliding her dress up over her head.

Alexander moaned at the site of her bent over shimming off her thong. He couldn't handle the torment, and was instantly behind her, pushing her forward until Kara hit some type of table.

She sucked in a deep breath as Alexander hooked both her arms around his neck. "You're driving me wildly insane my little temptress." He teased her ear with his tongue. "All I can think of is your moist wet heat welcoming me into your body." He cupped her breast, pinching and teasing her plump little nipple. His other hand worked its way down to those dark curls that begged for his attention. He found her still sensitized swollen clit, and flicked it.

Kara moaned with pleasure as Alexander slowly worked her body into a frenzy and when she came, it was with a burst of intensity that would have dropped her to her knees if Alexander hadn't been holding her.

Alexander knocked something off the table pushing her forward, and over it. Holding her hips, he submerged himself deep inside her with one strong thrust. Pulling back, he thrust forward sinking himself all the way to the hilt. "Oh, gods Kara. I'm never going to get enough of you. You feel so good wrapped around me. You're so hot and wet and tight. It makes me want to lose my seed just thinking about you."

The wood was cool and abrasive on her swollen nipples, and created all kinds of lusty sensations as Alexander pierced her neck and thrusted deep inside her. Kara's breathing was heavy as euphoria enveloped her just before her legs spasmed in another fierce release. With three more thrusts Alexander joined her, pulling her back against him, he moved backwards falling onto the bed. Still inside her, Alexander spooned them together.

Holding her protectively, Alexander watched her sleep, as he realized he'd never be able to live without her. Somehow in a mere couple of days this tiny woman had branded him.

"I'm sorry. Did I fall asleep?" She awakened rubbing her eyes.

Smiling, Alexander brushed Kara's hair away from her face. "You're quite cute when you sleep." He kissed her forehead. "I need to go downstairs for a little while. Would you like to stay here or come along?"

Kara slid up his body to kiss him. How she loved this man. "You keep doing that, and we'll end up staying here, and as much as I'd enjoy that, I really need to go downstairs." He teased.

Kara pouted. "We can't stay here tonight?" She ran her fingernail along the inside of his thigh "I haven't had enough of you." She purred. Kara laughed as Alexander cocked an eyebrow in disbelief.

Damn! This woman makes me hard.

Alexander couldn't get enough of her either. "I'm glad to hear that, and I have no intention of allowing you to return home tonight." Raising his eyebrow, "I'm far from done with you, my love, but it's very important we go downstairs before we retire for the night. You should also let your sisters know that you won't be returning home with them."

"Your right" Kara caved "but I'd prefer to stay naked with you."

"As would I, my love, as would I."

It was just after midnight when they made their way back downstairs. The club was still in full swing, with another dance tune pounding on the speakers. They found Becky, Alan, and Kasi sitting with Alexander's family.

"Well, it's about time." Becky teased. "Adelina told us what happened with Alexander's ex. Aren't you two just the pair? We all knew Kara had a psycho, but Alexander has one too. That *really* sucks."

Tiberius chuckled. "I've never heard Catherine referred to as a psycho, but it fits."

Kasi stood up and hugged Kara. "Hey sweetie. You ok?"

Kara gave her a squeeze, smiling. "I'm perfect. Why?" She was still holding Alexander's hand, as he looked down and smiled at her answer.

Kasi and Becky both noticed the look that passed between them. Something was up. After everything that had happened tonight, Kara was too calm.

"Why? Dealing with Steven is a challenge in itself, but also having to deal with Catherine." Kasi looked at her watch, "You were only upstairs a couple of hours. Your temper should still be blazing."

"Kasi's right." Becky interjected. "Two hours isn't long enough to calm your temper." They were looking at her suspiciously. "Explain!" They demanded.

"Becky, you see it?" Kasi asked.

"See what?" Adelina asked curiously. She hadn't really been paying much attention until now, but Kasi all of the sudden had her curious. "What do you two see?"

Alexander interrupted, "Excuse us ladies, Tiberius and I have some business to handle." He squeezed Kara's hand. "I'll be right back."

Kara was hoping Alexander's interruption would stop the third degree, but she wasn't so lucky. As soon as they left, Kasi glared accusingly at her. "You're hiding something."

Still confused Adelina asked, "What's she hiding?"

"We don't know" Becky was saying "but she's definitely hiding something. Look at her face she's……"

"SHIT!" Kasi yelled. "YOU'RE NOT A VIRGIN ANYMORE!"

"She was a virgin?" Adelina asked surprised. "Or is? How? Kara's what…mid-twenties?"

"23. Yesterday." Kasi answered angrily, "and yes, she was a virgin when we walked in here, and now she's not." Kasi eyed Kara up and down.

Kara knew she was bright red. She could feel the heat on her face. If only Kara could disown her family, SHE WOULD!!!! She was shocked silent by Kasi's outburst, but thank God they were in a secluded corner, or the whole club would know of her virginity, or lack thereof, status.

"How do you know that?" Kara could hear Adelina ask.

"I just do." Kasi snapped, still staring at Kara. "I'm her identical twin. We don't know why we know private things about each other, we just do. The doctors call it a twin thing." She glanced over her shoulder at Adelina, "So yes, I know." She looked back at Kara, "Don't I?"

The shock was wearing off as Kara's temper flared. Becky noticed her jaw flinching. "Alan, go find Kara's sisters'…quick."

Kara was trying to control herself. Deep breaths…in…out, just like her grandmother had taught her. Grinding her teeth, to try and stay calm, she said. "I can't believe you. What the hell were you thinking blurting that out?" She pushed Kasi back into the booth. "And you're wrong. I wasn't a virgin when I walked in here. I lost my virtue yesterday."

Becky stepped in front of Kara. "Deep breaths, Kara. She didn't mean to blurt it out. It was an accident. We were just shocked that's all. You know we're happy for you. We've wanted this for you. You know that."

Kasi stepped forward crying, grabbing Kara in a bear hug. "I'm sorry, Kara. I'm so sorry. I didn't mean to embarrass you, I really didn't. I was just so shocked. You always said you would wait for your soul-mate, and I was just angry that you didn't tell us. I'm sorry… really sorry…please forgive me."

Kali and Kami came running up with Alan behind them. "What's going on?" Kami demanded. Becky shook her head, giving them a warning.

"That's what I'd like to know." Adelina said. "I think your sister lost her virginity to my brother."

"What?" Kali and Kami said in unison turning to Becky.

Kasi looked over Kara's shoulder where she was still hugging her and gave them all a dirty look. She pulled Kara away from them into a dark hallway.

Becky went on to explain Kasi's outburst.

"She didn't." Kali said in disbelief. "In front of Nathaniel, Walter, and Adelina?" She asked waiving her hand towards them.

Becky nodded her head. "Yes, and Alan."

"Shit, Kasi's lucky to be alive." Kami blurted. "Poor Kara. She's such a private person, and she hates being embarrassed, especially about her big taboo topic…her virginity. She even hated it when we discussed it this afternoon."

"That's because she wasn't a virgin this afternoon." Becky pointed out. "Kara lied to us. She lost it yesterday."

Kami jumped up. "I'll be right back."

"Where are you going?" Kali asked.

"This is big news. I have to call mom." She said over her shoulder.

"I'm coming with you." Kali laughed running to catch up to her.

Adelina, Nathaniel, and Walter still looked confused over the whole situation, so Becky began explaining Kara's theory of a soul-mate and why she had kept herself a virgin this whole time, even though her family always teased her about it.

"You have to understand this is a big step for her. That's why we're all shocked. She's only known your brother a few days. Kara had been with Steven for over a year, Daisuke for eight months and Kevin for two years and she never gave herself to any of them. This is serious." Becky finished.

Becky looked around the table at the stunned looks. "Don't look at me that way. You guys asked." Becky shrugged her shoulders.

"More serious than you think." Nathaniel chuckled.

Adelina hit him hard, "Shut up!"

Becky looked between them, "What do you two know, that you're not telling me?"

Adelina wasn't sure if Kara knew about the blood bonding, and she didn't want to tip Becky off to information Kara didn't have.

Lie. Walter's voice shouted in Adelina's head.

Are you sure?

Yes! You can't risk Kara finding out something Alexander's not ready for her to know.

"Alexander hasn't been with a woman in over a century either, so if he slept with Kara, he must really care for her. That's all we're saying."

"Oh, that's good." Becky said relieved. "That's real good."

18

Kara awoke to arguing. It took her a moment to remember that Alexander had shifted her back to his home last night, where they had made love under the stars of the skylights.

Sitting up, she stretched, releasing every muscle in her body. She looked around the room, viewing it with new appreciation. She heard voices coming from the sitting room. Kara recognized one voice as Alexander's, and she thought the other might be his sister's, Adelina, but wasn't a hundred percent sure.

"I do like her, Xander." Kara heard Adelina saying. "All I'm saying, is you need to deal with Catherine. She's not going to take this lightly. I had a lot of trouble keeping her away from you last night. Even though she threatened Kara, Catherine knows better than to try to hurt her. She'll never go up against our family, but you still need to deal with her…yourself."

I could hear the anger in Alexander's voice. He was furious again. Who was this Catherine and why was it any of her business who Alexander is with now? They haven't been together in decades. *Right! That's what he said. Wasn't it?*

"Why?" Alexander snapped. "Catherine and I haven't been together in a century. You…of all people know that. I do not owe her an explanation, or anything else."

"Alexander, you know I completely agree with you, but you have to help Catherine except this. Remember how some people had trouble with Walter being my *Amara*. We were at war with the Lycans when I found him, some people will always remain prejudice. Catherine will be one of them simply because she wants you. You need to deal with her and the situation now…not later."

That Kara understood completely. Prejudice people will always find fault in things they don't understand. She thought she should let them know she was awake, but she was extremely interested in their conversation, so she kept silent.

"Have you told Kara we drink human blood? Is a human willing to accept that aspect of a Dark-Soul?"

"She knows what I am and doesn't seem to have any issue with it."

"But does she understand what it means to be *your Amara*?" Adelina's voice sounded concerned.

"Damn it, Adelina!" Alexander growled. "I fed from her last night. Is that what you want to know?"

"Good!" Adelina sighed. "Xander, don't be angry. I was just stating the obvious. Catherine is right on *that* one issue. Kara has to be able to take care of you. I'm sorry I upset you. *Really!* I am. I hadn't realized you were already explaining our ways to Kara. Although, I'm glad you are, and I'm very happy for both of you. Kara letting you feed is a huge step."

"I know." He sounded tired.

"Then you go handle Catherine and I'll take care of Kara until you return."

"Let her know, I'll be back soon."

Kara heard Alexander leave and decided it was time to get up and get dressed. She was confused about the conversation she'd heard. Who was Catherine to him? Obviously competition Kara hadn't known about. *I'm nothing compared to her.* She knew if there was really a competition between them, she couldn't win. Plus it sounds like some Dark-Souls wouldn't approve of a human as their princess. *Which means, I'll never be accepted. How can this work, when Alexander can have the gorgeous Catherine that every Dark-Soul would approve of.*

She was still sitting on the edge of the bed thinking, when Adelina cleared her throat. Kara pulled the sheet around her still naked body.

"Uh-hum…Good morning, Kara"

"Good morning, Adelina."

Adelina walked over and sat down next to her. "After we found you, Alexander and I did some wardrobe shopping. I hope you like them. Your clothes are in the walk-in closet, and your lingerie is in the dresser. I also made him buy some feminine beauty products, they're in the bathroom. I didn't think you'd want to smell like a guy."

Kara gave her an appreciative smile. "Thank you. Alexander showed me yesterday, and everything's beautiful. I've never had such exquisite clothing."

Adelina's face lit up. "I'm glad you like them. I pride myself in knowing current fashions." She stood up and strolled to the bathroom arch, content with whatever she saw, she stated. "I'll have your lunch brought up." Adelina winked at her teasingly. "You two slept most the day away, so you missed breakfast, and oh, by the way, Alexander has stepped out, but should return shortly."

"Adelina?"

"Yes?" Adelina turned back around to face her.

Kara wasn't sure if she should ask Adelina personal questions about Alexander or not, but she really wanted, no she *needed*, some answers. "Would you answer a question for me?"

"I can try." She frowned.

Kara bit her bottom lip. "I overheard the end of your conversation. I know Alexander went to see Catherine. Who is she to him?"

Adelina sighed, walking back over to sit back down next to Kara. "Catherine and Alexander had an off and on relationship for over 1000 years. A very complex relationship. To be honest, our parents always thought Alexander might take Catherine as his mate, but after Kelmar told him where to find you, Alexander decided he'd wait for you. Naturally, his choice hasn't made Catherine happy. She always believed they would end up together. She was sure she'd end up being Alexander's mate, and has been trying to change his mind ever since. You can understand why she wouldn't be happy that he's found his *Amara*."

"1000 years?" Kara thought out loud, while counting in her head. "Alexander was with her while he was married?"

"No!" Adelina looked up quickly. Startled by the thoughts she knew

Kara was having. She remembered what Chung had said about Kara's first boyfriend. He had cheated on her, and Kara has never forgiven him. Thank God Alexander believes in faithfulness. "My brother has many faults, but infidelity and adultery are not among them. He was with Catherine before his marriage and then they reunited a few years after his marriage ended. He was never with her *during* his marriage."

Kara was so relieved to hear that. She hadn't realized the panic that had started to envelope her, with the idea of him cheating. She couldn't be with someone that cheated. She just couldn't. Some women can, but she can't. "If they were together before, wasn't Catherine angry about his marriage?"

Adelina laughed. "I can only imagine, but personally I have no idea. I wasn't born yet, but I've been told by Dante, that she threw the biggest tantrum you've ever seen. She tried to have the marriage annulled, claiming she was with Alexander's child." Adelina saw Kara's confusion. Obviously, Alexander had explained the only way Cruetians can have children is with their *Amara's*. "Kara, before the curse, which happened at the end of Alexander's marriage to Fiona, Dark-Souls could have children with other Dark-Souls. If we married another race that wasn't Cruetian, we could change them into a Dark-Soul so that we could have children. That's what happened with my mother and father. My mother was human when my father, a Dark-Soul, fell in love with her. He married her, and then he changed her into a Dark-Soul, and they've been together ever since. You see, *Amaras* only happened after the curse was brought upon our people."

As understanding set in, and Kara's eyes lit up. "Wow! So, Catherine really has been after Alexander for a very long time. She's clearly obsessed with him."

"Catherine is nothing to worry about, Kara. Alexander will handle her. He's been dealing with Catherine's antics for centuries."

Kara didn't want to deceive Adelina, but she wanted to know if Alexander had told her everything, or had left something out of his explanations. "What exactly is an *Amara*? Alexander's tried to explain it to me, but you know how guys are. Their explanations suck."

Adelina agreed. "You can say that again. You're intelligent and perceptive…qualities I'm sure my brother adores about you. Our kind believes the fates or God, depending on your beliefs, has designed one woman specifically for each man. A Cruetian's chosen one. Each Dark-Soul is destined to have only one *Amara*, the one person in the world that will complete them, the one person who can make the Dark-Soul whole. Together they become one…two halves of a whole."

"A soul-mate." Kara sighed dreamily.

"It's more than a soul-mate, Kara. Their lives depend on each other. Once a Dark-Soul accepts their *Amara*, and they complete all three blood bonding ceremonies, they'll be together for life. They can never leave each other, it would mean their death. Their lives are no longer their own, they belong to each other. They're bound together for eternity. In the universe, there is no bond stronger."

Aghast Kara asked, "They would have to be with each other 24/7 or they would die? Wouldn't you get tired of each other? How would you go to work or out with friends?"

Laughing Adelina replied, "I didn't mean like that. I meant they could never change their minds. Humans believe in divorce. You always have a way out, but once you go through the *Amara* ceremony, that would never be possible. For an *Amara*, until death do us part, actually means just that."

"Why wouldn't everyone wait for their *Amara*? It sounds so perfect."

Kara heard the sadness in Adelina's tone as she explained. "The world is a very large place, Kara, with billions of beings living in it. What is the chance of being in the right place at the right time to find your *Amara*? Only a few of our kind actually find them. Most choose to find a mate, so they are not alone in the world."

"*You're* married, correct? I don't mean to be nosy, but are you an *Amara* or a mate?"

Adelina chuckled. You could never offend me Kara. "It's an honor to have an *Amara*, it's not something we hide, and yes, Walter *is* mine. In our kind, becoming an *Amara* is the greatest honor our people know. It's also the greatest satisfaction. An *Amara* knows more love than anyone else in the world."

"How long have you and Walter been married?" Kara continued to quiz.

"We were bonded 327 years ago."

Adelina giggled as Kara's eyes grew wide. She was actually enjoying this conversation with her.

Kara chewed on her bottom lip before responding. "Wow! That's a long time. It's hard for me to grasp that many years. How did you find each other?"

"That's a long story, that we don't have time for today, but ask me another time and I'll be happy to tell it to you." Adelina stood up, "You should get ready now. Alexander will return soon and I believe you're supposed to meet Becky tonight. It's already two, so you don't have much time."

Adelina turned around just before reaching the door. "Um… Kara, I love my brother. Please remember, we might be immortal, but we have feelings just as humans do. He already loves you, very much. I'm not sure a human can understand our type of love. I worry you might unintentionally hurt him. I know Alexander's afraid to show you how strongly he feels about you, because he's terrified he'll scare you away if he shows it too soon, but try to remember, we are not familiar with human dating rituals. When our kind finds their *Amara*; the pull is so great the relationship is immediately formed. Alexander understands that's not the case for humans, and he's trying to accommodate your feelings, but I ask *you* to please take into account my brothers feelings as well."

Is she joking? My pull to Alexander is like a fish to water.

"I have no intention of hurting your brother. He's the most amazing man I've ever met, and trust me; I feel the pull between us as well. It's true, I don't understand *it* the way you do, but I do feel it and I know it's something *very* special."

Adelina smiled. "I'm very glad to hear that, and the rest of my family will be too. I do like you Kara and when the time comes, I know you'll make a great addition to our family. Now go ahead and get ready. I'll have lunch sent up."

"Just one more question, please." Kara stopped her from leaving.

"Alright."

"Alexander told me about his marriage…his wife betrayed him… or something, and he executed her…was she his *Amara*?"

"No. There is only one *Amara* for each Dark-Soul. No more. It's a one shot deal." Adelina frowned. "That's why most take mates. Could you imagine searching your whole life and never finding them? It would be a very lonely existence." She looked at me with sadness in her eyes "Remember, I said the curse happened after Alexander's marriage. We didn't have *Amara's* when he married her. Alexander took a wife. It was an arranged marriage, but he ended up loving her. Fiona just didn't know the meaning of love and was unable to return it. What she did to Alexander's heart caused him to fear love for centuries."

Kara gasped. "Oh-my-god, what did she do to him?"

"I don't feel right telling you that. It's not my place, you need to ask Alexander."

After Adelina left the room, Kara went to the dresser and pulled out a sexy black and hot pink lacey matching bra and panties set and a pair of hot pink socks. She then went to the walk-in closet, finding a hot pink, low cut cashmere sweater that was cut to frame her curves perfectly. It was the exact same color as the socks she'd chosen, and it even matched the pink on the bra. She then found a pair of expensive fitted blue jeans with the same hot pink color jewels creating patterns on the pockets and down the sides. Sitting on a closet shelf was a pair of black K-Swiss tennis shoes. She took the underwear and went into the bathroom.

As Kara walked in, her breath caught in her throat. There was already a bath waiting for her, with red and white rose petals floating in the huge sunken tub. *That sweet man!* She felt the water, and to her surprise it was still hot. Slowly, she stepped into the tub, and the fragrance of the roses enveloped her. At the side of the tub was an expensive all natural rose shampoo, conditioner, and body scrub. She soaked for a while enjoying the relaxing fragrance. It was very soothing. Alexander had thought of everything, including makeup, which actually were the perfect colors for her skin tone. She had seen the makeup sitting on a grooming table the day before, but hadn't had time to look at. By the time Kara finished her daily ritual, and walked through the archway, Alexander had returned.

Adelina and Alexander were sitting on the couches in the middle of another conversation as Kara approached. Alexander looked up allowing a small gasp to escape his lips before he smiled. "You look absolutely stunning."

"You have good taste." She did a pirouette to show Alexander just how good his taste really was.

Alexander stood up. "Hungry?"

Kara closed the few steps between them and wrapped her arms around his neck. "I am, but not just for food." She stood on her tippy toes, looking up on him, teasing him with the desire showing in her big brown eyes.

Alexander understood what she needed, and bent down to make it easier for her. Kara gently kissed him, melting as soon as their lips touched. She pulled back, smiling up at him. "You smell wonderful." He whispered.

"Thanks to Adelina and you."

He sat back down, pulling Kara down onto the couch beside him. "You should eat now. You have to be hungry, it's almost three."

"I slept most the day? How odd. I never sleep this late." She blushed. "Of course, normally I don't have a reason to stay in bed."

Alexander handed Kara a plate filled with a selection of fruits and an omelet. It was delicious.

Adelina excused herself. "I think it's time for me to go. It was wonderful talking to you Kara. Alexander could you get me the reports you need me to deliver. I want to hurry up and deliver them, so I can spend some time with Walter, since he's off today."

Alexander smiled at Kara and winked. "I'll be right back."

While he was gone, Kara took the time to savor the food. She didn't know if Alexander or Adelina had cooked, but it was delicious. She'd heard Alexander was an amazing chef, but assumed Adelina was equally as talented. *I'm sure when you live hundreds of years you have plenty of time to perfect all your hobbies.* That one thought gave Kara more to contemplate. It kind of scared her, and made her feel very insignificant. What could she possibly bring to this relationship? What could she possibly give someone that has lived hundreds of years? She needed to discuss this with Alexander…She needed to understand more about him and his world…She needed him to realize that she's nothing compared to Catherine…and that she can't compete against her.

Alexander returned instantly sensing Kara's distress. He stroked her hair, "Kara? Love, what's wrong? I can feel you're upset."

"What?" She looked up confused.

"You were in deep thought. Do you want to talk about it?"

Alexander reached over and grabbed Kara's hand, entwining their fingers together. That simple physical contact, gave Kara the sense of coming home. The same feeling you get when you've been on vacation and you walk into your house to the feeling of security and warmth. That's what Alexander's touch does to her. *It's like I've came home.* Kara's whole family believes in Soul-mates. Both Kara's grandmothers had found theirs, and even her mom swears Kara's dad is hers. She's been taught her whole life about Soul-mates, and once you find yours, you grab a hold of him and never let go. If you follow this one rule, you guarantee yourself happiness for life, even if it means waiting for them, like Me-ma Sara had to do. It took her twenty years to finally marry Kara's grandpa. Grandpa Earl was so shy and focused on caring for his parents, that by the time he got around to asking Kara's grandmother to marry him he was drafted into World War II. Me-ma Sara had to wait until the war was over for him to finally claim her as his wife. A wait she says was well worth it.

Kara's other grandparents had it equally as difficult. Her grandmother Lalita is Greek and her grandfather Salvatore is Italian. Neither family was happy about them marrying outside of their cultures, so a month after they met they eloped, and it took three years of family fights to finally receive both families blessings.

As for Kara's parents, they had it easiest. They were high school sweethearts. They insist that from the moment they set eyes on each other, they knew they were each other's destiny, and since both sides of her grandparents believed in Soul-mates, they had no problem marrying right out of high school.

So why am I so afraid to tell my parents that I know for sure Alexander is my soul-mate? Is it because he's a Dark-Soul? They already know him. They even like him. Or is it because I would be the first sibling to actually marry? This is what I've waited for, so why am I afraid. Maybe it's because they use the word Amara and that's a word I don't understand, or maybe it's because it seems to be so much more than a soul-mate. Maybe it's just because I'm scared it won't last.

"Love, are you ok? You're in deep thought again."

Kara pulled away from her thoughts and squeezed Alexander's hand. She didn't want to burden him with all her worries. She still had a lot of questions that needed answered, before she could make sense out of her situation. "I was just thinking about my conversation with your sister today."

Alexander looked up frowning. What could they possibly have been discussing while he was gone? "I didn't realize you two had talked much."

"I had a few questions that Adelina was kind enough to answer. There was one question she said I'd need to ask you about however. She said it wasn't her place to explain it to me."

Kara felt Alexander's hand tighten around hers, as his frown became more pronounced. "What was the question?"

Kara felt Alexander's tension. His muscles had tensed up as stiff as a board. "I asked her if you loved your wife, and how exactly she was able to betray you."

Kara felt his anger before he dropped her hand. She didn't know why he was angry, but she knew he was. Alexander had fisted his hands so tight his knuckles were turning white. No, he wasn't angry, he was furious. Kara could feel it in every bone of her body. Alexander's anger and pain washed over her, sending goose-bumps up and down her skin. She could feel it. She could actually *feel* his emotions. She didn't want to look at him, she was too afraid of what she might see, but couldn't stop herself. Part of her wanted to apologize for being so nosy and inconsiderate of his feelings. The other part wanted to demand an answer. Kara glanced up noticing that Alexander's jaw was locked, displaying a prominent tic, like he was grinding his teeth.

Shiz-nat! He still loves her. Fiona might have betrayed him, but he still loves her. An acute wave of jealousy flowed through her so strong that it left her head spinning. *How could he be my soul-mate, if he loves another? He can't be. This will never work. A soul-mate is supposed to be yours. Not yours and another's...not half yours... but yours.* With that revelation tears filled Kara's eyes. She'd almost believed she'd found her fairytale. "I'm sorry, Alexander. I didn't mean to upset you. You must have loved her very much. I didn't mean to hurt you by bringing her up."

"LOVE HER?" Alexander spat furiously. "I can't *stand* the thought of her."

Kara choked back her tears more confused than ever. If he didn't love her, why was he so angry? "You *didn't* love her?"

"I did once, but Fiona taught me to hate her." Pushing back his pain and fury, Alexander realized he'd upset Kara. He felt her anguish. *Why? What did I say to make her upset?*

Alexander glanced over at Kara, but she refused to look at him, even though she could feel his burning glare. She hadn't quite pulled herself together yet, and wasn't about to admit how upset she was. Unexpectedly, he pulled her chin around noticing the glistening of unspent tears. She felt his hand brush her cheek, realizing a tear had escaped and he'd brushed it away.

"Why do you cry?" He asked softly. His whole demeanor instantly changing to the caring person she'd come to know.

"It doesn't matter. I was being s-s-stupid that's all."

"It matters to me. Did my *anger* scare you? I'm sorry if it did." Alexander knew his temper was quite intimidating, it was actually legendary. People have always feared his temper and with good reason.

"It wasn't your anger." Kara sniffled, and Alexander handed her his handkerchief. Kara looked at it as if she'd never seen one, and then wiped her nose with it. "Well, it was, but not for the same reason you're thinking." She admitted, feeling rather dumb being jealous of his *dead* wife. "This will probably sound really stupid, but I thought you still loved her, and that's why you were so angry that I asked about her. I mean…I know she was your wife, but women don't want to know that the person's heart they care about belongs to someone else."

Alexander burst out laughing, pulling Kara into his arms, and holding her close, as he continued to laugh. It stunned her; for she'd never heard him abandonly lose control, except when he's been angry. "OK. Ha-ha-ha. I knew it sounded stupid." She pulled away.

"Hold…on." Alexander gasped attempting to steady his breathing. "I'm not laughing at you, Kara. You're jealous! That makes me extremely happy." His next actions totally knocked Kara for a loop. He swiftly pulled her onto his lap into a deep passionate kiss. A kiss so incredible it rocked spasms from the top of her head to the tips of her toes. His tongue explored her mouth, plummeting her depths, teasing her tongue, until it agreed to dance with his.

"Only you hold my heart, Love." Kara barely heard him say against her lips, before diving back into the moist warmth of her mouth. Only after she was breathless did he finally pull away. This time it was Kara who emerged giggling.

"What's funny?"

"I was just thinking. It's pretty sad that every time your lips touch mine, I completely forget where I am. When you pull away, it takes me a few seconds to re-orientate myself."

Alexander cocked an eyebrow with a smug, arrogant, Oh! So-very-male smile. "Baby, if you liked *that*! I can make you forget your name, and who you are."

Kara waved her hand up and down, near the side of her face swooning. "Whoa! Adonis! You keep that up and we won't be leaving this room today."

Alexander raised his eyebrows chuckling. "You think I'm a god, do you? He smiled wickedly, "I do have some supernatural powers." He rubbed his fingers over Kara's jeans at the very heart of her molten heat. He pulled her close whispering in her ear, gliding her hand down to cup his hefty erection. "I also have some pretty amazing weapons."

Kara's breath was ragged as she nibbled his ear. "Baby, I'm not sure if I should call you Adonis or Hercules."

Kara's thoughts scattered as Alexander's tongue possessed her mouth in a demanding kiss. "Ahhhhhh!" She sighed, entwining her fists into his silky hair. Reciprocating Alexander's demanding tongue with her own, allowing herself to relish in his taste. Alexander replied to Kara's wickedly teasing tongue by plunging his tongue deeper into her mouth, taking control and melting her instantly.

"We need to stop." Alexander said against her lips.

Smiling seductively, Kara gently bit his bottom lip, "You sure?" She asked teasingly.

An amused smile spread across his face. "Love, we could stay here for the next century and I'd still never get enough of you." Alexander winked, "but…this afternoon I have business I need to attend to at the new club, and I was hoping you'd accompany me. Then I have guests arriving, before I meet you at Mel's, since you promised to meet Becky there tonight."

Kara stuck her bottom lip out in the cutest pout he'd ever seen. If he didn't have so many things to attend to, he'd nibble that tempting lip and keep her withering under him the rest of the day.

"You're right." She brushed his lips, "we should go."

~

Since it was the middle of the day, the club was dark and quiet as Alexander shifted them into it. She staggered briefly, still not used to shifting, but the dizziness was lessening each time. Kara looked around not seeing anyone. It was completely silent. After all the people who frequented the club last night, she hadn't expected it to be so clean, but it was spotless.

Kara followed Alexander to a back room which turned into an enormous sized office, and was quite surprised when a human, and he was definitely human, greeted them. "Good Afternoon, Dr. Conti, and this must be Kara."

Alexander smiled at the burly man, who reminded Kara of her brothers. "Hi Ted." He briefly introduced Kara then went about his business looking over some documents Ted had handed him. "How's your wife?"

"Our first is due in October." The man smiled an infectious smile that had Kara liking him instantly.

Alexander slapped him on his shoulder. "Congratulations! You take care of her. She's a wonderful woman." He handed him a hundred with his other hand.

"Don't you worry, Dr. Conti. Adelina made sure we have a good doctor. Thank you." Ted shoved the money in his pocket. "When you gonna settle down? My wife says a nice man like you is a catch, and any *smart* woman would grab a hold of you and never let go."

Alexander chuckled, glancing at Kara. "I don't know how great a catch I am, but tell your wife she's very kind."

"Oh, by the way, Nathaniel returned about a half hour ago. He said to tell you everything is set to your *exact* specifications. Whatever that means?" Ted let out a boisterous laugh. "All of today's deliveries have been put into stock and we're ready to open tonight."

"Thanks Ted, take care of that pretty little wife of yours."

Ted headed for the door. "Alexander, if it's ok, I'm going to follow Ted out and snoop around a little, while you work."

Alexander kissed Kara's knuckles, sending little waves of pleasure dashing over her. "Go ahead. Ted can turn on the music if you'd like. I won't be long."

Kara followed Ted out of Alexander's office. "Miss, would you like me to turn on the lights?" He asked.

Kara glanced around, but there was low lighting casting shadows around the empty room. "No, thank you. This is fine. If you can just turn the music on that would be great."

"Follow me, and I'll show you how to use the music system."

Kara was thrilled. She'd never seen such a technologically advanced system. She was programming a selection of songs, when she felt an ice cold fingernail draw a fine line down her neck. She felt a wave of nausea surge through her, as the hand gripped her neck and a wet slimy tongue struck out, licking a path along Kara's carotid artery. Kara shook with the disgusting feeling. "Little Bitch! I thought I might find you here. Didn't I tell you to stay away from Alexander?"

Catherine spat into her ear, tightening her grip around Kara's throat. "Didn't I?"

Kara gasped for air, nodding her head, knowing she wasn't taking in enough air to scream. She tried to position herself to break Catherine's hold. "You *stupid* little whore. You think you can escape me. I'm 1458 years old. I've broken more human necks than you've ever seen." To emphasize her strength, Catherine lifted her off the floor never releasing her grip on Kara's neck.

Kara thought her life was over, as she prayed to God for salvation. "I normally *don't* give second chances, but I'll make an exception this *one* time. I don't need Alexander's family angry with me, when I become his wife." Catherine tightened her grip even more, cutting off Kara's breathing completely. "Stay *away* from Alexander!" She dropped Kara like a bag of potatoes. Hitting the floor hard, Kara choked trying to breathe, as pain ripped through her body. Catherine reached down jerking Kara's chin to look at her, snarling she warned. "and if you ever *tell* Alexander about this little confrontation, I'll cut your tongue out."

Instantly Catherine shifted and was gone leaving Kara curled up in a ball crying. Kara couldn't think as she laid there on the cold tile floor of the sound booth. How ironic. The song playing was talking about how he used to rule the world. For a few days, Kara had actually believed that she'd finally ruled her own world. Tears were streaming freely when someone walked into the room picking her up and carrying her to the couch. She didn't know how long she'd been there, but she understood true fear for the first time in her life. Kara never doubted Catherine would follow through on her threats.

What am I going to do?

"You're going to complete your destiny. You're going to do what you were born to do."

Kara looked up into a beautiful woman's face. Her long black hair flowed around her, wrapping itself around her body. Her black eyes pierced Kara's soul. Kara wiped her tears away. "W-W-Who are you?"

She laughed. "*Only* a human would ask that question. I'm the Greek Goddess Hecate."

Kara's mouth fell open. "Y-Y-You *really* exist? I mean...like *really* exist. I know Alexander said...but I thought he meant...I didn't know he actually meant he physically talked to you."

"Yes. Pretty much all human myths exist in some fashion." Hecate sat down next to Kara. "You know humans used to believe in us too, until your real creator took you away from us. He is much more powerful than all the ancient pantheons put together, and thought we were abusing our power with *his* children. He sent his own Angels to watch over humans."

Kara rubbed her eyes. Was she dreaming? "No. You're not dreaming. I am very real. Let me explain why I'm here. Cruetians or as you call them, Dark-Souls are *my* people."

Kara sat and listened to Hecate explain how she helped the three Titan protectors escape Zeus and how they created the Cruetian people. Hecate told her that Alexander's father was the first and the strongest of all the Titan protectors, and that Avitus's blood line had many prophecies to fulfill. She said their destinies are intertwined with every being on earth, including humans, and that Kara's destiny was intertwined with Alexander's.

"Now do you understand why I am here? *You* are meant for Alexander. I cannot allow Catherine to scare you away. You are strong, and have a good heart, unlike his first wife. Search your feelings for Alexander. Accept them. Admit them. When you do, Darkness Falls and Catherine will *never* have the power to hurt you." Hecate kissed the top of Kara's head. The bruises on her neck instantly disappeared, erasing all physical evidence of Catherine's attack. "We would not want Alexander to know about Catherine's visit or mine."

With a flash Hecate was gone. Kara slowly took in a deep breath, letting everything she'd learned sink in. Hecate was right, she couldn't let Catherine win. Maybe the world depended on their mating, as Hecate had put it, but Kara's happiness depended on it too, and that was more important than anything else. With a renewed determination she got up and headed for Alexander.

Kara found Alexander standing over his desk, frowning at some reports. She walked up behind him encircling her arms around his waist. She heard him suck in a breath before she laid her cheek on his back. "Dance with me. I need to feel your arms around me."

He felt Kara's fear, she was trembling. "What's wrong?"

"Nothing." Alexander started to protest. "Please Alexander. I don't want to talk, just hold me." She drug him out onto the empty dance floor just as 'Only when we touch' began to play, a perfect song for their dance. Kara began singing as she swayed in Alexander's arms, and by the time 'I'll be following you' began to play; Kara was feeling her joyful self again. Safe in Alexander's arms as he spun them around the dance floor.

"You're a very accomplished dancer." She teased.

"I've had a long time to practice." Alexander winked, spinning Kara away from him then pulling her back into his embrace. Just as the song ended he dipped her, kissing her until her lips were swollen with his kisses, and she was flushed a lovely crimson red.

Alexander loved seeing Kara's eyes glow with passion from his touch. Seeing the burning fire in her eyes and knowing it was all for him. He was determined to make sure that she never lost that desire.

19

To assure Kara's protection, Alexander was awaiting the arrival of more of his Generals. They'd discovered Seth's assassins in Denver, which was closer than Alexander felt comfortable with. He still hadn't told Kara about the danger, but he might not have to at the rate their relationship was progressing.

He glanced at his watch, it was 6:30pm and Kara had left for Mel's a couple hours ago. His Generals would arrive in the next half-hour and then he would be able to join her. He hated being away from her, but her protection was more important than even his own desire to spend time with her. Alexander would never risk her life.

He looked down at his cell phone noticing he had two missed calls. Flipping it open he dialed his voice mail. The first message was letting him know three of his five commanders would arrive today, but the other two wouldn't arrive until the debriefing tomorrow. It was the second message that sent a wave of excitement through him. Kara had called. Oh, how he wished he had heard his phone. She had called for no other reason, than to let him know that she already missed him, and was looking forward to seeing him tonight. Such precious words leaving her lips, was heaven to his ears. Kara's voice sent his heart flying. This was the first time she'd called him, and for nothing more, than to tell him she couldn't wait to see him. The tenderness and sincerity in her voice stole his breath, and made him wish that his Generals would hurry up and arrive.

Kara strolled into Mel's around 6 pm, prepared to keep her promise to Becky, and help teach some of their friends how to dance, so they didn't embarrass her at her wedding.

Since Becky was still M.I.A., she sat down at a table near the dance floor wishing Alexander was with her, but knowing he'd join her as soon as his friends arrived, eased her anxiety.

"Whacha doin?" Becky teased as she plopped down, handing Kara a glass of Moscato. "Ooo, your blushing beet red. You're thinking about Alexander, aren't you?"

"No!" Kara rolled her eyes wishing Becky wasn't able to read her mind so clearly.

"Don't lie to me, bee-atch. I can see it all over your face, and you know what I think...I think you in looooove." Becky taunted her.

Kara smiled and punched her arm. "Just...Shut up!"

"So, what *did* you two do last night anyway?" Becky wagged her eyebrows.

"Actually, *Miss Nosy*, we were with *you* at Club Nouveau. Remember?"

She snorted. "Right! That was only part of the night, and I know you didn't go home last night."

Kara gave her a smug look. "So! What's your point?"

"Oh! I don't know. Maybe it wasn't *my* point you were thinking about." Becky giggled "but possibly some tall blonde's *point* you're remembering." Leaning across the table, she pointed at her "If you ask me, you're probably just making up for lost virgin time...your slut is finally making an appearance."

Kara couldn't help herself, as she burst out laughing. "Oh! Yeah! You have *no* idea how appetizing his body is." They both cracked up.

"So, you're telling me he looks just as delicious under those clothes, as he does in them?"

"Becky!" Kara blushed. "What I'm telling you is that man is hotter than Shiz-nat with his clothes on, but naked...he's just plain sex-on-a-stick. I just want to *devour* him."

"Oh...my...god!" Using her best California-Valley-Girl impersonation, Becky exclaimed. "You've gone from virgin to slut" snapping her fingers, "just...like...that!"

Kara snorted. "Yeah, like you're one to talk. If I remember correctly, I didn't see you for...what?...like two months after you met

Alan. So I don't want to hear it little *Miss Tramp* with a capital 'T'. Now if you don't mind gathering everyone together. I think it's time to start teaching, so when *"my sexy babe"* struts in, I can devote my time to him."

"Ohmygod! You have it bad." Becky chuckled as she turned to leave.

Kara watched Becky move through the crowd gathering people onto the dance floor. Becky always could see right through her, and she had been right. She *had* been thinking about Alexander and their time together last night. He had found the movie *Alexander* playing on cable and insisted watching it. Kara had enjoyed watching him more than the movie, as he became angry over how Hollywood portrayed the people of that time period. It was rather hysterical to watch him.

Kara mentioned that he hadn't even been alive during that time, but Alexander admonished her, explaining that his family had personal knowledge of '*Alexander*', and that Hollywood was not portraying him 100% accurately.

She couldn't stop thinking about Alexander. She knew it was crazy, but she couldn't get him out of her mind. The worst part was the *way* she kept thinking about him. Always Naked!

Maybe Becky's right. Maybe I have turned into a slut.

Because the things she imagined doing to him...Damn...they were probably illegal, and if they weren't, well...let's just say...they should be. In fact, Kara's body burned for him, it burned so bright that she sometimes felt like she was touching the sun. Even her dreams had become erotic as hell. She could swear she would feel his hands caressing her skin, and his tongue lathing her breasts, as he toyed with her in more ways than she had ever fantasized about.

Alexander had indulged one of Kara's fantasies just last night. She had fantasized about making love to him wearing his armor, specifically his Roman Centurion armor. She had teased him after the movie, telling him that she *now* understood why ancients were so open about sex, because men wearing *that* armor were guaranteed to get laid...a lot!

He had laughed and pulled her into his weapons room asking,

"Which one?" She had pointed to one of the glass cases. "Ah, yes. That's right, my Roman Centurion armor." He cocked an eyebrow, "Red...I should have remembered."

Kara bit her bottom lip shyly. "It is pretty sexy."

Alexander walked over to a touch pad and tapped in a set of numbers. Kara watched with anticipation, as she heard the lock click and the glass case opened. He pulled out his armor and headed for the bedroom. "Give me five minutes, and we'll test your theory."

She had continued admiring Alexander's swords and armor until she felt his return. She turned to find him standing in the archway looking as obscene as she had imagined. "Oh! Baby! My walking fantasy in the flesh!" She slowly surveyed him up and down, noticing how short it actually was. She could literally see a good portion of his inner thighs. "Um...um...um...Holy shit! The way you look I'm surprised Rome conquered anyone outside of the bedroom. Do you... like ...wear something under that?"

He gave her a wicked smile before answering. "We did, but I thought it would be...more appropriate to leave it off this time."

"Oh, you smart...smart man! You're going to be very happy you did that." She took a step towards him, and then realized he was granting her one of her fantasies, and she'd never asked about any of his. "Do you have a fantasy?"

He quickly closed the distance between them. "I'm *looking* at my 800 year fantasy."

Kara blushed, realizing Alexander was dead serious. In one fluid movement, before she could even let a small gasp escape; he had pushed her up against the wall, pushed her dress up around her waist, tore her thong off her body, and in one powerful thrust had buried himself deep inside her...all the way to his hilt.

Breathless she exclaimed, "So, this is how a Roman made love to his woman."

"Sweeting, we're just getting started. Romans had lots of stamina and Dark-Souls" he wagged his eyebrows "have even more."

And by God, Alexander had not been lying about that! She blushed, as she pushed the memory of last night into the back of her brain, and headed for the dance floor. As much as she wanted to dream about Alexander, right now she had a job to do.

Right! Teach Wedding dances to Becky's friends.

Alexander walked into Mel's finding Kara on the dance floor teaching ballroom dancing. She was currently helping Alan learn how to twirl her and bring her back into his arms. A wave of pride rushed over Alexander as he watched how graceful she was. Kara danced with an elegant fluid grace that even most professional dancers would kill for. As he guided his group to a table, he heard Becky snapping at Kara.

"Alright Ker, we *got* the basics." She sounded annoyed. "Now teach us to do *that* to 'Sway'. You promised."

"Ok! Ok!" Kara glanced around the dance floor. "Um...Darrius, please come here. I need a good dance partner to show everyone this." She yelled into the crowd.

"Damn, sis. Do I have to? You know I hate being your guinea pig." Darrius strolled forward with a young brunette on his arm. "Sorry, Maria. This will only take a few minutes." He pulled a chair out for her at a nearby table, so she could sit down, and then headed for Kara.

"This better not take very long."

"It won't!" Kara pulled him to the middle of the dance floor. "Hey Nancy, would you play 'Sway', and put it on repeat, please." Positioning Darrius where she wanted him, she turned her attention to the crowd. "Ok, everyone, we'll show you what this should look like, and then you can all try. I'll come around to assist anyone with questions afterwards."

As the music began, Darrius guided Kara around the floor in a sweeping, flowing display of Latin ballroom dancing. Alexander had to admit that Darrius was a pretty good dancer for a twenty-first century guy. Unlike gentleman of previous centuries that had to learn to dance to fit into society, the men of this last century didn't need to learn to dance unless they wanted to, and from what he'd seen so far, most of them did *not* want to.

"Dang, *adelfos* look at Kara move. If she wasn't your *Amara*, I'd be stealing her from you." Nathaniel said jokingly.

Alexander slapped the back of his head playfully and growled, "I would kill you if you tried."

The three new arrivals laughed. Conrad, Tycho, and Masaga were three of Alexander's best Commanders, he respected them and even considered them friends, but he would not have his brother teasing him in front of his Generals. It just wasn't proper.

Alexander heard Kara telling everyone it was their turn to try. He stood, excusing himself before making his way out onto the dance floor.

"Is that *really* the General's *Amara*?" Conrad asked Nathaniel, watching a petite, little sensuous blonde, enticing everyone with her hips.

"Yes, it is! So if I were you, I wouldn't piss her off. *Kyrios* doesn't like her getting upset." Nathaniel warned.

Kara was standing on the side of the dance floor, watching everyone try to mimic her and Darrius, when Alexander bent down and kissed her neck, spinning her back onto the dance floor. Laughing light heartedly, she instantly began swaying, picking up where Darrius and her had left off just minutes before.

"Are you aware, when you move that way I can't keep my hands off you?" Alexander whispered in her ear, pulling her into a hot kiss.

"Well, if you like this, you'll love the next song." She teased when he released her lips.

Kara wasn't exaggerating when a minute later 'Your Hips Don't Lie' began to play. Like the first day Alexander had met Kara, her hips started moving in that seductively hypnotic fashion that made his mouth water, but this time she took pity on him, putting his hands on her hips while she moved in rhythm to the music.

All of Alexander's blood raced from his brain to the straining member between his thighs. He was instantly so hot and hard he couldn't think straight. The sensation of Kara grinding against him drove every ounce of rational thinking out of his mind, and all he wanted was her *naked*...on the floor...against the wall...bent over a table...in his bed. He was imaging a hundred ways he wanted to take her, and another thousand ways he'd make her wriggle with pleasure, so she'd never doubt the sincerity of his desire for her. He dreamed of scooping her into his arms and shifting her home, so he could make sweet passionate love to her. He could keep her locked in his bedroom for days.

He groaned, and then another image entered his mind. Alexander imagined pushing her up against the nearest wall and taking her hard and fast like he'd done last night in his Armory. Of course, with Kara's temper it would probably just get him slapped, or worse, he might actually lose his member. So when the song ended, he discreetly adjusted himself, and pulled her towards his table so he could introduce her to his officers, and distract himself from these erotic thoughts.

Alexander was proud to see all his Generals stand at their approach. Of course, if they hadn't he would have raked them over the coals. Kara might not understand her position in his world, but his people did. "Kara, I'd like you to meet General Conrad Callaway, General Tycho, and General Masaga." He pointed to each man in turn. "Conrad is a Knight from Sixteenth Century England." Conrad placed one arm across his stomach and bowed.

"Wow!" Kara exclaimed. "A *real* Knight in Shining Armor." Conrad laughed.

"Tycho is an ancient Greek General from Thrace." Tycho kissed the back of Kara's hand. "*Kyria*."

"A Hoplite?" Kara inquired.

"Indeed, *Kyria*. I'm impressed with your historical knowledge." Tycho added, peering over her shoulder at Alexander as he continued with the introductions.

"And Masaga was a Samurai." Masaga bowed low at the waist.

She returned his bow. Then went on to say 'It's nice to meet you' in Japanese, shocking all of Alexander's Generals. "*Hajimemashite.*"

Masaga's head snapped up, piercing her eyes with his stare, asking if she spoke Japanese. "*nihongo hanase masu ka?*"

"*hai, su koshi dake.*" Kara explained, in broken Japanese that she only spoke a little.

"Interesting!" Masaga cocked an eyebrow and glanced at Alexander.

"My *Amara* is full of surprises." He admitted.

All of them were excruciatingly handsome. Conrad was as tall as Alexander with short curly dark hair and brown eyes. The only flaw on his body was a scar that ran across his left cheek. Tycho's features were closer to Alexander's. He was at least four inches taller than Alexander, with dark blonde hair and blue eyes, and like Alexander, another sample of God's perfection. Masaga reminded her a lot of Uncle Chung. He had that warrior demeanor about him. His black hair was long and he had it pulled back into a ponytail, he was shorter than everyone else by at least five inches, and his dark eyes looked almost black. There was no doubt this man was dangerous. Every one of his movements accentuated that fact. Naturally, as Dark-Souls, anyone of these men could grace the cover of GQ magazine, but not one of them, made her body burn with need the way Alexander did. That one fact alone sobered Kara. She had been worried, that her uncontrollable attraction to Alexander was simply because he's drop dead gorgeous. Now she knew the truth. The strong culminating desire inside her was solely for him. A fact that made her heart soar, with the realization that Alexander was *truly* her soul-mate. The one man she'd been waiting her whole life for.

"It's a pleasure to meet all of you." She said wrapping her arm around Alexander's waist. "Wow-Wow-Wow! The things you've all seen in your lifetimes. It has to be really fascinating. I'd love to discuss it with you all someday.

She turned to greet the rest of the table. Hey, Uncle Chung... Tiberius...Nathaniel, Ow!" Someone pinched her butt, and Kara swung around irritated, as the three Generals jumped up to protect her. "You *stupid* ass!" She yelled as Trent jumped back out of her way.

"Whooooaaaa...Sis...It's just me." Trent laughed with his hands held up in surrender. "Just an early birthday pinch to grow an inch, which we all know you need." He stuck his tongue out at her. "Although, I think you're getting old." He teased smiling. "Normally you'd have me by the balls, but you weren't even close." He snickered, slapping her cheeks playfully. "You missed!"

"It's just her brother." Alexander explained to his commanders, motioning them to sit back down. "She's not in any danger." He watched his Generals relax back down into their chairs before turning to Trent. "They're not used to human bantering" he pointed out.

"Yeah, it's just my *dead* brother if he does that again." Kara punched Trent's arm. "You *know* I'm still jumpy. What the hell are you thinking? Did you have a death wish or were you hoping I'd make you sterile?"

Trent gently punched her back. "You know...I *feel* for you, Alexander. Kara's the only one of my sisters, that's an *enemy* to a male's family jewels." He grimaced. "I wouldn't piss her off. It's the first thing she tends to grab for. Oh, and a warning. She has no qualms with twisting." He gave her a pointed look.

She patted Trent's cheek sarcastically, "Ah, poor-poor baby. You're just mad that men have a weakness, and I have no problem exploiting it."

There were chuckles around the table. "You guys can laugh now" Trent chided. "Just wait till you're on the receiving end." That shut them up. "You know *Miss Ball Breaker*. You were never this mean until after Steven screwed you over. He's still never experienced your *full* wrath. You were actually pretty gentle with him at the bar that night. Maybe if you grabbed a hold of him with *all* your strength, he'd leave you alone." He teased her. "Of course, we had fun knocking him around last night, so, maybe you should let us handle him."

"*Ball Breaker!*" Tycho mouthed to Nathaniel. Nathaniel nodded, leaning over to whisper. "You should have *seen* what she did to her ex. That guy's lucky it didn't shrivel up and fall off."

"What do you mean you knocked him around last night?" Kara stared at Trent accusingly.

"Becky called Trey and told him how Steven's been harassing you." He shrugged, "So, we handled it."

She glared at him. "Handled it...how exactly?"

"Don't give me that look, Ker. He's still alive. Barely! But he's still breathing, which equates to being alive." He chortled "and yes, he hit us first and we had witnesses to prove it."

Uncle Chung grabbed Kara's arm. "How many times a day is he calling you, and don't you *dare* try to lighten mood. How many?"

"It's not as bad as before." She replied, squirming out of her uncle's grip. "He's still much worse in person."

Alexander growled. "Kara, that did not answer the question, and why didn't you tell me?"

She rolled her eyes at him. "First of all, it doesn't concern you. Second, it wasn't a big deal. It was just a few stupid phone calls."

"It *is* my concern. You're my *Amara*. As your mate, it's *my* job to protect you." Alexander snarled.

Kara closed her eyes and gritted her teeth. Speaking under her breath, she ranted, "Arrogant men! I am surrounded by stupid arrogant men." Although it did her absolutely no good to say it under her breath, with their sensitive hearing every Dark-Soul present could hear her, just as if she was shouting it at them.

"In her defense," Trent stepped forward, "she didn't even tell us. Becky did." He gave Kara a disgusting look. "My sister obviously thinks she's invincible."

"Not invincible," She corrected, "just not helpless. I'm *not* one of those helpless little chits." She sarcastically smiled at all of them. "I'm the *Ball Breaker* remember. Now enough of Steven! I don't even want to think about him. As long as he's alive and none of you are in jail, I'm good." Kara looked around to see them all frowning at her. "You know. Right now, I think I need to get away from all this alpha-male-testosterone."

"Oh, shit!" Trent snapped. "That's why I came over here. Becky's asking for you to sing."

"Ugh! Now? Right, now?" He nodded. "Fine! Alright!" Kara stood on her tippy toes and pulled Alexander down into a kiss. "I'll be back." He pulled her tighter inhaling her sweet floral scent, before releasing her.

Alexander loved Kara's obvious display of affection. It lightened his heart, and had him feeling things he never thought was possible. *Maybe this would work out. Maybe Kara is different. Fiona never touched me willingly, especially never in public, but Kara doesn't seem to mind at all.* He smiled as he watched her walk to the stage, but became amused when she didn't get up on it. He knew how much she hated attention, in yet; she was so talented it begged for the spotlight.

Becky handed the wireless microphone to Kara and they started skimming through love songs for the wedding. Kara's voice was soft and gentle, but when she sang she held a passion that pulled at the very fabric of Alexander's being. He could listen to her for eternity, but right now, he had more important things to take care of. He needed to make sure she was fully protected, even from that dumb shit, Steven. He didn't give a damn if Kara was an independent woman or not. He was the man! *Her* man and *her* protector, and he would do his job, no matter how irritated she became.

"Trent, will Steven leave Kara alone or do we need to take more drastic measures to keep him away from her." Alexander asked.

Trent looked up from his conversation with Alexander's Generals, "Hey, don't worry about it. We've handled Steven before, and between Chung, my brothers, and me, we'll do it again. I don't think he'll come near Kara again for a while. Although, I have to admit he's a little delusional this time. He's somehow made up his mind that they were meant to be together." Trent snorted. "Trey gave him a black eye when he said that. I don't know how he can honestly believe that she would ever take him back."

"For that matter," Chung interrupted, "if Kara ever even considered it, we'd *kill* him. He took Kara's innocence away from her. She trusted everyone before he cheated on her, after that, she looked at every man suspiciously, waiting for them to hurt her. He was lucky I let him live then. If he keeps it up, he won't be so lucky this time."

Alexander's jaw ticked, as his hands fisted at his side. He was still unsure of Kara's feelings for him, but like hell would he let some asshole come between them. He'd kill Steven himself.

"Commander, do you want us to handle this?" Masaga asked looking between Conrad and Tycho

"No!" Alexander snapped more sternly than he should have. They were his trusted Generals, bound to protect the royal family, which now included Kara. Naturally, they would want to be involved.

Masaga put his hands up, "Sorry, Commander. We just thought......"

"No, General. I apologize." He sighed. "It's just that Kara is a......"

"Pain in the ass!" Trent filled in.

"No." Alexander chuckled. "Independent was the word I think I was looking for. She'd be angry if we went after him. She trusts in human laws, and would not approve of us using our beliefs in this instance. For right now, we'll watch and wait, but in the future, I might need your assistance in this matter."

Tycho combed his hand through his hair. "Damn *Kyrios*! You seem a little *soft* where she's concerned. Since when do you give a shit what a woman thinks, or for that matter what anyone thinks?" Alexander placed both his large hands on the table and leaned over, as Tycho recanted. "No disrespect, Commander. I didn't mean anything more than sometimes women don't always know what's best for them. You of all people know that."

Nathaniel slapped Tycho on the back. "I'd watch what you say around Kara. She's special, and she doesn't like..." He looked at Alexander for help. "How did she put it?...um...arrogant, domineering men."

"You can say that again." Chung chuckled.

They all started laughing. "Then how the *hell* is she going to put up with *Kyrios*." Conrad choked out between laughs.

"Shut up! All of you." Alexander warned, and they all immediately stopped laughing. They knew that look on their Commander's face. He wasn't joking, and none of them wanted to be on the receiving end of his anger. He would take them down without a second thought.

"Hey, it's ok Alexander. You don't have to be so defensive." Trent cut in, "My baby sister is a *royal* pain in the ass, and personally my whole family thinks you have a huge set of cojones just attempting to deal with her. Kara's so *damned* stubborn; we all lose any battle we try to wage against her. But Nathaniel's right, she's also special. She has strength that none of my other sisters have, but more importantly is her love, it's *truly* unconditional. That's why we all hate Steven so much. He ripped her apart. He shredded her. He shredded her heart, he shredded her mind, but most of all, he shredded her strength. She was like a little lost puppy, for a very long time after that happened. If you had seen her then, you wouldn't have recognized her."

"Trent's right. Steven didn't just break Kara's heart." Chung interjected. "He broke her spirit. None of us that lived through that time with her will ever let that happen again. He's also correct when he says that Kara loves unconditionally, but because she loves unconditionally, it makes her very vulnerable."

20

Alexander had heard Kara taking requests from the crowd, but hadn't realized she'd been singing for over an hour, until he heard her announce, "I appreciate everyone's support, but if I continue with the requests and dedications I'll lose my voice." He glanced over at Kara as she continued speaking, "and there is one dedication I need to make before my voice is completely gone, so I apologize if I've missed anyone's requests, but I promise to get to them next time. My last song tonight is dedicated to an incredible man that has recently become very important in my life." She turned to Nancy, "'Forever in Your Eyes' please."

Alexander's mouth fell open. He was stunned to the point he couldn't think to move. She was already singing when he finally pulled himself together. Kara was singing…for him? She'd announced to everyone that he was important to her, and she had to have been talking about him, because he was the only new man in her life… wasn't he?

Alexander couldn't breathe, as his mind grasped the realization of what Kara was doing. He locked onto Kara's eyes as she walked towards him.

"Look in my heart, and what do you see…I see you smiling back at me…the closer I look…the harder I fall…your love has healed my heart…I feel the heavens…each time in your arms…Your loving kisses are making me strong…and each and every time I look in your eyes… Forever is all that I see…"

She traced her fingernail along the back of Alexander's shoulders. His body immediately awakened to her touch, making him instantly

ANN MARIE KAZUTOMI

hard and straining with desire. Kara slowly circled him, sending chills
up and down his spine, before she sat on his trembling lap.

*"Suddenly now...I see the light...the darkness before...has turned
so bright...I look in your eyes and forever is all that I see...for your
love has healed that lonely girl inside me...Now that were one...our
hearts are bound...our love now grows strong...and it's out of our
hands...I no longer hide the love that I feel inside...for I see forever in
your beautiful deep blue eyes..."*

As the song ended she whispered in his ear, "I love you, Alexan......"
Before the last syllable left her mouth, Alexander growled capturing
her lips in the most desperate kiss she'd ever experienced. She felt his
excitement, relief, and something else she couldn't understand in his
kiss. Kara moaned in delight as his tongue invaded and dominated
hers.

Alexander groaned as he deepened their kiss tasting the true depth
of Kara's passion, her tenderness, her love for *him*. He growled with
the satisfaction of that knowledge. *She's accepted me.*

Kara was having trouble thinking with the intensity that Alexander
was kissing her. Her body burned for him and him alone. Every part
of Alexander invaded her mind, her heart, her body, until she was
spinning out of control with need.

She felt someone pull the microphone out of her hand. "Sorry, Ker.
Nancy needs this back." She heard Becky say, but Kara was too far
away to answer. Right now, all she was focusing on was the sensations
racing through her body from Alexander's kiss, the stroking of his
tongue against hers, his strong powerful hands holding her tight
against him, the hardness of her nipples pressed up against his rock
solid muscles, and the burning ache in her core. She was ready to
combust. Kara buried her hands deep in his silky hair, pulling him
even closer to her, wanting more.

Alexander gasped as he felt her pert nipples pressed against
his chest, his hands begged to cup each of them, while his mouth
anticipated suckling each rose bud deeply.

Kara felt the hot moisture pooling at the juncture of her thighs, as
his impressive cock pressed into her buttocks, sending thrills ravishing

290

her body in anticipation. Oh, how Kara wished she could sink down on him, right now, taking him deep inside her.

"Can they breathe? They've been that way for a while now." Conrad joked with the others at the table. "I guess we can all assume our commander is also skilled at kissing. Not that I really *needed* to know that."

"They do look pretty cozy, don't they?" Masaga stated. "Did anyone start timing them? This could be a new world record."

Nathaniel laughed, "No, I didn't. It never occurred to me that next to fighting, kissing was Alexander's greatest skill."

"Oh! I could have told you that." Chung chided, I've watched your brother entertain a good many women. All of who have dropped at his feet. In fact, he practiced pleasuring women, like he practiced his fighting skills. He truly made it a work of art."

Tycho gave them all a menacing stare. "You do know, when Alexander comes back to his senses, he's going to slap you all back to the first century." He reached across and gently shoved Alexander. "Commander, your *Amara* has adequately displayed the first stage of consent. Now you two should probably go get a room. You're making us all sick."

Alexander pulled back in response to the amusement in Tycho's voice. He chuckled as he caressed Kara's cheek with his thumb. "Yes, she has, hasn't she. Although, I can *assure* you she's unaware of it."

Kara blushed beet red, as the heat of the situation reached her cheeks. She'd completely forgotten they were in a crowded bar. When she kisses Alexander, it becomes just the two of them, nothing else in the world matters. Worse, she had obviously done something wrong.

"Hey Alexander, you know that's still my baby sister." Trent castigated. "I don't really enjoy watching your lips all over her."

"Shut up, Trent!" Irritated Kara snapped. "I don't need you flexing your muscles right now." She looked up at Alexander, "What did I do wrong? What *first* stage is Tycho talking about?" Alexander smiled at the dire look in Kara's eyes. "You did nothing wrong, love." He gently kissed her palm, "In ancient Rome for a woman to accept a man…in marriage. They had to perform three steps of consent. The first was a public display of affection. The second was reciting the vows of consent during the wedding ceremony, in front of a minimum of ten witnesses, and the third and final step was for the bride to repeat the consent chant again before being carried over the threshold." Alexander gave all of them a warning glare. "They were just teasing, love. No need for you to worry about anything. Everything is perfect." He brushed her lips with his. "You'll need to excuse me for a few minutes, sweetheart. Tiberius and I have a little business to attend to."

"Must you go?" She wiggled in his lap.

Alexander groaned. "You keep that up my little tease, and you'll be bent over my lap, giving Romans a *whole new* meaning to a woman's show of public acceptance."

Kara shyly smiled, biting her bottom lip, and almost sending Alexander to his knees. "All right then, but hurry back. I'll miss you."

Alexander gathered her against him placing a hard fiery kiss on her lips. "I'll be right back. Promise."

⟨✦⟩

Sorella! Alexander projected into Adelina's mind.

Alexander? What's happened? What's wrong? She answered back.

Nothing's wrong. In fact, everything's perfect! I'm going to propose to Kara.

Tonight?

Alexander smiled at the shocked tone of her voice in his mind.

Yes! She's at Mel's right now. Tiberius and I have left to get the ring. If you want to be there for this, you better hurry.

Alright! Walter and I will shift there now. Let Dante know.

I will.

After projecting his intentions to Dante, Alexander and Tiberius shifted outside of their family's vault in Italy. "I thought you were going to wait until tomorrow?" Tiberius commented placing his hand on the vault's scanner.

"That was my plan." Alexander placed his hand on the second

scanner. The royal vault required two family member's handprints to open it. "However, after Kara's recent display of affection, I think tonight's the perfect time. Don't you?"

"I don't know." Tiberius admitted. "Is she ready? Do you think she'll say yes?"

Alexander opened the red velvet box and looked at Kara's engagement ring.

"She'll love it." Tiberius assured him. "Although, Kara doesn't seem like the materialistic type." Tiberius hit Alexander on the back. "You never answered me. Do you think she'll say yes?"

Closing the box, Alexander glanced up at Tiberius. "I think she already has. That's what I meant, about tonight being the right time. Kara uses song's to express her feelings, and" A huge smile encompassed his face, "Kara just told me she loved me."

Tiberius grabbed Alexander into a bear hug. "Congratulations, *adelfos*. It's about time. Let's go put this on my little sister."

Not long after Alexander had left, Adelina, Walter, and Dante shifted into the hallway. Kara knew they had shifted, because she always watched her surroundings, and knew they hadn't been at Mel's tonight. Since they came out of a hallway that had no entrance, it was obvious they had shifted here. She was still getting used to them appearing and disappearing with that whole shifting thing, although it does come in handy when you need to get somewhere quick. She was surprised when they seemed to ignore her and made their way over to Becky and her sisters'.

Adelina could feel the confusion rolling off Kara, but wanted to talk to her family before Alexander returned. "Hi, Everyone."

"Hey, Adelina…Walter…Dante." Kami chirped. "We thought you weren't going to make it tonight. Thought you and your hubby wanted some alone time. What happened? Did you miss us?"

Adelina smiled amusingly. Knowing Alexander was about to propose to Kara. "No, but we didn't want to miss what's about to happen either, so we changed our plans."

Confused looks flashed towards Adelina from Kara's family "What's going to happen?" Darrius was the first to ask.

Adelina shook her head. "I'm not going to piss off Alexander by ruining his surprise. If you want to know, stick around, you'll witness it for yourself." She chuckled. "Follow me." She guided them over to the table where Kara was sitting with Alexander's Generals, and Nathaniel, Chung, and Trent. They pulled up chairs, just as Alexander strolled up beaming.

Alexander couldn't wait to put Kara's ring on her finger. He'd spent hours at the jeweler picking out the proper setting. The center was the five caret round pink diamond acquired from the Goddess Hecate specifically for his *Amara*. It's a one of a kind, just like Alexander's chosen one. He decided to have two, three caret princess diamonds mounted on either side of the pink diamond, and baguette diamonds embedded down the sides of the engagement ring. He just hoped Kara liked it. Alexander couldn't remember ever being this nervous. As he neared the table, he took the ring out of the velvet box, putting it in his mouth, and handed the box to Tiberius.

Oddly Kara was sitting between Nathaniel and Adelina. It was a lucky break for Alexander. He could easily make Nathaniel move with just a thought. *fratellino!* Nathaniel looked up at his brother. *I need to sit next to Kara. Move!* Nathaniel scooted out allowing Alexander to slide in next to Kara, before falling back in beside him. The rest of the crowd talked amongst themselves, as Alexander took Kara's left hand and slowly kissed and suckled each of her fingers, causing a deep blush to blossom across her cheeks.

Kara gasped as Alexander worked his magic on each of her fingers, leaving her panting with need and ardor. Alexander left Kara's ring finger for last. He slowly suckled her ring finger into his mouth then using his talented tongue, he slid the engagement ring onto her third finger.

Kara sucked in a deep breath as she felt a ring encircle her finger. As he released her hand from his mouth, he held it covering the ring.

Adelina kicked Becky under the table. *"Pay Attention!"* She silently mouthed, as Becky did the same thing to each of Kara's siblings. Becky wasn't sure what was happening, but she knew it must be important by the looks on all the Dark-Soul's faces.

Adelina held up a finger to her mouth telling them all "Shh!"

Kara couldn't breathe as she realized what Alexander was asking. She'd waited her whole life for this moment. She'd dreamed of this moment, the moment her soul-mate would make her his. The moment when she would *actually* belong to someone. The moment she would no longer ever be alone.

Alexander leaned down nipping her earlobe. *"Amaya,* marry me?" He used the Cruetian endearment 'my love'. A term he'd never called another woman. Not even his previous wife.

Kara sucked in a small amount of air, gasping as Alexander placed small kisses along her jaw. "I've waited 800 years for you. Please don't make me wait any longer. Please make me the happiest man on earth, by giving me the honor of being my bride. I promise you, you'll never regret it."

Bewildered! Kara was paralyzed by all the sensations and feelings running rampid around her mind and fluttering through her body. It wasn't until all the gasps and the "Oh-my-God! Alexander just proposed to Kara." That she was able to find her voice. Still dazed, Kara's tear filled eye's looked into the deep aqua ocean of Alexander's. They seemed lighter than normal and sparkled with anticipation. "Yes! Oh, Alexander, Yes!" He cupped the back of Kara's neck and kissed her passionately, deeply, allowing her to feel all the love he'd dreamed of giving a woman. All the love he dreamed of giving *this* woman. *His Amara!*

Alexander pulled back whispering in Kara's ear, "I hope you like this, but if not we'll change it." He released her hand enough to kiss her engagement ring, then held her hand out so she could fully view it.

Kara gasped. It was beautiful. She'd never seen anything like it, it was absolutely perfect. She threw her arms around his neck and kissed him breathless, as Alexander gathered her into his lap and laughed, "I take it you like it."

"Love it. It's truly exquisite." Kara purred, holding it out to admire it.

"Just like you." Alexander brushed back a strand of her hair.

Pride ripped through Kara as she realized Alexander really was *her* man. This was actually happening, and he would be *her* husband. Alexander was *her* future. She no longer had to search for it, it was staring her in the face. Kara looked around the table at her family, new and old, and blushed. Immediately realizing they had all been watching Alexander's proposal. Her sisters and Becky were all gawking. Everyone else was speechless.

Tiberius was the one who finally broke the silence. Reaching for Kara's left hand he kissed her ring, "Welcome to our family, little sister…*Kyria.*"

She shook her head, confused, why did they always say her name wrong. "Thank you. I'm…honored." Kara responded, as each of Alexander's family and General's repeated Tiberius's actions.

Alexander leaned into Kara and whispered, "It's tradition for our people to welcome a new addition to our family. If you don't mind, I'll take you to meet my parents tomorrow after your birthday party."

Kara kissed his cheek, letting Alexander know she would be honored to meet his parents. Now that she had accepted him and appeared to love her engagement ring, the pressure was off Alexander. For the first time in centuries, he sat back and relaxed. Draping his arm over Kara's shoulders protectively, he was at peace. *Finally*, his future, and his people's, looked promising.

Kasi was the first to speak on Kara's side. "Congratulations and Welcome to *our* family, Alexander. Um…our family has lots of traditions as well, and I'm sure you'll be immersed in all of them soon enough." she laughed.

"Your family and friends are now ours. They should *all* come to the birthday party tomorrow as well. This way we can not only get to know one another, but we can celebrate." Kami said with a little too much excitement. "Oh-my-Gosh! Kara *you're engaged*!"

Kali started crying, "You're engaged. My sister's *really* engaged." She laughed, wiping her tears with the back of her hand.

"As your best friend, I demand to see your ring first." Kara laughed at Becky's somber tone, and put her hand on the table. Becky pulled Kara's hand towards her to inspect it in detail.

"Oh, my…Is this…Is this really…a diamond?" Becky pointed to the pink stone.

Adelina nodded her head, "Yes, it's a very special pink diamond."

"A what?" Kara asked confused, she'd never heard of a pink diamond before. She'd thought it was a pink sapphire.

"Only you wouldn't know what a pink diamond was." Becky chided disapprovingly. "It's only the rarest diamond in the world."

Alexander smiled amusingly watching the shock spread across Kara's face. "It's a one of a kind. Just like *my Amara*." He said affectionately. "After Adelina found you, I spent most of the day at the jeweler designing your engagement ring. I had planned a romantic proposal after your birthday party, but after your revelation earlier, I thought tonight was a more appropriate time."

Kara cupped his cheek, looking deeply into his eyes. "You designed this ring *specifically* for me? *You* designed it?" She searched his eyes for her answer.

He nodded. "That I did." It warmed his heart to know that Kara was more interested in the fact that he designed it, then in the rare pink diamond. It confirmed his conclusions about her. Kara's heart was good and decent; she was a person with strong morals. This was the type of woman who wouldn't betray him. Unlike the others, Kara was not with him for his money or his stature. She had no idea how much he or his family was worth, and she never seemed greedy. She had actually been angry when she'd learned about the bonuses he'd given her employees to care for her store. The clubs were the only businesses Kara knew he owned. She didn't even seem to care that Alexander was a prince. She hadn't even mentioned it to any of her family and friends, which told him, she didn't think it was very important. She viewed it as just another job and nothing more. Kara *would not* betray him. He believed that now.

The fact that Alexander took the time to design Kara's engagement ring meant the world to her. Most men could care less, they'd buy whatever the salesperson suggested and be done with it. This ring proved Alexander viewed her as special. He treasured her. This was what she wanted from a husband, a man who respected *her*. This is the type of man who would never cheat on her.

"Thank you!" Kara gave Alexander a quick kiss. Glancing around the table, she demanded. "Please don't tell anyone. Alexander and I will announce it tomorrow, Ok?" Kara looked one by one at each of her family. "Promise me you won't tell anyone. Not mom…dad … grandparents…no one." They all hesitantly agreed in some form or another, and she let out a deep breath she had been holding. She didn't want anyone telling them before she had a chance to. She wanted to be the one to tell them her good news, not her siblings. Kara took Alexander's hand and interlaced their fingers. "We will meet you all tomorrow at the house, if you'll excuse us." She looked up at Alexander with desire in her eyes, and the intense need to be alone with him, "Are you ready?"

Alexander inhaled deeply. *Ahhhh! She's aroused…very aroused. My little tempting minx. You just striked a match, and have no idea how strong the fire is you're about to unleash.* He could smell Kara's arousal, so enticing, so delicious, if he wasn't careful he'd spill his seed with only her touch. Lost to her, he squeezed her hand, as Nathaniel moved to let them slide out.

Alexander glanced back smugly at his Generals. "By the way, *Kara* will collect my winnings." He looked over at Kara's siblings, "We'll see you tomorrow. Let your parents know my family and friends will attend your birthday party as well."

"I'll make sure everyone gets there." Adelina volunteered.

"Thanks, *sorella*." Alexander smiled, as she gave him a knowing smile back.

No one saw Steven hovering in the background watching the entire scene in complete fury, as he stepped away dialing his phone.

"You were right. It happened sooner than I thought, and you were right. She said yes. *Their engaged!*"

21

Kara awoke refreshed and sated to Alexander drawing a large heart over and over again on her stomach. His palms started under her breasts, and ended with the tip of the heart just under her navel. He was propped up against the headboard, with Kara leaning back against taut ropes of muscles that formed his remarkable chest.

It had been an incredible night. So much love, passion, and desire, there were times that she'd thought she would faint. Hoping it wasn't all a dream, she lifted her left hand. Nope! Not a dream! Kara was indeed engaged. Engaged to the most extraordinary man she'd ever known. Entwined in Alexander's strong arms, she finally had an optimistic vision of her future.

She giggled, "What are you doing?"

Alexander chuckled low and seductive in her ear. "Admiring perfection. Appreciating *this* exquisite body that the gods designed specifically for me, and *right now*, I'm paying homage to the womb that will house our children."

Kara laughed grabbing his arms and wrapping them tightly around her. "I really love the fact that God sent me such a blind man. Perfection? I wish!"

"Trust me, babe!" Alexander turned her, settling her astride his muscular thighs. "This body" he whispered in her ear, slowly caressing Kara's thighs as he moved his large hands upward, as his tongue laved a path from her ear down. Alexander felt the wetness of her hot core teasing his stomach, and knew she was more than ready for him again. Last night, he'd been so insatiable, he'd taken her so many times, he couldn't begin to account for all of them, and every time her appetite was just as strong as his. He didn't know why the gods had gifted him this amazing woman, but he vowed he'd spend eternity making her happy. "fits precisely with mine. We're like matching puzzle pieces." Positioning his thick staff at her entrance, he entered her in one powerful thrust, burying himself deep inside her. "See my point." He smirked wickedly.

Kara was still catching her breath from last night, when Alexander hadn't been able to keep his hands off her. Not that she was complaining, mind you, but he'd been like a kid visiting a candy store for the first time. After leaving Mel's, Alexander had shifted them into his atrium, taking Kara hard and fast in the fountain under the moonlight. All wet, she had challenged him to a race to his bedroom, without shifting. Kara had only made it half way up the first flight of stairs, when Alexander had caught her, proving stairs created a whole new depth to sexual pleasure. They christened numerous rooms, eventually making their way to his bedroom, where he had made slow, tender love to her.

A wicked smile spread across her face. "No!" She nipped his lip, "but I *feel* your point, and it's driving me crazy."

Alexander chuckled. He felt the exact same way. All he wanted was to slam into Kara's tight little body over and over again, feeling his balls slap against her soft, warm skin, but he had something he needed to prove to her first. Alexander laid small kisses across her forehead, and down to her ear. "This beautiful mind," he reached up laying his hand between her voluptuous breasts. "And this benevolent heart is the other half of mine. You make me whole Kara. In 2000 years, I never thought I'd know this feeling, but with you, I have a *true* feeling of contentment."

Kara felt all of Alexander's pain and hope. She watched both emotions flash through his radiant eyes, and heard the veracity in his voice. He truly believed everything he was saying, and for the life of her, Kara didn't understand why, but she felt the exact same way about Alexander.

Unable to control herself any longer, Kara began to move. She slowly rode Alexander, enjoying the sensation of being filled completely. She cupped his face between her hands, brushing her lips back and forth against his, whispering, "I feel the exact same way about you."

Alexander moaned with relief, burying his head in the crook of her neck. Kara had just thrown him his life line. *Oh! gods! How I'm going to love this woman. Yes, that's it!* Alexander realized. He loved this tiny incredible woman. In all his very long life, he had never felt this way for a woman. Not Fiona! Not Catherine! Not any of the other women he'd been with. He had cared for them, he'd even made himself believe it was love, but it *obviously* wasn't. The feelings Alexander felt for Kara, as unexpected as they are, he'd never felt them before. *This is what Love feels like. I Love Kara!* There was no longer any doubt in his mind. Somehow in the last few days, Kara had breached his hearts defenses, and claimed him as her own. "I'm never going to let you go." He whispered in her ear, nibbling on her earlobe. *Let's just hope she never betrays me. I would never survive her betrayal.*

Alexander rolled them over, pinning her underneath him with an extremely possessive, probing, and intensely hot kiss. A kiss that scattered all of Kara's thoughts, leaving her completely incoherent.

Alexander furiously pounded into her, over and over again. Completely lost in her floral scent, the silk of her skin, and the knowledge that he was claiming the woman he loved. He wasn't ready to admit this to anyone else, not even Kara, but he relished in his own revelation, and when he'd brought her to ecstasy again, screaming out his name, he followed her with his own release, declaring more fervidly than before, "Mine! You're *mine!*" Before collapsing on top of her fully sated.

Alexander's touch was a miracle on Kara's skin, how his touch could cause her such insanity was beyond her understanding, but the pleasure it brought was worth the delirium. Since high school, she'd never been a person to live her life passionately. She had become the sensible sibling, or that's at least what her family always called her, but right now her actions were *definitely* not sensible. No! They were out right wanton, and she loved it.

As their breathing finally evened out, he whispered in her ear sending goose-bumps up and down her spine...Again. "What time do we need to be at your birthday party?"

Dropping her hands away from his back, she moaned. "Ahh, Shiz-nat! I forgot that's today. Couldn't we just stay here?" She wiggled under him seductively, "I promise we'll have more fun." She taunted.

He rolled off her onto his back with a groan. "I don't doubt that, love. However, I also don't imagine your family would appreciate me keeping you from your own party."

Kara snorted. "You're right! They'd have no one to embarrass. Then what would they do?"

"What do you mean?"

"Never mind!" She snapped. "Let's just get this over with, shall we?"

Kara slid off the bed flashing him a teasing sensuous smile. "I'm in need of a bath, in that giant tub of yours. I could use a little help."

Alexander watched her luscious curves hurry off towards his bath-chamber. Damn! He couldn't think straight with her swaying that decadent body in front of him. He closed his eyes and groaned, before flipping off the bed, and trailing after her.

⟡⟡⟡

Two hours later, they were in his *Pagani* headed out of town towards the Spencer ranch. She still couldn't believe he was driving an *automobile* worth almost a million dollars to a ranch. She'd tried to convince him to shift them to her house and they'd take her Maxima instead, but he wouldn't hear of it. He saw absolutely no reason not to take the *Pagani*, as long as there were paved roads. What he failed to understand, was that her family would hound him with questions about it, and demand to ride in it. Alexander and the *Pagani* would probably end up being the 'family-amusement-park-ride' of the day.

When they arrived, Kara was surprised to see Alexander's family and friends already there. She found out that Trey and Tanya had brought them earlier, and that the two families were getting along marvelously.

Just as she had feared, her family was enthralled by the *Pagani*.

What astounded her was Alexander's reaction. Instead of being uptight, like most men, worried about their precious cars getting scratched, or dented, or any other small thing that could damage his *Pagani*, he threw his keys to Nathaniel and told him to let them drive it.

Kara grabbed his arm pulling him aside. "Are you crazy? You can't be serious! You're actually going to let my family drive the *Pagani*?"

"Why not?" He cocked one eyebrow. "I let my family drive it, and the way I see it, your family will soon be mine, so it's the same thing. Besides, it's just metal, Kara. It can be replaced."

"But...but it's...you paid......" Kara stammered. "its expensive metal and......"

Alexander's lips came down hard on hers stopping all her concerns and objections. He kissed her until he felt her melt against him, releasing all her built up tension. He'd felt her building frustration with every mile they drove towards her family. He still didn't understand their relationship, but he could feel that she truly loved them. He could see it when she talked about them. There was always tenderness and love in her eyes, but for some reason, she also feared them. That's the part he didn't understand. *What does she have to fear?*

"No! It's just a car, Kara. No more worrying." Alexander chided as he stepped back from her, wrapping his arm around her waist and pulling her to him. "Now it's time you introduced *your fiancé* to the rest of your family."

She let out an exasperated sigh and let him pull her towards her parent's house.

Kara's childhood home was everything Alexander had imagined and more. The instant he walked in, it had a homey feel to it. He could tell that in this home people were well loved. The house was filled with the smells of baked goods and spices, decorated with family pictures and trophies, and filled to its capacity with laughing humans. He could definitely feel the family love and camaraderie in the air.

Kara pulled him down to her and whispered in his ear. "I think we need to find my parents first."

Alexander nodded, and listened until he found her father's voice coming from a back room. "This way!" He pointed.

She followed him to the game room, which they had added years ago onto the back of the house. It was adjacent to their large kitchen, where she spotted her mother cooking, as they passed through. Kara yelled to her to gather her grandparents and follow them, as she continued following Alexander.

In the game room they discovered her father playing chess with Alexander's brother, Dante. Kara was delighted to see both their families getting along so well. Nothing could have made her happier. Well…maybe not coming. That would have topped it.

"Hi, Dante!" Kara crooned. "Dad!" She kissed his cheek.

"Hi sweetie! What has you in such a good mood today?" Edward, her father asked, as Alexander shook his hand and teased his brother. "If this is your doing, Alexander, we're going to keep you around. Kara hasn't been this happy to attend a family gathering in years."

"What has Alexander done?" Kara's mom, Melody asked as she and Kara's grandparents approached them.

Edward chuckled. "I was just telling Alexander, that if it's his presence that has our Kara in such a good mood all the time, then we're going to demand that he sticks around."

Alexander greeted everyone shaking their hands, as he playfully answered. "I can't take all the credit, but I do hope some of her happiness is from me. It's why we're all standing here away from the rest of your guests." He looked down at Kara, "Would you like to share our news?"

Kara held up her left hand, proudly displaying her engagement ring. "We wanted you all to know before everyone here figures it out. We're engaged."

With tears in her eyes, Melody stepped forward hugging her daughter and her fiancé. "I am so happy for you both. Welcome to our insane family, Alexander."

"Alexander…Son." Edward cupped his shoulder. "I know it must sound strange to you, having me call you son, and you are no doubt much older than me, but at least you look younger, and you'll have to get used to it, because you're marrying my daughter, so as far as I'm concerned that makes you my son. Congratulations! We're keeping you after all."

"Thank you, sir. It would be an honor to be considered your son."

Kara's grandparents gave their congratulations, and then Edward stole Alexander to introduce his future son-in-law to the rest of their family and friends. It was well after lunch, before they had anytime alone together. Kara's father, Edward, had suggested that she give Alexander a tour of the ranch, although they hadn't quite made it past the back lawn yet.

They had been walking out towards the stables, when Kara was trampled by two beasts that reminded Alexander of bears. Kara was down for the count being licked to death by these two savage creatures.

"Ok! Ok!" She was laughing. "Enough! Enough you two! Lay down!"

Instantly the two fur balls laid down in the grass next to her.

"I was wondering where you two were." Kara scratched their heads. "Were you hiding out from all the chaos?"

The black fur ball leaned back and licked Kara's cheek. "Well then, let me introduce you to a wonderful man. Alexander, meet my Chow Chows." She pointed to the black ball of fur. "This is Misty, and this is Sunny." She pointed to the gold ball of fur. "They're my babies." She stated proudly.

Alexander stretched out next to Kara. "Well then, I guess it's time for them to get to know me, since we'll be spending a lot of time together." He reached out, letting them smell his hands, before scratching them behind their ears.

Kara laughed as the dogs jumped up and licked Alexander's face. "Well, look at that. It looks like you've past my Chow Chow's test. They like you."

They sat playing with the Chow's talking about how temperamental they could be, but how they'd raised them to be sociable. Kara told him why Chow's tongues are blue-black and how they were the Emperors' guard dogs.

Alexander was quite impressed with Kara's passion for animals. She was amused by the fact that in 2000 years he'd never taken time to have a dog of his own. Not that he didn't like them, quite the contrary; he'd just never had time for them. Besides, the Cruetian castle had many dogs hanging around, so he really didn't need his own. Kara then informed him that she was already committed to one of Misty's pups, so they would have to have dogs when they married. Not that he'd mind. Her Chow's had grown on him.

"I'm sorry." Kara apologized. "I should have warned you about how many people would be here today. I didn't mean to immerse you into our chaos."

"No need to apologize." Alexander replied. "I'm having fun, and you're not even close to duplicating my family."

"Really?" She glanced up hopeful.

Alexander smiled, as he realized she was nervous about his reaction to the size of her family. "When you have 33 siblings and are immortal, your family only continues to grow. Just wait until our wedding. This is nothing."

Kara laughed. Releasing all the stress that had been building since they'd arrived. She was glad to hear her family didn't scare him. Most people she brought home criticize the size of her family. They can't fathom how her parents could have had so many kids. "I guess you're right. I never thought of it in that way."

"Although," Alexander laughed, rubbing his index finger back and forth over his chin. "It did take my parents 2300 years to have 33 children, it took your parents less than 10 years to have almost a third that many."

"Oh!" Kara punched him playfully. "You're bad!"

Alexander grabbed her hand pulling her up into a kiss. "Come! Show me the rest of your family's home."

As they toured the ranch, Alexander was surprised to see Kara with her animals. She cared for them as she would people. She'd introduced him to her family's Chow Chows, two big fluffy dogs that reminded him of bears, a red male named Sunny, and a black female named Misty. Kara's horses, 4 beautiful stallions. She had a beautiful black Arabian named Caesar, a Palomino Quarter horse named Adonis, a grey Dartmoor Pony named Wellington, and a rare white Miniature named Napoleon, that truly was a horse, but fully grown was only a couple inches taller than her dogs. Alexander was amused that she'd named all her horses after important figures in history. She continued with her Chinchillas. She had so many he couldn't even remember their names. Overall, he'd learned a lot about her, by watching her care for her animals. The best part was riding with her. It had been a long time since Alexander had a woman on his horse, and riding Caesar with Kara wrapped in his arms felt like pure ecstasy. They hadn't ridden far since they had to return for cake and ice cream, but they planned on taking both Caesar and Adonis out afterwards for a longer ride across the Spencer fields.

It gave him an idea for a birthday present for her. He'd been racking his brains trying to figure out what to give her, and now he knew. He'd give her some of his family's land next to the castle's stables, and have her own private stables built. This way she could use the land anyway she liked, and have as many animals and she wanted on it.

Kara sucked in a deep breath trying to come to terms with all the strange feelings running wild inside her. So much had changed in just a few days. She'd finally faced the reality that Alexander was her true soul-mate, and that somewhere along the last few days, she'd fallen head over heels in love with him. Now she was facing the reality that she really didn't know this man. It wasn't the three ceremonies of the blood bonding that bothered her, or the three Roman acceptance steps, although she didn't know if they had to do those, or if Tycho had just been joking about the Ancient Roman ceremony, but either way those didn't scare her. Kara was actually pleased that they had taken the first step. She had every intention of completing the Cruetian ceremonies with Alexander, so completing the Roman ceremony wouldn't bother her either. What did scare her was their difference in age. Listening today to his family's banter, realization struck her, and she became very aware of just how many lifetimes he'd actually lived, and how immature she must appear to him. How could she ever be intellectual enough to hold him? How could she keep him interested? Everyone knows men stray when they get bored. Could she possibly be enough for him?

Kara came out of her own thoughts, listening to the current conversation about cars. A typical male conversation, but luckily one that she could hold her own in. She spent two years after high school selling Nissan's to help pay for college. At the moment, Nathaniel and Masaga were arguing over which car was faster, the M6 coupe or the GT-R.

"We all know that European engineering is superior to Japanese when it comes to cars." Nathaniel was stating.

"Um…actually you would be wrong. Car magazines clock the GT-R, going from 0-60 at 3.2 seconds. The M6 takes 4.5 seconds, and its $20,000 more. Personally, I love Japanese engineering. Not only is the performance comparable to any European made car, but it costs a lot less to service. I'd buy a Japanese car over a European car any day." Kara glanced around as they all gawked at her except her brothers. "What?" she asked innocently.

"You know *cars*?" Alexander looked dumb founded.

"Sorry!" Trent cringed. "I should have warned you all. Kara used to sell cars. Salesman……" He saw the angry look on Kara's face and rebuked his statement. "I mean salesperson of the year. She probably knows more about cars than all of us put together."

Alexander shook his head in defeat, "I had no idea."

"I worked at a dealership to help pay for college. First year I sold cars, the second year I was a finance manager. It was difficult working full time and going to school, so I quit and started focusing more on the tea store." Kara explained with pride.

"What *is* she?" Nathaniel asked sarcastically.

Alexander rolled his eyes. "I think I should take Kara inside, before all of you irritate her. It's been a long day, and we still have the horses to take out. Besides, I think she's still recovering from her attack."

"I feel *completely* fine. I'm totally healed." She argued.

"Doctor's orders. Rest! Or I have the ability to admit you to the hospital." Alexander demanded.

Kara huffed. "Fine!" She grumbled reluctantly, warning, "You'll pay for being so bossy when I'm back to full power."

"I'm sure I will, but it *will not* be today." He said amused. "Besides shouldn't we go for our ride?"

"Whatever!" Kara huffed again and stomped inside.

"Hey, Alexander." He looked over at Trent, "Walk with us a moment." Trent pointed to Kara's brothers.

"Sure!" Alexander headed in their direction, as they guided him through the wraparound porch to the other side of the house.

Trent began. "We like you. In fact, my whole family likes you, but the last time my sister sang a song for someone like she did for you last night, and I'm not talking about a request or a dedication. I'm talking about her dedicating to someone, was five years ago after Steven crushed her. She sang 'Try it on my own', and that was dedicated to all of us." He swung his arm around the crowd. "Her family and friends. The next day she moved out, and has been on her own, and independent ever since." Trent put his hand on Alexander's shoulder, "It took a lot for her to give you her heart. Please, don't hurt her. None of us want to fight you, but we will if we have to, to protect Kara."

"She never even sang for Kevin." Trey stepped forward, "and they were together for two years. As much as we like you, and we really do, we don't think she'd be able to handle another heart break……"

"So just be warned," Darrius interjected, "we will protect her if we have to, even from her own feelings."

Alexander offered them his hand. As each of them shook it, he assured them, "We all know women, and how fickle they can be, so I cannot promise I will never make her angry, but I will *never* deliberately hurt her. That much I can assure you. We all know she's independent and stubborn as hell, so I can't promise misunderstandings, but I will always be faithful, and I will always try to make sure she is happy." They nodded in understanding and each of them slapped him on the back and truly welcomed him into the family. "Now I need to get back to her before *I* irritate her." They all laughed and motioned him on.

Alexander knew sooner or later this conversation would come, and was glad it was over and done with. He was glad they were concerned with Kara's future and he respected their candidness. All of them having an understanding was far better for his and Kara's relationship. It would limit the misunderstandings and save numerous arguments.

He finally found Kara out in the stables saddling two stallions.

"You're sure you want to ride Adonis?" Kara asked. "I just started breaking him, and so far I've been the only person he's allowed on his back."

"Kara…Please." Alexander said annoyed. "Automobiles have only been around for a century, before that, *all 2200 years*, I rode horses. I've broken some of the most stubborn horses that have ever lived. I'm really quite the horseman. Trust me."

"Ok, fine. You win. That sounded pretty dumb didn't it." She admitted. "It's hard for me to think it terms of centuries. You definitely have more experience with horses than I do, so let's see what you can do with Adonis."

It took a little while for Adonis to succumb to Alexander, but in the end he did. Of course, not before it attracted attention from the house, and by the time Adonis capitulated, Alexander had a full applauding audience.

Alexander bowed to Kara as she mounted Caesar. He heard her declare, "Show off!" He laughed feeling her exasperation.

They headed across a pasture and then out a back gate connecting to a path that Kara explained would lead to a stream that winded along the back of the ranch. At first it was pretty open fields, but after a while they were walking through some beautiful old trees.

Alexander finally broke their silence. "I'm sorry if I embarrassed you in front of your family by breaking Adonis."

"No, it's OK." Kara looked over and smiled at him. "I was probably just a little jealous that you accomplished it so quickly. It took me days to get on him, but I have to admit, it was quite impressive watching you." She admitted with a shy smile.

"He's a great horse." He continued the conversation, answering her smile with one of his own.

"That's why I bought him. He'll make a great barrel horse."

"He's actually…yours? Not your parents?" Alexander asked shocked.

"That's right. All the horses I showed you are mine. The others in the stables are owned by my parents or siblings." Kara laughed. "Don't look so shocked. It's taken me a long time to save the money for my horses. I recently bought Adonis because my childhood barrel horse was ready for pasture, so it was time to buy another. I'm currently saving for a Thoroughbred, so I can start jumping and then a Tennessee Walking Horse, and after I have both of them…well, let's just say I already have a long list. She turned and smiled at him. Haven't you noticed how much I love animals? My obsession probably comes from growing up on a ranch, but either way, I love animals, all animals."

He chuckled. "It's a good thing my homes all have large stables."

Kara stared at him, as a gigantic smile crept across her face. "You'd let me bring my animals to your home."

"Well…let's see. First of all," Alexander said in a teasing voice, "as my wife, it will also be your home. Second, I can't imagine you being separated from anything that you love, and third, I want my wife happy. Whatever, makes her that way, is fine with me."

He looked over to see tears in her eyes. "You're too good to be true, Alexander, but I do love you, and even though you paint a fairytale marriage, even if it's *not* quite perfect, I'll be happy just to be with you." She glanced up realizing they were getting closer to the stream. "I'll race you to the water." She kicked Caesar's flanks and he took off in a full out gallop.

22

Alexander was stunned motionless over what she had said. *I'm enough. Kara said I was enough. She doesn't need anything else. Just me! She only needs me. Oh, gods, thank you! She'll never betray me.* He kicked Adonis's flanks, but heard a gunshot up ahead, as he watched in horror as Caesar spooked, throwing Kara. She was so far ahead that a human wouldn't have been able to see her, but his Cruetian eyesight let him see for miles. He kicked Adonis harder, but they were already in a full gallop. He could see three men step out of the trees walking towards her.

Kalab...Nathaniel...Tiberius...Dante...Chung...Tycho...Conrad... Masaga...Walter! Shift to me NOW!! When you shift, if I'm still riding, look for Kara and shift to her. She's rode ahead of me. He projected into their minds.

Kara heard the shot and knew Caesar would freak. He'd never been around guns. She tried to rein him in, but it was too late. She flew, landing with a thump, as pain seared through her body.

Who the hell is shooting on our property? Idiots! She started to move, as another stabbing pain shot through her leg. She tried to move it. To her relief she could, so she knew it wasn't broken. She probably just twisted it. *Stupid Idiots!* Kara knew Alexander was behind her and would be here soon. The best thing she could do was lay here and wait until he arrived.

Kara had just closed her eyes, when her blood turned to ice in her veins. She could here footsteps and voices. Not just any voices, but the same voices of her previous attackers.

Who the hell are these guys, and what do they want with me?

"We need to hurry and get her out of here." One of the voices said.

"You better hope she's not hurt. The boss wants her alive." Another voice answered.

"I didn't know the gun would spook the horse. I only wanted her to stop. I don't know why the boss cares anyway; he's just going to kill her." A third voice stated, very matter of fact.

Kara laid completely still, hoping to give Alexander time to get to her. Adonis was fast, but she'd never clocked him, so she wasn't sure how far behind her he actually was, but she hoped not too far.

"What the hell? What are you doing here and who the hell is she?" Kara heard the first voice ask.

"The boss sent her."

Son of a Bitch! I know that voice. Steven! That Bastard! He's behind this? I should have let my brothers kill him.

"She came after you left and told me to bring her here." Steven continued.

"The boss says he's not risking another mishap. We're to take her to him immediately." A familiar woman's voice stated, but Kara couldn't put her finger on whose it was. She knew that voice, but from where she couldn't remember.

It took all of Kara's concentration not to squirm or pull away when they started tying her hands and feet together, she was preparing to fight, when to her relief she heard hooves racing towards them.

"Too late! That's Alexander and his posse." The woman's voice shrieked. "I'll send for help. Keep her from them."

"Just take her now." Steven argued.

"NO! He can see us. He'd shift to her. We need to keep him busy to make our escape." The woman snapped.

"Fine! But, don't forget, she bites." Steven snickered. "Stuff something in her mouth."

Asshole! I'm going to cut your balls off when this is over. My brothers won't have to, I'll kill you myself.

Alexander came around a corner and saw four men carrying Kara into the trees. He pulled back on the reins, jumping off Adonis, he threw the reins around a tree branch, and shifted to Kara the same moment his team arrived, and the exact same moment fifteen vampires surrounded her. Instead of being next to Kara, he ended up facing a sword.

As the fight broke out, Adelina appeared with swords. Thank the gods for the *Amara* bond. Since Walter was with them, as soon as he knew what was happening, so did Adelina. She immediately shifted to Alexander's armory bringing them weapons.

Kara's eyes were open, but when they gagged her, they'd also blind folded her, so she couldn't see anything. She heard metal hitting metal and instantly knew they were battling with swords.

Who the hell are these people? No one except Dark-Souls fight with swords, Do they? and what the hell do they want with me?

Alexander was fighting his way towards Kara but every time he got close, another vampire stepped in. Each of his men was having the same problem. No one was able to get to her. No matter how hard they fought, more vampires kept coming. They had her completely surrounded, so no one could even shift next to her, and if they shifted in front of her guards, their backs would be to the vampires they were fighting.

"Son of a Bitch!" Alexander cursed. When they had first arrived, Kara had been calm, but now he could feel her shear panic. She was scared, and there wasn't a damn thing he could do about it. Some protector he was turning out to be.

Alexander lunged forward, catching his enemy square in the chest, slicing through skin, muscle, and bone. Not a killing blow by any means, but a blow that would require time to heal, sending the vampire shifting back to his home. Wherever that was!

Again and again Alexander tried to reach Kara, only to be blocked. Furious with a rage he hadn't felt in centuries, he screamed a battle cry he hadn't used in a millennium. *"vinco vici victum!"* Conquer!

Alexander felt the shock of his men, before he heard them answer his demand, screaming the same battle cry, with sword blades hitting harder and stronger than they had a minute earlier. Just as they were making head way, Alexander saw a cloaked figure step into the fold next to Kara, the person touched her, and she was gone.

Alexander let out a heart wrenching scream, as Kara's emotions left him. Instantaneous grief overwhelmed him, replacing Kara's emotions that had become so much a part of his life. Insanity gripped him, as he reverted to an extremely vengeful warrior, beheading both the vampires near him. He turned and caught another one in the chest as he roared. He shifted behind one of her human captors, ready to slit his throat, as he disappeared with the vampire next to him.

Chung knew his commander was lost. He felt his despair, and knew every Dark-Soul on earth that was connected with Alexander, was feeling his pain at this very moment. He didn't know how to help him, when he was barely holding back his own grief. Kara was gone. In the hands of vampires she'd never survive, and they had been too late. Too late to protect her! Too late to save her! They were just *TOO LATE!*

Alexander looked up as each human and vampire disappeared, the last human standing caught his hard gaze. He wore a smirk on his face that immediately turned into an evil smile.

"She's mine!" He mouthed, hitting his chest with his fist.

Instantaneously, Alexander recognized him. *"Steveeeeen!"* He roared charging forward, as Steven disappeared with the vampire standing next to him.

Every one of them had shifted away. As fast as the battle had begun, it had ended, taking Kara with them. *Kara's gone.* He threw back his head and roared. His pain lashed out, affecting everyone in its wake. *She's gone, damn it! She's really gone.* He dropped to his knees, holding his head in his hands, cursing himself. Cursing himself for not being with her. Cursing himself for taking too long to get to her. Cursing himself for letting his guard down. Cursing himself for allowing himself to become so weak. During wars, he'd always been suspicious, but during a more peaceful time, he'd allowed himself to become weak, and look what his weakness had cost him.

Kara! gods, NO! Please. NO! I need her. Kara! I'm sorry.

How had he let this happen? Why hadn't he stopped the horse and immediately shifted to her? *Why? Why?* He knew why. He never anticipated vampires being involved, because he never anticipated

Steven, or any other human working with them. A mistake that might have just cost him his life, because that is what Kara had become to him. She *was* his life, and he didn't want to live without her. He screamed again, holding back tears that hovered near the surface, just ready to escape if he allowed them to. He had never cried for a woman before, not even for Fiona, but then again, he'd never felt the gaping hole that he now felt in his chest either.

Alexander rocked back and forth, unable to clear his mind, unable to do anything, but allow his grief and despair to overcome him. That's how Adelina found him, when she bent down and wrapped her arms around him, and felt hot drops hit her arms. She choked back her own tears, determined to comfort Alexander. She didn't even think he realized he was crying or rocking back and forth, he seemed so alone, and his pain was so intense it was crippling.

"How did this happen? How the *hell* did we allow this happen?" Tiberius asked to know one in particular.

Avitus and Hypatia immediately felt their children's agony, and their debilitating pain. They immediately shifted to them, shifting into a tree grove, as they watched their son, Tiberius, slump against a tree trunk, and slide down landing on the ground.

General Chung had his forehead leaned against a tree, pounding his fist into it over and over and over repeatedly.

Their son, Nathaniel, was in a squat, holding his face in his hands, moaning, "No-No-No!"

General Conrad was on his hands and knees praying.

Their son-in-law, Walter had changed into a wolf and was pacing around the trees.

Their son Dante, was leaning back against a tree, slamming the back of his head against it over and over again.

General Masaga and General Tycho were standing like statues with their heads bent looking at the ground.

They spotted their son Alexander on his knees, holding his head in his hands while their daughter, Adelina held him. Kalab hovered protectively nearby, but one look at his face, and you knew he was in the same amount of agony as the others.

Oh, gods! She can't be dead. Hypatia thought.

Let's hope not, akribos. For Alexander's sake, gods, let's hope not.

Adelina glanced up, as her mother shifted next to her, finally allowing her own tears flow. Hypatia bent down and wrapped her arms around both of them. Shocked to realize Alexander was crying. Her strong, ruthless son was utterly, and entirely broken.

Is Kara dead? Hypatia projected to Adelina.

We don't know. Vampires took her. Adelina let out an anguished cry. *We couldn't stop them. We couldn't get to her. We tried. Matris, we tried.*

Shh! We know you all did as much as you could have. Shh!

Alexander felt his mother's arms around him, but even that couldn't diminish his pain. The usual comfort his mother's embrace encircled him with was non-existent.

Avitus dealt with his Generals first. They were his best Vici Warriors and he needed them strong right now. There would be time for grief later. He listened to them explain the battle, but none of them really knew what had happened prior to being summoned by Alexander. He knelt beside one of the vampire bodies that Alexander had beheaded. Rolled him over and tore his shirt off.

No viper tattoo!

"These are *not* Seth's Warriors." Avitus pointed to the vampire's stomach.

"Who else would want Kara?" Conrad asked. "It has to be Seth. He's the only person that would have need of her death."

Tycho pinched his nose thinking. "Maybe Seth's using uninitiated vampires to throw us off his trail."

"Why?" Masaga growled. "What would be the purpose? If it's Seth, he'd want to rub Alexander's face in Kara's death. He'd want Alexander to suffer and he'd want to witness Alexander's pain."

Avitus scrubbed his hand back and forth over his chin. "We need to gather information, before we can analyze who is behind this and why." He sent all the Generals except General Chung to incinerate the vampire bodies, and scour the area for clues. He then turned his attention to Alexander motioning Hypatia and Adelina away.

"*filius*, you need to tell me what happened." Alexander didn't speak, he just continued to rock back and forth. Avitus knew his son was devastated. He was completely consumed with grief. Grief he'd never experienced before, but Kara's life depended on the Commander, the strong cold hearted General that beat through his son's veins. The Crown Prince that only knew duty. This is who would save Kara.

"Commander!" Avitus said using his King voice, putting every ounce of authority his title gave him.

Alexander's head snapped up for the first time since Kara had been taken. Seeing his father standing tall before him, he jumped to attention.

"Yes, *Regis*!"

Using that same authority, Avitus had every one of his sons, Kalab and General Chung standing before him at attention. He then recalled the other Generals.

"I know you're all hurting. I can feel each of your guilt, each of your despair, but Kara might still be alive. Are we going to sit here and allow her to be killed, or are we going to fight to save her?" Avitus demanded.

"Fight!" They said in unison.

"Good!" Avitus paced in front of them. "Kara is the Cruetian future. She is Alexander's future. She is *your* Crown Princess. It is time we brought her home. Alexander! Is she still alive?"

Alexander's eyes jerked towards his father's gaze. "*Regis*?" He looked questionly at his father. "We never completed the second blood bonding ceremony. When they took her, they took her far enough away, that I can't sense her emotions any longer. She's out of my range."

Avitus walked back again, wearing a path on the ground. "If you have only completed the first blood bonding ceremony, then you truly do have a very limited range and only the empathy connection. So, she could......"

"*Regis*!" Nathaniel cut in. "Alexander and Kara's bond is much stronger than the average *Amara's* after the first step. He was even able to shift to her within hours of their first kiss, before their first blood bonding."

"*Kyrios*, Is that true?" Avitus stopped dead in his tracks, spinning around to walk back in front of Alexander.

"Yes!" Alexander looked ashamed. "I failed! I could have shifted to her, but I did not. I knew humans were no match for us, so I saw no reason to expose our way of transportation to them."

Avitus reached forward laying his hand on his son's shoulder. "*Kyrios*, you were protecting our people. You were right in your actions. There was no way for you to know that these humans knew our ways. You did what was necessary to protect other Dark-Souls and Magikos beings. You did your job. No one can blame you for that."

"So I exchanged my *Amara's* life for my people. How fitting!" Alexander said sarcastically. "I keep killing my wives...for *my* people."

"Commander!" Avitus bellowed into Alexander's face. "You are a Warrior! Act like one! Warriors do not engage in self-pity. I did not mention your bonding to have you berate yourself. I mentioned it so that we could narrow down where they might have taken her. How far can you sense her?"

"*rumex, Regis!*" Alexander apologized understanding his father was only trying to help. If only he could grasp onto the fury and despair that ran wild through his soul. Maybe then he could become the ruthless General he'd always been. "I was able to sense her as far as Denver a couple days ago. I'm sure our bond is stronger now."

"Alright! Now we're getting somewhere." Avitus stopped in front of his men again. "Let us not assume this is Seth. The vampires Alexander killed did not display the viper tattoo. That does not mean he has not changed his tactics, but we need to look at all options. I want the remainder of our Vici Generals, as well as the Elite Generals in the Fort Collins villa in one hour." Using a softer voice, he turned to his wife, Hypatia, and gave her, her orders. "*akribos*, Adelina will take you to Kara's family. Let them know what has happened, but do not give to many details. Assure them we are doing everything to find her."

Adelina stepped forward. She knew her father didn't view her as a warrior, even though she'd fought in numerous wars, including the Lycanthrope war, where she'd met her husband, but she was not about to stay out of the search for Kara. "*Regis!* Kara's father and brothers will not stay out of this. They will demand involvement. Steven, a human that was among her captors has been an antagonist of the family for years. I can help them on the human side. We can meet you at Alexander's villa at the designated time, and work both the human and vampire sides together."

"Fine! Take your mother to Kara's family and then if the males insist on being involved, bring them to the villa." Avitus turned to Alexander. "*Kyrios*, summon the Phoenix and the Dragon. Namorita will arrive when the Vici Warriors are summoned." Alexander nodded, and Avitus stepped back to encompass all his men into his vision. "Let us bring back our *Kyria*." He shouted.

"*vinco vici victum!*" They shouted in unison just before they all vanished.

23

Kara knew the feeling of being shifted, and she definitely had just been shifted. Not by Alexander or his people though. She wasn't naïve enough to believe *that*. But who? Why would Dark-Souls help her attackers, and what is Steven's involvement in this?

Kara continued to pretend that falling from Caesar had knocked her out, staying completely limp and still. She had no idea where she'd been shifted to, or what they wanted from her. She'd hoped that while pretending to be knocked out that they would reveal some of their plans, but so far, all they'd talked about is booze, gambling, women, and the occasional mention of 'their boss'.

Idiots! These men are completely stupid! That's all they can talk about? They must have brains the size of peas. Morons! Talk about something important, like what you're going to do with me. I need to know. I need to figure out where I am, and how I can get away.

They were descending, while following Steven. Kara lost count of the flights of stairs they had went down, four, possibly five. Her leg was still throbbing, but she knew Alexander's blood would heal her fairly quickly. Wherever they were, it smelled damp and musty, and the temperature had dropped considerably. *Maybe a basement?* But that wouldn't account for the numerous flights of stairs.

"We need to shackle her in this interrogation chamber and then wait for the others to arrive." Steven ordered.

Shackles? He can't be serious, can he?

"How are we to chain her to that wall, when she's passed out?" One of the cowboys asked.

"Just do it!" Steven snapped. "I've been assured she isn't

unconscious. She'll stand once you chain her, or she'll dangle like a marionette. Either way, it's her choice."

Asshole! and to think, I actually liked him once.

Kara felt her arms lifted above her head, and clamped into thin metal cuffs. Then they spread her legs, and clamped her ankles to the wall. Now panic set in. She never thought they were serious. She wanted to yell, to scream, but her gag muffled even her strongest shrills, and *who* were they waiting for?

Kara hadn't had time to ponder her dilemma, when a hand closed around her throat squeezing off her air supply.

"I *warned* you to stay away from him, but you didn't listen. You chose to gamble with your life instead. Now you'll pay!"

Shivers ran up Kara's spine, slightly jerking her body. *Catherine! It's...Catherine! That's the voice I heard.*

"Scared? You should be." Catherine mocked her, then followed it with a chilling laugh.

"Catherine, you promised." Steven warned. "Kara's mine!"

"Shut up!" Catherine growled. "You think you're a match for me, Steven? Please try! I'll sic my vampires on you without a second thought."

"Eh, Excuse me." One of the cowboys interjected. "Seth plans on killing her anyway, but he wants the pleasure of watching her be drained. He wants her alive."

Catherine secretly motioned to three vampires. "Shut up, Fools!" She shouted. "I'm *not* giving her to Seth. Idiots! Seth will use her to kill Alexander, and I don't want Alexander hurt. I love him. HE'S MINE!"

The three cowboys exchanged knowing looks, and lunged for Catherine and Steven at the same time, but were captured by their necks before they could get far. Struggling to get free proved useless, as their legs swung under them before they finally passed out from lack of oxygen.

"Take them down to the next level and put them in the prison chamber." Catherine ordered. "Now! Kara-Kara-Kara!" She tsked. "Where should we start?"

Kara heard the menacing tone in Catherine's voice, and her blood ran cold as ice with panic. How would she escape this? She felt Catherine's long cold fingers untying her blind fold.

"I want to see your fear, and the pain I cause in your eyes, as I strip you forever from Alexander's life."

Oh, God! Oh, God! Oh, God! Kara couldn't breathe as tears filled her eyes. I'm really going to die.

"Catherine!" Steven begged. "You promised."

"Steven-Steven-Steven!" Catherine tsked. "You didn't *honestly* believe I could let her live, did you? The only way, an *Amara's* bond is broken, is for the Dark-Soul's *Amara* to die. Her life is now linked with his...so she must die."

Steven gazed around the room. "Don't even think about it?" Catherine threatened. "If you even attempt to help her escape, you'll become our local blood bank."

Catherine released her blind fold, as Kara watched Steven shrink onto a sofa, situated in the center of the room. It was the only thing in sight. The rest of the room was solid grey concrete walls. Kara almost felt sorry for Steven. His face was all scrunched up in pain, but she couldn't...not since *she* was the one about to die.

"Ah, isn't that sweet." Catherine taunted. "She's crying. Do you want to beg for your life?"

Kara nodded, angry at herself for her weakness. Uncle Chung had always told her 'never-show-weakness', but in this situation, she couldn't help herself.

"Too late! But don't worry." Catherine slapped her cheek, hard enough that her head swung around hitting the wall, and leaving a bruise on each cheek. "I'll play with you first. I want you to feel the same pain I've felt thinking of you with my mate." She pulled out a small ancient dagger, running her thumb across its edge. "I've even agreed for the vampires to feed on you for a few days...before I dispose of you."

Catherine spun around so quickly, Kara wasn't ready for the blade that slashed across her cheek. Pain tore through her mind as blood gushed down her cheek, her neck and pooled onto her shirt.

Catherine wiped her finger across the gash. Suckling it. "You really are delicious, but I don't want any part of you inside me. When Alexander takes my neck, I don't want any part of your essence reminding him of you."

Catherine whirled around chuckling, and then headed for the door. "She's all yours Erwin. Just make sure your vamps don't drain her. I want her alive. At least, for a few more days. I'll kill you *all* if she ends up dead before I'm ready. Also…No Sex!" Erwin raised a curious eyebrow at that demand. "At least…not…yet. Not until I'm able to witness her pain and humiliation, and I'm too tired tonight."

"Nooooooooo!" Steven screamed leaping towards them.

Kara watched in horror as Catherine backhanded him into the nearest wall, where he hit with a thud, silently falling to the floor. Was he…was he…dead? Tears surged in Kara's eyes. How had she ended up here? How had she ended up with such a ruthless creature?

Erwin left returning with three others. As they stalked towards her, she tried to scream, but the gag muted them, allowing only moans to escaped. She jerked from side to side, pulling on the chains, as tears rolled down her cheeks, stinging the cut.

No-No-No-No-No-No-NO! Kara chanted in her head. *Please God. Please don't let them do this. Please God. Please Help Me!*

"It won't hurt as much if you stop fighting us." Erwin said softly into her ear.

Like he cares! Kara closed her eyes tight, as the little hairs on the back of her neck stood up.

Kara screamed inside as her jeans were stripped away, and cold hands swarmed all over her body, just before she simultaneously felt teeth bite into her skin on each of her inner thighs, her throat, and her wrist.

꧁꧂

Alexander had been *ordered,* by his father to get some rest. This was the third night Kara had been missing, and he hadn't slept a wink since her capture. He shifted into his office, entirely to wound up for sleep. How could his father possibly think he'd rest, when they still hadn't found any sign of Kara or Steven? He didn't want to sleep, or eat. He didn't want to do anything but search for Kara.

So many horrible thoughts had been surfacing in his mind. Was Kara Ok? Had they hurt her? What was she enduring? Would Steven try to force himself on her?

I'll kill him! I'll kill all of them! Let's see how they like being hunted down like the dogs they are. If they've hurt her...I'll slowly rip every limb from their bodies. They'll wish for death long before I'll grant it to them. Torture is my specialty!

Hence his nickname during the wars. *Algor!* 'The Cold!' As in… No emotions…No feelings…Absolutely ruthless…Completely *COLD*! Granted, it had been decades since he'd utilized his *unique* talents, but the knowledge remained. Kara's kidnappers better pray they don't give him a reason to revive his skills.

Avitus had taken the Commander-in-chief position, allowing Alexander to actively participate in the search for his *Amara*, but Avitus had went searching on his own, shifting to every known location Seth had ever occupied, hoping to feel Kara's presence, which he had imprinted on his own senses from Alexander. He then started shifting to major world cities…still nothing.

Where could she be? There's something I'm overlooking. I just don't know what.

Alexander had met that very afternoon with Namorita, his Lunarian Vici Warrior; Kelmar, The Phoenix; and Drake, The Dragon. He hadn't seen Drake in years, and was surprised at his new look. He'd cut his Dark hair short, looking more like an English Gentleman then the Dragon he truly was. Although his height and muscular build, would instill fear in anyone who thought to stand in his way.

Overall, the meeting went quite well. They all agreed that Kara was definitely still alive. What they couldn't agree on was her condition or location, but at least they all had felt her presence.

Thank the gods for that. I need her. I actually need her. I know that now. I'm not afraid of her betraying me. I'm only afraid of losing her.

By the gods grace, please help me find her. Please give me the chance to tell her.

Needing to find some way to feel close to her, Alexander went online and pulled up the lyrics to the song Kara had dedicated to him, and the song Trent had informed him, was the last song she had dedicated to her family. As he sat there reading both songs words, he understood their significance. Since Kara expresses herself through songs, both of these made complete sense to him. Trent mentioned 'Try it on my own' was the last song she had dedicated to anyone. It was dedicated to her family and friends. The words to this song, declares control over her life after being hurt by someone. 'Forever in your eyes' is her acceptance of her feelings for him. He bought and downloaded both songs, hoping he'd get to hear Kara sing them again. Playing them, he settled back in his chair and dosed off.

For the first time in centuries Alexander fell into a pleasant dream. It was not a memory, but a dream of his future.

Alexander was standing before the alter in his family's chapel, holding a small hand with skin as exotic as satin, and the strength of a warrior. He turned, looking down into the most beautiful big brown eyes he'd ever had the honor to behold. She smiled, melting the ice encircling his heart and giving him something incredible to live for. He looked up expecting to see the vicar, but instead it was the Goddess Hecate.

"Alexander! Go to New York. You must hurry. Kara needs you. Go to the Adirondack Mountains. Kara's will is fading; I cannot protect her from her worst fear much longer. Go now, or this image will never come to pass." Hecate demanded his awareness. She demanded him to wake up.

Alexander jumped up out of a deep sleep, trying to catch his staggering breath. *Hecate!* He scrubbed his hand over his face, clearing his mind. *I have to go!* He shifted to his closet, throwing off his dirty clothes, and replacing them with his Cruetian battle armor. A solid black Kevlar, one piece body suit. Designed specifically for each warrior, hugging every one of his sharp planes, it encased each of his rock hard muscles, proving his powerful strength with just one glance and intimidating anyone whose gaze crossed his path. Black! The only color anywhere on the suit, except the gold band that each Dark-Soul wore on their left bicep. Engraved and studded with jewels, it was their only identifying mark, a symbol of their warrior rank within the Cruetian military.

It was the first time in days he'd felt any type of hope at all. The feeling enveloped him, ripping forth his powerful strength, and empowering the warrior within. He shifted to his armory, arming himself to the hilt. He strapped numerous daggers around his thighs and biceps, including his Sword-Breaker, then he strapped on two sword belts. One wrapped around his waist, holding the sword Hecate had given him, on the day he'd executed Fiona; the other over his shoulders, placing his favorite Gladius down his back. Grabbing his duster, he jerked it on concealing his weapons. Glancing in a mirror, the hard merciless warrior he'd always been stared back at him. He was ready. Ready for battle! Ready to kill! Ready to bring his *Amara* home! Since he awoke, he'd been in constant contact with Avitus, a benefit of their mind connection. Avitus and their warriors were ready and waiting. Alexander shifted to his father.

⁂

Kara was startled awake by the broth being forced into her mouth. She choked, spitting some of it out.

"Whoa!" Steven caressed her cheek. "Come on, a little at a time, those vamps drank a little too much of your blood last night. You passed out." Steven softly explained, putting the spoon back to her mouth. "Let me feed you. It'll help you regain your strength."

I don't want my strength. I just want to die. Kara thought, but didn't say anything to Steven.

At first, Kara had been relieved at Steven's recovery from Catherine's hit, but then she became furious knowing he had helped put her here. He was equally responsible for her suffering. Ultimately, his recovery was a blessing, since he fought Catherine for permission to take care of her. He fed her, gently cleaned her wounds, which were always too numerous to count, and made sure the vampires never took sexual advantage of her, but he wasn't able to stop her humiliation, the pain, or the fact that Catherine *would* eventually kill her. Kara had come to realize her death was something Steven would be unable to prevent.

Kara had been captured three nights ago, by the deranged, lovesick Catherine, and had since learned that Alexander, her so called *wonderful* fiancé, had not been 100% forthcoming about the life she would live as his wife. No! In fact, he never once mentioned there would be a bounty on his *Amara's* head.

It would appear that the three cowboys traipsing all over Fort Collins, attempting to kidnap her, works for Alexander's cousin, Seth. The same Seth that Fiona, Alexander's executed wife, had been in cahoots with. Catherine had relished in the knowledge that Kara had no idea Seth wanted her dead. She had made a big deal explaining Seth's ambition to steal the Cruetian crown, and how Seth viewed Kara as a threat to his desires. Catherine expounded on the fact that as Kara *was* Alexander's *Amara*, they'd be able to have children together, which could lead to the conception of Alexander's heir. The Cruetian heir!

"Seth will never allow that to happen." Catherine had confided in her. "This means…you are a liability to Alexander's life. So, you see, there are two reasons your death is required. First, he's *my* mate, and you're an interference. The Fates screwed up putting his mark on you. It *should* have been me. It has *always* been me. For the last 1000 years, I've been the one in his bed."

Kara cringed. She didn't like the idea of Alexander having another woman in his bed. The image of his hands and lips caressing another's skin, or his tongue working its magic on another woman's breast, or worse sending her to ecstasy with his wicked tongue, as it strokes her clit, it sent her blood boiling, especially the thought of him with Catherine.

"Yes, Alexander might break it off between us from time to time," Catherine had continued unaware of Kara's anger, "but he always comes back. He comes back to *me*. Second, you're dangerous. You'll attract his enemies far and wide, putting his life in danger, because he'll feel obligated to protect you."

As much as Kara loved Alexander, this isn't what she signed up for. It might make her sick to think of him in bed with another woman, but Catherine's daily torture was bad enough. Others like Catherine searching for her? That was just plain horror.

When Catherine had returned the following day to find Kara's cheek completely healed, she recognized that Kara had obviously already drank Alexander's blood, that they had already began the steps of the *Amara* blood bonding. Catherine lost it! She went completely crazy, snapping Kara's arm like a twig then using her as a punching bag, leaving no part of Kara's body without a purple-bluish tinge.

Steven continued to spoon feed her the broth. She wished he wouldn't. Kara was ready to die. She didn't have the strength to fight anymore, and she didn't want to. Every morning Catherine took pleasure in torturing her until Kara passed out from the pain, or was so mangled she couldn't find any other place to hurt her. Each evening she was humiliated, when the vampires returned to feed off her, leaving her feeling physically weak and mentally disgraced.

Yesterday after Catherine left her bloody and beaten, Kara started humming, trying to keep her mind off the pain. She recognized the song her mind had chosen. 'When is it Over'.

"When is the fight over?...When is it time to forgive?...When is the time to die...more important than to live?... Lay down your weapons... Lay down your soul...Let God make the decisions...when it's your time to go..."

She understood what her mind was telling her...what God was telling her. She couldn't win this battle. She was destined to die... here...by Catherine's hands. It was time to stop fighting, and accept her fate. She just hoped that Alexander would realize who'd killed her, and stay away from that *Evil Bitch*.

In the last couple of days, Kara had made peace with God and herself. She was ready to meet her maker, ready to end her constant pain and humiliation. There was no need to wait. Catherine had assured her that Alexander would never find her. She'd shifted her far enough away from Fort Collins that the connection of the first bonding would never work. Alexander was unable to sense her, a blessing from God if you asked Kara. At least, he wouldn't feel her pain. At least he wouldn't feel her weaknesses or her helplessness. His memories would always be her feelings of love and happiness.

Thank the Lord for that!

During her healing yesterday, Kara had derived a plan to end her life. Catherine wanted her engagement ring. She wanted it so bad she'd screamed when it wouldn't come off. She'd said she didn't want Kara having anything of Alexander's, and that the ring should have been hers anyway. Catherine tried numerous times to remove it from her finger, even trying to cut it off before finally giving up, breaking Kara's finger out of spite. She finally decided that Alexander must have had the witches put a spell on it, attaching it to Kara. Kara knew she was able to take it off, she'd taken it off, and passed it around at her birthday party, but instead of telling Catherine, she figured she could use it to end her life. Catherine's desire for her ring might be the only way to end her suffering.

"Sooooo! The *little bitch* still lives." With a sadistic smirk, Catherine stalked towards Kara. "I heard the vampires got a little carried away last night." She slapped her hard across the face, splitting her lip. "You're such a little blood *whore*. I'm sure you *actually* enjoyed it."

Catherine twirled a small dagger between her fingers. Kara bit her lip refusing to cry. Again. Catherine slowly nestled the dagger between Kara's breasts, scrapping its tip down to her navel. Kara gritted her teeth, as tears swelled in her eyes then with one fluid movement, Catherine cut Kara's shirt in half, leaving it gaping. Now fully exposed, except for her bra and panties, Kara couldn't hold back her whimper.

"Oh!" Catherine exclaimed. "What is this?" She pulled harshly on Kara's belly ring. "Does Alexander like this?"

Kara didn't respond.

Catherine pulled on it again, slightly tearing her skin, sending pain along her abdomen. "I asked you a question. Does Alexander like this?"

"Y-Y-Y-Yes!" Kara stammered.

Catherine smiled a very wicked smile. "Good! I'll have to get me one then. I wouldn't want him to be deprived of anything he likes."

Catherine continued to taunt her, moving the dagger across the top of Kara's breasts. "I think…tonight…I'll allow the vampires to make you the *whore you really* are."

NOOOOOOO! Kara's tears escaped creating a flowing river running down her front. *I can't do this! I can't! I really can't! I'm not strong enough. Please God help me. I beg you. Help me. Just let me die. I can't be raped. I'll never survive it. Please…just…let…me…die. Take me home! Take me now! Take me to live with you Lord, please. Please! Please! Please!*

Kara screamed as Catherine's dagger sliced across her breast. "Oops!" Catherine covered her mouth in shock, mocking Kara. "Oh! Pity! I can't leave them unbalanced. I should make them a matching pair. What do you think?" Kara screamed again, as the blade sliced across her other breast.

"Please!" Kara begged.

Catherine instantly stopped, as a smirk stretched across her lips. "She speaks."

"I know how you can get the engagement ring off my finger." Kara admitted. "You have to kill me! If you kill me, the spell will be broken." Or at least Kara hoped that's how spells worked. "Why wait to kill me? Kill me now and you can have it."

Catherine threw back her head, and diabolically laughed. "Oh! How sweet. She's begging for her own death. How quaint?"

Alexander instantly grabbed his forehead, falling to his knees with a gasp, as he shifted into the Adirondack Mountains, with a contingency of his family, Kara's family, and his Generals.

"Kara's here...and she's alive!" He choked out, as her pain and weakness washed over him, crippling him with her fear and suffering... her agony...her torment...her despair, and worse her hopelessness. She'd given up.

Kara! I'm here. Don't give up! I'm coming to get you. There is hope! I'm here!

Alexander tried to project his feelings towards Kara, but he knew she wasn't used to using their empathy connection. He had to find her. *Quick!* He had to get to her. *Now!* He advised his father of Kara's feelings, and they decided their contingency would wait at their current location, until Alexander found Kara's prison.

Alexander shifted more than twenty times before he finally found himself standing outside a large log cabin in a clearing. From the outside, it didn't look like anything more than a hunter's cabin, but this was definitely Kara's prison.

Kara's here!

I found her! He projected to his father, Avitus.

Seconds later, he was surrounded with their contingency, readying themselves for the battle to come. Kara *was* alive, and he *would* save her. There was no longer any doubt in Alexander's mind. He *is* a warrior, and this was a life he completely understood.

Avitus sent two Cruetian Warriors to scout out the house, while posting ten more in the forest, encircling the clearing.

"*Regis!* I can shift directly to Kara." Alexander conferred with Avitus. "You know her family will demand to come along. I can take one of her brothers with me, but then each of you who are connected to me will have to shift to *my* location once I'm inside."

"That's a great plan, *Kyrios.*" Avitus agreed. "Then the rest of our men can shift to their connected Generals after we're in. Kalab! You will immediately follow my son. Do not wait for any of us. Your sole job as always is to protect Alexander." Kalab nodded, before Avitus turned to Kara's father, Edward. "There are vampires inside, so only one human will go with Alexander, the rest of you *must* stay here. We won't have time to worry about all of you while we're trying to save your daughter. Understand? The vampires, knowing we'll protect humans, will come after each of you first trying to distract us. We know you'll want family representation inside, so only one of you will accompany Alexander, so choose. Now! Every minute could cost your daughter her life."

⊙〰〰〰〰⊙

As usual, Catherine was brutal. Kara had given up, focusing what little energy she had left on prayers. The last hour, she had been singing 'My Prayer' over and over again in her mind. Hoping, God would hurry up and give her salvation.

"Lord, I pray that you can hear me...that you understand my plea...I can't live this way anymore...the pain is drowning me...I ask that you have mercy...and take my grieving soul...I need you more than ever...please lord...take me home..."

The dagger fell clanking to the floor, as Catherine's head snapped up gasping. She had just made a long cut up the inside of Kara's thigh, when she felt *his* presence. "He's here! Shit! Steven! Alexander is here!"

What do I do? What do I do? He'll kill me, he will! I need a new plan...a new plan...a...Got it!

"Erwin!" Catherine bellowed. "Shift the other three humans in here. NOW!"

Kara was totally confused. Could Alexander really be here? Catherine was in an extreme state of hysteria, so it was a good possibility. In the three days she had been here, Catherine had always been calm and extremely cold hearted. Nothing seemed to upset her, but then again, this could be just another trick, just another way to torture her. Give her hope, and then steal it away.

No! I'm not going to give Catherine that satisfaction. I will not hope!

Catherine ran around the room knocking over the sofa, making it look like there had been a struggle. She punched Steven a couple of times for good measure, assuring him it was part of her *new* plan. She then shifted to the kitchen where she retrieved a knife, then shifted back, wiping it in Kara's blood then dropping it on the floor in front of her. She had just completed staging the fight scene, when Erwin and his vampires shifted in with the three cowboys.

"Drain them!" Catherine commanded, as Kara watched in horror.

Kara understood the pain they were feeling. The vampires were literally sucking the life out of them. She'd felt it every night since her capture. The tears that never seemed to stop became more pronounced flowing stronger and harder, until her vision was blurry. As much as she hated those men, they didn't deserve to die this way. She barely saw them slump when Catherine slit two of their necks, and ran the other one through with her dagger.

"Place them so they look like they were in a fight." Catherine demanded. "Then *all* of you shift away from here. I'll catch up with you later."

Alexander shifted into a concrete room with his sword already drawn. His heart broke at the sight of Kara chained to the wall next to him, badly beaten, with cuts all over her body, and very evident vampire bites. Rage wracked his body. He barely looked up in time to see Steven slide down the far wall from a blow that appeared delivered from Catherine.

What is she doing here?

But he didn't have time to question her before five vampires appeared. "Trent! Stay behind me, but protect Kara. Our contingency should be here......"

Alexander's words faded away as Kalab shifted next to him and his contingency started shifting in around him.

Alexander jumped forward engaging the vampire nearest him in swordplay. He saw Kalab engage another. Metal striking metal Alexander understood, for he was an accomplished swordsman. Very few men, it didn't matter their race, could come close to his skill. He pushed forward, leaping over the sofa to corner the vampire.

I will help Trent with Kara! Avitus projected to Alexander. *Lead the fight!*

Avitus saw the disbelief in Kara's face as Trent tried to hug her, covering her nearly naked body. It seemed to him that she could hardly believe what she was seeing. It was as if she was in a trance.

Kara watched the chaos over her brother's shoulder, letting him comfort her, for the first time since she was a small child. She noticed a tall, handsome, well-muscled man, strutting towards them with the same confidant, aristocratic swagger she'd come to associate with Alexander, but his features were more like Nathaniel's and Dante's. *Maybe another of Alexander's brothers.*

"Hello, Kara! I am Avitus, Alexander's father. I am here to help you." Avitus said in a soft, but commanding voice.

Alexander's father? Wow! He doesn't look any older than Alexander and his brothers.

Kara couldn't find the will to say anything as Avitus reached up and broke her cuffs with his bare hands. She fell into Trent's arms like a sack of potatoes. Seconds later, her legs were free and they had gently laid her on the floor. Avitus took off his coat and covered her, searching out her injuries.

"Trent, she's in shock. Keep her warm." Avitus directed.

With so many of Alexander's men in attendance, it never really was much of a fight. They had taken down four of the five vampires in minutes, and he had dispatched his men to search the rest of the building. His only regret was not getting to the fifth vampire before he'd shifted away with Steven, but Alexander assured himself neither Steven, nor *that* vampire, would live long.

Alexander sheathed his sword walking over to Kara. She looked so small and fragile lying under his father's coat. Her face was swollen with bruises. She had a cut on her lip, and her cheeks were raw from crying. Her hair was all ratted, and her eyes were dull with resignation. The lively woman of three days ago didn't seem to exist. Alexander locked his jaw and closed his eyes, trying to contain the fury that waited to lash out. He took another step forward, noticing her throat. It was healing, but he could tell it had been savagely bit. *Bastards!* He jerked off his duster. "*patris,* will you lift her."

Avitus carefully picked Kara up off the floor while Alexander wrapped his duster around her. Then he handed Kara to Alexander.

Trent stepped forward with his arms open, but Alexander shook his head. He knew he was being selfish, but at this moment, he needed to feel her next to him. To feel that she *was* still alive. He needed to know that he hadn't lost her.

Alexander held her so close. So close, Kara thought he'd break her ribs, but even the pain of a few broken ribs would have been worth this moment. He'd saved her.

Thank you, Lord! Kara chanted in her head, unable, and unwilling to stop her gratitude. For instead of allowing Catherine to take her life, the Lord had brought Alexander to her.

"Kara, I am so very sorry." Alexander nuzzled her hair…her neck… her cheek. He couldn't get her close enough. To have almost lost her. Tears swelled, but he pushed them back. "Look at what they've done to you."

Not wanting to scare Kara, Alexander screamed inside. These bastards had earned Alexander's wrath, and he vowed to release his revenge with a rage worthy of his nickname. *Algor!* Kara was bleeding in so many places, he couldn't even count them. They had used knife play, so would he, but his way. He might even find dull daggers. They enjoyed using their fists on his *Amara*. Well, Romans were known for the ruthless torture of their enemies. How else did he come by his nickname? These bastards would understand the meaning of Roman torture. *It's too bad we no longer crucify criminals.* It'd be his pleasure to nail them to a cross.

Avitus laid his hand on Alexander's shoulder. "*filius*, she's been blood raped. Severely…blood raped. It looks like…continuously."

Alexander fisted his hands so tight, his knuckles turned white, as he shook with fury. His *Amara* had been *blood raped*. Repeatedly! They *would* slowly die by his hands!

"Not now!" Avitus said sternly. "Right now, Kara needs you. We'll deal with the other later. I've sent for food, water, and clothing for her. It should arrive momentarily."

"Thank you!" Alexander said through his teeth.

"Blood raped?" Trent scowled, sitting down near Kara's feet. "I don't like the sound of that."

"I have a little stronger feeling than that." Alexander growled. "I'm going to kill them. *All* of them."

Trent shouldn't have been shocked after seeing Alexander the Warrior, but he was. The venom in Alexander's voice, made Trent appreciate that he was not one of Alexander's enemies.

Nathaniel leaned over the sofa, gently brushing Kara's cheek. "Good to have you back." Kara tried to give him a faint smile, and then just nodded. "Alexander." He continued. "The vampires we just killed *were* Seth's warriors. They display the viper."

Alexander nodded in understanding, as Kara tried to shake her head, but couldn't drum up enough strength to complete the task.

It's not Seth's men. It's Catherine! But Kara could only think the words. She couldn't get them out.

Alexander wouldn't let go of Kara. He had her sitting on his lap, holding her close to his chest. Burying his face in her hair, he allowed his pores to be saturated with her scent. He had to get her to agree to complete the second blood bonding ceremony, so they never had to go through this again. With the second ceremony completed, he'd be able to trace her anywhere on earth. He'd almost lost her, and he'd never allow that to happen again. Fury raged in his blood, wanting revenge, as relief ran through his veins, knowing she was still alive, but she'd been badly hurt both physically and mentally. It would take time for her to heal. Physically his blood would heal her completely in a few hours. Mentally, he didn't know how long it would take. His blood couldn't erase her horrible memories.

He gently kissed her lips, surprised when she tightened her grip on the front of his shirt, attempting to hold onto him.

"I truly am sorry." He said against her lips.

"I know." He barely heard Kara reply with tears in her eyes, she was so weak; it was breaking Alexander's heart.

Damn it! Damn Seth to Hades! To hell! He didn't care which, as long as he suffered forever.

For the second time in three days, and in 2000 years, Alexander allowed his father to take control of the situation. He listened and watched as he held Kara in his lap, until Adelina and Tanya appeared with her clothes, bandages, food, and water.

Alexander gently laid Kara on the sofa, and allowed the women to take care of her, still hovering over her protectively, near her head at the arm of sofa, while Trent hovered at her feet. He glanced around the room until he found Catherine.

What was she doing here?

Calling her over, he began quizzing her on why she was there, and what had happened.

By the time Alexander motioned her to him, Catherine had perfected her story. She explained that she had overheard Steven's plans to kidnap Kara at *Club Nouveau*. She said Steven was quite obsessed with Kara, but originally thought he was just bluffing. Then when she heard Kara had been kidnapped, she remembered he had said something about a place in upstate New York, so she began an investigation that led her here.

"Why didn't you tell my family? You knew we were searching for her." Alexander demanded.

"I'm sorry, *Kyrios*." Catherine bowed her head in remorse. "I didn't know Seth was involved. I knew I could handle the humans, and I wanted to make up for my actions at the club that night. I'm really sorry." She looked up with tears running down her cheeks. "I *did* save her."

"Yes, you did!" Alexander softened his tone, opening his arms to her. "I'm sorry. Come here." He kissed her forehead. "Thank you! I can never repay you enough for saving her life."

Kara couldn't believe the lies coming out of Catherine's mouth, or the really great actress she was, and when she stepped into Alexander's embrace, a surge of fury ripped through her soul so intense, it hovered on complete madness. The frenzy charged through her blood giving her a renewed amount of strength. Like hell was Catherine going to get away with what she'd done to her. Maybe they were all buying her heroic bullshit, but she knew the truth, and that evil woman would pay.

Kara jolted off the sofa screaming, as Alexander caught her. "Liar! Liar! Liar! Tell them the truth you stupid bitch. *You're* the one who kidnapped me. Tell them how you tortured me. How you continuously cut me, beat me, allowed your vampire friends to feed on me. Tell them how you were going to let them rape me. *Tell them!* Tell them how you enjoyed it. Tell them how furious you were when you found out Alexander had given me his blood. Tell them you *bitch*. Tell them the truth!" Kara screamed hysterically, while tears streamed down her cheeks.

"Kara, I saved you." Catherine stated innocently. "She must be in shock. It looks like she's lost a lot of blood, she's gone completely crazy."

Kara roared, as she lunged forward swinging, getting one good punch in, before Alexander caught her around the waist, pulling her back into his embrace. "Tell him! Tell him how you're so jealous you swore to kill me. Tell him the only way you can have him is to kill his *Amara*. Tell him you stupid bitch. *Tell him what you did to me!*" Kara collapsed sobbing. "Tell him. Just tell him the truth."

"I don't know what you're talking about." Catherine said sounding hurt.

What a fucking actress!

"Kara, I know you and Catherine have issues, but she saved your life. *You're* wrong about her. *You* should be thanking her right now. We all need to be thanking her right now." Alexander said stroking her hair. "I think she's right. You're in shock, and don't know what you're saying."

Kara froze, as she looked up into his beautiful eyes, and saw the truth. He didn't believe her. He believed Catherine. Kara choked back her tears, barely able to find the words, she finally whispered. "The first time I ask you to trust me, and you don't. You're not who I thought you were, Alexander. You're *not* my soul-mate. If you were, you'd believe me. I know what happened to me. I lived it! I…never mind!" Tears rolled down her cheeks. "Just…stay away from me." She pushed away from him. "Uncle Chung…Tanya…can someone…*please* take Trent and me home."

"Kara? Catherine saved you. I know you're confused right now, but……" Alexander tried to explain, but Kara didn't want to hear it. His betrayal stung. How could he believe Catherine?

How could he not have believed me? How can he choose her over me?

Kara pushed him with what little strength she had left. "I don't care what you're saying. Stay the fuck away from me. You believe Catherine then have her. You never even had the decency to tell me about the danger I was in. She had to taunt me with it."

Kara looked at Catherine. "You were right all along. He *is* obviously yours. He's protecting you, like I thought he was supposed to protect me." Kara wiped the tears out of her eyes. "Just remember. I know what you did." Kara sneered at her. "He might believe your stupid lies, *Bitch*. But I'll *always* know the truth. *You* kidnapped me, *you* tortured me, and *you* would have killed me if they hadn't arrived. Ultimately, *you* won. You got your way. You can have Alexander." Kara glanced around the room, "Now, *all* of you can stay out of my life."

Kara took off her ring and handed it to Catherine. "You *wanted* this so damn bad, well now it's all yours."

"NO!" Alexander screamed, cursing under his breath while pushing his hand through his hair. "Kara, please. You don't know what you're saying."

"You had your chance!" Kara gritted her teeth holding back more tears. "Bye, Alexander, have a good life with Catherine."

24

"What in Hades just happened?" Avitus bellowed with frustration.

Alexander couldn't say a word; his eyes were still frozen on the spot Kara had just occupied. What the hell *did* just happen? They had saved Kara. He had felt her relief, her happiness, her love for him, and then everything fell apart. Her anger dominated her, causing her to lash out at Catherine. Was Kara jealous? He hadn't felt any jealousy in her emotions, just raw fury...towards Catherine. *Why?* Why could she not appreciate what Catherine had done for her? Catherine *had* saved her life.

Catherine began to sob. "I'm sorry, *Kyrios*. I'm sorry you lost your *Amara* because of me. I'm truly sorry. I just wanted to help."

Alexander wrapped his arms around her, guiding her to the sofa, where he sat down pulling her into his lap. "Shh, it's Ok, Catherine. It'll be Ok." He murmured in her ear trying to comfort her, hoping that was true. He bent down to kiss her cheek, but she turned, and captured his mouth.

Alexander jerked back stunned, but assumed it was an accident until he heard her next words. "You're right, Alexander. It will be alright. I will make you a great mate. I promise!"

Alexander sat Catherine next to him, and silently moved farther away from her. "Catherine, I think you're as distraught as Kara is. Kara's my *Amara*. She's in shock right now, but I'm sure she'll apologize to you, and thank you for saving her life, just as soon as she's back to her old self again."

"But she said......" Catherine began shaking her head. "She gave me this." She held out Kara's engagement ring.

Alexander plucked it from her hand. "She was distressed. Kara just went through a horrible ordeal, and is still in shock. She didn't mean what she said. She loves me, and I love her. We'll work it out, and I guarantee you, she'll end up apologizing to you for her accusations."

"I don't think she will." Venom flowed through Tiberius's words as he stood up from kneeling over the human bodies.

Catherine saw the accusation in Tiberius's eyes, and noticed Kalab, Nathaniel, Dante, Nicholas and Sebastian hovering in a corner. *They know!* And when the hell did Sebastian and Nicholas get here? She hadn't noticed that two more of Alexander's younger brother's had joined them. Both had the 'Maximus-Conti heart-breaking features. Sebastian with his black hair and emerald green eyes, and Nicholas with his dark chestnut hair and deep blue eyes, but at this very moment they were Catherine's worst nightmare. These two brothers of Alexander's were the best Cruetian investigators, and trackers their world had ever seen. This was not what Catherine needed right now. Before Tiberius had a chance to shift to her, she shifted away, making her escape.

"What the hell?" Alexander growled as Tiberius stood before him. Sebastian and Nicolas strolled forward, with a remorseful expression on their faces.

Avitus glanced around, as everyone crowded around the small group near the sofa. "Generals! Relieve your warriors back to their normal duties, but you will remain here. It looks like we're not quite through with our investigation." He waited until every warrior had shifted away, except his Generals. "Alright!" He walked into the middle of the circle. "Tell us what you've found."

Sebastian cleared his throat. "We hate to be the bearer of bad news, but something is definitely not right with Catherine's account of the facts."

"Kara might have been telling the truth, Alexander." Nicolas concluded.

"You think Catherine kidnapped Kara." Avitus asked. He was shocked, but as a commander would never show the emotion on his face, or in his tone of voice. "Her father is a dear friend of mine.

Demitrius was the man who brought your grandmother to Rome. He saved your mother. I have a hard time believing his child would betray our family, or commit treason."

"I agree!" Alexander said forcefully. "We've known Catherine her entire life. I've personally been extremely close to her off and on over the last 1000 years. I cannot believe she would hurt me, or our family. Granted she's selfish, and extremely jealous of me, but like *patris*, I do not believe she would commit treason."

"That's where I disagree with you, *adelfos*." Adelina stepped forward. "You've heard the saying 'Hell hath no fury like a woman scorned.' Well, Catherine has felt scorned for decades. What you call jealously, I call an obsession."

"One more thing," Nathanial spoke up, "even though we haven't known Kara very long, I find her to be a very honest person, someone who doesn't throw out accusations without some type of basis to them."

"Of course you're right." Alexander agreed. "I just assumed she was in shock, and didn't realize what she was saying."

Tiberius shook his head. "No! What you did, *adelfos*, is choose Catherine over Kara, or at least that's how Kara views it."

Avitus saw the understanding hit Alexander's face, and he realized, his son never actually thought Kara believed he had chosen Catherine over her, until now. His poor son still had a lot to learn about women. "Well, what is done is done. We cannot change what has already taken place. Alexander will have to work out his relationship with his *Amara* at a later time. Right now, we need to know what Sebastian and Nicolas discovered, so we can bring Kara's kidnappers to justice."

Alexander only heard bits and pieces of Sebastian and Nicolas's explanations. The information he did digest truly shocked him. Catherine had blatantly lied. The humans were drained before being sliced open with Catherine's dagger, and since Catherine did not have a red ring around her eyes, she could not have been the one who drained them, and since Seth's Warriors arrived after Alexander had, none of them could have drained them either. As soon as a Dark-Soul drains a human body, killing them, their eyes immediately have a red ring around the iris, making them a vampire. A Dark-Soul criminal!

Furthermore, even the fifth warrior, who kept to the corner during the fight, couldn't have drained three human adults by himself. There had to have been at least three vampires here prior to the one's they had killed. One for each human adult!

ᎾᏍᏲᎾ

It had been two weeks since Kara walked out Alexander's life. Fourteen…extremely long and agonizing days. Three-hundred-and-thirty-six hours to punish himself for his stupidity. Twenty-thousand-one-hundred-and-sixty minutes of complete and utter agony. One-million-two-hundred-nine-thousand-and-six-hundred seconds that Kara had refused to speak with him.

The first week she completely locked herself inside her home, refusing to speak to anyone, including her own family. At first, her family wanted nothing to do with him. They were as angry as Kara was because he had hurt her.

"You promised you wouldn't hurt her." Kara's brothers said in unison. Making him feel even more of a traitor than Adelina had already made him feel, for she had made it obviously clear she was on Kara's side.

"You were an idiot, *adelfos*." Adelina chided him. "You should have never castigated Kara in front of Catherine, even if you thought she was wrong. After what she had gone through, you should have brought her home and comforted her. If you had, Sebastian and Nicolas would have known Catherine was a traitor, and Kara would never have known you didn't believe her. This is your own fault, and I have no sympathy for you."

Well, he didn't have any sympathy for himself either. He did finally explain to her family what had happened, and why he'd felt so strongly of Catherine's innocence. Her parents were the first to understand and give him their forgiveness, and then within a couple of days, the rest of the family forgave him as well.

Since Kara refused to speak to anyone, Alexander shifted into her room each night, after she'd gone to bed, and checked on her. Her family was appreciative to know that she was doing alright, but it killed him to be so close to her, and not be able to hold her. He knew she'd been crying. He not only saw her tear stained cheeks, but he felt her sadness, her anger, and her loss. Sadly, Alexander felt the same exact way.

If only she'd let me explain. Let me apologize for being such a jackass.

Kara had cried for hours. Hours that had turned into days. She knew she couldn't hide at home forever. She'd been through this pain enough times to know, that someday it would turn to anger and hate, and she'd move on. Move on alone! Again! She burst into tears.

I love him. I honestly believed he was my soul-mate.

She wiped the tears from her eyes, and stuck out her chin. She would beat this, just like she had the last three times. He wasn't the *one*. She knew that now. He just wasn't her soul-mate.

It was Friday night, and had been a little over two and a half weeks when Alexander felt Kara's emotions change. Happiness! Excitement! Passion? Not the intense desire he knew she felt when they were together, but it was still passion. What had brought on this change? She had begun talking with her family, had even met once with Adelina, and another time with Chung. They had all explained what had happened, and why he'd done such a stupid thing. They told her how sorry he was, and begged her just to listen to him, but she continually refused. He tried to send her flowers each day, but each time they were returned to the florist. When Adelina met with her, he'd sent a dozen yellow roses. Adelina brought them back with each bud broken from its stem.

"Chung warned you, Alex." Adelina taunted. "Kara doesn't except apologies very easily, and I think she made that clear with your roses."

Alexander sent a puppy with Chung. It was a beautiful blue chow-chow female. When Chung returned with the puppy, at least it wasn't dead. Chung handed him the pup. "Kara says that was a low blow, but she said to tell you she did name her for you. Her name is 'Yume'. Japanese...for dream. She said to tell you to... *'Dream on!'*"

So what was Kara doing that made her so happy, while he sat in his atrium so miserable? Was she with her family? He dialed Trent, but Trent said all his family was at home, and that no one had heard from her tonight. Was she with Becky then? No! Trent assured him. Becky and Alan had left for Las Vegas to get information to plan their wedding. So why the hell is she so happy? Then a thought ripped through his mind that shook the very fabric of his being. Could she be with another man? She was feeling...passionate.

To hell with this! This is completely ridiculous. It's time I took a stand. She has to talk to me.

Alexander shifted a little ways away from Kara finding himself in the middle of Mel's bar. He quickly shifted himself into a quiet corner, so Kara wouldn't discover his intrusion. He caught site of her on the dance floor with......

Son of a bitch! She's with Kevin. She's with that stupid bastard that left her to experience worldly women. What the hell is she thinking?

Kara knew the instant Alexander had arrived. That same sparkling electricity that always encompassed him, wrapped around her instantly when he appeared. She had glanced around the bar, but never actually saw him. She didn't need to. She knew he was there, and she had every intention of making him pay for choosing Catherine over her.

When Kara had come to Mel's tonight, she'd known that none of her family, nor Becky and Alan would be here. Her family was at home awaiting a new colt to join their stables, and Becky was in Las Vegas, so she figured it would be a good time to work her way back into the human world, or at least work her way back into her old life, her life before Alexander and all his bullshit. What she hadn't anticipated was finding Kevin here. Not that she was interested in him, but he did make her laugh, and she would always care about him, and since Alexander had shown up, she might as well act like she was elated to be here with Kevin. Maybe then he'd understand how she felt.

Alexander watched as Kevin bent down and said something in Kara's ear and she laughed. He felt her happiness. He watched as Kevin's hands roamed over her body as they danced. He felt her excitement. He watched as Kevin bent down and kissed her. He felt her passion. Even though it was just a hint of passion, it made his blood boil, then turn ice cold as it ran through his veins. He had to get out of here, or he was going to *kill* Kevin. Kara was his, damn it, and Kevin had her in his arms. Every instinct told him to kill Kevin. Run over grab Kara, and pull a dagger across Kevin's throat. Instead, he shifted to Italy.

Kara sensed the moment Alexander left. She had been dancing, and actually enjoying herself, when she felt loneliness. A hole opened in her chest, and she knew he was definitely gone. She should be happy. It's what she wanted. Wasn't it? It's all she'd thought about for the last week. She'd relayed time and time again with his messengers that she wouldn't forgive him. So, why did her heart hurt? Why had she felt excitement and anticipation when she'd realized he was here? Had she thought he'd come here because of her? Maybe he just came for a drink. He had become a regular here since they'd met. Maybe he just came to see Mel and Nancy, and why did that make her so damn depressed?

Alexander was pacing the Gallery when his mother flowed into the room.

"Conversing with your ancestors?" Hypatia asked.

Alexander looked down releasing a long breath, and then smiled at his mother. "No! Just trying to understand women."

"*gios,* considering the gods themselves do not understand their women, how do *you* propose to be wiser than them." Hypatia teased.

"I just don't understand Kara, *matris.* She won't even let me apologize, and then tonight……" Alexander's voice broke.

Hypatia saw how heartbroken her son truly was. She'd never seen him in so much distress, and she wasn't even sure she could help him. She understood Kara's feelings. Her son had been extremely stupid believing Catherine over his own *Amara,* and women tend to view these things as a betrayal. From what her husband, Avitus, told her of Kara's reaction, she was deeply hurt; and as stubborn as Adelina had described Kara, she might never forgive Alexander.

Hypatia dragged Alexander to a chaise and pushed him down upon it. "Tell me what happened tonight." She demanded.

Kara was back to dancing to drown out her misery. Kevin was being a good sport. Other than the one kiss, he'd caught her off guard with, he'd been a complete gentleman, but there was still something missing. She decided maybe she needed to sing to let off a little of the steam.

Alexander shifted back into Mel's after having an extremely enlightening conversation with his mother. She'd confided in him that sometimes with a strong and stubborn woman, their pride refused to allow their minds to see what was in their hearts. If he wanted Kara, he was going to have to fight for her. He had to fight her mind with her heart. He would have to find a way for her to let her heart rule, instead of her mind, at least long enough to prove himself worthy of her.

Alexander immediately recognized Kara's voice. She was singing. She had just finished a song when he found a table in a dark corner and sat down. She began singing 'What is My Life Without You?'

"What is my life without you?...How will I go on from here?...Did I make a mistake...saying goodbye...Everyone fights...Everyone has issues...No one is perfect...Did I make a mistake...because...I can't imagine my life without you..."

Confounded, Alexander sat in a daze. He didn't know if he should hit something or jump with joy. She wasn't taking dedications tonight, so those were her feelings. It could easily be about him...or...Kevin. Which one he had no idea, should he be thrilled, or should he be infuriated? Then as she began singing her next song, 'Your Touch', he could have sworn that she saw him, because for just one moment their gazes seemed to lock, and in that one instant he felt her desire. Desire he was sure was still for him.

"In the heat of a moment...Insecurities rear their head...I judged you completely...without listening to what you said...it might not make any sense to you...but my pride was on the line...our love was still so new to me...that the real you is hard to find...the hurt that burns inside of me...wants your touch to heal the pain...but your betrayal eats away at my heart...until my anger is all that remains...but maybe with your touch... if you could just hold me right now...and erase all these painful doubts...you could kiss me until the pain disappears and

goes away...If your touch could just heal...all the fear that I feel...it seems only natural...that our love could survive this day..."

Alexander was sure this was about him. Kara's feelings of loss were too new, to raw, to be from Kevin. He could feel her emotions, as if they were his own, and if he wanted to be honest with himself they *were* his, for he felt the same way. His mother was right. Kara's pride will never allow her to forgive him. It was time he took a stand. It was time he forced her to see reason, or at least to feel what's in her heart.

Alexander shifted into Kara's bedroom, and for the first time since they'd met, he searched her condo. He looked around her quaint home. It felt like Kara in every way, from the color combinations, of red, white, and black, to the decorating that seemed to have a lot of sentimental artifacts lying about. It was pure Kara. On his left was her kitchen with a nook, where he sat a bottle of wine and strawberries, on an antique cherry wood dining table. The table was out of place among the modern look of the kitchen with its black marble counters, dark mahogany cabinets, and stainless steel appliances. Her living room held a beautiful black marble fireplace, with a flat screen above it. Red pillow couches surrounded them with a glass coffee table in the middle.

He went back to her bedroom and removed his clothes, hanging them in her closet. He was *not* leaving here tonight, until they had resolved their issues.

Alexander found a quiet place in the shadows near the front door to wait for Kara to come home.

Kara shut the door as an arm encircled her waist, ripping free her purse. Locking her wrists behind her back with one of his large hands, he pushed her forward until her knees hit the couch and she was conveniently bent over the arm. Already naked he shoved her dress out of the way, and ripped her panties off. Fighting she tried to pull herself over the couch, but he plunged mercilessly into her sweet moist heat, that same tight sheath that drove him wild. "Kara!" Alexander whispered in her ear. "Let go of your anger. Feel me! Love me! Forgive me for being such an idiot. Listen to your heart, *Amaya*. Enjoy the feeling of me inside you, and then try and tell me there's nothing between us."

"Asshole! Bastard! I don't want this!" Kara claimed breathlessly.

"Don't you?" Alexander chuckled. "Your body deceives you, love." He slid out of her and briefly filled her with two of his fingers, before his cock was back inside her. "Feel that!" He glazed his wet fingers along her bottom. "You're already so wet for me. Your body is definitely tattling on you."

"You stupid jackass!" Kara spat, but with no more conviction than a newborns whimper.

"Oh, Baby! I'd prefer you leave out the stupid part, but that's the nicest compliment anyone's ever given me. I never realized I was *that* big." Alexander slammed into her, moving his hips in a circular motion.

Alexander knew he'd won a huge round. The emotions emanating from Kara was not the same feelings her mouth was expressing. She loved him. He could feel it, and now he'd make her admit it.

"Oh! Shit!" *That felt so good. I should not be letting him get away with this, but Shiz-nat! It feels too good.* Kara panted heavily.

"Right!" Alexander softly chuckled. "You don't want this anymore than I do." He nibbled her earlobe, as Kara squirmed. "Remember one thing tonight, love. I'm going to pound into you, until the pleasure I give you makes you forget your anger towards me."

Kara moaned as he reached around and found her swollen nub. He massaged and pinched it between two of his long fingers, until she screamed and he felt her inner muscle convulse around him, squeezing his cock, milking it, until he couldn't wait any longer. "Hold on, sweetheart." He staggered out. "It's been so long, this time could be a rough ride." He pulled back and slammed into her, seating himself deep inside her warm, wet heat. Over and over he drove himself into her all the way to his hilt.

When he'd finally spent himself, his thighs were trembling. Still inside her he lifted her, and moved them around the couch, so she was sitting on his lap, where he wrapped his arms tightly around her. "Kara, I'm truly sorry. I've missed you so much. These last couple of weeks has been a living hell. It's been horrible. Please forgive, an ancients high-handed short comings. Please, don't sentence me to a life without you. I can't live that life. I can't bear living without you. I need you. I know I screwed up, but if you'd just allow me to make it up to you. I swear to the gods I will never doubt you again."

Kara sighed. "Damn you, Alexander! Damn you! I don't want to forgive you. You hurt me. You chose Catherine over me." She slid off him and stood up, but just as Alexander went to reach for her she sat back down on his lap facing him astride his thighs.

"How would you have felt if I had chosen Steven or Kevin over you?" Kara closed her eyes, as a tear ran down her cheek.

"I was an idiot, Kara." Alexander kissed the tear from her cheek. "I didn't want to believe that Catherine, someone I've trusted for 1000 years would betray me. I didn't want to believe that I had been that stupid again, to allow another woman, whom I trusted to betray me." He lifted Kara's chin so she'd look at him. "It was easier to think you were in shock, than to believe Catherine was like Fiona. I'm truly sorry. I Love you, Kara, I don't want to lose you." He hugged her to his chest, stroking her hair, her back. "When I saw you taken, I didn't think I could function. My father had to lead our troops. That's been my job, since I was 20 years old. He's never had to step in before, but when I saw you shift away from me, I thought a dagger had cut out my heart. I didn't want to live. I need you, *Amaya.* You make me whole, and I need you to survive. I'm sorry for not telling you about Seth. I just didn't want you to be afraid, to live your life in fear, and I'm sorry for not trusting you, and for not being here to help you through your recovery." He pulled her back enough to touch his forehead to hers. "Please forgive me. I can't promise I won't mistakes, but I can promise I'll never be *this* stupid again."

Kara felt his sincerity as if it were her own. An odd sensation to say the least, but she understood he wasn't lying. She also understood how afraid he was of being betrayed by women he trusted. *"Amayo!"* Alexander smiled, as the male version of the Cruetian word for 'my love' rolled off her tongue. He never knew how pleasing one word could be, or how soothing when spoken by the right person.

"Don't make promises......"

Alexander's smile turned into a deep frown, as he started his rebuttal, but Kara held her finger to his mouth. "Let me finish." She smiled, before biting her bottom lip. "Don't make promises you can't keep, because males are known to be constantly doing something stupid. Just promise to never again put someone above me, and I'll forgive you…this time."

In one sweeping movement he captured her lips. "That I can promise." He kissed her again, this time he wasn't in a hurry, his tongue played with hers, slowly building their anticipation, until there was a knock at the door.

"Just a minute." Kara yelled.

Alexander had already shifted to her bedroom and dressed, when he shifted back and answered the door.

Kara leaned back on the couch and closed her eyes, completely content with the world. Even after her horrible kidnapping, having Alexander here made her feel protected. She was relishing in the knowledge that Alexander was back in her life, when she heard Kevin's angry voice at the door.

"What are you doing here?" Kevin demanded.

Alexander had no intention of explaining himself to this pathetic human. "I could ask you the same thing."

"I came to check on Kara, and see if she'd give me a second chance, since you two aren't together anymore." Kevin snapped. "Not that it's any of *your* business."

"Actually, *my* fiancée is my business, and as for your second chance that will *never* happen. We are currently working on *our* relationship." Alexander chided.

Kara jumped off the couch and headed for the door. She knew the testosterone was about to fly, and she was the only one who could stop it.

"Down boys!" Kara yelled as she reached the two of them. "Kevin, I'm sorry if I gave you the wrong impression tonight, I was just enjoying your friendship. I want to be your friend, but that's all. Alexander's correct, we *are* currently involved." She placed herself between them, as they glared at each other.

"Engaged involved?" Kevin inquired.

"Yes!" Alexander stated bluntly.

"We're working out the details as we speak." Kara rebuttaled.

Kevin leaned into Kara before he spoke. "Just remember...I want you...and I've vanquished the demons that took me away from you once. They'll never hurt you again."

"*I* have no demons, and *I* would never leave Kara to skirt about." Alexander declared, as Kevin gave him a this-isn't-over smile and left.

Kara rolled her eyes.

"I don't." Alexander said innocently. "I have *no* demons."

Kara shut the door and spun around facing Alexander. "All men have demons." She lectured. "It just depends on the woman, what demons *she's* willing to put up with."

Alexander scooped her up and headed for the bedroom. "Kara, I want us to complete the second blood bonding ceremony. If we had, you wouldn't have been tortured. I could have shifted directly to you anywhere on earth. Furthermore, you would have known my feelings, and understood that I wasn't taking Catherine's side. You can feel them now if you try hard enough, but with the second step, you'll have no doubts. We'll be able to project, or talk into each other's minds. We can allow each other to read our thoughts if we choose to. I would have let you, and you would have understood that I was just shocked, and I was trying to understand *everything*, before condemning Catherine to death. That is her punishment, you know, when we find her. No one threatens the royal family and lives." He kissed her deeply. "No one hurts you and lives. The last 2 weeks have been a living hell for me, and I never want to be away from you again. The thought of losing you, just about killed me."

"Take me to bed, and I'll think about it." Kara kissed a trail down his strong, extremely sexy neck with satisfaction. Satisfaction that Alexander was back in her life.

25

A week later, Kara was still undecided on if she wanted to complete the second blood bonding ceremony with Alexander. It wasn't from aversion, or fear of the idea. Nor was her hesitation due to any uncertainty that they would eventually marry. Her reluctance was a direct result of her independence. Over the last week, Tanya, Namorita, and Adelina had taught Kara how to open her mind to the empathy connection that Alexander and her shared. At first, it was an intriguing sensation, feeling Alexander's emotions, especially when they were apart, then it turned to fascination, wondering what he was thinking about when she felt his anger, or when she felt him exhilarated, but in the last couple of days, she began to feel uneasy with the thought of Alexander knowing every emotion she felt. There's really no privacy, and if they complete the second *Amara* ceremony, they'll be able to speak into each other's minds, giving them very little privacy. Would she still be able to be independent? Would her thoughts still be her own? She'd never thought about it in these terms before. Alexander assures her that with the second step, they're still not fully bound. Unlike the third blood bonding ceremony, which unites their life forces together as one, allowing them full access to each other's minds, the second ceremony only allows a mind connection. They have to project their thoughts into each other's minds, and they have to agree to open their minds to each other's thoughts. It's not automatic like after the third ceremony. What Alexander explained made sense, but just last week, she didn't even think they still had a future. Could she actually give him that much power over her?

Alexander was working in the emergency room today. Since the day Adelina had found Kara, he'd slacked on his 'human' duties, as he called them. Duties and a human career that had begun specifically to locate his *Amara*, Kara. Now that he'd found her, he could probably give up the charade, and allow other doctors to take over his research, but he'd spent years studying to earn his human degree, and actually found he enjoyed being a doctor. Not necessarily the research, but he enjoyed helping humans. There's something to be said about the satisfaction you feel when you're able to save a life, or at least help someone have a more productive life, and since Kara recently seemed to need a little time by herself, Alexander had put himself back onto the emergency room rotation.

Over the last week, he had felt Kara's turmoil and indecision. Her reluctance, every time he had mentioned moving forward with their relationship. He'd accepted that there was a battle raging between her mind and her heart, and understood that she was the only one that could declare a victor, but it still drove him insane with worry. They needed to complete the second step. Only then would he feel that he could protect her efficiently.

Since he was scheduled today at the hospital, they'd agreed to spend the day apart. A day for Kara to deliberate over everything that had happened over the last few weeks, time for her to contemplate their future, and time for her to decide when she would be ready for them to take their next step, to perform the second blood bonding of the *Amara* ceremony. Ultimately, Kara would decide a victor today.

Kara had a decision to make, and decided she needed to get away from everyone to think. Since her kidnapping, she'd neglected her horses. Taking them out proved to be a great way to escape. When she gave free rein to her Palomino, Adonis, he took off in a full gallop. He seemed to enjoy the beautiful Colorado summer day as much as she did. They made their way along paths and trails, until she pulled back the reins near a stream in the foothills. Dismounting, she secured Adonis to a tree, patted his neck, and went to get him some water. After taking care of Adonis, she sat down next to the stream with a small cooler that she had strapped to her saddle.

"You can come out and join me if you'd like. I know you're here." Kara shouted.

Since her kidnapping, either Alexander or one of his brothers was always nearby watching her. The first time she realized Alexander had procured her a bodyguard scared the wholly-be-gee-bees out of her.

It was the night Alexander had forced her to forgive him. The night she had left Mel's and found Alexander in her house. Early the next morning, she'd been awoken by the heebie-jeebies. Grabbing the dagger Uncle Chung had given her, she quietly made her way down the hallway to her living room. Terrified, when the man stepped out of the shadows, she didn't wait to see who it was or why they were in her house. He was an intruder. She lunged forward plunging the dagger straight into his heart. It wasn't until he slumped to the floor that she recognized Tiberius. She was so shocked she just stood there dumb founded. It wasn't until minutes later when Tiberius handed her dagger back, that she broke down apologizing.

"Where the hell did you learn to do that?" Tiberius still gripped his chest.

Sobbing, Kara choked out. "I'm…s-s-sorry…I d-d-didn't…k-k-know…it was you."

"Come here!" With his free hand Tiberius pulled her into a hug. "It'll be OK. It won't kill me. It hurts like hell, but it won't kill me."

"I-I-I know." Kara wiped the heel of her palm across her eyes. "U-u-uncle C-Chung told me. After my kidnapping, he taught me how to stab a vampire through the heart. He said it wouldn't kill them, but it would briefly incapacitate them, possibly helping me to escape. He also gave me that," Kara's tears began to flow again, "that d-d-dagger."

Kara had tried to convince Alexander to call off his dogs, she was afraid she might hurt someone else, but he insisted that he would never jeopardize her life again, so until they were husband and wife, she would always have a bodyguard. If she liked it or not! Damn! She sometimes hated his high-handed ways.

"Good afternoon, Kara." Dante stepped out of the trees. "I hope I haven't disturbed you today, as per your request, I've tried to keep my distance." He smirked. "I wouldn't want to end up with an extra hole in my heart like my brother."

Kara didn't know Dante very well, but from what she could tell, all the Conti men have a great sense of humor. "Ha-Ha-Ha! Very funny. If certain Dark-Souls wouldn't skulk around in the shadows, they wouldn't have to worry about being irrigated."

Dante laughed, and shifted the distance between them. "Did you truly bring enough lunch for both of us?"

Kara slyly smiled. "I would never let my protectors starve."

Dante let out a boisterous laugh taking the cooler from her, and walking to a small patch of grass shaded by Aspen trees. "You're too kind, Kara. We all know you don't want us hovering over you, in yet, you still tend to our comforts. Yesterday, Nathaniel said when you were outside training Yume in the park, it started raining, and you had an umbrella for him; and Tiberius says when Alexander leaves for work and he takes his place, there's always a blanket and pillow on your couch for him. We all really appreciate your generosity. Especially when we know, you don't really want us around."

Kara turned her head, fidgeting with the sandwich he'd handed her. "It's not that I don't like you guys. You're all really nice, but I happen to like my privacy."

"Is that why you're refusing to take the next step with Alexander?" Dante asked handing her a bag of grapes.

Kara's head whipped back around. "Did he send you to ask me that?" Her eyes pierced him accusingly.

"No! Actually," Dante smiled amusingly. "it was my mother."

"Your mother? Hypatia? Why?"

Dante chuckled. "Why?" He said amused. "Because she is our family's matriarch, and her job is to protect her family. You're part of our family now, Kara, if you want to admit it or not."

Speechless, Kara watched him eat his sandwich, until he spoke again. She noticed how much he looked like his father with his black hair and blue eyes, but as sexy as Alexander's brothers were, not once, had she felt any desire for them. Only Alexander had the ability to make her feel giddy.

"My mother said she met you last night, when Alexander took you to the Opera in Rome."

Kara nodded. "Yes, Alexander took me to the Teatro dell'opera de Roma, it was amazing." Dante noticed the sparkle in her eyes. He'd have to tell Alexander she enjoyed it. "Your mother's a beautiful woman. Seeing Avitus and Hypatia together, I now know where all your sibling's features come from. You and Nathaniel look like your father, where Alexander and Tiberius look more like your mother."

"True! But wait until you meet the rest of our siblings. The color combinations are endless." He winked. "It confuses everyone." He clucked his tongue against the roof of his mouth. "Oh! No! You don't!" He laughed. "Alexander said you were good at changing the subject when you didn't want to talk about something, but you're not winning this one." He swung his index finger back and forth. "I'm not here to lecture you. I'm here to offer transportation to visit my mother."

Kara started to shake her head......

"Hold on, before you say no. My mother was once in the same situation you are. She was a human that loved a Dark-Soul, and had a similar decision to make. She's simply offering you her experiences, and her advice on a subject she has lived through. All you have to do is listen. Afterwards, you can make your own decision."

Kara didn't move while she analyzed the situation. She did remember Alexander saying his mother was once human, and it would help to know about her experience. She's lived both lives. How could it hurt? It wouldn't change her mind one way or the other, and since she couldn't seem to make up her own mind anyway...What the hell!

"OK! Let me take Adonis home, and then you can shift me to your mother."

Dante jumped up smiling. "Good girl! Mount up!"

It was early evening by the time Dante shifted her back to her family's stables and Kara still needed to ride Caesar. She grabbed her saddle and headed towards her stallion, thinking about everything she'd learned this afternoon. Dante hadn't exaggerated. Alexander's family already thought of her as one of their own. At this minute, Catherine was being hunted down, even by her own father, who was a longtime family friend. Shocked at this revelation and learning what Catherine's father had done for Alexander's grandmother, Kara had a moment of compassion. She asked for leniency. She asked for them *not* to execute Catherine, but to see if they could reform her.

With amusement in her eyes, Hypatia replied. "*Kyria*, if that is your wish, and Catherine is taken alive, then we'll grant it."

Kara laughed to herself, as she remembered how regal and noble Hypatia appeared, with her golden blonde hair, and those same intelligent aqua eyes that she'd given to her son, but she was not supercilious. No! Alexander's mother, was compassionate and sincere, and had a great sense of humor. No wonder her children had such great personalities.

Kara had Caesar galloping before they'd left her parents ranch. She headed back into the foothills, but turned south instead of north, as she had with Adonis earlier in the day. She was still digesting all the information she'd learned from Hypatia, when she noticed where she was headed, towards Alexander's ranch.

Or is it a villa. Ranch...Villa does it really matter? More like a fortress. She giggled. I'm almost there. Do I want to see him tonight? Did I come this way on purpose? I do feel much more confident about our situation.

Hypatia had explained the connection between herself and her husband, Avitus. She explained that they would never be able to have the connection Alexander and Kara would have after the third ceremony, because their marriage happened before the Cruetian curse. Before their curse, Cruetians had to change their spouse into a Cruetian to have children. Which is why Hypatia must drink blood, just like her husband and children, but since Avitus changed her, she has the same type of connection Kara will have with Alexander after their second ceremony. Hypatia and Avitus can converse within their minds. They can feel each other's emotions, and they can allow each other into their thoughts. She said it's the most comforting and intimate connection she's ever had, and she wouldn't give it up for any amount of privacy.

"Besides, you should not hide things from your spouse." Hypatia confided in Kara. "Except maybe a surprise gift, and Adelina can teach you how to do that, even after you're fully blood bonded."

Yes! I definitely feel more confident, and I think...I'm ready!

Alexander was sitting down to dinner, with his family and house guests, when all the alarms went off simultaneously, but before he could move, Dante appeared next to him.

"Will...You...Shut...Those...Off!" Dante shouted. "Caesar set them off, and it'll scare him."

Alexander didn't have time to understand the nonsense Dante was shouting, but if his brother said there's no danger, then he'd turn them off, and wasn't he supposed to be with Kara. Alexander tapped in the code shutting off the alarms, and then another code to reactivate the system.

"What the hell is going on, Dante? Aren't you supposed to be protecting Kara?" Alexander interrogated.

Alexander was sitting there with one of his arrogant, commanding looks on his face. The kind of look that warned Dante he was about to be reprimanded. No wonder Kara wasn't sure if she wanted to perform the next ceremony. Alexander could sometimes be a total ass.

"I am!" Dante growled. "Think about what I just said. Caesar... set...off...the alarms. Her horse! I've followed her all the way here."

Alexander was stunned silent. A first if Dante could remember one, so to antagonize his older brother a little more, he cocked an eyebrow and smirked. "Any further questions, *Kyrios*."

Alexander was still stunned when he glanced up into his brother's amused face, and realized how on edge the situation with Kara had made him. He was snapping at people for no apparent reason, yelling when he should be thanking them and just overall being a royal pain in the ass. "No!" He slapped his brother on the shoulder. "Sit down and have some dinner. You brought Kara to me, your jobs done for the day."

"Actually!" Dante rubbed the back of his neck, with a grimace on his face. "I didn't bring her to you. She started riding and ended up here."

Alexander laughed punching his brother hard in the shoulder. "Either way, Kara is here, and you made sure she got here. That's good enough for me. Now I don't want to keep her waiting. Kalab come with me. We need to put Caesar's DNA into the alarm system, and then you can take him down to the stables."

Kara had gradually reined in Caesar, bringing him first down to a trot, then to a walk before they'd arrived at Alexander's front door. She was surprised to see Alexander and Kalab waiting for her.

"How'd you know I was here?" Kara asked, as she dismounted. "I thought you said I'm programmed into the alarm."

Kalab scowled at her, before taking Caesar's reins. "You are. Your horse is not."

Kara's laugh turned into gawking, when she saw how serious Kalab's face was. "You're serious?"

"Yes. I'm serious." Kalab grumbled. "Morfians are shapeshifters and are our enemies. We don't take any chances, Kara."

Kara bent her head in shame. "I'm really sorry, Kalab. I didn't mean to make your life difficult. I know how hard you said it was to reset the alarm, after someone sets it off. Please forgive me."

Behind her, Alexander was trying to stifle a laugh. "Kalab told you that?" He asked. "In reality, all it takes is punching in two codes." He burst out laughing.

Kara turned around, and punched Kalab as hard as she could. For now he was laughing as hard as Alexander was. "Sometimes, Kara you're so gullible, I couldn't help myself."

Kara was shaking her head as she walked towards Alexander. "Just you wait, Kalab. Someday I'm going to understand your world, as well as mine, and then we'll see whose laughing. For the person, who laughs last, laughs hardest."

"We'll see, *Kyria*. We'll see." Kalab continued to laugh. "But right now, I'm going to tend to Caesar, and put his DNA into the alarm."

As soon as Kalab was out of sight, Alexander pulled Kara into his arms, finding her mouth already open and eager to accept his kiss. He ravaged her mouth, allowing his tongue to wreak havoc on her senses, and when she actively took part suckling his tongue, he groaned loud and proud, for he knew why she was here.

"You're ready!" It wasn't a question, it was a statement, so when they broke apart, she wasn't surprised to see them in his home in Greece, in the second blood bonding bedroom.

Kara didn't waste time as her hands slid under his shirt, gliding over his steel muscled chest, and pushing his shirt up and over his head. With amusement in his eyes, Alexander grabbed hers and pulled it off. She gasped. "Fairs, fair." He flashed that sexy smile of his that sent moisture pooling between her thighs. She ran her fingers over his taut nipples, relishing in his moans, before moving downward, playing with the tiny hairs that ran from his navel, disappearing into his jeans. Kara looked up Alexander's body to see him watching her through his hooded gaze. She smiled seductively, just before she reached down releasing him from his jeans. The sight of him so large, and fully aroused, made her ache for her own pleasures. Alexander was amused as she struggled getting his jeans off, and when she completed the task, she wanted to jump up and down with satisfaction, for there was nothing sexier than Alexander completely naked.

Alexander scooped her up and tossed her onto his bed, enjoying the way her breasts bounced as she landed. He kneeled beside her as he shimmied off her jeans and panties, leaving her as naked and aroused as he was. He could feel her arousal, desire, and passion. It was infectious, and he knew it was for him and him alone. He covered her, capturing her mouth with a hot, deep, provocative kiss. A kiss that went on and on, as their tongues stroked and played with each other, and when the pleasure had them shaking, they both pulled back rasping for breath.

Alexander released her bra in one elegant sweep of his fingers, and sucked in a sharp breath at the site of her plump pink nipples, before suckling one, and then the other deep into his mouth. He enjoyed Kara's squeals and moans, and how she wiggled under him. "I Love you, Kara! He said as he laved his way down her belly. Tears stung her eyes. She was stunned and ecstatic at the same time. He'd said it before, but now she could truly feel it. Alexander loved her. He truly loved *her*. He had said it again, and he didn't have to. She had already agreed to this ceremony. Her heart was pounding with joy when she answered him, "I love you too, Alexander.

Alexander was so energized by Kara's declaration that by the time he'd worked his way down to her triangle of curls, he could barely control himself as he lapped, suckled, and teased her clit into the sweetest release he'd ever tasted. It was the sweetest nectar, and he had to have more. He plunged his tongue deep into her moist heat over and over, and after her third orgasm, she was begging for mercy, and he was enjoying every moment of it.

Alexander slowly kissed his way back up her body, savoring every moan, gasp, and scream that escaped her lips.

"You're always so wet and ready for me. You drive me insane." Alexander's low rumble caressed her ears. "I need to be deep inside you, *Amaya*, but before I do, I need to make sure you understand once we do this there's no turning back. We will have completed the betrothal ceremony, and Kara...this is not to be taken lightly. Breaking a betrothal is almost as difficult as a divorce for my people. Do you understand?"

Kara cupped both his cheeks and pulled him down into a hard kiss. "I want you!"

Alexander let out a deep breath, and kissed her. "Lay your marked hand next to your head."

Kara brought it up, so that her palm was facing up. She felt Alexander slide her engagement ring back onto her finger. "I asked you once to marry me, and you agreed to be my wife. This belongs to you, for it represents my love. It belongs on no one else. Don't...ever... forget that." Alexander wrapped his marked hand around hers, and entwined their fingers.

"Next is the tricky part, love. I have to slide inside you, but I can't take my release until we've completed our vows, so I need your help not to move too much, because I want you hard and fast right...now, and it'll take all my control to go slow."

Tormenting himself, Alexander slowly seated himself deep inside Kara, reveling in her soft, moist, heat that sheathed him perfectly.

"*Amaya*, we need to finish the betrothal ceremony." He barely choked out, as a whisper. "You need to repeat after me. OK?"

She kissed his chest. "I'm ready."

"Kara, I offer myself to you, freely and willingly." Alexander stated as he thrust hard against her once.

Kara repeated. "Alexander, I offer myself to you, freely and willingly."

"Kara, I accept you exactly as you are. Today, we start down the path that will unite our lives. A path that will end, the day we become forever one."

Kara repeated the vow, as Alexander thrust against her slowly, rhythmically. She closed her eyes rejoicing in the feeling of him inside her. He was so strong and thick; he filled her completely, and stretched her beyond sanity.

"Kara, open your eyes." Alexander demanded. "I want to see you come in my arms, our minds will begin uniting when we climax and I take your blood. Look in my eyes. Watch us unite." He bit his wrist. "You will need to take my blood as I take yours."

He brought her wrist to his mouth, thrusting faster, he bit her wrist, at the same time she licked the blood off his. Instantly, they were both flying in complete heavenly bliss. Their release was stronger than either had ever imagined. Kara screamed his name, as he roared deep in his throat. Their bodies soared as Kara felt the oddest sensation, as if their souls had actually touched. She could feel Alexander's satisfaction, happiness, and contentment more pronounced than they'd been before. Then she heard it. *I Love You, Amaya.* Alexander's voice in her head.

I Love You, Too, Amayo.

Kara knew he heard her from the smile that spread across his face.

Alexander rolled over draping Kara across his body. It seemed like days before they came back down from their high. Kara laid there too exhausted to move. Alexander spooned up behind her, wrapping his strong arms around her, and draping his large thigh over her, allowing his body to envelope her in a protective cocoon.

Completely satisfied, Alexander held Kara as she slept in his arms. Her breathing was soft and soothing, as he drew little patterns on her stomach. He had never been this sated in his extremely long life. There was no doubt she completed him. The darkness that had lived inside him for centuries had somehow disappeared, and he no longer felt the darkness in Kara. What had Kelmar said… Darkness Falls. Yes, both their darkness's had fallen, they had each other and together they brought forth the light.

After tonight, Alexander would never be able to live without Kara, and not Seth or Catherine, would ever take her away from him, he would make sure of that. There was nothing more precious to him, and he would protect her with his life.

EPILOGUE

Steven sat in his prison cell terrified. He had no idea where he was, except that he was in a cold old dungeon. When he had shifted, he had thought Catherine had saved him, but no, he had been captured instead, and this vampire, Seth, is one seriously demented vampire. He wants Kara dead, and will do anything to accomplish it, including kidnapping Catherine.

Steven had been here a week, when he heard Catherine drug in. He'd overheard her interrogation and had come to realize, Seth was a hundred times worse than Catherine ever was. A few things he'd learned, was that as far as Seth is concerned, Catherine is an interference, an interference in his plans that had to be stopped. He'd promised not to kill her; he said he'd never behead one of his own kind. He just needed to detain her, until after his *business* had been completed. Steven didn't believe any of it. He'd heard Catherine's screams, much worse than Kara's ever were. He'd watched horrible things go in and out of her cell. Demons and Shapeshifters. Things that shouldn't exist in real life. No, this guy is nuts, he's completely mental. He's allied with the devil himself, and the only way Steven could possibly save Kara from this deranged psychopath, was to gain his trust and become one of Seth's myrmidons. The thought terrified him, but he owed Kara. It was his fault she was in this mess. He should have never listened to Catherine in the first place, but that was his mistake, not Kara's. He had to find a way to save her.

1 month later, Italy!

Kara was enjoying her engagement party. Her family, Becky's family and *all* of Alexander's family were celebrating in Italy, at the Maximus castle. Kara had never seen anything so magnificent. She didn't even know where to begin to explain the beauty of it all.

Becky had Alan running around taking pictures of everything and everyone, while Kara just tried to remember everyone's names. She was happy that she'd finally met *all* of Alexander's siblings, now she wouldn't feel *so* surprised when they popped in on them, but for the life of her, she couldn't remember all of their names.

Alexander had surprised her by learning to two-step, and then actually singing a song to her.

> *"You know you're not my first love…and I know I'm not yours…but of all the others before…I remember no one but you…when my lips touch yours…when we are skin to skin…I remember no one but you…when I hold you in my arms…when I look into your eyes…I know…*
> *I have never loved another the way I love you…"*

"You sing!" Kara laughed accusingly.

Alexander grabbed her up and swung her onto the dance floor with a wicked glint in his eyes. "I lived through the Renaissance, didn't I?"

With happy tears blurring her sight, Kara choked out. "Thank you! This is perfect!"

"Well…I have a confession to make. I had help. Becky sent list after list of songs, until I found the one I wanted." Bending down he planted a sweet kiss on her lips, just as someone came screaming through the great hall.

"Regis! Kyrios!"

Alexander shifted them next to Avitus, as the man ran up placing a square wooden box down in front of them.

"An engagement present, my lord." He opened the box and Kara saw Alexander and Avitus grimace.

"Shut it!" Avitus snarled. "Who's…sword?"

Before Avitus could finish his question, the man answered. "Her own father's, my lord. Demitrius, himself! The warriors with him said she left him little choice. It was either him or her."

Alexander felt Kara's distress, and glanced up as her face paled.

Catherine's dead, isn't she? That small box was her...... Kara couldn't say her head as she projected the words into Alexander's mind.

Yes, Amaya! Catherine...is...dead!

MAGIKOS DICTIONARY

In the *Magikos* world, these races have lived hundreds, of thousands of years. Over time, they have picked up human words, and adapted them to be their own, as well as, creating their own languages. Below is a list of terms that might be helpful while traveling through the *Magikos* world.

adelfos:
A respectful term for an older brother. Stems from a Greek word.

Adora:
A Magusians beloved. The one person to complete their powers, making them stronger.

Agerikian:
A race that is composed of many different types of elves.

akribos:
An endearment, such as sweetheart, stemming from an ancient Greek word.

Amara:
A Cruetian's chosen one. The one person given to them by the gods to love and cherish. The only person they can completely bond with.

Amaya:
The female Cruetian word for "my love".

Amayo:
The male Cruetian word for "my love".

Auraian:
A weaker race of otherworldly beings that has the sight.

bao-bei:
An endearment for a child (daughter, son, etc.). Stems from an old Chinese dialect.

Basila:
The title given to a Cruetian princess, except the Crown princess, see *Kyria*.

Basilo:
The title given to a Cruetian prince, except the Crown prince, see *Kyrios*.

Cruetian:
An immortal race, who were created by the three Titan protectors. They drink human blood to survive. See *Dark-Souls* and *Vampires*.

Daemon:
A race of demons made up of the many different Demon clans.

Dark-Soul:
Another term used for a *Cruetian*, to distinguish themselves from their criminals, they are known to humans as *Dark-Souls*. A term given to the *Cruetian* people by ancient humans.

Elite Warriors:
Highest ranking *Cruetian* warriors. Their sole responsibility is to protect the royal family.

filius:
Son; stemming from a Latin word.

fratellino:
A respectful term for younger brother. Stems from an Italian word.

ge-ge:

A respectful term for older brother. Stems from a Chinese dialect.

gios:
   Son; stemming from a Greek word.

Imperatess:
   The title given to the wife of the *Magikos Alliance* leader.

Imperator:
   The title given to the leader of the *Magikos Alliance*.

Kyria:
   The title of the Crown Princess of the Cruetian people.

Kyrios:
   The title of the Crown Prince of the Cruetian people.

Lunarians:
   A race of women warriors created by the Morrigan to cull her Morfians. Their power comes from the Blue Moon.

Lycanthrope:
   A race of Shapeshifters who can only shift into wolves. Werewolves.

Magikos:
   The name used for all otherworldly races.

Magikos Alliance:
   A council of the otherworldly races. Each holds a representation on the council. They vote on otherworldly laws, and unite to protect all otherworldly races that are a part of the Alliance.

Magusians:
   A race of the many different types of fairies.

matris:
   Mother; stemming from a Latin word.

Me-ma:
What Kara calls her grandmothers.

Morfians: A race of shapeshifters, created by the Morrigan. They can shift into anything, including inanimate objects.

patris:
Father; stemming from a Latin word.

Putalla:
Highest form of insult in the *Cruetian* language.

Regina:
The title given to the Cruetian Queen.

Regis:
The title given to the Cruetian King.

rumex:
Sorry; A strong apology, stemming from a Latin word.

sorella:
A respectful term for younger sister. Stems from an Italian word.

Stregians:
A race of witches made up of many different witch covens.

Therianthropes:
A race of shapeshifters who can only shift into animals. (except wolves. See *Lycanthorpes*). Werebears, Werecats, etc.

topolina:
A term of endearment stemming from Italian.

Vampires:
Cruetian criminals. A *Cruetian* who drinks humans dry, killing them.

Vavorians:
A race composed of many different types of dwarfs.

Vici Warriors:
   Highest ranking Generals within the *Magikos Alliance*. Their
   job is to protect the Magikos world.

vinco vici victum:
   Conquer! Stemmed from an ancient Roman battle cry. Latin.

Watch for the next book in the
Dark-Souls Series.

Darkness United

The continuing story of
Alexander and Kara.

Watch for it in 2014

annmariekazutomi@gmail.com

www.ingramcontent.com/pod-product-compliance
Lightning Source LLC
Chambersburg PA
CBHW050313030726
47505CB00003B/680